A KING CALLED ARTHOR

AND OTHER MORCEAUX

D. Sidney-Fryer has written or edited the following books:

Poems in Prose, by Clark Ashton Smith (1965)
Etchings in Ivory, poems in prose by Robert E. Howard (1968)
Other Dimensions, short stories by Clark Ashton Smith (1970)
Songs and Sonnets Atlantean: The First Series (1971)
Selected Poems, omnibus by Clark Ashton Smith (1971)
The Last of the Great Romantic Poets, i.e., Clark Ashton Smith (1973)
Emperor of Dreams: A Clark Ashton Smith Bibliography (1978)
The Black Book of Clark Ashton Smith, his commonplace book (1979)
A Vision of Doom, poems by Ambrose Bierce (1980)
The City of the Singing Flame, tales by Clark Ashton Smith (1981)
The Last Incantation, tales by Clark Ashton Smith (1982)
The Monster of the Prophecy, tales by Clark Ashton Smith (1983)
Strange Shadows: The Uncollected Fiction and Essays of Clark Ashton Smith, edited
    by Steve Behrends with Donald Sidney-Fryer and Rah Hoffman (1989)
The Hashish-Eater; or, The Apocalypse of Evil, 1922 version, by Clark Ashton
    Smith (1990; with CD 2008 performed by D. Sidney-Fryer)
As Green as Emeraude: The Collected Poems of Margo Skinner (1990)
The Devil's Notebook (complete epigrams and apothegms) by Clark Ashton
    Smith, edited with Don Herron (1990)
Songs and Sonnets Atlantean: The Second Series (2003)
Gaspard de la Nuit, by Aloysius Bertrand, translation (2004)
Songs and Sonnets Atlantean: The Third Series (2005)
The Atlantis Fragments: The "Songs and Sonnets Atlantean," omnibus (2008,
    2009)
The Outer Gate: The Collected Poems of Nora May French (2009)
*The Golden State Phastasticks: The California Romantics and Related Subjects:
    Collected Essays and Reviews,* edited with Leo Grin and Alan Gullette (2011)
*The Atlantis Fragments, The Novel: The Existing Chronicle: A Vision of the
    Final Days* (2011)
Hobgoblin Apollo: The Autobiography of Donald Sidney-Fryer (2016)
Odds & Ends (poetry, 2016)
West of Wherevermore and Other Travel Writings (2016)
Aesthetics Ho! Essays on Art, Literature, and Theatre (2017)
Ends and Odds (poetry, 2017)
*The Case of the Light Fantastic Toe: The Romantic Ballet and Signor Maestro
    Cesare Pugni—A Chronicle and Source Book* (magnum opus, 2018)
West of Wherevermore and Other Essays (second version, 2019) /
    The Miscellaneon (poetry, 2019)
A King Called Arthor and Other Morceaux (2020)
Random Notes, Random Lines (2021)
Astral Debris (2022)

A KING CALLED ARTHOR

AND OTHER MORCEAUX

———

Donald Sidney-Fryer

Hippocampus Press

New York

See page 403 for acknowledgements.

Published by Hippocampus Press
P.O. Box 641, New York, NY 10156
www.hippocampuspress.com

Cover art/design, map, and "Key to Names" by Daniel V. Sauer,
dansauerdesign.com. Cover based in part on artwork by Gustave Doré.
Hippocampus Press logo designed by Anastasia Damianakos.

First Edition
3 5 7 9 8 6 4 2

ISBN 978-1-61498-294-4

To the triumvirate who have made most of my recent
books objectively tangible:

Derrick Hussey as publisher,
Alan Gullette as first editor, and
David E. Schultz as last editor and as typesetter.

Contents

A KING CALLED ARTHOR

a chronicle

A KING CALLED ARTHOR, a chronicle by D. Sidney-Fryer

This experimental novel is a radical retelling of the King Arthur story, but based on the historical Dux Bellorum of the fifth century A.D., and thus minus the trappings of myth and legend that accrued in the latter Middle Ages (c. 500–1500), that is, after 800 (the imperial coronation of Charlemagne at Rome) as well as during the eleventh, twelfth, and thirteenth centuries.

Besides foraging in various books on the subject (mostly by Geoffrey Ashe and Leslie Alcock), the author made a special research trip abroad in the early 1970s, visiting with a close friend the major sites associated with the Arthur of the 400s in the West Country of Great Britain, including Wales, Somerset, Dorset, and Cornwall.

Artorius, Arthurius, or Arthur Rex?

As mobile cataphractarius chief,
Or perhaps even more, as king, or kyning,
Did he but lead, then hold estates in fief?
As Dux Bellorum, seeming always winning,
He ever led the armies on his inning,
His turn at power, across a varied clime—
The clash of arms and armor ever dinning,
Still deafening across the waste of time,
And this was when the world still seemed pristine and fresh and prime.

With echoes that ring on and on, however thin and thinning,
The cosmos yet maintains its pulse, its rhythm and its rime,
1Kaleidoscope of sight and sound that keeps the head a-spinning.

When by an empire's vanished sun, then and thereafter litten,
Was he that Rhiothamus who ruled Brittany and Britain?

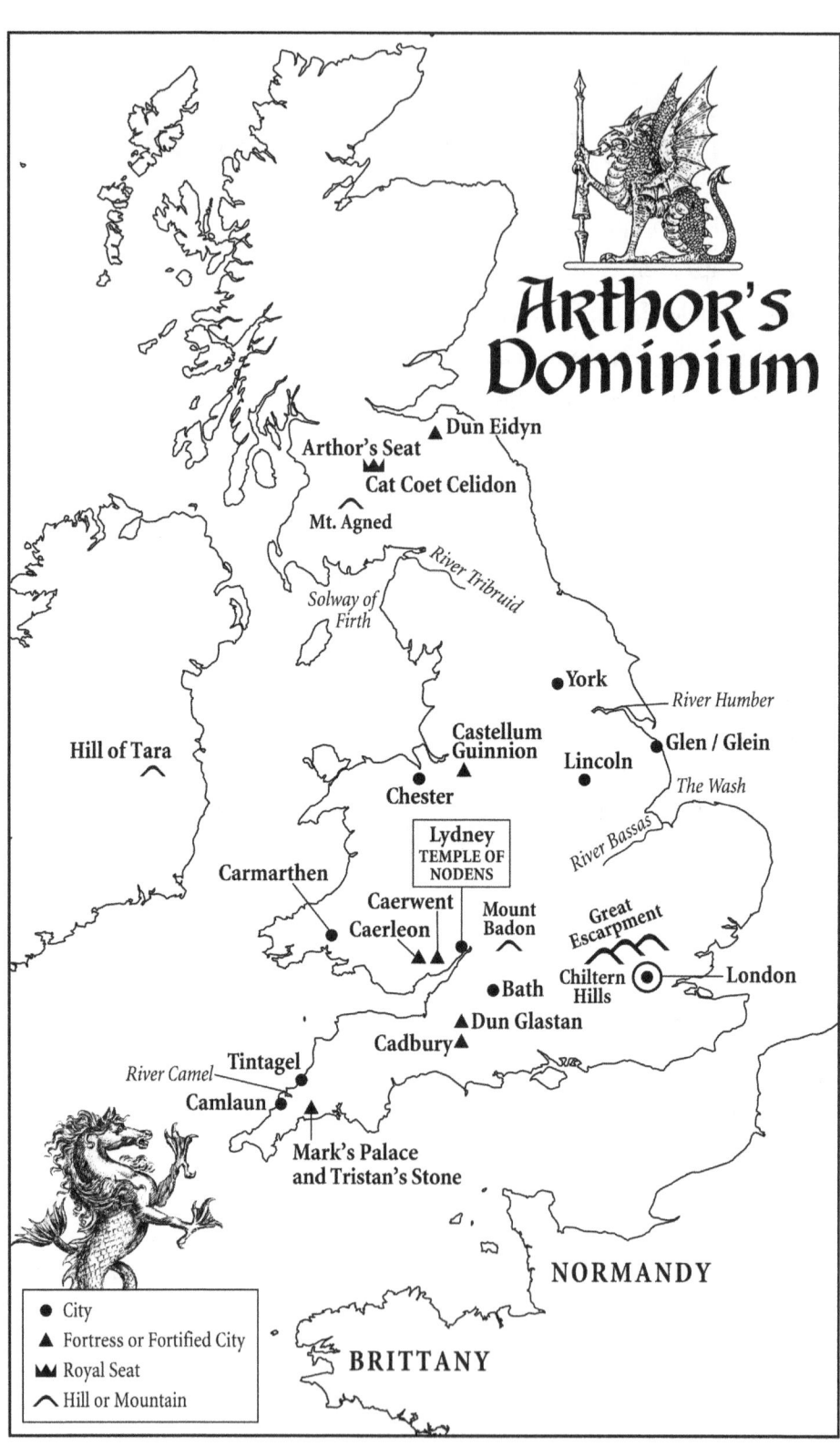

Arthor's Dominium

Dun Eidyn ▲

Arthor's Seat �

Cat Coet Celidon ⌃

Mt. Agned ⌃

River Tribruid

Solway of Firth

York ●

River Humber

Castellum Guinnion ▲

Glen / Glein ●

Lincoln ●

The Wash

Hill of Tara ⌃

Chester ●

Lydney
TEMPLE OF NODENS

River Bassas

Carmarthen ●

Caerwent
Caerleon ▲▲

Mount Badon ⌃

Great Escarpment ⌒⌒⌒

Bath ●

Chiltern Hills ◉ — London

▲Dun Glastan

Cadbury ▲

Tintagel ▲

River Camel

Camlaun ▲

Mark's Palace
and Tristan's Stone

NORMANDY

BRITTANY

● City
▲ Fortress or Fortified City
� Royal Seat
⌃ Hill or Mountain

Key to Names
Arthorian vs. Modern

Din, Dun, Dunum (Roman fort) means fortress or fortified place

car = caer (car or cayer) means a fort or fortified or stout-walled or city

Bath = Caer Vadon

Brittany = Armorica Inferior

Carmarthen = Caer Marthen

Caer Gwent = Caerwent

Caerleon (Caer Leon on Usk) = Isca Silurum, in southeast Cambria, modern Wales

Chester = Caer Leon on Dee, former legionary fortress (small "city")

Din Tagell = Tintagel

Dun Cadan = Cadbury (Castle)

Dun Eidyn = Edinburgh

Dun Glastan = Glastonbury

Ireland = Eire = Hibernia

Lincoln = Lind Colin = Lindum Colonia

London = Londinium

Mount Badon = Mons Badonicus

Normandy = Armorica Superior

Rennium = Rennes, at eastern edge of Brittany

Temple of Nodens = Templum Nodentis

York = Caer Ebrauc = Caer Eboracum

A King Called Arthor

a chronicle

PART ONE
WARRIOR APPRENTICE

Contents

CHAPTER I. Review, Revision, Reappraisal

Let us begin at the beginning. By us, I mean *we,* the writer and the reader. I assume no lofty editorial *us* being but one humble scrivener and poet among hundreds, nay thousands, even if not hundreds of thousands. We speak in terms of our planet Earth, as reconfigured by Ptolemy, one Claudius Ptolemaeus of Alexandria, sometime back in the 100s A.D., as now dated by the Christian monks.

But this usage of *us, we, ourselves* appears rather advantageous, lest some critics might otherwise accuse me, Merlin, or Myrdin, of any untoward egomania. By default, if by nothing else, I remain the elder who dates from the time when the administration of the Western Empire seemed to abandon, albeit inadvertently, the diocese, or province, of Great Britain, or Britannia Major. Let us position our narrative in time and space.

The midafternoon sunlight slants through the open front door of our humble but sturdy house. This early autumn in Brittany, or Little Britain, or Britannia Minor, across the Narrow Seas from Cornuae, still retains considerable warmth, above all on a rare, clear, and sunlit day such as this. The warmth lingers on within the wide space with kitchen garden long since cleared in front of our dwelling that faces west.

Apart from the big clearing the dark and shadowy forest of oaks and beeches rises up on all sides, the Forest of Broceliande, or the Selva Broceliandis. Largely and aptly built of oak, both walls and roof, the structure stands on the eastern side of the clearing, centered as it is in the midst of a clump of some huge and ancient oak trees that surround and protect the house on all sides except the west. Suitably named, and in fact rebuilt several times in whole or in part, the Domus Quercus has long preceded in place its current inhabitants. Here the original builders and residents had located it in a safe and secure site somewhat raised up on a mound.

It stands well inland of the vast and illimitable waters of the Ocean Sea, between the westernmost part of the peninsula that constitutes Brittany, and the ancient Roman capital Rennium further to the east. That fortified city had functioned for hundreds of years as the chief town of the main and southern part of Armorica, or Armorica Inferior. This, together with Armorica Superior on the north, makes up the entire old province of Armorica proper. These two peninsulas represent the northwesternmost part of the overall province or country of Gaul. They lie between the two rivers, the Sequana [Seine] to the north and the Liger [Loire] to the south.

The immediate locale thus keeps our house free from danger and damage. Between the outer front door and the hearth of the inner fireplace there stands a large and long oak table, or desk, piled with scrolls of vellum arranged more or less in some kind of order. An old, nay more, an ancient man sits in a sturdy oak chair, and midmost of the side away from the outer door. Tall and broad but thin, with an immense white beard flowing down over his abdomen, and with a full white head of hair covering the shoulders and then down over his back almost to the waist,—this is Merlin, who holds a scroll unrolled before him on the table-desk. His face manifests a stern set of chiselled features as of an old Roman senator, as if carved in stone. The light by which he reads comes in from both the open front door and from the several small windows in this front chamber, windows that hold real glass, but unusually thick. Curtains, now drawn to either side, can be closed at night, to baffle curious eyes, and to maintain privacy.

On the old man's right there sits in a similar oak armchair a much younger man, middle-aged, with trim beard and short hair down to his neck and covering his ears. His handsome face bespeaks an aristocratic origin. This is his assistant and general secretary Glirid Selevinid. Both men wear woolen tunics and breeches, and capacious woolen cloaks over those, secured at the right shoulder with large ornamented pins, or brooches, of bronze.

The older man speaks rather slowly, but loud enough, in a deep bass voice, and Glirid responds in a modulated baritone. From time to time they will smile and nod at each other. Merlin speaks. "Alas, that now I become somewhat easily confused. At over one hundred and twenty-five years my old age is finally catching up with me. My hearing and my vision remain exceptional. I can still achieve a decent script. I can still think and write with some real clarity. And where and when I cannot, you can guide and correct me, my thanks to you." The older man smiled as he turned his head toward Glirid, who smiled and nodded back to Merlin.

At the top of the scroll spread out before him, the vellum bore in big square letters the single word PROLEGOMENON, that is, the foreword that set up the narrative, its origin and place in time and geography, so that the curious reader could grasp in advance something of its plan and layout.

The old man spoke again, "Let me locate us in time and space, as a proper author should, forming his memories into proper memoirs. Let us begin at the beginning with a proper introduction." Here he cleared his throat before he continued.

> We, Merlin, or Myrdin, or more properly Merlinus Merlinius, begin our tale in 525 A.D., according to this new-fangled style or system of dating introduced by the monks, the Christian clerics. Thus this takes place in the middle of the 520s, figuring from the birth of their still new god Jesus Christus. Even if it goes a little against our own grain, we might just as well use it ourselves, rather than the older imperial dating used throughout the Empire, a system with which we grew up. That is, *Ab Urbe Condita,* from the Founding of the City, Rome, Roma Maternalis, Rome the Mother. The foundation must have happened then around 753 B.C., that is, figuring from the birth of Jesus of Nazareth, otherwise Jesus Christ. Our great and good secretary here with us by our side will correct any mistakes that we make in our rough and ready calculations: to wit, Glirid Selevinid, or more properly Gliridaeus Selevinidaeus.

Here Merlin paused again and looked up at Glirid, while the latter looked back at him, nodding in assent. "Have no fear, *meus carus magister,* indeed my dear old master. So far, so good, as when you first began a year or so agone."

Merlin frowned, and spoke. "Yes, I shall use this damnable new system of dating. Even then we have no guarantee that our calculations will be other than approximate, given that now some further new complications have come about from their even yet further system of dating, as we have heard via trade and other exchanges from the Continent, from the rest of Europe. Damn!"

Glirid assented. "Please let me sum up the situation once again for you, dear Merlin, and refresh your understanding. As recalculated, the Christian monks now figure that Jesus of Nazareth was born in 6 B.C., and to have died in 29 A.D., give or take a few years either way. He lived for some forty years before his crucifixion under the term of office for Pontius Pilate, the Roman procurator at that time in Judaea.

Even these recalculations are not certain, as it always appears to happen when a minor or marginal person transmutes into a major one."

Merlin nodded back at him before Glirid continued. "First of all, in 417 or 457, a Christian monk, one Victorinus of Aquitania, introduced the first system as calculated from the *death* of Jesus Christ. Then almost yesteryear another monk, one Dionysius Exiguus, introduced a yet newer system, but this time recalculated from the *birth* of Jesus Christ. We just happened to learn of it by chance from a merchant passing our way, going west from the old capital Rennium. Thus all these good monks, these exemplary clerics, will now have a busy time of it, recalculating all the new dates thus far established in their archives, as well as in otherwise established history pertaining to the Romans and the Greeks. In this manner, the Founding of Rome the City has changed from c. 713 to c. 753 B.C."

Merlin responded, "Yes, and this new system, recalculating many other systems along with it, will give far future generations much to ponder, to calibrate, to compute. One does not need my prophetic powers to predict that. Damn, but I wish that the clerics would reconvene, and make up their mind once and for all. Nothing is now certain. We should never have given up the old imperial system, *Ab Urbe Condita,* or A.U.C. It had long since attained universal acceptance and certainty, and had firmly established itself per Roman custom, per Roman history, and per Roman law."

The old man paused again, turned in his chair, then looked at once at Glirid, almost with tears in his eyes and voice. "Glirid, my dear young friend, what would I do without you?!" (Here Glirid embraced his master to reassure him, before Merlin continued.) "As I have said many times before, I still think it an unprecedented anomaly that your pre-eminent Roman Briton family should have named themselves, especially you, after the humble dormouse, as it exists somewhere between the field mouse and the squirrel."

Glirid immediately replied with a rueful smile. "We did not want to tempt the gods to punish us, to invite their anger at any undue pride of family, tribe, or social position on our part."

Merlin commented, "Well, maybe that was the better part of wisdom. Let us go a little bit further with our foreword, and our discussion, and then we shall call it a day. We have made a good start in our necessary review.

"Oh, please close the outer door. It is getting a little bit chill. We still have some daylight left, and we do not need any candles yet."

Glirid got up, closed the door, and sat down again close to his master.

Midmorning of the following day found the venerable elder and his youthful assistant seated once more at their table-desk, dressed more or less the same. They had each consumed their meager breakfast, a cup of wine and a few crusts of bread. That would hold them over until a more solid lunch around noon or earliest afternoon. Merlin turned to his assistant.

"My dear Glirid, when I woke up this morning I noted to myself that I want to insert something after my opening that I read aloud late yesterday afternoon. I dislike handling dates and systems of dating, at least in writing, to the utmost extent. But since we have come up against the problem, I have decided to discuss the problem head-on in the text of this very first section. Please put what I say directly into the text on a small piece of vellum or on the back of the present scroll if there is room."

Glirid nodded, as Merlin continued. "I think that I should lay out here according to this new system concocted by Dionysius Exiguus the overall period of time against which these memoirs take place. Please listen carefully to what I have to say, and put it all into proper shape for me." Merlin sat still, as he plunged into thought. Then he spoke.

During the early 400s a number of tribal chieftains had established their own fiefdoms and had set themselves up as kings and princes over their domains. All this happened before Honorius issued the Rescript of 412, directing us to take care of our defenses, that is, of Britannia, and to take up arms. The Britons had already done so. It was a matter of life and death and simple survival.

By 440 I had attained my later thirties and had gained a reputation as a man of great wisdom and as an astute counsellor. Kings and officials, no less than common people, consulted with me. My advice led to very positive results. Early on in my own life my parents and I realized that I had the gift of second sight, of prophecy. The family moved between our holdings in Cornuae, southern Cambria, and in the hills north of Aquae Sulis, now Caer Vadon.

My reputation as a wizard grew, and wherever I went, people came to ask my counsel. This I gave, and for this I received payment in kind, that is, in goods, food, wine, and other necessities, but rarely payment in coins of gold, silver, or bronze. Without money coming in from the Continent, we had fallen back on trade and barter.

In 440, while our family was living in Cornuae, at our fortified palace on Din Tagell Headland, Uthor Pendragon, the former supreme commander, took refuge with us, alongside his princess Ygurna. Not long after their arrival Ygurna gave birth to the boy Arthor. Uthor had been fighting his campaigns against the Saxons and their allies from the Continent. But he shared the command with the general Ambrosius Aurelianus, or rather the then Dux Bellorum.

Uthor and Ygurna gave Arthor over into my care, or rather into that of the women in the household. We were all distant relatives, and Arthur became part of our family. In this way I became both tutor and stepfather to him. Thus I knew the acknowledged son of Uthor and Ygurna from his birth in 440 to his death in 520. Uthor would later perish in an ambush, and Ygurna came to live with us wherever our family happened to be living. Her grown son would join up with the Dux Bellorum.

All during the time Arthor was fighting under the command of Ambrosius Aurelianus, he fought at his side. This took place from 455, when Arthor was fifteen, until 470, at age thirty, until the death in battle of Aurelianus in that same last year. Arthor had begun his training in arms at ten, and by 470 he had become as the new Dux Bellorum the greatest warrior in Britain. From ten to fifteen he had studied the martial arts, thus during six years. He had lived and studied with me for fifteen years. He had also become a man of great wisdom like myself. He treated both allies and enemies with equal fairness. All this is by way of prelude as you know, but it is important that we rehearse it all in advance to keep everything clear. Now let us return to the latter half of the Christians' fourth century.

Merlin finished his long discourse and sighed. Glirid now spoke up. "Master, we should have some lunch—the women signal that it is ready—and then we should have some rest. Later this afternoon, we can continue." Merlin assented, and they went into the eating area further on in the house.

By midafternoon Merlin and Glirid had seated themselves back at the table-desk in the front room of the house. They had both read over to themselves what Merlin had more or less dictated earlier that same day. "Glirid, I am not unhappy with my discourse, but please improve it when you rewrite it for me, as you usually do." Glirid nodded his head. "I must now mention something that happened before I came on the scene, and you know what it is, as narrated to me by the elders in the family. This is the next material that I want you to redact." Again the secretary nodded. Again Merlin became still and silent, plunged in deep thought before he began.

"In 367, as closely as I can remember, an enormous disaster struck our Britain, the great Barbarian Conspiracy, the Conspiratio Barbarica. The Scotti and Attacotti came over from Hibernia, from the west. The Picti came down from the north, from the highlands of Caledonia. The Franks, the Angles, and the Saxons attacked the frontier and coast of Gaul, and then harried the eastern and southern coasts of our own Britain. From all this devastation and chaos the great and good Count Theodosius rescued us during 369–70. Luckily our own family did not directly suffer, but many of our friends and their families did.

"Our holdings in Cornuae, and those in southern Cambria, lying west and inland of Caer Leon on Usk, lay too far out of the way for the invading barbarian tribes to attack and loot. And the estate north of Aquae Sulis just happened to avoid any damage by sheer coincidence. Theodosius restored order, and everything appeared to revert to the normal peace that our province had enjoyed for years. But between the restoration effected by Theodosius and the year that I was born, to wit, 400 A.D., the condition of the province greatly worsened in regard to security.

"The emperors or would-be emperors had removed so many troops from Britain to the Continent—for the defense of the Empire there—that circumstances forced the Britons to take up arms and form themselves into little armies everywhere. People moved into the fortified cities wherever they could, and they refortified the old ancestral and abandoned hill-forts extant from when before the Romans took over Britain. We re-used them as habitation. All this happened before Honorius and his Rescript of 412."

The old man peered solemnly at Glirid, who looked back at him in the same way. "Those years of turmoil and chaos, especially the great Barbarian Conspiracy, have profoundly affected us all. I was born in 400, and that invasion became the chief topic of conversation since that time. But our people somehow survived and went on with their lives. The shock of 367 shaped us forever after that catastrophe. We could never go back to our former way of life.

"The strategic counterthrust launched by Uther Pendragon, Ambrosius Aurelianus, and then by Arthor Pendragon ensured the long period of peace from 490 to 520. But we all knew that it would not last forever, above all after Arthor's death in Cornuae in the battle with Medraut, and then after Arthor's interment at Ynis Avalon. And that is why we find ourselves here in Brittany at Domus Quercus. We left as soon as we could, aided as always by my prophetic insight. I cannot speak for you, but rehearsing all this tragic history has left me quite exhausted. Let us call it a day."

CHAPTER II. Beginnings

As already stated, I came into this world of Romanized Britain and Brittany almost at the end of the fourth Christian century, give or take a year or so, during January and under the Sign of the Capricorn. This was also the sign or symbol of the Second Augustan Legion, which built and inhabited the grand legionary fortress at what we now call Caer Leon on Usk, but also and first known as Isca Silurum. In popular usage the name went from Castra Legionis to Caer Leon, but more than one town with the latter name still exists in Britannia.

Even if I, Merlinus Merlinius, identified more with Caer Leon than any other—my family had a fine estate, a villa that survived for many years, northwest and inland of that fortress in southeast Cambria—I was born in the stone palace complex long since built on the fortified headland, almost an island, called Din or Dun Tagell not far from the Land's End of Cornuae. In fact our family name, the Cornuarii, reflected our long association with southwest Britain, or Prydain.

I do not, or cannot, remember my siblings very well, but I did have brothers and sister. My parents proved to be a passionate couple, and their many children mostly survived the diseases and rigors of childhood, not always a guaranteed condition. We were a very close and affectionate family, and my siblings made much of me as a cute little tyke. As I recall, we maintained our status as a wealthy, happy, and healthy family, including our servants. All our estates had permanent staffs, but our personal servants, of course, went with us from place to place.

Din Tagell by its very location seemed always a cold residence to me as a child, and the wind! It was almost always howling and screaming within and without whether by night or by day. On occasion a calm sunlit day might happen, but such always appeared like a miracle! Our other estates did not have nearly as much rain or wind. What a balm it turned out whenever we moved to our other holdings, just to get away from that wind!

Apart from our kitchen garden just outside the house in the best sunlit and sheltered spot; and apart from the food that came in from outside the headland; agriculture did not especially prosper in our part of Cornuae. We did maintain a few sturdy fruit trees here and there. Instead of regular crops, the family had long since raised food in the form of cattle, dairy cows, goats, pigs, and sheep. The sheep above all provided the wool that the household wove into our clothing.

As ever and as everywhere, the women in the household accomplished everything with the help and under the supervision of the menfolk. They raised the children and nursed the sick. They made the meals and kept up the larder. They wove the wool and made the clothes. In those days, as now, families living outside the towns had to be as self-sufficient as possible, but even more so now. The many imports from the Continent had long since ceased, apart from the occasional shipment of wine, olive oil, and processed fish packed in olive oil inside large and sealed ceramic jars, all shipped in from the Mediterranean. We also made our own wine from grapes and other fruit.

We rotated among our three chief estates, the one at Din Tagell, the one to the northwest of Isca Silurum, and the one among the high hills north of Aquae Sulis, or as we now call it, Caer Vadon. In fact, this last estate lies not far from the highest elevation Mount Badon, or Mons Badonicus—rendered immortal some thirty years or more ago because of the late great Arthor as the Dux Bellorum and his crushing victory there against the Saxons and their allies. That victory purchased for us the Britons a long period of peace. Nonetheless, by means of my second sight I knew that the Pax Britannica would not last forever, and that furnished the main reason why we moved here, safe inside the forests of Brittany, to this old ancestral dwelling of Domus Quercus.

My family tolerated the new religion of Christianity but continued to believe in, and rely on, the old gods whether Graeco-Roman or especially Keltic. To our own old gods they and I ascribed my rare gift of prophecy. I had undergone the usual training in arms and fighting that had become obligatory for all able-bodied males. I could put up a good fight to defend myself and others. But obviously my career did not include a military vocation!

When I turned fifteen, my parents took me east of Caer Leon on Usk to the great temple complex of Nodens, our great god of the abyss (and of illimitable space). Some local countrymen had refortified an old tribal fort, and in it had constructed an enormous temple to Nodens, in addition to the needed out-buildings. By an odd coincidence this construction happened in the same year, 367, as the great Barbarian Conspiracy.

There at the grand and still new temple my parents and I met the then high priest, Merlinus Nodentis, and he happily accepted me as his apprentice, perceiving my extraordinary powers now more than in embryo. Under his benign instruction I developed my second sight, and soon the local people began to consult with me. I never made a wrong prediction or prophecy, and my name and fame grew. Soon local officials and chieftains came to consult with me at Templum Nodentis. After about five or six years Merlinis Nodentis died at an advanced age, handing over his priestly office to me.

I mourned his passing: he had become another one of my dear parents. But I now needed to move from place to place, and in turn I handed over the office of high priest to the most capable and promising of the several acolytes who served us. From there I returned to Caer Leon on Usk and to the family estate that lay safely inland northeast of the legionary city. My family welcomed me to the old villa, which I now proceeded to make into my new headquarters.

Thus the family continued rotating among our estates, including the smaller one to the north of Aquae Sulis, or Caer Vadon, where the local people still used the thermal baths as best they could, even if the once beautiful town lay damaged and almost abandoned. The site was too exposed. Everywhere I continued to employ my prophetic gifts to help the local officials, princes, and regular citizens. Britain surely had strategic need of them. Life continued onward somehow even without the central administration of the Western Empire, such as it was, limping along as it could.

Meanwhile, far to the east the capital Constantinople presided supreme over the Eastern Empire, safe and secure within its massive fortifications. But for us in Britain, like the Sword of Damocles always overhead, suspended by that single hair, there inhered the unrelenting threat and expanding pressure of the Saxons and their allies, quite well established in the southeast, the northeast, and in and around London. Only a series of brilliant commanders managed to keep them at bay. We Britons held the rest of the island south of Hadrian's Wall.

To be fair to the invaders or the new inhabitants, the long-lived and self-proclaimed High King, Vortigurn, at his court in London, had purposely invited the Saxons into the country to man the Saxon Shore. But soon the defenders became the invaders, the conquerors. We the Kelts, the original Britons, had perforce to tolerate them as a necessary evil, while we stood firm in the west, in the southwest, and in most of the northwest. That is how the situation stands to this day.

For some compelling reason that I cannot recall, the family had moved back to the fortified palace on Din Tagell, at least for the coldest part of the winter, January of 440. We gave hospitality that month to some very special guests. This in turn compelled some long-enduring consequences, above all for me. Meanwhile I urged the family to leave the headland as soon as possible, which we did the next month. Quite apart from the physical discomfort of the location, it turned out as a very poor place for the local people to consult with me there; that is, a poor locus for me to conduct my business of prophecy. The villa north of Caer Vadon and the estate northwest of Caer Leon on Usk proved always much better.

After a louring day of scudding clouds and gusting winds that shook the headland from time to time, the watchman at the outer tower and gate, across the walled isthmus leading to our family palace, called out. A mounted party of some eminent people was approaching Din Tagell. The late afternoon still had plenty of light by which to see, but the clouds and wind gave promise of a dark and stormy night. Several outriders were carrying lances from which unfurled light green banners emblazoned with red-purple dragons.

I had come out from the palace. I stood at the inner tower and gate at our end of the isthmus. I had recognized the group at once as Uthor Pendragon with his armed escort, hardy warriors all. The largest man of the party proclaimed in a stentorian voice that even I could hear. He and a woman wore leather cloaks, the others only woolen ones. They had come up to the outer gate and greeted the watchman on duty.

"Uthor Pendragon salutes the family of the Cornuarii. He requests, as a kinsman and fellow Briton, hospitality and refuge." The word refuge caught my attention. Speaking for the family, I proclaimed in a voice not less than stentorian myself: "Let them enter." The watchmen at both ends of the isthmus opened the gates. The mounted group clattered over the cobbled way to where I stood smiling. I had opened my arms in a warm gesture.

"Greetings, Uthor Pendragon. I, Merlin Merlinius, welcome you and your fellow kinfolk to Din Tagell. May you honor our house with your presence for as long as you need or wish to remain with us."

The entire group dismounted, Uthor helping a pregnant woman down from her horse. I went up to Uthor and embraced him warmly. Our household servants took the horses to the stables for food and rest. Uthor, meanwhile, introduced me to the other person wearing a leather cloak. "Please meet my wife, the princess Ygurna." I bowed and kissed the hand of the strong and beautiful woman. She wore a narrow circlet of gold around her head atop a leather cap secured by ear pieces, tied under her chin, no less than a rich red-purple gown or tunic down to her ankles, warmly dressed against the wind, the rain, the cold.

The entire family had all come out from the house and warmly embraced our kinsmen and fellow countrymen. My parents and the others escorted everyone into the house. As we gathered around the open hearth in the main inner chamber, some of us seating themselves on little chairs and stools, my father spoke out; both my parents and siblings were broadly smiling.

"We are greatly honored and pleasured that you grace our home. All the more so because we well know the part that you play against the outlanders that Vortigurn invited into our midst."

Uthor bowed to my parents. I noted what a handsome couple Uthor and Ygurna made, he with his ample hair and beard, with his stalwart frame (who thought of shaving when almost always in combat mode?), and she in her sheath of a gown, and with her long and abundant hair that she let loose after she took off her cap, and replaced the golden circlet back on her head. Uthor removed his coronetted helmet, and they took off their leather cloaks. We had all seated ourselves around the steady fire on the open hearth below the egress for the smoke in the roof, adequate but shielded on the outside from wind and rain.

Uthor spoke again. "My wife Ygurna is carrying our child. She has reached her term. She will soon give birth. We chose to come back here as in the past, a safe and secure spot. We were traveling not far away, and could no longer delay in finding a refuge."

My father spoke again. "We are thrice honored: with Uthor, with Ygurna, and with your child. But let us have drink and food. Then we can all rest. You and your party must be very tired after riding all day."

Ygurna herself did not eat, but did drink a little wine that we had just received in a shipment from Aquitania. She had reached her full term. Her pains had already begun. At midnight she gave birth to what seemed a strong and healthy boy. We all felt elated, his parents, of course, above everyone else. We all rejoiced, embraced, and congratulated one another, the happy parents above all. Their visit had turned into a celebration. Mother and child had emerged out of the birthing in excellent shape. Albeit Ygurna could indeed suckle the child, and indeed did do so at first, yet a wet nurse in the household took over the newborn baby and suckled it. The child lay quietly in her arms, calm and content.

Completely exhausted from the long day of riding, and then by giving birth, Ygurna could now sleep and recover from her double ordeal. A cup of wine mixed in with some opium in powdered form helped her out with any lingering pain and safely put her into slumber.

Uthor stayed up with the menfolk for a little while, drinking several more toasts in their company, although also quite fatigued. Then we all retired. Uthor would sleep in the same bed as Ygurna by her side, or as close as possible. Even if it had in fact turned into a dark and stormy night, the birth of the healthy child, and the survival of the mother, provided us all with a welcome interlude of celebration, a time of inner light made manifest.

The Pendragon remained with us for several weeks or more, to rejoice in the arrival of his newborn and healthy son. Although nominally a Christian, Uthor still worshipped the old gods in his heart, and Nodens above all, the god of the abyss, of the black hole, of illimitable space, whether as perceived on our planet or out in the cosmic void. With that salient god or force I had made, of course, my own pact while an apprentice under the care of Merlinus Nodentis, and while residing at that magnific fane, now just a little bit less than a hundred years old.

Uthor would need to return, to rejoin forces with Ambrosius Aurelianus in their off-and-on-again but seemingly endless campaign against the Saxons and their allies. They mostly kept to the east, the southeast, and the south but not beyond the midcoast. Vortigurn still exercised some sort of influence over them, possibly because of some lingering respect for Romanitas, that indefinable essence yet surviving throughout the former Imperium, even in the western half, which had fallen away from the new capital Constantinople. However, that new resplendent metropolis could not have seemed further away than it was. Mother Rome, Roma Maternalis, had apparently but inadvertently abandoned Britannia.

In late January the family decided to move on from Cornuae to Caer Leon, and from there to our estate northwest and inland. We would leave in early February. One morning at Uthor's request the elders had a solemn gathering and palaver with him, and with no less than Ygurna herself. We had all seated ourselves around the central hearth in the main room of the palace. We had not barred the rest of the family from standing or sitting outside our circle.

Uthor spoke first. "I cannot postpone much further my return to our British headquarters, to join forces with Ambrosius Aurelianus. But I would like with your permission to leave Ygurna with you for the nonce, wherever you make your home."

The elders all signified "Yes," and nodded at Uthor. He continued, as he looked at his wife sitting in our midst and suckling Arthor, who made no disturbance as usual. "Ygurna must bond with our son for several months before she can hand him over to any available wet nurse. Eventually she will depart, to join me and Aurelianus, traveling with an armed escort, of course."

We sat and talked among ourselves; my parents, my siblings yet living with them, and I, Merlin, reached an accord at once, to have Ygurna remain with us as long as needed. We had already become quite fond of Arthor and his mother, ever graceful and gracious. She had enormous charm and beauty, and she smiled and bowed her head a little to us in acknowledgment of our decision.

Uthor spoke again, looking directly at me. "I give mother and child into the care of the family at large. The women in the household can give them help whenever they have need. I charge Merlin with the instruction and care of my son as soon as he can talk, that is, if Merlin agrees."

I tried to look startled, but my second sight had warned me to expect such a request. I stood up and walked over to the other side of the circle, to where Uthor sat. He got up and approached me. He put his hands on my shoulders and looked profoundly into my eyes, as I did into his.

Merlin: "I accept this honor and this responsibility and shall discharge it to the best of my power."

Uthor: "In essence, beside agreeing to become his tutor, you will also become in effect his legal stepfather, his legal father, in case anything should happen to me, my death or severe injury."

At this point we firmly embraced each other, deeply moved. We both had tears in our eyes.

Uthor now spoke once more. "I shall accompany you and the family to Caer Leon, from Cornuae to southern Cambria, with my armed and mounted escort. Then I shall head east to join Aurelianus." With that our circle broke up. The solemn conjuration had ended. Everyone arose and joined with everyone else inside or outside the circle. Everyone embraced, old and young alike. As Romano-Britons we stood united.

CHAPTER III. Education, Military and Otherwise

On a rare clear and calm day, with plenty of sunlight but still quite cold, of course, our family group started out from Din Tagell, in addition to Uthor and his escort. Such a clear day in early February seemed all the more a miracle, and we interpreted it as a fortunate omen. Gathered in the wide space on the mainland beyond the outer gate, we made a brave and imposing spectacle, albeit not intentionally. We had all mounted our particular horses. Our personal servants had mounted their hardy asses as usual. They had securely packed gear and equipment on extra pack animals of all kinds, including wine and other provisions.

Most of the family's able-bodied men had leather armor on their torsos under the woolen cloaks. We all had our long and short swords at our sides, left and right, plus round wooden shields on our backs, but easily removed for action. Just in case of attack the women carried short swords or daggers. Most of them could use them effectively if needed.

Uthor and his escort would ride ahead of us, our family procession, while some of his guard would ride behind us. In full battle mode they wore their long and short swords just as we did, wooden shields like ours at their backs. Whereas our shields had spikes in the middle, theirs had wide metal reinforcement around the rims, and with a strong spiked metal hub at the center.

With our motley cloaks further patterned by bold curvilinear Keltic designs, we made a brave show. Outriders before and behind the family procession carried large banners unfurled from lances. Uthor's escort displayed the red-purple dragons denoting the Pendragon. The family's own outriders also carried banners from lances, but on theirs they displayed the symbol of the Capricorn once designating the Second Legion at Caer Leon on Usk. We had long since adopted the device as our own.

Only we had made the horns much larger and recurved, that is, curving backward and/or inward. This was the symbol that we claimed Caer Leon and its traditions as ours, and as the family of the Cornuarii of Din Tagell we also claimed as our home the multipronged, or multihorned, peninsula of Cornuae, its overall horn pointing southwest to Land's End.

Around midmorning we had made everything ready. By common consent the adults in the family had given the command to Uthor. He proclaimed in his stentorian voice, "Forward ho!" At last our caravan moved ahead, our older children on their own mounts, the younger children carried by the women in a special device at their back.

We would be overnighting with friends and allies along our route. This itinerary Uthor and we had plotted to cover the distance between Din Tagell and Caer Leon as directly as possible, using all the old Roman roads and bridges that we could, especially over the largest streams. We would ford them as little as possible.

We had sent messages ahead to let our hosts know that we would overnight with them. They also knew that we would be carrying extra provisions with us. Good guests know just when to help out, so as not to overwhelm their hosts! It would require a good week or more to reach Caer Leon with no serious accidents along the way. There we would take refuge inside the stout, re-strengthened walls of the old legionary fortress. Behind those walls most of the local people had long since created perforce a new town. The old vicus, the once luxurious civil settlement outside the walls, had long since disappeared. The local people had removed the stones and bricks to build their new town or structures inside the fortress.

Once we reached Caer Leon, and after a suitable interlude therewithin, the family could continue onward to its estate inland to the northwest of Isca Silurum. Meanwhile I would remain in the old fortress-town, where I could ply far better my wonted business of prediction and superior wisdom for whatever clientele would come to my door. Meanwhile also, Uthor with his mounted escort would return to join forces with Ambrosius Aurelianus. However, in winter time the battle tide or thrust from the invading outlanders established in and around London usually ebbed to its lowest point.

I do not always use my prophetic skills for the family's activities, for something as routine as moving among our three (or four) estates. We had planned a good week or more to reach Caer Leon, moving across the countryside. Despite our start in fair weather when leaving

Din Tagell, our itinerary took much longer than planned. It required a full two weeks and a little more. Stormy weather with heavy rains and winds prolonged our travels, although drinking and feasting enlivened our way.

We did not, of course, travel during the worst weather, that is, during the actual storms, but stayed on with whatever hosts were giving us hospitality. We moved on only on the days that turned out relatively clear.

We stuck as much as possible to the old Roman bridges and roadways, the latter fortunately raised up above the lowest surrounding terrain. To us the full two weeks and more seemed like an eternity, but we finally arrived without serious accidents while traveling, in itself a miracle. We made our grand entrance into Caer Leon. Never had the fortress appeared so comforting or reassuring to us, with its battlements, no less than the towers and turrets that the inhabitants had added over time, in fact since the great Barbarian Conspiracy of 367.

Our family of the Cornuarii remained here overnight for several days. It seemed to take forever for all the woolen clothing to dry out! I literally set up shop (as it were) in a former wine merchant's quarters. When the family moved on to the estate within the mountains of southern Cambria, I did not join them. I had been rotating among our several estates ever since my childhood. I no longer wanted to do that.

I reassured my parents that I would assist the family whenever I could, but I would no longer join them on their travels among their several holdings. They understood. Uthor and escort departed, while Ygurna and Arthor remained with the family at the mountain villa. Life among us Keltoi managed as ever to move forward. We stayed firmly ensconced in our domains in the north, the west, the midsouth, and the southwest.

I remained alone in Caer Leon with my personal servants who ran the little household. Apart from the occasional excursion outside the walls as needed, I had found myself a breathing space where I could conduct my business at my own pace or leisure. I had removed myself at last from the comforting but distracting routines of our family. My business did not always demand prophetic skills so much as it did clear thinking for clients too enmeshed in their problems emotional and otherwise to perceive their way out of them or resolve them on their own. I provided the counsel or advice external to them that they could not. No great magick, but it worked.

Caer Leon still remained in part on a money economy using coins old and new. This made financial transactions much easier. Like everyone else I welcomed barter or trade. In addition to the local people, princes and magistrates came to my door. I helped them to resolve affairs of state; thus my fame and business grew.

Of course, I kept in touch with my family, who mostly maintained themselves at the mountain villa in the next few years, rarely sojourning at Din Tagell or near Caer Vadon.

Infrequently I would go to see clients, much older people, who could not move about readily. This involved several trips to the villa near Vadon, when I would also avail myself of the old baths there, somehow still extant and functioning. I always came back to the household at Caer Leon with a sense of relief. By prior arrangement with the family, and according to the charge laid on me by Uthor, I as a kind of stepfather assumed the task of raising Arthor, after one of my returns from Vadon.

This happened around 446 when Arthor turned five. The family and I had agreed that I would begin discharging this task as soon as Ygurna had weaned Arthor, and as soon as he could speak well and coherently. Now she could join her husband wherever he was fighting against the Saxons. For the sake of their only child she had stayed put for the first five years of his life.

Ygurna with a few family members now brought Arthor to my household within Caer Leon. As soon as I met or re-met Arthor, a sturdy and handsome little boy, I realized that what I had feared could turn into an onerous task would result in an unmitigated pleasure. What a wonderful surprise!

After Ygurna greeted and embraced me, Arthor spoke, and in the basic British language that we spoke throughout our Keltic world whether in Britain or Brittany. "Greetings and salutations, Magister Myrdin," and here, dressed in tunic, breeches, and cloak, he bowed to me. Such spontaneous grace utterly charmed me! I went over to him at once, embraced him, and had him sit with Ygurna and myself as an adult, and as one among equals.

Looking deep into his eyes, I spoke next. "Just call me Merlin. I am your new parent, as requested by your father. I shall be your tutor, your private instructor, until you leave here when you turn fifteen, a decade or so from now. But we need not think about that at this moment. That is a long, long time off in the future." Arthor nodded. He understood.

The family had sent a courier to Uthor, to the headquarters that he shared with Aurelianus in the Chiltern Hills. There the twain could exercise a better surveillance over the regions with the troublesome outlanders, and wage effective military action against them. Our family let Uthor know that Ygurna had weaned their son and had entrusted Arthor to my care, as we had all agreed some five or six years agone at Din Tagell. Sojourning with me at Caer Leon, she could now rejoin him at long last. Apart from an infrequent visit, Uthor had hardly ever had the time, or could have taken it, to spend any occasion with us in the west or southwest. Love still existed between the parents.

After several days her mounted escort arrived, and Ygurna left us. She said goodbye to me with a simple admonition, "Take good care of my son." I smiled in acquiescence. Arthor took the parting from her, and then her departure, with calm and good grace. He did weep a little while he embraced her just before she rode off, surrounded by her mounted guardians.

My prolonged instruction for Arthor commenced. He was an astute and enthusiastic student and learned fast, an ideal situation for me. We soon began conversing in Latin with facility, and I showed him how to form his letters with ink and quill on an old piece of vellum, often erased and used again, a true palimpsest, from such as I myself had learned long ago.

Soon we would graduate from simple exercises in simple, straightforward Latin to Caesar's *Commentaries on the Gallic Wars* and then on to the simpler orations of Cicero, the standard texts for beginners. Arthur's progress appeared to me phenomenal. Linguistically he seemed a genius at least, but I also made sure that he got plenty of physical exercise. I let him roam throughout the town and form his own circle of companions his own age. Some of these later became part of his trusted cataphractarii. Invariably he led his own pack and always seemed fair and evenhanded, as far as I could observe. He turned out to be a genuine leader by his very nature, one whom the others could trust for sensible guidance.

Physically tough, he took after Uthor in rough-and-tumble games, in the mock battles and combat that the boys instinctively undertook. When he turned nine or ten, I handed Arthor over to one Junius Maximus, a trained military teacher, an experienced man or master at arms. Junius thoroughly indoctrinated him in all aspects of arms and fighting. The use of the long sword, the short sword, the spear, the big shield and the buckler, that is, the smaller shield, no less than the dagger.

One early morning, soon after Ygurna's departure, Arthor and I found ourselves at the table-desk in the main chamber of my property in Caer Leon, alone at last apart from the personal servants who managed the household and the meals. Our impromptu classroom had formerly served as the chief tasting room for the wine merchant and his amphorae filled with vintages from all over the Mediterranean world.

Arthor looked at me with a little bit of diffidence, no less than deference, and then he spoke. "Merlin, may I please also call you master? I am accustomed to address my elders, men in particular, in this way, as carefully taught by my mother." I responded at once, "Of course, dear child, you may do so, even if we need between us to stand on no ceremony. But let us attend to our learning for the day, no less than many days ahead of us." Arthor nodded. He understood.

Merlin: "Your mother has already taught you your Latin alphabet, the sounds, and how you speak and write them. You already know how to speak our British tongue, and now you must learn Latin itself. This is essential. You will become a warrior and a leader of warriors. As a leader or a statesman, you must have the Latin, in order to speak with the other members of the Roman Empire, even if our ties to it no longer exist, or are somewhat frayed."

Arthor nodded again and smiled eagerly. "So we now begin to learn Latin grammar, its conjugations for the verbs, and its declensions for the nouns and adjectives." I, Merlin, had spoken.

Often I watched the master at arms and Arthor sparring with each other. They both wore leather armor with little metal rings or scales firmly attached, to deflect a sword or dagger blow. Whereas the leather armor protected the upper body, small simple leather caps with lappets tied under the chin defended the head, also reinforced with rings or scales of metal.

One day they would spar with big shield and long sword. Another day they would feint with buckler and short sword, the old legionary gladius. To my wonder and gratification Arthor appeared a natural-born fighter. Although not quite full grown, being only in his early adolescence, he seemed more than capable of defending himself, as well as going on the offensive. Such a deep relief did I feel at having my second sight corroborated about him, that he would become a great warrior.

Then on a day when all seemed quiet, no classes in language or literature, no training in arms, Junius came to confer with me privately. Arthur was by now but fourteen, but appeared nearly full grown. I paid acute attention to what Junius had to say.

"Young Arthor can soon join his father and Ambrosius Aurelianus at their headquarters in the Chiltern Hills. I would gauge that he can do so when he turns fifteen, or soon after that. It is a subject that only you two can decide between you. I cannot teach him much more. He can already beat me in regular combat. He is quick and can adapt himself at once as things change in battle. He is already a full-fledged warrior, and now he needs only experience in the field, in battle with the Saxons. But best of all, he keeps a level head on him while fighting. Please tell him what I have just confided in you about him."

I countered, "No, thank you, but you tell him while in my presence. Let me summon him; he should be back from roaming around town." It was done. Arthor embraced his instructor at arms. He seemed more than eager to join his father and the others in those central hills. As I then told him, "Arthor, my son and student, your education is complete. Neither Junius nor myself can teach you anything more. You choose the time when you want to leave, and the family will send a courier to Uthor. He can then order a mounted guard to fetch and bring you to him."

All three of us embraced. How proud I became of Arthor, no less than for him.

CHAPTER IV. Warrior Apprentice

In case I have not mentioned it before, Arthur would not need to shave until his early twenties. He wanted to look clean-shaven like his idol Alexander the Great. He would look very different when he became the sole Dux Bellorum and let his beard and hair grow as they would. He would have them trimmed only to keep them out of his eyes, out of his way. How different he would look during the last thirty years or so of his life!

As a young man he seemed strong and stalwart, garbed as usual in tunic, cross-gartered breeches, with a brown cloak thrown around him. This provided some camouflage when in any forest, and made him less of a target for enemy eyes. Although spring had arrived, and many trees had already leafed in much of southern Britain, it still remained cool at times.

If I do say so myself, Arthur was more than merely handsome. He was what the Greeks and Romans would have called a beautiful youth. In fact, he resembled his idol distant in time, Alexandros Megalos. That is, as we had perceived his face on old Greek coins, and as I had portrayed him from Greek and Latin literature. Arthor's great ambition? He wanted to imitate, perhaps to equal, Alexander as a fearless fighter, a genuine warrior, but also, if he could, to cultivate a sense of compassion like Alexander's.

After several days of steady riding, overnighting where they could, Arthor and his mounted escort had arrived at the southwest edge of the forest covering most of the Chilterns. Here, as prearranged, they would meet another mounted escort. With their forces joined, they would proceed to the headquarters of Uthor and Aurelianus deep in the higher hills.

As the head of the detachment escorting Arthur with a few of his personal but well-armed servants, Caspar broke his usual silence and spoke. "Let us dismount here while we wait on Hilarius and his troop."

They did so, and let their mounts crop the grass and other plants here and there. But the men kept a close eye on them so that they should not wander too far off. In fact, they stayed close to the Britons.

All of a sudden, out of the forest a sizeable group of Saxon warriors appeared and began encircling the Britons. The latter grabbed their horses as fast as they could and mounted them. As the Saxons rushed up to attack them, Caspar and Arthor began to fight with their long swords, deploying their shields as best they could.

Caught on the defensive, Arthor went on the offensive at once, Caspar by his side. The other warriors rallied behind them and boldly charged the leading Saxons. Even if the latter had no horses, they put up a formidable fight. Moreover, they clearly outnumbered the Britons. Blow followed blow, and the Saxons might have overwhelmed them by sheer numbers, despite the skill and bravery displayed by the Britons.

Just at that moment, riding out of the forest, Hilarius and his detachment of mounted fighters appeared. Immediately they joined Arthur and his escort. Now the tide of combat quickly turned against the Saxons, but they continued fighting. At last their line broke, and a few fled back into the woods.

Arthor faced a young man his own age and would have dispatched him, but right then his enemy stumbled and fell. In perfectly good British speech the youth shouted, "I yield!" He lay there without sword or shield. Arthor spoke: "I spare your life, but only if you join us and our cause. Right now!"

The young man somehow managed to speak in a hoarse throaty voice. "I agree, and accept your offer." Again he said this in perfectly good British. Arthor helped him to his feet. The youth shook Arthor's right hand; for that one moment neither was holding a weapon.

The other Saxons lay dead or had vanished back into the forest. The Britons did not bother to pursue them. Miraculously they had suffered no deaths or serious wounds. After regrouping, they proceeded along the old Roman road leading into the hills, into the deeper woods. They all found themselves eager to meet and to report back to Uthor and the other Dux Bellorum.

I record this episode as Arthor later remembered it. It served as his first real fight against an enemy force. He had passed his first test. How very different from training to fight, merely training to do so! Nevertheless, Arthor's long preparation in arms had more than served him well, or much more than well. Yes, that preparation, plus above all else his own spirit and bravery. His decision to spare the Saxon youth also served to demonstrate Arthor's inherent magnanimity. Onward now to the British headquarters deep in the *selva obscura,* indeed, the dark forest.

Arthor cast a glance back at the site of the skirmish. Some dozen Britons stayed behind to bury the dead Saxons, rather than to leave them exposed for dogs, wolves, or bears to eat. Arthor had the Saxon youth ride behind a big Briton on an especially large charger, following at once Arthor and his personal servants, positioned with the vanguard. Arthor planned to use the Saxon recruit as another personal assistant, intrigued as Arthor was by the Saxon's command of the British tongue. He wanted to know how that had come about. He had also noted the Saxon's youthful beauty, his blond hair and his blue eyes, strikingly distinct from the darker Britons.

Just before they skirted the Great Escarpment that runs roughly southwest to northeast, Arthor and his party stopped in a well-shaded spot to water and to rest their mounts from their moderate but steady pace. The Great Escarpment divided the higher part of the hills from the somewhat lower terrain beneath the great forest cover.

Arthor came over to the Saxon youth and asked him his name. He answered forthrightly, "My people call me Everherd. I primarily have guarded our flocks, cows and goats and sheep. Although I can fight, I am not a warrior in the first place. Our tribal chieftain recruited me. The rest you know."

Arthor commented, "You speak very good British. How did that come about? I am intrigued."

Everherd replied, "Count Theodosius recruited my family along with other families, whether Saxons or Angles, to man the Litus Saxonicus. He settled us along the Saxon Shore from southeast Britain to the south-central coast. Invited into Britain, it was my great-grandfather who established us here. We have been settled here since just after what you British call the great Barbarian Conspiracy."

Arthor responded, "I am happy that you yielded, and that I spared you. I need an assistant, not so much to fight by my side, but someone who can act as an interpretor and liaison with the Angles and the Saxons, a kind of secretary. Do you think that you could handle the job?"

Everherd answered, "I think so. I shall try my best. You spared my life. You are now my master." They both smiled and shook each other's right hand, signaling that neither held a weapon whether sword or dagger.

The party mounted up at a signal from Arthor and continued on its itinerary.

Arthor had relocated from Caer Leon to a region some thirty miles or so west or northwest of the old fortified City of London, the Civitas Londinium, within the original walls that went up only late in the third Christian century at the command of that other Aurelianus, the Roman emperor Lucius Domitius Aurelianus. Had the walls gone up almost as soon as the Romans had founded the city, they might have withstood the grim war waged by the British queen Boadicea, when with very good reason she rebelled against the new central authority from the Continent. Boadicea's rebellion happened around the middle of the then first Christian century. But the most urgent need for the walls only came about in the time of Aurelianus as emperor, or a little before his reign.

In the same way Caer Leon, as Arthor's former home with me, Merlin himself, lay some eighty miles or so due west of London, but in southeast Cambria the much earlier walls had gone up as part of the legionary fortress, now since turned into a civilian town. However, it was from the old capital of the overall province of Britannia that the long-lived Vortigurn, the self-proclaimed High King, still held sway more or less as the protector or the prisoner of the Germanic tribes. Those he had invited onto the island from the Continent across the Narrow Seas.

As Arthor and his party approached the headquarters held in common by Uthor and Ambrosius, the day was waning. They reached the central building a little before sunset. Underlings relieved the group of their horses at the entrance of the main structure. The Britons had made their encampment out of wood. They had sited it amid an old ancestral hillfort. They perforce abandoned it at the time of the Roman invasion and conquest. Then in the late fourth century they had refortified it, with walls of earth and wood.

The chief structure featured that kind of wooden architecture notable for its intricacy whether inside or outside. This was the style that had prevailed before the buildings of tile, stone, brick, and mortar favored by the Romans. By comparison it could but appear as fantastical or fantasticated. Arthor noted the rather complicated craftsmanship with awe and astonished admiration, above all when he entered the main chamber. It was a great hall like a great barn with columns made out of the entire trunks of lofty trees, and above the heads of the entering party there extended a bewildering kaleidoscope of rafters at successive levels with diagonal beams connecting them to the ridgepole.

Arthor only had a moment to note this bewilderment of carven wood before the people in the hall called him back to himself. Some outriders had gone ahead to tell of the imminent arrival of Arthor and his party. They had prepared everyone for Arthor's appearance. Scarcely had he managed to survive his kaleidoscopic impression of the great hall with its extensive circular hearth in the very middle than he faced his father, the Pendragon, somewhat older and more battle-scarred than ever, but still exuding tremendous energy. He embraced his only official son with vehemence. Then his mother, the princess Ygurna, did the same. And then the very Roman-resembling "General" Ambrosius Aurelianus, as introduced to Arthor by Uthor, also embraced him no less warmly than had his parents.

A chorus of "Welcome, twice welcome, thrice welcome!" assailed Arthor's ears. In a sense he felt that he had indeed come home at last like the Prodigal Son in the biblical fable. What an exuberant sensation overwhelmed him all at once. No drug could have acted more powerfully. Now beyond any doubt he had entered the world of endless combat, of endless battle, beyond what any warrior could ever have wished.

As it occurred often in the course of Merlin reading to Glirid aloud, thus during that long year c. 425 or 426—not to mention his digressions and his direct asides to his own secretary—the venerable gentleman and magician would sometimes pause and return to himself, as if overwhelmed by his memories or some emotion incited by those recollections. He did not always finish up in tears, but sometimes with chuckles, guffaws, or outright raucous laughter. On the present occasion he just sat there, absorbed in some pensive moment that had taken place but beyond words. Glirid already knew the account pretty well. After all, he had redacted it from Merlin's ever-deliberate dictation onto successive scrolls of thin supple vellum.

CHAPTER V. Full-Fledged Warrior and Dux Bellorum

Merlin had purposely stopped, even if what he now said appeared no more than a paraphrase of what lay redacted on the literal manuscript, beautifully formed in Glirid's hand-printing.

"Here I give up, I surrender, attempting to give a straightforward account of Arthor's life and career, from about 455 to 490. This covers the period when he became a full-fledged warrior and leader of warriors, then a kind of assistant general (first to his father Uthor, second to Aurelianus), next at long last *the* Dux Bellorum by himself alone.

"Here he falls out of my own direct purview. Here I must perforce depend on what I can recall from his then reports on papyrus, or delivered in person whenever he could come back to Caer Leon on Usk. Please excuse what must seem like no more than redundant summaries. I need to make them from time to time to keep myself focussed and unconfused.

"In Arthor's further life and career I cannot keep up with the flux of events, of that endless cavalcade of random skirmishes, of major combats between posses of Britons and Saxons, of pitched battles at least twelve, perhaps more. Twelve battles worthy of being immortalized in some Virgilian epic divided into twelve books. To do justice to all that, the writer would have to qualify as an official herald, or yet better, as a practiced bard or other professional poet.

"Even if I have loved poetry all my life and can still turn out a competent long line imitating Virgil in his *Aeneid* or his *Georgics,* I would not, I could not, create an epic poem worthy of Arthor as an undoubted hero. Who could hope to capture or to match his actions in mere words and meter? What he and Uthor and Aurelianus achieved remains a monumental catalogue, an unparalleled procession of activities.

"In Arthor's case as Dux Bellorum alone, by himself in collaboration with several generations of warriors, what did he manage to accomplish? As an official general elected to that position by common consent of all the British kings of his time, he countered the ever-expanding thrust of the Saxons and others all along Britain's eastern coast from Din Eidyn in the north, and then all along the southern coast from Kent to the isle of Vectis, that is, all along the fortified Saxon Shore, and then inland of there northwest to Caer Vadon and Mount Badon, an extended front to defend time and again.

"He gave us, his fellow Britons, as Romanized Kelts, a breathing space. Practical and realistic, as advised by myself as Merlin, Arthor realized in advance that he could never restore Britannia to what it became under direct Roman rule. That rule or dominion lasted from the middle of the first century until the end of the fourth, when Rome inadvertently had to abandon the province to look to her own defenses as well as devices.

"From the time of his great victory, his triumph at Mount Badon in 490, over the Saxons and all their allies attempting to invade and inhabit our island, he held high court for thirty years until his death in 520 or so. He died in battle with his own son Medraut at Camlann in Cornuae, at the little village of Camlann, near the mouth of the river Cam or Camel. That last great battle marked the end of the peace, the Pax Britannica, that had endured as long as his unprecedented reign as High King after the death of Vortigurn in London about the same time as the victory at Mount Badon.

"Even if I and others have hardly mentioned it, there was one other major, if not paramount, condition that played a determining part in Britain's destiny: the occasional but awful plagues that came in from the Mediterranean basin from its far eastern shore. They came in by means of the vessels with the merchants who arrived here to trade in the western and southern parts of our island. First came the plague that happened around the middle of the 300s, and that decimated both the cities and the countryside. Then another after the great Barbarian Conspiracy in 367, that is, soon after the restoration of Britain by Count Theodosius during 369–70.

"The late 360s marked a strategic development in our British history, even without Theodosius: a large number of Romano-Britons left much of the eastern and southern parts of our common domain. They had become discouraged and exhausted by the instability of life in Britain. They emigrated and settled in Brittany, to take refuge under that peninsula's vast and protecting forest cover. This large-scale emigration especially served to depopulate our own original realms. Then sometimes during the first third of the 400s another plague, or series of plagues of different kinds, came in as always from the eastern Mediterranean, further devastating the island.

"Britain thus lay nearly undefended and underpopulated from plague and other natural disasters. To the Germanic tribes along the Gallic littoral across the Narrow Seas, the island must have appeared almost unpopulated, a tempting prize to invade and occupy as their new homeland relatively safe from the unceasing political and military troubles on the Continent throughout the Western Empire.

"Only the militant intervention, the defense of Britain, by Uthor, Aurelianus, and Arthur gave us any real hope, those of us Kelts still managing to hold on, to endure, and that only in the north, the west, and the southwest."

Well, Virgilian epic or not, Ciceronian prose or not, Merlin had already launched himself on into his account of Arthor's extremely long military career first from 455 to 470, and then from 470 to 490. After his election as High King by all the British kings, princes, or chieftains, he would both reign and rule from 490 to 520. He would have a rather long life overall, dying about eighty, maybe a little more.

PART TWO
Dux Bellorum

Contents

CHAPTER I. Full-Fledged Warrior and Leader of Warriors

Arthor and others took the occasion to wash up before an early supper. That evening, after the meal, everyone had seated themselves around the great circular hearth in the great hall. Many held cups or goblets filled with the wine that Arthor and his escort had brought with them from Caer Leon. Uthor, Ygurna, and Arthor sat to one side in a little group of their own.

Caspar had just related to Arthor's parents how some Saxons appearing out of the forest had ambushed and almost overwhelmed the Britons, but how Hilarius and his escort had come upon the skirmish in time to assist and save Arthor and his warriors. They defeated the Saxons, killing most of them in direct combat, while a few managed to escape. Both Caspar and Hilarius described Arthor as if he had already made himself into a seasoned warrior. They praised his valor, no less than the exceptional skill in arms he had shown.

Uthor: "Between them Merlin and Junius Maximus did quite a good job at preparing you to join us here. Congratulations! I am proud of you, my son. In the next few days either Ambrosius or I shall take you out on patrol with us along the edges of the forest. You will have plenty of chance to show more skill and bravery in other skirmishes. The Saxons and their allies are as determined as we Britons are."

Arthor's parents had noted how powerful their handsome son appeared. He had his father's body but his mother's face and comeliness. The latter seemed all the more noticeable because as yet he had no facial hair, and the hair on his head came down only to his neck but covered his ears. No long flowing locks would impede his vision and his fighting.

Already and immediately Arthor had introduced Everherd to the Britons, claiming a special status for him as Arthor's own interpretor and liaison for dealing with the Saxons. He related how Everherd had stumbled and fallen, how he yielded, and how Arthor had spared his life. More than that, he claimed a further special condition for the Saxon youth. With the permission of his parents, readily granted, Arthor formally adopted him as a blood brother.

They performed the little ceremony, and everyone drank a toast to the adoption. Standing stalwartly, Everherd bowed his head slightly, smiled graciously, and thanked everyone present for the honor. All could see that he was well born and well bred, even if not aristocratic. But Arthor also made a yet further special condition. Everherd did not need to fight at his side, or anyone's side among the Britons, unless an emergency might arise in the field, as it often did.

Thus it was in this way that Arthor began his life as a man of arms, and a man at arms, fighting along his fellow Britons as Combrogians, as countrymen as well as brothers. Several weeks passed with this routine, patrolling these hills with the occasional skirmish or more extended combat. But the Saxons in general avoided the forested hills in favor of open fields and river valleys.

Meanwhile Arthor continued to nurse and nourish an idea that Merlin and he discussed before Arthor left Caer Leon. He told Merlin that he would broach the idea to his fellow Britons in the Chiltern Hills when the time seemed ripe. That moment had come, and Arthor asked to address a small assemblage of the leaders like Uthor and Ambrosius, no less than the elders among them, in privacy within a smaller separate chamber, and not in the great hall until they had argued it among themselves. They agreed, intrigued by what Arthor had to discuss or propose.

They had convened, and everyone sat around the great oval table in the smaller separate chamber chosen for the meeting. All waited in eager anticipation. Arthor stood up and addressed the assemblage.

"Respected elders, let me propose at once an idea that Merlin in his infallible wisdom often discussed with me before I left Caer Leon to join you here at this headquarters. In fact, I first mentioned it, but Merlin had long pondered the subject by himself: the concept of an additional headquarters.

"Whether we like it or not, it seems that the Saxons and their allies have come into Britain to stay. Theodosius, when he was Count and before he became Emperor, first officially invited them here. But some had already settled here and there along the Saxon Shore somewhat before then, and as part of the regular military assignment in the Western Empire.

"They have now become established in Britain for at least three quarters of a century in the southeast of the island, but mostly in and around London, as further invited by Vortigurn as his own self-proclaimed High King. Given that these so-called outlanders are firmly established along the eastern and southern coasts, they would not leave easily. They make a worthy foe. Merlin and I suggest that we work to accommodate them here in Britain, after such a long settlement on their part, even if we must keep on fighting them.

"But the chief thing that Merlin and I propose is that we set up an additional headquarters but southwest of the old watering place of Aquae Sulis, or Caer Vadon, and south of Dun Glastan. The new locale is an ancient ancestral fortress of great size, perforce abandoned after the Romans arrived, took over, and settled here. The local people call it Dun Cadan.

"It would make an easier locale from which to counter the continuing thrust of the Anglo-Saxons. Merlin and I do not propose that you abandon the headquarters here, but we urge you to set up an added command post at Dun Cadan. Leave London to Vortigurn and the Anglo-Saxons. This is our proposal. Please discuss it among yourselves."

Arthor sat himself down and continued looking at the assemblage with a serious mien. The voices of the elders rose up at once in anger and irritation, in loud and vigorous dispute and argument. Arthor had anticipated the wrath, as if he had implied something overtly treasonous. Uthor and Aurelianus conceded privately to each other that Arthor had shown great courage to propose something so much against the grain. They also conceded that he had a sense of humor, albeit cloaked carefully with due and respectful solemnity.

Following apt and prolonged colloquy the elders announced that they might pursue the proposal, but that Arthor could also prosecute the matter on his own, as time and circumstance might permit. Arthor thanked the council of elders for their answer and vowed to himself that he would do so as he could.

For me personally it is a supreme irony that I, Merlinus Merlinius, the least militaristic person that I could imagine, must relate the manifold military deeds of Arthor, now perceived as one of the great-

est military geniuses of all time, bearing comparison with his own supreme idol Alexander Magnus, all proportions guarded. Even if Britain might seem insignificant compared to Persia, no less than India,
the overall British terrain provided a more than adequate challenge
considering the vastly reduced forces and resources that Arthor had at
his command in Britain or in Brittany. More than once, circumstances called Arthor to defend that country's eastern marches.

It is true that at one time I could summon up the past, the present, and the future, but those erstwhile powers have waned. I must
rely on my strength of memory alone, however insufficient and inadequate. Honesty compels me to admit these weakened faculties. But
let me attempt the task!

How can I even begin to call up all those unending skirmishes, all
those ambushes, all those combats, all those battles beyond what any
warrior could ever have wished? And this involved Arthor as one of
the greatest warriors of all time! I can hardly summon up the strength
to admit my patent inability. However, I shall try to invoke his twelve
great battles in some form or fashion, that is, after he became *the* Dux
Bellorum around 470.

Meanwhile, on his own, Arthor surveyed again the terrain and
surroundings of Dun Cadan for future use, and with such restricted
money resources as he had, including some old Roman coinage. He
began to urge and reimburse the local people to start refortifying the
four surrounding walls of earth, of wood, and often still of stone. This
also involved the ditches between and below the walls. The site remains a remarkable place even after Arthor.

The coinage derived from my own searches and researches in
and around Caer Leon. The coins came in much handier and easier
for negotiation than barter or trade. Beyond the money or other
payment, all our fellow countrymen appeared more than eager to
help. After all, it implicated them and their own survival, their own
well-being, as much as possible. Arthor would see to the further development of the site somewhat later on. In the meantime the local
people had taken shelter in a little village of their own at the top level,
the ridge area, of the extensive plateau.

Much occurred before Arthor became the sole Dux Bellorum,
albeit reluctantly and rather sagely. He never manifested any greed

for power, but accepted it as his destiny and his natural inheritance. His father Uthor gave up the ghost when unwisely he rode forth on his own, on reconnaissance in and around the hills. A posse of Saxons ambushed and killed him, but they did not dishonor or mutilate his body. Once the Britons recovered the body and embalmed it, Arthor and others escorted the body back to Dun Glastan for interment in Ynis Avalon in the midst of that swamp. The princess Ygurna in sable mourning accompanied Arthor, and from there she joined the family, that is, the Cornuarii, at our estate northwest of Caer Leon. This happened around 460.

Thus Arthor continued to fight alongside, and otherwise aid and abet, the then almost venerable Ambrosius Aurelianus, who died in another skirmish with the Saxons or other outlanders, as the Britons preferred to call them. They buried him somewhere in the Chiltern Hills not far from the British headquarters, but in an unmarked grave, unmarked save by subtle features of the landscape and known only among the Combrogians. This happened about 470.

Arthor now moved his own headquarters from those hills west or northwest of London to the new location at Dun Cadan. Most of the warriors followed him of their own volition, leaving about only a hundred men or more there behind them, all hardy and seasoned fighters. The local people at Dun Cadan in the interim of 460 through 470 had constructed at Arthor's request, or command, a series of buildings for his use and that of his own standing army, perhaps about a thousand men or less, not always in place there at Arthor's side. His warriors had their own lives and families to which they had to attend, as often dispersed throughout the British-held territory, an extensive terrain.

As already and cautiously expressed, even if I could not evoke just a tiny percentage of Arthor's multifarious exploits, I shall attempt the task of at least *naming* his twelve great battles and indicating where they happened to take place, typically near the rivers, which afforded the easiest entrance into Britain.

CHAPTER II. A Register of Noteworthy Combats

Another day, another addendum to Merlin's memoirs, but as usual dealing with Arthor and his exploits. Midmorning, and already seated in their solid oak armchairs, at the long, large oak table, are the wizard Merlin; and close to him on his right, his indispensable secretary Glirid.

"Glirid, kind friend, please find for me that wide old chart made at the time of that other Aurelianus. The old map that shows from left to right, west to east, the coastlines of Hibernia, Britannia, and Gaul, plus the other notable features, the towns, the rivers, the mountains.

"I need it to make sure that I have my register of Arthor's twelve great battles in correct chronological order vis-à-vis the locales where they happened."

The secretary finds the scroll, and unrolls it where it covers the other half of the table, laying it out over the other scrolls piled in some kind of regular order. Merlin appears to pull back for a moment into himself, and then begins his discourse.

"Yes, Arthor's twelve great battles! Worthy to be relived and presented in some Virgilian epic poem in proper form and meter, and failing that, at least in decent Ciceronian prose! But failing even that, all that I have attempted here is a simple register as correlated with certain sites noted on the map." Glirid nods and smiles encouragement at his master.

"The first battle occurred at the mouth of the river Glein, the Gline, the Glean. That would be the Glen, the stream that flows not far from the town of Lind Colin, the old Lindum Colonia, now largely abandoned by the British, by us.

"The next four battles, numbers two, three, four, and five, took place on the banks of the river Dubglas, in the region Linnuis, to the north of Lind Colin. Here Arthor and his army had to fight long and hard to defeat and discourage successive waves of invaders, a determined series of warriors.

"The sixth battle happened on the banks of the river Bassas, to the south of Lind Colin. Another hard and hotly contested struggle!

"The seventh big fight occurred at Cat Coet Celidon. That is the vast forest in the Caledonian Lowlands. As far as I can recall, some thirty miles southwest of Dun Eidyn. Given the nature of those woods, this resulted in an arduous and awkward contest. But again the British came out as the victors despite heavy losses.

"The eighth battle, another particularly hard one, took place by that castle, the Castellum Guinnion, east of the Caer Leon on the river Dee in northern Cambria proper.

"The ninth struggle occurred at Caer Leon on Usk, unless it happened again at Caer Leon on Dee, as claimed by some historians, or even at that older town that began as another legionary fortress, Eboracum, now Caer Ebrauc. As you know, that lies far to the northeast of Caer Leon on Dee, by some ninety miles. But lesser combats also took place not far from both Caer Ebrauc and Caer Leon on Dee.

"The tenth battle came about on the banks of the river Tribruit, which (as I recall) flows into the western sea somewhere south of Cat Coet Celidon, and north of Caer Luell, the Luguvallium of Roman days, as well as of Roman nights.

"The eleventh battle took place at or near the great hill of Agned, or Mons Agned. Another hotly contested battle, like the one on the river Tribruit. Difficult ground once again, and closer to Dun Eidyn.

"But as you know, the greatest struggle of all, which would give us peace for some thirty or even fifty years, turned out to be the battle fought in the hills north of Caer Vadon. Invaders and enemies from all over had conspired to gather by land and by sea. This happened in 490, a year no Briton can ever forget. It was as great a conspiracy as the great Barbarian Conspiracy of 367. But this came together more than a century later, at least.

"The barbarians once again had entered into a clandestine pact to challenge us, the Britons, in the open region at or near the foot of Mount Badon, or Mons Badonicus. Ah, how that last lovely Latin consoles us!

"Our widespread web of spies had kept Arthor and his army well informed as to this new barbarian pact. They confronted the outlanders, the invaders, the enemies arriving from all over, but they, the Britons, with a combined army as great as theirs. And it was the cavalry, Arthor and his cataphractarians, that played the decisive role in crushing all these enemies. It resulted in our greatest victory, and at long last our enemies left us in peace, at least for a good long while.

"The other great result of the triumph at Mount Badon: it had united all the Britons in common cause against the common enemy. And we, the Britons, remained united for several generations. Given our strong preference for, as well as emphasis on, individuality, that unification proved a triumph as great as the battle itself. The Britons could not have achieved what they did without Arthor and his brilliance as paramount warrior and *the* Dux Bellorum, the leader of leaders nonpareil!

"Vortigurn, the self-proclaimed High King, died at London in the same year as the victory at Mount Badon, and of extreme old age, but few true British mourned his passing. To them he seemed a traitor by inviting even more Saxons and their allies on into our contested island.

"It was only justice that after this greatest victory of Arthor's that all the surviving British kings, princes, and chieftains unanimously elected him as High King. He would rule and reign alternately from Dun Cadan and Caer Leon on Usk, but largely from the latter for some thirty years more or less."

Merlin had completed his long discourse and he seemed, and was in fact, very tired. The recital of Arthor's twelve great battles had outworn him a bit more than what Merlin and his secretary had anticipated. Merlin spoke.

"Well, dear Glirid, I trust that I did a passable job of locating the battles and correlating them with the map." Glirid nods with due solemnity and says, "Yes, you have, in fact and in deed!"

Merlin heaves a big sigh and replies, "Thank you. Please help me into my bedroom, where I must have a rest before we continue later this afternoon."

CHAPTER III. The Princess Gueneveria

It must not be thought that all during that long spell from about 450 to 490 Arthor did nothing but fight. He did have on occasion various bowers of solace and intimate enchantment as afforded by various enchantresses, as he liked to call them. There was no British woman of suitable age, whether unmarried or married (even the latter proved no barrier if the husband agreed), who would not have bedded Arthor in a trice. When he was between his mid-adolescence and his early twenties, before he let his later voluminous beard and head hair flourish as they would, Arthor as a beautiful youth appeared radiant.

Quite apart from the beauty and regularity of his face and well-muscled body (he had inherited Ygurna's beauty of face), he seemed to project a light around him, a veritable aura nearly golden in its effect on others. Coupled with his qualities as charismatic leader, he seemed irresistible to men and women alike. But as he told all people who bedded him (even if he bedded them apparently at first), they took responsibility for any children that resulted from any liaison betwixt him and any ardent maiden. They all accorded with this condition, and this did not appear surprising.

On occasion an exceptional woman or man would claim Arthor's attention exclusively, even when it did not involve anything erotic, but it usually did. Such proved the case when he met up with a certain young woman of high degree, of great intelligence and great beauty. She was the daughter of a king, a certain Voël, who ruled over the southwest region of Cambria proper, his capital established in the old walled city of Caer Marthen. How many names or spellings do we have for that beautiful young woman of high degree! Guinevere, Gwynwhyfar, Guenhevaer, Ganhumara, Guenhumara, Guynhumara! But the name that Merlin preferred of all these variations was Guen(h)everia, a name as elegant as the princess herself!

She happened to be studying in Isca Silurum with various teachers, including Merlin (myself or himself). On one of the rare occasions when Arthor was visiting in Caer Leon with me, Gueneveria and he just happened to meet. It must have been love at first sight. At once they engaged each other in conversation.

"In whose gracious presence am I so fortunate to find myself, pray tell? I am Arthor, son of Uthor Pendragon and the princess Ygurna, as well as an enlightened student of Merlinus Merlinius, as you yourself appear to be." He flashed his most radiant smile at the young lady, who returned the radiance with a smile of her own.

A heightening of light seemed to hover and linger in the air around the three of us in Merlin's boutique of enchantment and prophecy. Before she could answer, the elder excused himself to go to the back of the shop on some errand, leaving the young people to themselves.

She spoke, "I am the princess Gueneveria, the eldest daughter of Ohoupen Voël, the king of Caer Marthen. Merlin has often spoken of you, and I am honored to meet you." She bowed her head more than a little toward him. He returned the compliment by grasping her right hand and briefly placing his forehead onto the hand. The spontaneous act of courtesy and homage, totally new to her but agreeable, amazed and enchanted her.

Gueneveria was wearing a motley green and blue tunic, a sheath of some Egyptian cotton, down to her ankles, and a slim golden circlet around the top of her head. Her unbound black hair hung down to her waist in the back. With her dark blue eyes she looked into Arthor's eyes of deep green, and he looked back into hers.

He smiled one of his most radiant smiles, and then he spoke. "I am happy that you live so far from the eternal battlefront between Britons and Saxons, whether safe in your father's court or here under the tutelage of my own teacher and foster parent. Merlin taught and raised me from the age of five until the age of fifteen. You are safe here with him, quite apart from his so-called magic powers."

Gueneveria countered with a question and a smile. "Since the collapse of the Western Empire, is there any place in Britain left that is truly safe?"

Struck by her astute response, Arthor answered, "Except in a relative sense, no! But you are much safer here than in the Chiltern Hills."

She nodded. "That is true." At that moment Merlin came back and asked them if they would join him each with a cup of some rare pomegranate wine that had just come in by ship from North Africa.

They agreed to his proposal and sat at a little table to one side of that front chamber, the former wine-tasting area. The wine had mercifully not gone off during the sea voyage. They all agreed that the wine had a subtle as well as exquisite pomegranate bouquet.

*   *   *

The meeting and then the falling in love between the two young people happened not long after the death of Uthor Pendragon by Saxon ambush in the Chiltern forest, oddly not far from the very British headquarters. Despite his experience as a great warrior, Uthor should never have gone riding by himself on unofficial reconnaissance in such equivocal territory. After Uthor's burial in Ynis Avalon at Dun Glastan with understated pomp and ritual, the princess Ygurna as his official wife and widow came sometimes to live with Merlin at Caer Leon or with Merlin's family at their fortified villa northwest and inland of the same Isca Silurum.

The meeting between Arthor and Gueneveria under Merlin's auspices took place after Arthor had become assistant Dux Bellorum to Ambrosius Aurelianus, if not actually a co-equal one, given the latter's failing health at long last, no less than his death in battle or in some skirmish around 470. This left Arthor alone as the supreme leader against the Saxons and other enemies.

Sometime after Uthor's burial Arthor and Gueneveria married in Caer Leon, and as in the case of his father's interment, with understated pomp and ceremony. To this official unionization Gueneveria's parents, the king and queen of Caer Marthen, together with other family members, journeyed from southwest Cambria proper to Caer Leon to celebrate the event. Her parents had already given their formal consent via an exchange of couriers between Arthor at Caer Leon and Gueneveria's family at Caer Marthen, about sixty miles as the bird flies west to east.

As Arthor's wife and queen Gueneveria would now divide her time between Caer Leon and Merlin's family estate northwest of the old legionary fortress that had become a civilian town. But most often she resided with Arthor in the Chiltern Hills. Wherever they went in that forest northwest of London, Everherd went with them as their interpreter and liaison with the Saxons and their allies. The Saxon youth enjoyed thus a special status among both the British and the outlanders as a neutral entity, as a Saxon who had become Arthor's blood brother after the Dux Bellorum had spared his life in battle.

Later, of course, when Arthor moved his main headquarters to Dun Cadon, to the rebuilt fortress there, Gueneveria and Everherd accompanied him and the army of warriors that went along with him.

CHAPTER IV. Another Great Barbarian Conspiracy

During their long and mostly faithful marriage, Gueneveria and Arthor never produced any children. His queen was barren, although she took care of various foster children and in a sense adopted them. Meanwhile Arthor fathered children by other women, to which his queen did not object. She and Arthor continued to make love, nonetheless. A persistent rumor alleged that the Dux Bellorum had fathered the troublemaker but valiant warrior Medraut.

Whatever else Arthor may have done before 470 and the death of Ambrosius Aurelianus as co-equal general, or military leader, and however else Arthor may have fought before that landmark death, everything now paled before Arthor's activity between 470 and 490. Moving to his new headquarters at Dun Cadan, and with the use of his mobile force of cataphractarians as headed by himself, Arthor soon came to know, like no one before him, the terrain of Britannia, its breadth and its length. He seemed to ride and fight everywhere, fending off one attack after another, which could originate from any and every quarter, by would-be invaders, in an unbroken series first in and around Lindum Colonia.

Then Arthor and his mounted warriors went much further north, into the Caledonian Lowlands. Next they backtracked to the northern area of Cambria proper, in and around Caer Leon on Dee. Thereupon Caer Leon on Usk itself came under attack by invaders from Hibernia. Arthor came to the old town's rescue while under siege by the outlanders, and those Hibernians that his army did not slay fled back to their native island to the west. This threat to Isca Silurum touched Arthor deeply. He regarded Caer Leon on Usk in some real sense as his own hometown. He had no such feeling for any other cities.

Whereupon events in the Caledonian Lowlands called him back, first to the river Tribruit and second to Mount Agned. We have already gone over Arthor's twelve great battles. Need we mention the unending skirmishes and minor battles that could take place anywhere at any time along the uneasy frontier between the British and the outlanders?

But everything else that had occurred beforehand now paled in comparison to that final great battle just north of Caer Vadon. By land and by sea a huge mass of alien warriors came swarming onto the plain, the level ground, immediately to the south of Mount Badon, despite its being just the largest hill among all those hills.

Informed by his web of spies, Arthor had expected this invasion and let the enemy forces gather, determined as they were to wipe out the Britons and take over as much of their island as they could. But Arthor remained as determined as they that he would not let this permanent occupation come to pass.

The great Barbarian Conspiracy of 490 became a repeat of that previous great plot of 367, now more than a hundred years beforehand. From Hibernia once again came the Attacotti and the Scotti. From the Caledonian Highlands once again came the Picts, and from the Caledonian Lowlands came that other group of Scotti who had settled there from Hibernia some generations back. Again the Saxons from London and southeast Britain, no less than the Franks from northwest Gaul across the Narrow Seas, all these groups came together north of Caer Vadon.

Meanwhile, from far and near Arthor had assembled his own forces in the hills north of Mount Badon, a terrain that his countrymen knew as well as their own shields and swords. Summoned by his couriers, able-bodied Britons came from all over the island and flocked to his banners, to the same light-green banners with the red-purple dragon that his father Uthor Pendragon had used until his death around 460, and that his official son had adopted as his own. But Arthor also used the Capricorn of the Second Legion on some of his banners, the legion that had built Caer Leon on Usk hundreds of years before.

All the Britons knew that the upcoming battle was an utmost matter of life and death, and that their very survival depended on them, the British warriors, and on them alone. No one among the British, certainly not Arthor himself, needed to say this aloud. Everyone felt it. And this was how the great battle began, and in what order.

Amassed onto the great open space between old Aquae Sulis, now Caer Vadon, and the biggest hill just north of that plain, Mount Badon, the outlanders had grouped themselves as usual under their commanders or chieftains, each group being the expanded comitatus, or special guard of warrior-companions fiercely attached around some little king, not so little if a great fighter.

As with the Britons the overall mass of the outlanders had elected a supreme leader, in this case an astute and valiant Saxon, Ironhenge, as he had become rightfully called. Informed by his own web of spies, he and the outlanders expected the Britons to emerge out from the little valleys under the forest that covered the hills further to the north. As always the Saxons and their allies preferred the open plains and wide alluvial valleys to the dark and cryptic woods.

The outlanders with prudent respect had filled the wide southern half of the plain south of Mount Badon. Even if they planned, and hoped, to wipe the British out in the course of this strategic battle, they well knew not to underestimate or disrespect the British, above all with their special force of mobile horsemen.

For the most part Ironhenge and his allies had no horses or other mounts, not even asses and other pack animals. Like the great mass of the British, the Saxons and other outlanders functioned best by navigating on foot. The outlanders had all faced expectantly toward the north. An odd sound had alerted them.

A strident chorus of Roman military trumpets at once made itself heard, and startled the outlanders. The sound made their hearts leap up, but also excited and enheartened them. The great mass of the Britons now descended out of the hills in a deliberate manner. At the center Arthor and his comitatus, his cataphractarians, rode beside and around him. Foot soldiers followed.

Immediately to Arthor's right and left a dozen or less buccinators, or Roman-style trumpeters, escorted him, blowing upon their raucous instruments. How much time had transpired since that sound had made itself heard under a Roman administration! Arthor had garbed himself in the armor of a Roman general. He had inherited this armor directly from Ambrosius Aurelianus at the latter's death in 470. Even if only two decades ago, Arthor had not worn it before. This was a special occasion.

At a little distance to the west and east other groups of British warriors or foot soldiers now came out of the little valleys between the hills. These were added battalions under the direction of Arthor's two special companions, or high officers, Kay and Bedevyr, subsidiary generals to Arthor's own supreme one. The sheer number of Britons assembled and organized made the outlanders realize that they and the islanders had achieved parity. It all promised an incredible struggle one on one on both sides. If any fear made itself palpable, it only added to the overall excitement.

With awesome dignity and true Roman gravitas, Arthor and his companion cataphractarians rode up to the central Saxon position, where the alien Dux Bellorum stood with long sword and shield, with his own comitatus to either side and behind him. Arthor dismounted while a warrior held his horse. With sword and shield Arthor went up to Ironhenge, who also held himself at the ready. Arthor lifted up both sword and shield to signal that he challenged Ironhenge to single combat. The Saxon leader nodded his head in acknowledgment.

The alien Dux Bellorum had attained some thirty years of age, whereas Arthor some fifty, a significant variable between them indeed. Ironhenge had relative youth in his favor, while Arthor had much more experience, particularly fighting almost exclusively with the same outlanders. What factor would weigh the most in the contest just ahead?

Arthor lifted his sword and forthrightly struck at Ironhenge, who met the stroke with his own sword. Between sword and shield on both sides, the clangor seemed much louder than any thunder nearby. Blinding sparks in truth leaped up from both Arthor and Ironhenge, from their arms and armor. Arthor appeared to feint, but moved back at once, as if retreating. Ironhenge advanced to seek advantage of this evident withdrawal. Arthor then pushed Ironhenge back with a series of almost lightning-rapid strokes, and then moved back again.

Both combatants knew that each of them had a formidable and worthwhile foe. As it evolved, Ironhenge did not necessarily have a greater strength because of his relative youth, or a greater advantage because of that same relative state. Arthor at fifty still had greater strength and greater resilience, not to mention far greater experience. When Ironhenge charged him again, Arthor moved aside with incredible speed and ran Ironhenge through with one swift push of the sword, and thus also through his leather armor. The push or thrust went up from the Saxon's gut up through the heart. He died almost at once.

The single combat had finished, but not the battle. Evidently the outlanders did not grasp or know that the outcome of single combat between two champions—in this case the leaders representing the two enemy sides—had decided the overall combat or battle. Some of the enemy warriors charged Arthor and his escort immediately. This led the Britons to countercharge to protect Arthor and his escort, his cataphractarians. The regular battle overall between the two sides had begun with a vengeance, literally with revenge as the motive for the action or reaction taken by the Saxons and allies.

The latter in fact fought hard, fought very hard, but the Britons fought back just as hard, if not harder. How many blows and strokes did the Saxons and the Britons not exchange that day of days! Almost at sunset the Britons emerged victorious, their losses much less than those of their enemies. The field, the open space, between Aquae Sulis and Mount Badon resembled nothing so much as an unending shambles, an endless butcher's meat market, an outdoor slaughterhouse of vast extent.

The Britons felt no elation, only exhaustion. The captured members of their enemies, the Britons forced to burn and bury all the dead, all the bodies ruptured or ripped apart by sword, spear, or giant dagger. A tremendous and messy task, handling blood-saturated bodies and parts of bodies, arms, legs, hands, heads, brains, and intestines, everything thrown together. The survivors had no choice but to dispatch those most severely wounded, whether friend or foe, the better part of mercy.

Such turned into the finish of another day of strife. Starting on the morrow, the Britons could survey the scene, no less than the result of their victory or triumph, as accomplished by Arthor and his fellow warriors.

CHAPTER V. In the Wake of Mount Badon

To speak in the abstract, we may state that the military makes or establishes the nation. Without it and the defense it provides, no state can long exist. If it is a small country, it seeks the aid of another and bigger country, that is, of its military. It takes refuge under its wing. As for a major country, the first thing that it does to found itself is to set up its military, unless already evolved in place.

A great amount of money, energy, and material is essential to recruit and maintain that military presence. Much of the enormous wealth of our Roman Empire has always gone to support that Imperium, which always involves the military. Without it no state can long exist, or exist at all. In saying this, we do not propose anything radical or revolutionary, but only something basic or elementary, typically overlooked, or taken for granted, because of its fundamental or foundational quality.

Nonetheless, it serves a real purpose to remind ourselves of that which is fundamental, or elementary, lest we overlook the basic role that it plays in all our lives whether directly or indirectly. The British triumph at Mount Badon reminds us of this basic truth, and why we must reiterate it here.

Another obvious truth about a major set or intentional battle: victory is determined on an obvious premise, the more enemy fighters that one side kills, the more assured the continuing existence of the victors. If one kills enough enemy warriors, one does not need to fight them ever again.

Only the fact that the British forces killed so many members of the alien armies guaranteed the long period of peace that followed the triumph at Mount Badon, a period that has endured now for at least thirty years since then and may last not quite a full fifty years; if I, Merlin, may here invoke my prophetic skills, if I may make a simple prediction, on behalf of the unknown future—unknown at least to most people—speaking as I do from the fulcrum of an always equivocal present.

Many or most of Arthor's warriors could now return to their homes, to their own lives and families, but only after such a prolonged period of near constant struggle against a common enemy. The British had no desire to reconstitute Britannia as it was, and no desire to reclaim London and southeast Britain. Circumstances had forced the British to become established in the northwest, the west, and the southwest, and to remain there now for several generations.

After their great victory the British forces had briefly regrouped behind the substantial defenses of Dun Cadan, before dispersing to other places. The inner core of the British army would remain with Arthor. On a rare sunlit noon before that dispersal elsewhere—which occurred over several days—everyone had gathered within the very large expanse of ground at the top of the fortress, about 18 acres.

Kings, princes, kinglets, chieftains, and other leaders of all sorts or groups had assembled in that space by prearrangement with Arthor as the Dux Bellorum. The rank and file of the other warriors had gathered around them. The leaders and other warriors just about covered the entire expanse of ground. It made for a huge concourse.

Kay and Bedevyr as Arthor's two chief officers, or as assistant generals to his pre-eminent one, commanded everyone's attention and respectful silence. They spoke in unison, rather unusually, a prepared speech from a small piece of well-worn vellum, but they had virtually memorized it. They both announced in loud ringing tones what they had to say. This was the gist of it.

"We have an important proclamation to make. By the authority vested in us by Arthor and all the other leaders gathered here, and by unanimous vote of every other leader except Arthor, we all together elect Arthor as High King, as the supreme ruler over Britain and the British. He will maintain his two principal centers of authority here at Dun Cadan and at Caer Leon on Usk as well."

When they had completed their announcement, Kay and Bedevyr nodded to the crowd to indicate that they had made their momentous proclamation. A gravid moment of silence ensued. Then everyone began to shout in vehement acclamation and agreement. They directed their gaze and their voices at Arthor. The Dux Bellorum stood at the center of the concourse. He bowed his head a little in acknowledgment of the speech and the uproar of jubilation. Over and over again, everyone shouted out the same thing.

"Praise him with great praise!"

Everyone turned to everyone else and began embracing one another. Arthor and many others were openly but joyfully weeping. Together they had all done their extraordinary deed. They had completed their arduous and apparently unending struggle all along that uneasy frontier that had sundered their island. They had achieved this deed only through their united strength and their united forces.

Meanwhile, before the huge numbers of alien warriors had amassed themselves there on that open space between Caer Vadon and Mons Badonicus, Arthor had taken various precautions. He had sent his wife under escort to stay with Merlin at his ample abode in Caer Leon for the duration of what promised to turn into the biggest battle of all.

Also meanwhile, Arthor's mother Ygurna came down from Merlin's family estate northwest of Isca Silurum to stay with Merlin for the duration. After the victory at Mount Badon, at Arthor's request, both Ygurna and Gueneveria with Merlin rode by horseback from Caer Leon to Dun Cadan under military escort.

As expected, of course, much celebration had already taken place at Dun Cadan, but Merlin advised Arthor to hold it all in check until his coronation at Caer Leon as High King, or Amheraudur, as Imperator, or Emperor (in his role as commander in chief). Merlin planned this for the end of summer before the rains of autumn would arrive.

PART THREE
HIGH KING

Contents

CHAPTER I. A Coronation at Caer Leon

By some miracle or magic Merlin managed to have everything ready by the end of summer for Arthor's coronation before the rains of autumn arrived. He managed to accomplish everything needed for this truly grand event of universal jubilation among the British. This preparation included several adjustments or constructions inside the fortress walls. For once, and publicly, Merlin lived up to his reputation not just as a prophet and magician but moreover as a great magician, a genuine, a true thaumaturgist.

At his especial request to make everything go forward with all due speed—he only had three or four months to do all that was needed—Arthor invested Merlin with all due powers plenipotentiary that he would require for the great event to happen in Caer Leon. This encompassed where the banquet or series of banquets would be held, in what structures that were still extant or in those needing construction or rebuilding.

First Merlin commandeered Arthur's assistant generals to look after the provisions, the drink and food, including the beer and wine from whatever source, domestic or imported. Thus Bedevyr became the caterer or supplier of the provisions from wherever in Britain or Brittany they could come. Thus Kay became the seneschal or steward in charge of the provisions for the banquets, the meats, the breads, the beers, the wines, and by what staff that would serve them.

To assist them with methods of payment faster than barter or trade, Merlin had found other sources of good Roman coinage of gold, silver, and bronze. He had discovered further caches of old coins long since buried by their owners, who had either died or had fled to the protective umbrage of the Selva Broceliandis in Little Britain.

Thus it occurred that Britain and Brittany, or at least parts of them, returned briefly to a money economy, even if those receiving such payment stashed them away in their own turn! To those familiar with the concept of Romanitas, with Roman things and customs, the following explanation about Roman camps and major forts will perhaps appear superfluous. To those not familiar with such matters, the reader or student should con this discussion with great care. It involved how Merlin prepared Caer Leon as the new British capital for the coronation.

As a well-known matter of unembellished fact, all full-scale Roman camps or fortresses are laid out in the same way, the same shape, the same ground plan. Whether a temporary encampment or a series of solid structures in stone, the overall shape is a rectangle, a third longer than it is wide, the proportions of any size being three by four.

All the erections within the rectangle—whether leather tents, or buildings of wood, or edifices of tile, stone, brick, and mortar—always exist in the same layout in terms of the relative position of one structure to the rest of the others. A soldier or other inhabitant can find their way easily from one place to the next whether by day or night, wherever the legion would have pitched the encampment.

The Romans, that is, those of the Second Legion, had laid out the original legionary fortress in the same way as a matter of course, a few hundred years ago, back in the first Christian century. The fortress became known as Isca Silurum, the Isca (or Usk) of the Silures, of the Silurian tribe long resident there in the southeast region of Cambria proper. The present-day British call it Caer Leon on Usk, the name closely derived from the Latin.

But at some point after they had occupied the fortress for only a few hundred years, the Romans decommissioned the not so old military base and also dismantled much of it, the principal buildings used by the commander. These edifices included the praetorium, an imperial palace, where the commander usually lived when resident in the fortress.

If a genuine Roman emperor, that is, from Rome herself, passed through the region or stayed overnight in the fortress, then the commander would lodge him in the praetorium, giving up his own chambers for the emperor's use. Now Merlin had the bright idea to rebuild the former structure—by magic?—on the same terrain where the legionary soldiers had razed it. Much of the materials from the dismantling, the local people had re-used for new, more modest buildings inside the fortress walls, to which they had added towers and turrets.

To suit the location, instead of orienting the rectangle of the fortress strictly to the four cardinal points of north, south, east, and west, the authorities had tilted it so that the southwest bastion at that corner faced literally due south, with the other corner bastions arranged accordingly and appropriately. Just off the southwest bastion the Second Legion had built their oval amphitheatre, which could serve for military manoeuvers, public discussions, gladiatorial contests, and so forth. All suchlike had indeed happened therein, but ceased when the legion finally moved on into another part of the empire.

The local people thereupon used it for their own events, as expected. They maintained the structure's fabric and kept it in good repair. Of course, Merlin planned to use it for the actual ceremony of Arthor's coronation. It could hold at least six thousand seated men, the original number contained in the early Roman legion. Many more people could stand in the aisles and any other empty spaces. The paved space around the amphitheatre could contain any overflow from the building itself.

As for the praetorium, it had stood (in the fortress's northern swath, or broad strip or belt) virtually opposite the northern gate in the middle of the northern walls. When they had first constructed Isca Silurum, the Romans had built it temporarily out of solid wood, that is, out of hardwood trees. Later they had replaced the wood with substantial edifices and outer walls of tile, stone, and brick. It would remain in this condition until the partial dismantling, and then the reuse, of the original materials by local people for their houses within the walls, as we have already recorded.

The dismantling of the praetorium represented a poignant loss. When rebuilt, it had boasted fine veneers of limestone, marble, and granite, imported from Italy. The veneers sheathed the walls of the most important rooms. The palace—it was nothing less—possessed a grand central entrance and vestibule, then an enormous colonnaded courtyard, and next the inner praetorium with its sizeable and imposing basilica, or central hall, with massive columns of basalt or granite. To the local people the praetorium in particular seemed like something out of an exotic dream.

To the reconstitution of the praetorium, but in wood made and painted to look like stone, Merlin directed his vision and his energy. To that end he hired a large army of carpenters and skilled woodworkers from Britain and from Brittany. He supplied the architectural plans for the construction crews under the direction of the master builder and his assistants. Everyone involved had completed their task just prior to the end of summer. They had accomplished an impressive job in record time.

Merlin, Kay, and Bedevyr in fact had everything ready for the grand event. Now Merlin as Arthor's chief counsellor summoned

Arthor, Ygurna, and Gueneveria to Caer Leon from Dun Cadan. Meanwhile the troop of the permanent garrison at Dun Cadan would man and maintain that unique fortress. Later Arthor temporarily would replace them with another troop from Caer Leon so that the regular garrison could partake in the ongoing festivities at Isca Silurum.

Arthor with his wife and his mother, and surrounded by a suitable escort of warriors no less tested than he, made an imposing entrance into Caer Leon through the streets to the praetorium. He had garbed himself in the Roman armor and helmet of Ambrosius Aurelianus, which he had worn during the battle at Mount Badon. The people in the streets noted this and cheered Arthor and his group all the more vehemently. The helmet still fit him despite his full beard and head of hair, but nothing as voluminous as those worn by Merlin. The local folk appreciated Arthor's armor and what it represented, no less than the proud helmet of a Roman general.

In the interim, in response to the couriers dispatched throughout Britain, as well as to those by boat throughout Brittany and other parts of the Continent, people flocked to Caer Leon from everywhere, from near and far, on the island and from Europe. Embassies from Brittany and from Gaul at large, from city states in Hispania and Italy, and strangest but most impressive of all, the one from *the* Roman emperor situated in Byzantium, or Constantinople. Never before had so many ships from so many countries docked along the Usk. Given the limited shelter that Caer Leon could muster, many of the crews perforce stayed overnight on their own ships.

That last embassy, from Byzantium, provided a source of amazement, but no less of trepidation, inasmuch as no one wanted Arthor's coronation as the said Imperator Hesternalis, or Western Emperor, to be misconstrued as a challenge to the imperial presence and authority far away in the northeast sector of the Mediterranean world. Luckily, no one did in fact misconstrue what was after all no more than a geographical designation. The Britons did have the legal fact or authorization from the Rescript of 412 direct from Honorius himself to back them up.

Most knowledgeable people know that Augustus Caesar founded the Roman Empire in 27 B.C., and that Diocletian had realistically divided the Empire for practical reasons of governance in 395 A.D. into Western and Eastern.

Fortunately the day set aside for Arthor's coronation turned out clear, warm, and sunlit, neither hot nor cold. In the late morning Arthor rode forth with his mother and with his wife from the praetorium to the amphitheatre. Whereas his appearance as a Roman general when he rode into Caer Leon had gratified and pleased everyone, now his new appearance more than amazed and astonished all those assembled. Bareheaded, that is, without cap or helmet, he had had his long hair cut, his beard and moustache removed, and his face clean-shaven. For all the world he looked like a Roman senator or a Roman emperor.

Arthor wore an old-fashioned imperial toga made of white linen. A narrow border of imperial purple ran around the bottom edges of his robes. Over the toga he had put on a flowing mantle of purple silk (secured with an elaborate Roman brooch), the cloth having traveled all the way from the fabulous empire of Serica located in the furthest east, where it fronts on an enormous ocean. As advised by Merlin, who had suggested the garments for the event, and had had them created, Arthor wore this outfit only for the ceremony in the amphitheatre. Later, when back in the praetorium, Arthor would change as soon as possible into a cool and simple tunic and kilt, once again made of white linen.

Despite the pomp and ceremony the coronation itself went fast and smoothly. Preceded by the buccinators—who had accompanied Arthor to his single combat with Ironhenge at the start of the battle at Mount Badon—Arthor with his small family did indeed make a grand entrance into the amphitheatre, to the cheers and shouts of the people assembled there.

No sooner had the buccinators finished their raucous fanfares than a huge bellowing as from some gigantic monster made itself heard, and astounded the people even more than ever. Merlin had reconstructed the hydraulis that he had found inside one of the vaults, with keyboard still intact under the amphitheatre.

Just as the Romans had featured the hydraulis at the games in the Colosseum at Rome herself—for entrances and exits, for the appearance of the emperor, and so forth—so now the Britons under Merlin's tutelage were highlighting its use, its redeployment, in the legionary amphitheatre at Caer Leon, just outside that southwest bastion! The outré sound made everyone tremble with wonder and not a little fear.

In what Merlin had altered into an imperial box for its especial employment, Arthor and his family had sat them down. At the pre-arranged signal from his chief counsellor, Arthor arose and stood at the box's edge, facing into the arena, and looking around him. Whereupon Merlin had him kneel, while he placed upon the head of his former student the special crown that the counsellor had had created out of gold mixed with silver: a low nine-spiked crown with a spear's head as its central point. All this while the hydraulis accompanied the ceremony with its bizarre and ear-shattering music, playing the old imperial hymn. Suddenly it stopped.

Merlin in a deep voice that he had made curiously loud (as if with a megaphone) by some arcane magic spoke. "We, Merlin, proclaim Arthor High King of Britain and Brittany, elected by unanimous vote of all our people, no less than Imperator Hesternalis, or the Emperor of the Far West!" Then a great silence ensued, but broken soon only by the acclamations of everyone.

"Praise him with great praise!" The people shouted it over and over again.

The ceremony had concluded, and everyone dispersed out of the amphitheatre. They went back to the praetorium and to the open space, the open ground, the plaza, just south of it. There the first of the celebratory banquets would take place at the trestle tables that Merlin with Kay and Bedevyr had set up in advance, no less than with the essential energy and labor of a special crew.

That night the British held high feast in honor of their victory at Mount Badon and of Arthor's coronation, and celebrated these events one evening after another for one entire month. When he sent his couriers throughout Britain and the Continent, Merlin suggested that visitors or guests might bring with them both drink and food as appropriate gifts, given Britain's depleted condition after fighting a war that had lasted more than a hundred years.

Neither Arthor as High King nor the Britons as his own people commanded the wealth and resources of the Byzantine Emperor hundreds, nay, thousands, of miles away to the east. Merlin's hint, well given and well received, created an abundance. All the ample feasting shared between host and guest passed into myth and legend, and not unlike a golden cup transmitted from the sun to haunt the planet Earth.

CHAPTER II. A Giant Boar Hunt in Brittany

As much of the large island that is Britain became underpopulated of humans whether British or non-British, the wildlife, the flora and fauna, flourished and recovered from all the depredations inflicted by people. On the other hand, the human life on the Continent did not appear to diminish to any great extent. For what it was, full as it had become of the now settled and well established Roman British refugees, Brittany itself seemed to prosper, but yet looked to Arthor Pendragon as High King and Amheraudur, the Imperator Hesternalis. When some crisis arose, the people of Brittany would send a special delegation to Caer Leon, asking for help or advice, whether from Arthor or Merlin, or from both, as the case often happened. Merlin had served as Arthor's tutor and foster parent during his childhood and adolescence until Arthor's coming of age, when he left to become a warrior fighting alongside his father Uthor and then Ambrosius Aurelianus as the official Dux Bellorum, even if both served in that role, working as a pair. Then Merlin served as Arthor's all-purpose counsellor, that is, apart from purely military matters, which did not strictly fall under his purview. Next, and currently, Merlin served as Arthor's court minister whether in the rebuilt praetorium or at Merlin's own residence, all this at Caer Leon for the most part, but sometimes at Dun Cadan.

To Arthor's credit it must be recorded that he functioned very well and worthily in his governance as a ruler, always acting in a fair and evenhanded manner, always doing much good, as much as possible, to aid and abet his people, wherever they had established themselves. He turned into as good or great a ruler as he had served as Dux Bellorum. Unlike the usurpers of imperial power who preceded him, Albinus, Carausius, and Magnus Maximus, Arthor did not overstep himself and seek to set himself up on the Continent at large, thereby saving his people from considerable grief.

The High King also found or made the time to do things that he never had the chance to do beforehand, preoccupied as he was as warrior or Dux Bellorum. While Merlin attended to the court at Caer Leon, Arthor with Gueneveria went on a visit to the old stone palace at Din Tagell during a clear and warm summer, accompanied by a mounted guard of honor. From that headland they rode some one hundred miles along the coast all the way to the Land's End pointing southwest. From this locus they could easily perceive the tiny islands that some have identified as the remnant isles of Lyonnesse. There at Land's End Arthor and his party sojourned for several days while they savored the grandeur where the land eternally confronts the ocean.

After they returned to Caer Leon, a special delegation, nay, an embassage if you will, now came from Rennium that still availed as the capital of Brittany not far from its eastern marches. Merlin came forward at once as soon as the newcomers had entered the basilica, or great hall, of the praetorium, to welcome them warmly, and with due deference. He had noted at once the almost familial similitude between the British of Greater Britannia and those of Lesser Britannia whether in bearing, speech, clothing. He guided them into Arthur's presence, where he sat on the grand chair, or cathedra, when he conducted his daily business, and when the court was in session.

The leading man of the delegation, the embassador, came forward, bowing his head in respect before Arthor. He spoke in a loud clear voice, first in Latin and then in British.

"To Arthor, High King of Britain and Brittany, Amheraudur of the British, greetings from Julius Questus, governor of Brittany! I, Marcus Pentius, his embassador plenipotentiary, speak for him in his name. For a month or more a scourge, a monster, has deeply troubled our province, from west to east, from south to north. This monster is a gigantic boar. He ravages our crops and our kitchen gardens. He suddenly materialized, and continues to materialize, out of our Selva Broceliandis. He attacks people; he has even killed more than a few. We beg you yourself to sail over to Brittany, you as a renowned huntsman, to hunt down, to kill this tusked prodigy. The efforts of our own huntsmen have had no success."

Further palaver occurred. Arthor spoke first in Latin, and then changed to British. He spoke, "I consent to help you, as soon as I can make my arrangements for Merlin to take over my duties here in Britain. I am eager to find myself again under the protective cover of your great forest. I shall arrive with a sizeable contingent of my own huntsmen." As before, and as had often happened, the adroit counsellor would indeed attend to any business or problems in Arthor's absence.

It was true, it was fact: Arthor had turned into as great a huntsman as a Dux Bellorum. Until his great victory at Mount Badon, he almost never had the occasion to hunt, but he soon became an adept at the art. The vast woodlands of Britannia provided an abundance of wild game, fox, wolf, bear, wildcat, boar, and so forth, not to mention the plentiful game birds everywhere. Like most huntsmen, the High King used primarily the spear as well as the bow and arrow. Hunting soon became one of Arthor's chief pleasures or passions, quite apart from the taste and savor of roasted wild animals and roasted wild birds.

Sailing down from Caer Leon, and then out into the western or southwestern sea, going around the Land's End of Cornuae, the ship carrying Arthur and his huntsmen docked in a safe and secure harbor located in the midst of the broad blunt nose or forehead of Brittany's westernmost land mass. When Arthor and his contingent disembarked at what once had served as a Roman port, a special delegation met them with all due ceremony. The delegation reassured them that they had made all the arrangements for hospitality, for room and board, wherever Arthor and his men would need to go. Who would not give hospitality to the great hero of Mount Badon?

First they had to find the enormous boar before they could hunt him, and corner him, unless he cornered them. All the reports emphasized his height, his breadth, his weight, no less his wiliness and ferocity. The huntsmen would have to exercise care and caution. They had an extremely large area to canvas, a giant peninsula, some 150 miles west to east, some 80 miles broad at the western end, and some 120 miles wide at the eastern end. First they would cover the northern half of the peninsula, heading toward Rennium, that is, going east. Second they would head back west, going through the southern half of the peninsula. However, the awesome beast had waxed quiescent, and had vanished back into the woodlands. At least the great boar hunt had actually commenced!

*   *   *

Evidently the giant boar found enough to forage in the woodlands at large. He ceased to raid the crop fields or the kitchen gardens; he did not attack or kill anyone; he had just disappeared. No one had lately seen him. Did he have preternatural faculties that warned him about the great huntsman and his companion hunters who were actively looking for him? If so, then they had a more than formidable beast to handle. A certain subtle chill of awe and fear began to grip the huntsmen, even Arthor. They had a greater foe than what they could imagine.

True, they had formulated an adequate plan, but as we know, dint of circumstance often dictates otherwise than what a theory and/or a plan might. So it turned out in the present case. No sooner had they made some progress heading east through the peninsula's northern half than a report came from the southern half, a report of a sighting and the near death of several humans. Accordingly they headed south but found nothing, nor trace nor track. Then came a report of a sighting in the north and the devastation of several farms with their crops. Despite their plans and best intentions the reports forced them to zigzag back and forth, a process at once annoying and frustrating. All this zigzagging, and chasing after rumors and reports, took much longer than planned. Almost a month had gone by, and they themselves had found neither hide nor hair to justify their search, and give them some impetus to continue.

Arthor and fellow hunters had covered about half the distance toward Rennium, when the chief huntsman suddenly remembered what Merlin had confided to him. The counsellor's family had a small property somewhere in the middle of the great peninsula. Distant relatives lived there, subsistence farmers. On this property stood a substantial but curious house all made out of oak, and accordantly called the Domus Quercus. The dwelling might have run some risk of wildfires if the great forest cover did not invite and undergo frequent rains from off the illimitable Ocean Sea to the west. Arthor wanted to find the house with Merlin's relatives. After a search and numerous inquiries Arthor and his companions did in fact find it, on the northern side of a great open space among the woodlands.

The family residing there, and tending the crops that they grew in the middle of the large glade, welcomed Arthor and his huntsmen with notable warmth. Yes, they acknowledged who he was, and noted that they had a distant but genuine relationship with the Cornuarii, Merlin in especial, of whom they had heard marvelous things indeed. Realizing their limited means, the Britons from Britannia did not linger there with this family for more than a few nights.

When Arthor and companions left, he gave them a small but heavy pouch of gold and silver coins of high value. He said to the good and frugal people that Merlin wanted him to make this gesture. However, Arthor alone had come up with the idea. His men knew the true situation, but verbally seconded Arthor's gesture as if instructed or inspired by Merlin. The family thus endowed with the cache of money seemed stunned and thanked Arthor (and Merlin through him) with tears in their eyes and with voices strained by emotion.

When Arthor and his companions proceeded east again, as ever on horseback, they eventually reached another large clearing but without house or family. They would bivouac for a night or so before seeking out regular shelter from their fellow Britons, those who had settled in the lower but larger part of ancient Armorica. Even if late in the day, they had an unexpected visitor.

To date the entire experience of the High King when hunting under official conditions could not have differed more than it did compared to the present situation. An official hunt involved many people, perhaps two hundred or so, outriders, personal escorts, a concourse of people on foot, people carrying drink or food on pack animals, etc., so that a considerable company of all types of specialized professionals took part. Contrasted with all these folk en masse, the prey per se did not have a chance whatever form it assumed—fox, wolf, bear, wildcat, wild boar, or whatever. A small army versus a single mammal, what chance did the latter have? Not very much. However, this current hunt in Brittany, as elemental and simple as it might appear to an outsider, proved inherently more primitive and atavistic. It could not help but do so, particularly when it came to that unexpected visitor. The giant boar!

The oversized boar suddenly trotted into the extensive glade as if it had been looking for Arthor and his companions. It stopped at some little distance from the humans. It did not make a move as if it would charge. Arthor and the other huntsmen did not panic, but remained calm and collected, even if all their hearts beat faster with as much force as a battle drum. They all picked up their spears immediately and stood their ground without fear or fuss: seasoned hunters, no less than seasoned warriors. The gigantic boar stayed where it had stopped and faced them in the same way as they faced him.

Truly this boar had mutated far beyond the ordinary limits of his species. He possessed the same relative size as a bull of the forest, a bison or buffalo. The same height, the same breadth, and it would seem the same weight. Was there ever before or since such a magnificent specimen? He seemed a bull himself, albeit no more than an oversized hog. He had the large head and the heavy forequarters of a male bison but no beard and no horns. Instead he had several pairs of sizeable tusks on either side of his mouth, protruding out of his mouth and through his jaws. These tusks looked lethal enough. No need of demonstration!

As it was, it required all the will power of the huntsmen to stand their ground and not to run off, or not to climb the nearest tree. Even Arthor himself experienced a twinge, a mere touch, of panic looking into the eyes of what seemed a creature beyond ferocity.

Arthor spoke, and softly, but they all could hear him. "Very well. All of you lift up your spears. When I say *Strike!*—hurl them with all your strength at this creature." The giant boar continued to look at them all impassively. When Arthor commanded, "Strike!" the boar suddenly came to life and snorted, pawed the ground, but before he could move the spears hurled by two dozen very strong arms struck him and hit home. The volley stopped him dead in his tracks.

Most of the spear shafts remained projecting out from all over the boar's bulk, above all in his forequarters. The impact from the spears had proven so total and overwhelming that the beast did not have enough energy to charge Arthor and his companions, to try to toss them around with his large head armed with those deadly-looking tusks. He stood standing for several minutes, and then, quite overcome at last, he collapsed on the spot where he had been standing his ground.

Everyone heaved a sigh as a huge feeling of relief swept over and flooded everyone. They also felt a certain regret that they had needed to kill the creature. Arthor fully shared the same feelings. Tomorrow they would go to the nearest town or village to make arrangements to have the body of the bison-boar transported to the palace and court of the governor Julius Questus, as proof that Arthor and his huntsmen had in fact killed the beast who had become a dreaded scourge throughout Brittany. Never might not such a creature emerge again!

The meat itself, properly marinated and roasted, would serve as the main course for whatever feast or celebration that Julius Questus or Arthor himself might command. Thus had unfurled the unparalleled hunt that ended with the giant boar's death. As Arthor and his huntsmen escorted the dead beast in an open wagon of great size and strength, mounted grooms directed and managed the two dozen horses that pulled the wagon, arranged in six rows of four each abreast. The grooms rode the front line of horses. It required several weeks of slow and careful conveyance for the convoy to reach its goal.

The whole company whether mounted or afoot deliberately wended its way to the old Roman capital, to Rennium, going along the old Roman roads and bridges eastward through the woodlands. People would gather alongside the roadway, to gape in awe at the dead beast and to marvel at its untoward bulk, unprecedented for a wild boar. Even Julius Questus and Marcus Pentius could not hold back their surprise and wonder at the beast, and their admiration for Arthur and his four-and-twenty huntsmen for what they had accomplished. After the due feasting and celebration Arthor and his contingent of hunting specialists would return in due course, and in triumph, to Caer Leon, but still a long journey by land and by sea back to Britain. All that Arthor asked of his hosts as a kind of recompense, they gave him without demur: the boar's large preserved head with the several pairs of oversized tusks.

CHAPTER III. Drustanus and Essylt

Some twenty or twenty-five miles due south of Din Tagell as the bird
flies, a little to the south-southeast, extends the tiny fiefdom, kingdom
if you will, of Foy, or Phoé. Does the name, sounded out, not evoke
the long-term presence of the Phoenicians, or Foy-nicians, in this region as former and long-term collaborators from afar on the spot, in
that spot, in this locale?

Who can deny the presence of historical memory in defining
what has taken place before us, in terms of what created us? People
cannot deny what created them, that is, themselves in a physical
sense. Is that not true? Without what created them they could not
find themselves here with us at all.

Because of its wealth, no less than its consequent importance because of that wealth, Foy in retrospect has assumed an even greater
significance, above all due to King Mark. A tall and stalwart man, he
eschewed completely the role of warrior, or as a warrior leading other
warriors. He did this in accordance with his preoccupation as a financial wizard, even akin to me, Merlin, as a non-financial wizard, even if
I could, and did, advise other people well relative to their investments
thanks to my second sight.

The ambivalence or ambiguity that comes with age, how do we
say no to it? We do not. We accept it as part and parcel created by
the rigamarole of one's own time and place. Confusing and kaleidoscopic mixture! But King Mark had made a sensible decision to make
the financial world (trade and barter) the essential feature, or the key,
to his own survival, as well as that of his chief son Drustan, or Tristan.

In the final analysis commerce reigns or prevails at the highest
level of human activity. There is thus no place or point for the arts,
except as a private or public religion! All brave endeavor founds itself
in conjunction with the money resources of its time. Without that enlightened patronage nothing heroic or adventurous could exist, could
come into being! Such is a central fact for our life in the far future, or
as of now! The latter includes Phoé, or Foy.

The river, especially the lower river, the estuary, and the peninsula
bearing the same name, all belong to the domain of King Mark. Even if

the tiny kingdom does not measure much more than ten miles by ten miles, covering both sides of the estuary and more, it retains its importance only because of its wealth, including coinage from the Continent, a status disproportionate to its mere size. It was a long-term trade center since at least the last one thousand years of ancient Egypt, as of when the Foy-nicians first came to trade and barter and buy.

The trade and commerce poured in, as they do to this day, from all over the Mediterranean basin, from Gaul, Hispania, North Africa, and the British Isles themselves. Thus King Mark's palace became some real time agone a true focus for trade and money exchange. The Phoé estuary with its depth and width makes a perfect harbor for ships of all types and sizes that arrived with all kinds of cargo and fraughtage. The outer courtyard of Castell Dor, as our Gallic friends call it, between the inner and outer walls became the focus for traders, even if best known among the Romanized Britons as the Castellum Aureum, the House of Gold.

The background for Essylt, or Yseult, needs a little bit of detail here as one of the daughters fathered by the then High King of Eire, or Hibernia, generally resident at his fortified palace maintained at Tara, where it stands well inside that emerald isle. As a young and beautiful woman Essylt became the second wife of King Mark, of Marcus Cunomorus, or Quonomorius, that is, following the death of his first wife, the mother of Drustan, or Drustanus. The two kings arranged the marriage to foster both trade and friendship between their two kingdoms, one a large island, and the other a tiny fiefdom.

Even if neither King Mark nor his son Drustan volunteered themselves as warriors for Arthor's final great battle, that is, of Mount Badon—Drustan was too young in any case at the time—the father sent both men and materials to the Dux Bellorum for that signal encounter. Mark recruited and outfitted a sizeable contingent of mercenary warriors to help the British cause. Even if only mercenaries, they bore themselves exemplarily during that battle to end all battles, and most of them survived.

However, he did not send any of his rather large comitatus, or band of companions, almost a small army that he very much needed to defend his castle, or palace, on the river that passed through Phoé. The Castellum Aureum sits on its low ridge, as bounded on the east by the river's estuary. The overall area circumscribed by its double circular ramparts measures about five hundred feet across at its widest. The inner area inside the inner circle or barrier measures about two hundred twenty feet across.

Within this latter circle rose up the porter's lodge, twenty-four feet by eighteen feet, standing just inside that inner entrance, and adequate for him and his family. The compound inside the inner circle contained two sizeable halls, but the larger one could hold a considerable number of people. The main enclosure, the aisled great hall, measured ninety feet by forty feet. The entire trunks of lofty trees did duty as the columns for that enclosed space.

At one end of the great hall, that is, outside, stood a small gabled building that served as the kitchen for the feasts, the celebrations with drink and food, inside the great hall. That grand enclosure became famous for its size, as well as for the gorgeous ornamentation that Mark had lavished on its walls and columns, metallic sheets (decorated with Keltic patterns) and other ornaments that suggested gold, and looked and glittered like it.

The king had had the structure built out of hard wood with wooden floors, and with a ridged roof remarkable for the intricacy of its large beams at various levels connecting with the rafters. It created a breathtaking ensemble that invariably astounded people when seeing it for the very first time. Lest I forget, the compound had other buildings, separate ones with bedrooms for sleeping, and for the sick people.

This was how I, Merlin, perceived not only the great hall but the entire compound on several occasions as the guest of the king and his queen, his first wife and the mother of Drustanus among other children, even if he remained the king's chief son and heir to the throne and kingdom.

(Here I have given this detailed and extended account of King Mark's Palace, or Castell Dor, in order to reassure our fellow Britons who emigrated over to Brittany that something of the old ways and the old years has in fact survived in Britannia Major. The miniature dominion centered in the Castellum Aureum provides us with a perfect example.)

But let us return to that same Drustan and Essylt, as they have already become celebrated in song and story. That two such beautiful
young people should have fallen in love makes no great surprise, even
if Essylt, a passionate young woman if ever there was one, did her
conjugal duties by Mark with fervor, and then some. It certainly went
a long way to create an intriguing narrative, inasmuch as Tristan
should have fallen in love with his father's own bride soon after the
marriage between the king and the Irish princess, if not beforehand.

Since Drustan himself journeyed to Eire with princely escort to
fetch the princess, it follows that they might have fallen mutually in
love. The two spent some significant time together while Drustan was
sojourning at Tara, then during the trip overland from Tara, and next
during the sea voyage from Hibernia to Phoé! Later King Mark as
Drustan's father, despite his legitimate wrath at his own son for dallying
with the woman destined as his own wife, had to admit that his son
had not really betrayed him the father before the king had married
her. That explains much of the mischief, the main problem. Certainly, when King Mark, Drustan, and Essylt came to Caer Leon aboard
their own special ship, to attend Arthor's coronation with all the festivities, everything seemed well with the family, and nothing marred
the surface of things, or else Drustan and Essylt kept their own emotions under control by acting as they should per custom and law.

The Irish are the Irish, and the British are the British, but as fellow
Kelts they have much in common. They speak almost the same language, close enough to communicate somewhat. For all their different
cultures, they have far more in common than differences. Still they
function as two separate nations or peoples, and subtle distinctions exist
between them. Drustan's task consisted in grasping these differences
himself, and then in explaining them to the princess. He already knew
some Irish, and she some British, thus both enabled somewhat to
speak with some finesse and some genuine understanding.

On a beautiful sunlit late morning they left the compound of her
father the High King's fortified palace through the main gate all by
themselves. Although Drustan carried his dagger at his left side, there
was no real danger, and he did not need to carry arms or armor. No
need for a chaperone. As his father's own embassador he held a special status, and people expected him to act as protector and chaper-

one all in one if alone with the princess away from the court or other people. The twain walked slowly, enjoying the beautiful day without the usual rain. They came to a small parklike forest and entered.

They found two clear-cut tree stumps and sat down on them. She thought she had never before seen such a beautiful young man. In his own turn he thought he had never before seen such a beautiful young woman. That was to say quite a bit, since the Irish among them do not lack for beautiful young men, and the British do not lack for beautiful young women. She had long dark-red hair, and he had short dark-brown hair that covered his ears down to his neck.

Essylt smiled shyly but slyly at Drustan, and he did the same back to her. She asked, "What is your father like? What type of man is he?"

He responded, "My father King Mark is tall and stalwart. He is accounted a very handsome man. He is very kind and gentle to his own family, but can be a stern disciplinarian. I take after him physically, albeit somewhat smaller, and I have my mother's looks."

At this Essylt commented, "Then she must have been quite a beautiful queen." He nodded, and said, "Yes, so she was—and thank you for the compliment," blushing a little.

She reached out over to Drustan and lightly touched him on his arm. He said nothing, but reached out in his own turn and placed his hand on her arm, and then her hand. He bent his head over it and lightly brushed his lips on it. Then she did the same back to him. The tree stumps sat close, and so did the two young people. They leaned their upper bodies into each other. They mutually put their arms around each other and kissed, at first lightly. Then they both stood up and kissed passionately, their hearts beating faster.

He suddenly broke just a little away from her and spoke softly, "I love you, Essylt, but you are promised to my father. Perhaps we should stop at this point while we can."

She reluctantly agreed. They both had to fight themselves, but managed to regain their balance. They somehow regained control over themselves and their emotions, but it was a real struggle for both of them. She said, "Well, all right. You are wise, and I should follow your example. Still," and here she looked up at him with a serious face, "there is the future. Who knows what it might not bring about?" Drustan looked back at her also with a serious face and repeated,

"Yes, who knows what it might not bring about?" As they spoke, they had disengaged.

They walked slowly back to the High King's residence, somehow not unhappy despite their mutual frustration. Several days later, with an armed escort, Drustan and Essylt departed from Tara and went to where he had left his ship at the harbor that faced over to the southwest point of Cambria proper, the kingdom of Caer Marthen, the shortest passage over to Britain.

The twain embarked, and the ship sailed first to Caer Marthen, and then across the huge estuary of the river Severn, or Sabrina, over to the northern coast of Cornuae. Keeping a safe distance from the rocks and promontories, the ship navigated around Land's End, and finally reached Phoé and her harbor-estuary, after a fast, safe, and smooth passage overall without storm or other incident. However, our twain managed to keep their strong emotions to themselves. But whenever they met on board in the course of that passage, their hearts would beat faster. If they touched each other even just lightly, it seemed to make an almost electric shock pass through them, and again mutually.

Keeping their emotions in check, and acting as if nothing roiled their inner being, proved a greater strain than anticipated. Drustan and Essylt felt greatly relieved when they attained the shelter of Castell Dor and could busy themselves with other matters. They avoided each other as much as possible, unobtrusively. It made it all so much easier for them.

Both King Mark and his bride-to-be, and soon his wife and queen, became enamored of each other. He had waived any dowry from the High King of Eire as quite unnecessary. He had more than enough wealth for both of them. The wedding, the nuptial celebration, and the marriage all seemed a success. Meanwhile the love that Drustan and Essylt still felt for each other only grew stronger for being suppressed and nurtured in silence.

After Essylt's life at court with King Mark had settled into a routine as expected, Drustan began unobtrusively spending more time in her company, as well as dancing attendance on her. It all happened so gradually that no one paid any particular attention. Soon with or without others they began to take little walks together into such little forested areas as the tiny kingdom possessed. One thing innocently led into another. One day when completely alone, and in a sylvan locus where none could observe them, the twain finally succumbed to their passion. They finally made love to each other. The exchange turned out superlatively.

Alas, instead of assuaging or quenching their thirst for each other, it only made the flames of passion rage all the more violently. Despite the care and caution that they exercised with wisdom and forethought, someone inevitably would come upon them *in flagrante delicto.* It just so happened that it was the king himself who discovered them, and almost in the act of love itself.

Removing their clothes, they had used them as cover over the natural grass. They had completed their breathless hour but had not regarbed themselves. The king came upon them while they remained naked. He also noted their youthful beauty. Despite his instant wrath he had the maturity and the presence of mind to control his anger. Meanwhile his face became suffused with red, the red of his wrath. He had left his Castell Dor by himself. No one else attended the exchange among father, second wife, and son.

Mark: "Well, well, well, what a lovely picture! So here I am betrayed by both of you, my wife with my son! How do you expect me to react except in anger?"

Drustan: "Father, pray pardon me, but I take responsibility for the passion between Yseult and myself. We fell in love while in Eire, but avoided, on purpose, making love at that time. This we did out of deference and respect for you, our benefactor. Please try to understand!"

Yseult: "Mark, a person can love more than one person at a time, no?"

Mark: "Yes, I concede that might be so. I did notice this in my own youth not so long ago."

Drustan: "We do not ask that you condone what we have done, but beg you to understand and grant us indulgence."

Mastering himself, Mark responded calmly. "I grant you that indulgence. I owe it to both of you. After all, one of you is my wife and one of you is my son, but I am profoundly disappointed. I have decided on the spot right now. I banish you, Drustan, to Brittany for one year: you will have ample funds, do not worry. And you, Yseult, will continue here, fulfilling your obligations as wife and queen. Come!"

During this exchange the lovers had reclothed themselves, and together the three of them returned to the Castellum Aureum. As dictated by the king, Drustan sailed over to Brittany, where he became attached to the service of the governor Julius Questus and his right-hand man, Marcus Pentius. He served them both with diligence no less than with distinction. Meanwhile he fell in love with another Essylt, or Yseult.

Eventually King Mark recalled his chief son back to his court across the Narrow Seas. Perforce he brought this other Essylt back with him. They had married, and she was already carrying their child. The affair between him and the first Essylt had become a dead issue. In due course the second Essylt gave birth to a healthy son. It delighted King Mark to have another grandchild, especially a beautiful new grandson. While Drustan had absented himself in Rennium, the old capital of Brittany, the first Essylt had also given birth to a child, a son, or perhaps a grandson. He resembled both King Mark and Drustan. Who then was the actual father? It made no difference.

Sometime after this the king died, even if not that old, hardly more than middle age. He had no premonition of his decease, and he suffered no lingering illness before he died. Drustan and the second Essylt became the new king and queen of Phoé, and the first Essylt became the dowager, albeit quite young to assume that senior status. The love affair between Drustan and the first Essylt did not prove the tragedy depicted in song and story, so much as it did a major awkwardness or difficulty. Sic transit gloria mundi? No, sic transit gloria amoris!

CHAPTER IV. Lancelus and Gueneveria

Presently we turn from a pair of younger lovers, nominally Drustan and Essylt, to a pair of somewhat older ones, nominally Lancelus and Gueneveria. We had the tale of Drustan and Essylt from the original couple themselves, first Drustan and secondarily from the first Essylt. Even following *the* King Mark and his floruit, they continued in existence. Meanwhile Lancelus and Gueneveria came to know each other mutually, and moreover with Arthor's knowledge and approval.

Warriors and champions, the latter the upper level of warriors, flocked to Arthor's banners that he assumed as the official son of Uthor Pendragon, and acknowledged at large by the public, as was fitting and proper. Among the warriors attracted to Arthor as Dux Bellorum and High King, one champion stood out, one Caesarion Lancelus, either pure old-time Gallic or a mixture of Gallic with the new Frankish overlordship. As it developed, the Franks displayed great aptitude for, and eager acceptance of, the Romanitas, the Latinity, the Latin culture of the Gaul that, following their conquest and occupation, came as a natural and perhaps inevitable consequence.

Among the newcomers to Arthor's court at Caer Leon, this Caesarian, or Little Caesar, stood out pre-eminently. He derived from an aristocratic family famous for their skill in arms, not only the long sword and the short sword, the full shield and the buckler, not to mention the dagger, even the bow and arrow, but above all the arrow-headed spear, the lance. From this especial skill came his name of Lancelus.

Even before the endless little skirmishes between the factions in the new half-Gallic and half-Frankish hegemony, Lancelus had shown his proficiency with the lance either in martial exercises held in public, or in the large-scale hunting enterprises that the new aristocracy loved to put into action. Whether he launched the spear into the enemy fighter, or into bear or boar or wolf, Lancelus proved equally fearless. Invariably he hurled his lances with impeccable accuracy and success.

Once he arrived in Caer Leon, during the martial displays held in the amphitheatre, Lancelus displayed his proficiency with unerring strength and marksmanship. Arthor seemed quite honored and happy to welcome this new champion into the special circle at his dining table or in the old legionary arena. In the relatively few skirmishes with the Saxons, at least for the nonce, Lancelus appeared fearless and a formidable antagonist indeed.

As soon as Lancelus and Gueneveria met and exchanged signals and basic values, the queen demonstrated a marked predilection for his company, nay, his companionship. She sought out Arthor for a private interview and expressed her desire for this new companionship.

Arthor smiled, embraced her, and told her with great warmth, "I could not approve more. You could not choose a better champion than myself."

Gueneveria warmly embraced him back and simply said, "Thank you, dear friend and husband." Apart from hunting and the needed exercises in the amphitheatre, that is, for Lancelus, the two new companions passed much of their remaining time together. Certainly Arthor would not, could not, have complained. Gueneveria otherwise spent much time with him when in public at large. In his many needed absences from Gueneveria, to fight his then endless wars and battles, circumstances had allowed him to make love with many women more than eager to spend the night with Arthor. In this manner he had fathered many children, all of whom he acknowledged when they would come forward. But he did officially recognize Medraut as his son and heir, to take over his dominion after his demise.

Lancelus and Gueneveria soon began taking extended promenades here and there, leaving the praetorium through the northern gate of the great legionary fortress metamorphosed into a civilian town. They developed in particular a marked fondness for a then heavily wooded and rounded hill northwest of Caer Leon.

No one seemed to linger there, and so the twain had unlimited access to this enchanted place. The twain called it "The Hill of Dreams," truly a magical ambiance, a special sylvan paradise. It might have functioned long agone as an ancestral hill-fort, but they could not easily discover any remnants of ditches and ramparts, as in the case of Dun Cadan.

No matter, as their attention more or most often than not, focussed on each other. Nonetheless, they loved the ambiance for its freshness and natural beauty. From certain selected spots they commanded an unparalleled perspective of the river terrain around and below them: the other and older houses, some still in use and inhabited; the river Usk, or Isca, continuing down on the south to the sea; but above all else the legionary fortress with its towers and turrets, its corner bastions.

At that point, although perforce we (that is, Merlin in his presence at large) had to spend much time at court in the praetorium, as *the* court minister in fact, we still passed as much time as we could otherwise at our own place, the former wine shop, where we still conducted our business of advice, comfort, consolation, and prophecy. This arrangement continued all through Arthor's reign as High King, approximately from 490 on into 520.

One day, musing as she often did, Gueneveria suddenly spoke up, but softly, as usual. "However harsh the conquest and occupation of Britain by the Romans proved initially, still their colonization did turn out in the long run as a great good thing for Britain and the British."

Lancelus considered what she had said, pausing and pondering before he spoke in turn. "On careful reflection—I have thought about it often before—I must be in accord with what you have stated. For us, too, in Gaul it resulted in a huge step forward for both us Gallic people and the Franks who followed after the Romans. For all the peoples who formed part of it, the collapse of the Western Empire has proven a disaster, a calamity, a catastrophe, an unprecedented misfortune. Just as Britannia shall not go back to her former status, so neither can the Western Empire return to her former self.

"It has taken over one hundred years for us to realize that fact. But at least we have survived so far, and we have an entire novel world that we can create out of the ruins. That should give us hope and strength. In the meantime much of our older life does in fact endure, and shall endure. We can also take encouragement from those conditions, no?"

He smiled at Gueneveria. She nodded back, and they held hands. They never spoke of the subject again.

As we have already stated, although many British had become nominally Christian, yet many remained pagans at heart. They still believed in the older British pantheon, not to mention what they had inherited from Greece and Rome, that is, before the first muted appearance of Christianity out of Judaea. Perhaps like Constantine the Great [280?–337: emperor of Rome, 306–37] they were merely hedging their spiritual bets, just in case one religion proved more veracious than the other. Even after declaring Christianity the state religion of the overall Roman Empire, Constantine himself did not convert to the official new faith until his deathbed.

Nominally Lancelus and Gueneveria passed as Christians, but in their hearts they still believed in the older gods. This remained another special issue that they shared, as they privately confessed to each other. With these and other shared values, they began taking little trips by horseback here and there and, usually with a mounted escort of heavily armed and leather-armored warriors, with no pomp or ceremony. (The Saxons had not yet cultivated horses to any notable extent.) First, they visited the fortified villa belonging to Merlin's family northwest of Caer Leon. Second, they visited almost clandestinely the Temple of Nodens to the east or the northeast of Isca Silurum, but not far away. The priests there still maintained the great fane for the still considerable number of adherents remaining in and around the sacred ambiance.

Third, they visited that other principal home of the Cornuarii, Din Tagell, as arranged by Merlin in advance. From there they went to spend a few days and nights at Land's End, to renew contact with eternal things. Finally, well pleased by all this sightseeing, they returned to Arthur's court at Caer Leon. They had returned to the rebuilt praetorium by no more than a few months when a courier arrived, a younger brother to Lancelus, from their family home in Brittany. He advised Lancelus to return there with all possible haste. Their two elderly parents were failing at last after an unusually long life.

Gueneveria and Lancelus said farewell. Without his speaking it, she knew that he would return to her as soon as possible, that is, as the family circumstances would allow him. Perhaps a matter of a month, or several months. She, of course, expressed her complete sympathy to her dear Lancelus. The two brothers departed almost at once, leaving by ship from Caer Leon, crossing over to Cornuae, and then around Land's End crossing over to Brittany thus via the widest expanse of the Narrow Seas, as luck and happenstance would have it.

One month. Two months. Three months. No message and no Lancelus. Gueneveria would have sent over to Brittany her own courier with written message in the earliest part of the fourth month. Then one day, before she could effect this, the younger brother to Lancelus, Lucianus Quintus—whom Gueneveria had met just three months or so before—suddenly showed up when he came into her presence in the praetorium, *the* courier from her dear, dear lover. Her heart leapt up when he came up to her, and then dropped, when she noted his calm but subdued expression. When she first observed him, she did a double take: how much he now looked like Lancelus, only a much younger version! Quintus asked to interview her in a private chamber. She set this up at once, and they sat opposite each other across a small table. He reached out and touched her hand.

Quintus now spoke deliberately. "Our parents died a month or so after Lancelus returned. Then, during the obsequies, Lancelus became gravely ill. The doctors diagnosed some internal complaint." He had planned and wished to return to Gueneveria as soon as possible, but decided to wait out his malady. However, he only waxed sicker and sicker. Then one morning the family found him utterly lifeless in bed. He would not be returning to Caer Leon and Gueneveria. When she heard this report, she herself wanted to die, and at once. Quintus and she stood up. They embraced as they both began to weep and sob. He had loved his big brother as a very special person, almost as a god, albeit in a way different from how Gueneveria loved him.

Lucianus had brought with him a special note on vellum that he gave to her. Lancelus had managed to write this message on the evening before he died, and moreover with great effort. It read: "My dearest Gueneveria, when you receive this from my brother Quintus, I shall be dead from this internal complaint. Please do not grieve. We shall meet again in some future life. This is not a promise, it is a statement. Fare you well until we meet again on the further shores of time and space. Undying love to you! Lancelus."

After a few days Quintus returned to the family home in Brittany via the same ship that had brought him to Britain. Before he left, he gave Arthor's queen a simple ring, a band of electrum, of silver and gold, that Lancelus had often worn. He wanted Gueneveria to have this memento of him and the love they had shared. Indeed, she would wear it until the day she died. Once again, it was not a case of sic transit gloria mundi, but sic transit gloria amoris.

Chapter V. A Battle at Camlaun

At long last we come to the final and saddest part of Arthor's long life (440–520), his long career (455–520), and his long reign (490–520). And it was his official son and heir, Medraut, who caused the final decade of Arthor's floruit to turn into the saddest part. Arthor had fathered his official son via some Romano-Keltic noblewoman of the West Country. She had raised Medraut himself until she sent him to his father's court at Caer Leon when the son attained his tenth year. Despite the boon that the peace and prosperity Arthor gained for his fellow Britons during his reign, many petty kings and chieftains, certainly his own son, chafed against the restraint and restrictions imposed by Arthor. They preferred some conflict so that they could exercise their martial skills, to win and garner glory on the field of battle. How could they do this when Arthor kept the peace, kept such a tight lid on everything, and rigorously so?

Medraut felt the same way, but felt it even more. He must have attained his mid-adolescence at the time of the enormous triumph won by Arthor and his allies against the Saxons and theirs at Mount Badon. Medraut, a good warrior (I shall grant him that), especially chafed under the long reign of his father, and wished very much to inherit the supreme power, that is, if all the kings, princes, and chieftains agreed to elect him as High King following Arthor's demise, whenever that might happen.

Perhaps someone or something clandestine could help that along, to help Medraut attain his goal, all quite innocently, of course. During the third and final decade of Arthor's reign Medraut was passing through his thirties. Thus it came about that Medraut began to cultivate the Keltic leaders and warriors disaffected by Arthor's formidably maintained peace and armistice. Medraut and all those disaffected began planning a *coup d'état* to remove Arthor and to elevate Medraut to his father's place, even if it meant Arthor's murder.

Medraut even went so far in his turpitude and treason to foster negotiations with the Saxons and their allies in southeast Britain, and in and around London. Their numbers had by now significantly increased since Mount Badon, bringing recruits or immigrants from the

Continent. The disaffected leaders, including Medraut, swore themselves to secrecy. What they planned was pure treason and rebellion.
Thus they plotted and planned all through that decade from 510 into
520. The overt flames of rebellion would not break out until sometime during Arthor's last year.

The death of Caesarion Lancelus in such a quiet and unheroic
fashion left poor Gueneveria devastated, nay more, desolated. She
doubted that she would ever have another lover like Lancelus, not
just physically stalwart and forthright, but above all in his rank as an
ingratiatingly delectable companion. They had enjoyed so many marvelous, even transcendent occasions together. That would not, that
could not, happen again for Gueneveria. To be honest, she surprised
herself when she felt vague stirrings of desire as she visited with Quintus Lucianus, when he came over from Gaul, from Brittany, to give
her the melancholy news of his older brother's quite unexpected passing. How much Quintus resembled his older brother, whom he still
worshipped, even though deceased!

Gueneveria still felt the same as Quintus, but her life now needed
to take a new course. Her thoughts continued to revert from time to
time to Lancelus, as she pondered the almost contradiction: that he
and his family claimed to be both Gallic and Frankish, but claimed
Brittany just as much as their ancestral domain. The queen attached
herself closely once again to her husband. She dedicated herself once
again to him and to his governance of his now far-flung dominium,
meaning above all Brittany with her many offshore islets, distant at the
widest extent of the Narrow Seas. At least no immediate attack threatened from the Saxons and their allies, even where firmly settled in
southeast Britain.

The queen continued to reach out to Medraut as a kind of adopted son, but although deferent and gallant, he kept to himself, or was
gone elsewhere much of the time, well out of Caer Leon and its
courtly orbit. So it was that she turned to her foster children or grand-
children. She also concerned herself with running the household that
maintained the praetorium. She busied herself as well with weaving,
employing the little hand-looms that one found in most households.
Like all weavers Gueneveria became expert at changing the raw wool

into the cloth that almost everyone wore, into the garments of every-day use.

Arthor gallantly showed himself as compassionate to the queen's loss of Caesarion Lancelus, and manifested his appreciation of the care and attention that she was now paying to him and his concerns of governance. This renewed relationship, almost in the manner of nup-tial vows restated and restarted, went a long way toward sustaining both the High King and the High Queen, as he lightheartedly called her in private, even if not an official title.

Much of what I (or we, Merlin) now relate, I did not know for obvious reasons at the time, given the circumstances. I only found out somewhat after Arthor's death, above all as it reflects the clandestine activity sponsored by Arthor's heir.

Once again, and this on the third occasion overall, Medraut was paying a visit to the leading Saxons (not to mention the Jutes and An-gles) headquartered in London. Always it seemed that he with his mounted escort, and under a flag of truce—yes, as always, a plain white banner—reached London after sunset and after twilight. At that time of night only several beacon fires here and there were burning inside the towers and turrets of the solid walls that protected the City, the Civitas Londinium, the original square mile of London.

The circuit of the original walls had gone up only as late as the reign of Aurelian (215?-275), his reign of 270-75: Aurelian, or to give him his full name, as it is apt and proper for a Roman emperor, Lucius Domitius Aurelianus. After reuniting the overall Imperium Romanum, especially by bringing back into the fold the kingdom or empire of Zenobia, Queen of Palmyra (some hundred miles or so east of the Mediterranean), this astute emperor commanded walls to rise up around many towns, villages, and cities. That is, when they did not already have them, such as the Civitas Londinium, and in that case, an outstanding lack, or deficiency.

When he first visited *the* City, Medraut remembered how keen he had been to see London's original square mile, the original 640 acres. (The Britons had adopted the Anglo-Saxon acre, or 43,560 square feet.) Because he had mostly known Caer Leon as a city, no less the City of the Legion, the difference in scale between Isca Silurum and Civitas Londinium rather startled him. While the 60 acres of Caer Leon did not deserve any disdain, they could not compare with London's acreage, at something less than one-tenth of that latter expanse. And knowledgeable people had informed him that the truly grand cities of the empire extended far beyond the size of the former capital of Britain. Those truly grandiose municipalities included Rome herself, Alexandria in Egypt, Antioch on the Orontes in Syria, and not to leave out Constantinople as the new magnificent capital of the overall empire. Medraut would have to take their word for it!

As always, when entering London through the main gate on the west, Medraut found the place eerie, a ghost town, a spectral civitas. He could imagine with ease what it was like as the former administrative and financial capital of Britain!—its bustle, its merchantry, its variety of people from all over the island, not to mention the overall empire! Nowadays, or nowanights with so little illumination, it appeared a deserted city, haunted by its past. Although somewhat neglected for something like a hundred years, most of the principal structures remained in relatively good shape, free of trees and bushes, the sure sign of abandonment. The official palace of the procurator, a grand edifice north of the forum, had retained its use as the center and residence of the leading Saxon king, Axel Aesca.

Going past the forum lying on the east en route to the palace, the immense colonnaded courtyard as the forum's heart—400 square feet with the basilica serving as the main part of the northern wing's quite solid fabric—struck Medraut all over again, lit as it was here and there by only a few lanterns that could but accentuate its empty vastitude.

A small delegation of Saxon officials had met Medraut and his mounted escort at the chief western gate and were guiding them to the procurator's former headquarters. Some officials had lanterns, but most of them carried flaming torches. A few were holding ornamental flambeaux, devices made of metal, keeping in their sockets upright burning sticks of resinous wood. These burned well and steadily, and created strange shapes and shadows. In this way the Saxons and the Britons proceeded through the city's thoroughfares in a silent procession broken only by the occasional snorting and stamping of the British horses.

As a mark of trust and courtesy the Saxons allowed the Britons to keep their weapons. After they alighted outside the main entrance to the palace, several British grooms who accompanied the mounted escort attended to the horses in some stables nearby. The Saxon delegation ushered the Britons into the basilica of the procuratorial palace, which the Saxons used as a throne room and a banqueting hall. The two ethnic groups greeted each other in a reserved but friendly manner. Despite their ethnic differences they all dressed more or less the same in wool clothing, but the cloaks of the British bore typical Keltic curvilinear patterns. Both groups had their bilingual interpretors who could translate both Saxon and British.

First the hosts offered the guests some drink and food, which the guests accepted, but drank and ate only minimally, and fast. Everyone wanted to get down to business as soon as possible, even if the guests would be staying overnight before departing in the morning to return to the British domains to the west.

All had seated themselves around a large oval table with sturdy chairs, everything of obvious Roman design. The Saxon leader, Axel Aesca, spoke first. "Welcome! Tonight, as planned, we shall make final our mutual arrangements for your *coup d'état.*"

Medraut and the others bowed their heads in respect and agreement. The British crown prince (if so we may call him) spoke next. "As soon as you and your allies create your special 'disturbance,' and Arthor's own spies report it as the sizeable gathering that it will turn out to be—as if threatening to advance west against him and his forces—then Arthor will head southeast to this area, expecting to find you and your army. But you will all have retreated back into London. When he comes east, you might explain under a flag of truce that his own scouts had misinterpreted the gathering and had misinformed him, that the gathering was only that of several tribes or clans for family reasons, and that you had no intention of advancing against him and of upsetting the armistice or the status quo."

Here Medraut paused as if gathering his thoughts before speaking again. "Then our British countergroup will take over, and secure, Caer Leon; and we shall amass our forces near Caer Vadon. We shall remain in touch with our mounted couriers. When Arthor learns of our countergroup, he will head back to the West Country, expecting to engage me and our forces, those of our countergroup, at or near

Caer Vadon. But meanwhile we shall all retreat to a certain place on the coast in Cornuae. This locus as a place for battle will give our countergroup with lesser forces a decided advantage over those of my father."

Here Medraut paused again before going on. "I cannot predict how this battle near the village of Camlaun on the river Camel in Cornuae shall result. But if our countergroup with myself as one of the chief leaders should win out, then we shall achieve all that we have promised you. My rule will recognize your settlement here in and around London as permanent and legitimate. We shall also confer the other benefits as already discussed. Agreed?"

Axel Aesca and the other Saxon leaders nodded solemnly. More palaver, more discussion, more agreement. Medraut made a final speech. "I shall meet as soon as possible with the other leaders of our countergroup at the Temple of Nodens. Once we make our own preparations among us, we shall send you word via several couriers. That will be the signal for you to start. We are agreed?"

Everyone had agreed to everything. The great *coup d'état* would begin as soon as everyone could put all the other plans into effect. Everyone retired to various chambers to sleep, and the Britons would leave in the morning for their own dominions.

When I stated earlier that I (or we, Merlin) had no clue or concept as to Medraut's treason and rebellion (as well as involving many other Britons), it is obvious that I did not consult my second sight, or that my prophetic powers failed me. I neglected to make use of them in this case, and suspected nothing amiss. Events overtook me as they did Arthor, and eventually Medraut himself, no less than those other leaders in his countergroup.

Meanwhile, under the eternal forest canopy that seems to cover much of the big island that we call Britain, Medraut continued his campaign against his own father. Albeit indirectly and inadvertently, Arthor had aided and abetted his own son in his machinations always going forward.

Once again Medraut had met his co-conspirators at the grand and expansive Temple of Nodens east or northeast of Caer Leon—under that protective deity's especial care—as I, Merlin, had investigated, inspired, and shepherded the emanation of that same elder and all-inclusive deity, that divinity of unending space whether on our planet Earth or in the illimitable profounds of outer space, of the cosmos at large.

Once again, after initially meeting inside the temple itself (on behalf of some ceremony to help Medraut and his countergroup), they had convened in that certain forest glade not far away. Medraut addressed the countergroup that made up his eager support, still sworn to secrecy as well as to their particular common purpose.

"I have fully reported to you what occurred between myself and the Saxons with their allies in London. They stand with us, and we must not betray that trust. As soon as we finish our final preparations here under the protective surveillance of our own indigenous divinity Nodens, I shall inform them to begin their disturbance in southeast Britain to draw the Dux Bellorum away from the West Country. In the meantime we shall gather our own forces north of Caer Vadon.

"Once my father realizes that the greatest challenge lies once more here in the west, he will return to Caer Leon or Caer Vadon, to confront or pursue us, while we retreat into Cornuae. There we plan to confront and fight him at the mouth of the river Camel near the little walled village of Camlaun. If Arthor suspects any collusion between the Saxons and ourselves as a countergroup and counterthrust to him and his hegemony, it will make no difference. We must confront each other and battle it out, whichever side emerges as the victor. Let me know your decision. As soon as possible, I shall alert our allies, the Saxons in southeast Britain, by special couriers." Medraut concluded, as ever under Britain's eviternal forest canopy.

As soon as the countergroup had come to an agreement, Medraut sent his couriers to London in order to incite that initial disturbance. It came to pass. Meanwhile Medraut and his countergroup began assembling their forces near Caer Vadon. Thus in spite of everything that might have gone wrong, everything at first concerning Medraut and his countergroup went right. Everything functioned just like the machinery for the clepsydra, or water clock.

After being baffled by the Saxon disturbance in southeast Britain, Arthor and his army turned his full attention to Medraut and the forces of his countergroup in the west, a tedious but fatiguing journey by horse and by foot. The countergroup had invested and secured Caer Leon as Arthor's chief capital. Medraut and his forces had withdrawn to Cornuae, in turn compelling Arthor to follow them in pursuit.

At long last we come to the great battle that happened not far from the little walled village of Camlaun at the mouth of the river Camel, just north of the sizeable estuary, about the same size as that of the river Foy on the other, or eastern, side of the overall peninsula of Cornuae, by some twenty or twenty-five miles. The headland of Din Tagell itself stood out from the coast only ten miles or so north of Camlaun.

There a considerable plain, or flat area, extends much wider east and west than north and south. It constitutes an adequate surface for a major combat, or a pitched battle. It would seem that other great combats had occurred in this place, but before the Roman conquest and occupation from about 50 to 410 A.D. The little village itself lies somewhat elevated on the other, or southern, side of the river.

Medraut and his forces did not bypass Din Tagell, but made it their headquarters in the stone palace still impregnable as ever. Here they would wait until the inevitable arrival of Arthor himself with his army. Arrive he did, and with his full complement of seasoned warriors. Both Medraut and Arthor had kept themselves fully informed via their respective scouts about the movements of each other and their respective armies. Medraut had already set up an encampment on the northern side of the plain with his back toward the higher elevation. Arthor then set up his camp with his warriors on the more than adequate ground south of where Medraut and his troops had established themselves.

The weather itself cooperated and held good at least for a little while. The vernal rains had finished more or less, and the days had turned out warm and sunny.

At midmorning, on the day of battle, Arthor with the other leaders came forth from his pavilion, announced by a new set of buccinators, or trumpet players. The two sides advanced to the middle of the open ground, facing each other. Arthor stood in the middle of his chief officers, opposite where Medraut stood in the middle of his own leading men. Medraut went up to Arthor, raised his long sword, and struck forthrightly at his father, who struck back at once. Each side then surged upon and into the other, engaging in a hot and heavy exchange with sword, shield, and spear.

Arthor still had love in his heart somewhere for Medraut as his official son and heir, but on this day rage and wrath had replaced the love. At his age of eighty or so he did not appreciate the challenge to his power from his very own son and his conspirators. Arthor had not done anything to deserve what Medraut and allies were attempting. He saw their motivation only as vanity. But Medraut felt that he had right and righteousness on his side. After chafing for years and years under his father's rule and reign, as well as his restrictions, Medraut felt that his father should have resigned, retired, or deceased long since. Each in his own way felt animated by a higher morality than mere power, or the lust for power.

The battle had begun, and it continued until about early afternoon when most of the leaders had perished. Arthor and Medraut had mutually killed each other almost at the exact same time, each driving his sword into the gut and upward into the heart of the other— Arthor first with his last energy, and then Medraut with all his anger, irritation, and younger energy enabling him to drive his sword into his father's gut and heart in the same way. The slaughter on both sides, as it developed, turned out to be tremendous. The armies on both sides had killed so much of each other that not enough warriors on either side remained to claim the victory. When the sun finally set that day on that battle of battles, it saw nothing but an immense mass of bodies dead and dying. Thus ended Arthor's last great battle. Everyone had put up a colossal fight, but most of them perished, and nobody won the victory except Death himself.

FINIS

Author's Note

In compiling this new chronicle translated and redacted from the original version of *Merlin's Memoirs* (multiple handwritten scrolls during 525-26 A.D.), we faced at once the same problems relative to dating and mileage (the mile as a unit of linear measure) that he did.

In redacting his own memoirs (mostly recounting the life and career of that singular individual best and later known as King Arthur), Merlin himself complained about the aequivocal and unsettled state of the new Christian chronology. Victorinus of Aquitane in 457 introduced the system of dating as calculated from the *death* of Jesus Christ; and Dionysius Exiguus in 525 in turn introduced his own system of dating from the *birth* of Jesus Christ. The relative dates for him are now standardized as circa 6 B.C. and 30 A.D., a lifetime of some forty years or less.

Merlin would have preferred the continued usage of A.U.C., *Ab Urbe Condita,* or *Anno Urbis Conditæ,* that is, from the founding of the city, *the* City, Rome, the Civitas Roma, dated 753 B.C. The new dating attendant on the Christian Era only became widespread as the new Christian faith itself spread throughout the former or then actual Roman Empire after the collapse of the western half.

The other major problem concerns that of geographical distance as related to Britannia Major, or Great Britain, as calculated in miles as the chief unit of linear measure, and with the aid of modern maps. Modern British (English-speaking) and American people use the English statute mile of 5280 feet, whereas Merlin would have used the standard Roman mile of c. 4860 feet, even if the Roman foot might have measured out somewhat differently.

The Roman mile is the thousand paces (each pace about a yard) by the Roman legionary soldier in transit by foot, that is, when marching from one locus to another in order to travel. For one example, the difference of circa 420 feet between an English mile and a Roman mile, say, as multiplied by ten, yields 4200 feet, thus almost an extra mile for each ten Roman miles. In general terms, perhaps not significant. Therefore, to avoid useless pedantry, we have made our distances in miles deliberately approximate. We have indicated this less than exact geography by such terms as "about thirty miles" or "some twenty miles," and so forth. The real distance between the Roman and the English miles would not amount to much, even if the individual were traveling on foot. If traveling on horseback it would seem different, or it would total out differently.

DONALD SIDNEY-FRYER

East Sandwich, Massachusetts
Saturday noon, 22 June 2019

A MEDLEY OF NONFICTION

Introduction to
Etchings in Ivory: Poems in Prose

Among those writers who contributed to *Weird Tales* (1923-54) and
helped make it memorable, there were at least five who more than
any others truly made it "The Unique Magazine" (as its quondam
subtitle ran) and who gained thereby a unique reputation for themselves: Henry St. Clair Whitehead (1882-1932), Howard Phillips
Lovecraft (1890-1937), Clark Ashton Smith (1893-1961), Robert
Ervin Howard (1906-1936), and Ray Bradbury (1920-2012). The
two outstanding poets of this group, whether in verse or in prose,
were the Californian Clark Ashton Smith and the Texan Robert Ervin
Howard. Smith had gained an outstanding reputation for himself as a
lyric poet before he began to contribute regularly to *Weird Tales.*
Howard may have made his first reputation through *Weird Tales,*
but he went on to write successfully for virtually every major type of
pulp magazine of his time—a considerable accomplishment. Moreover,
he used his writings not merely to make a living as a pulp writer but also to express his life-attitude and life-philosophy. His death at the age
of thirty is often held to have cut short a career of great promise, but
many commentators underestimate the fact that he had had a career of
considerable achievement by the time he died. In Howard's best prose
and verse, there inheres a wonderful and liberating sense of imagination and adventure, a uniquely healthy gesture reaching outward, as
well as a pulse, a rhythm, that is as vigorous as it is invigorating.

Howard was descended of pioneer forebears, and one senses a
certain homeric quality of the frontier and the frontiersman in his best
writings. Just as much as his Texas forebears, Howard was a pioneer,
but in his own way. Where they had hewed and fought with axe and
gun to build a life for themselves from an often hostile environment,
Howard in his turn used his typewriter to wrest a living for himself in
the face of what was assuredly not a sympathetic environment. He
showed his fellow citizens of Cross Plains, Texas, that a man could
make a living for himself through his writing. What sweat and tears
and blood the dedicated writer of vision and responsibility must
sometime shed so that through his pain he can create pleasure and

enlightenment for others, only the initiated can discover and know for themselves. But where the old pioneers had at least enjoyed a hearty and warm companionship in their adventure, Howard had in his adventure virtually no kindred spirits living near him, and in an interior sense lived virtually alone—sustaining himself spiritually through literature, his own or that created by others, and through correspondence with a few of his fellow writers for *Weird Tales* and other magazines. The amazing thing is that, with or without the immediate physical presence of kindred spirits, he managed to create as much as he did in the short period of time at his disposal as a professional writer.

Today, more than ever before, there is a large and growing audience for Howard's fine adventure stories, as demonstrated by what will evidently evolve into a complete line of Howard paperbacks published by Lancer Books of New York. Just as his finest verses—with their pulsing rhythm, their incantatory rime, their vivid and colorful imagery—make one think instinctively of the poet in his primal role as a witch-doctor or magician invoking spirits good and evil for the benefit of his people or to the harm of their enemies, human or otherwise; so do Howard's finest stories evoke for us the presence of the campfire narrator, or the antique bard in flowing bardic robes, who keeps his fellow tribesmen or adventurers enthralled and thrilled with epic narratives of men battling against seemingly insuperable odds, perhaps eventually to triumph or, even if defeated, to triumph still in their own dark will. More than any other writer except perhaps Jack London (one of his favorite authors), Howard stands alone in twentieth-century literature in his ability to envision and portray elementary red-blooded struggle in "perilous untried barbaric lands." He is often unsurpassed in his power to invoke primordial gods or forces greater and older than man. His best short stories—with their vigorous and rhythmical prose, their sense of a larger context than man's own immediate environment, their strong and sweeping narratives, their often striking and poignant imagery--are akin to the plays and poems of the Elizabethans, with their similar sense of adventure spiritual and physical, their sense of breathless discovery and exploration, and their consciousness of the macrocosmos. Some of his best stories, such as "The Mirrors of Tuzun Thune," are virtual prose-poems in the manner of Poe's masterpiece, "The Masque of the Red Death."

Akin to Howard's best prose fiction is this unique sequence of prose-poems never before imprinted, the very titles of which open up magic portals of mystery and imaginative speculation: "Flaming Marble," "Skulls and Orchids," "Medallions in the Moon," "The Gods That Men Forget," "Bloodstones and Ebony." Verily, these are titles to conjure with! According to Glenn Lord, now deservedly and at long last the literary executor of Howard's estate, the author created these poems in prose comparatively early in his career as a professional writer, sometime around 1928 or 1929, to judge from the manuscripts. From where did R.E.H. derive his models for these prose-poems? One is tempted at first glance—noting similarities in vision, in rhythm, in subject-matter, in the love of color and of picturesque detail, even in titles—to see something of an influence from the prose-poems of Clark Ashton Smith, twenty-nine of which were first published in 1922 in his *Ebony and Crystal,* in the final section entitled "Poems in Prose." By virtue of these last, Smith had shown himself as the sovereign master of the prose-poem in English. However, it was not until the early summer of 1933 that Howard bought himself a copy of *Ebony and Crystal* directly from the author-publisher, although he may have seen a copy earlier. But, to judge from Howard's considerable and highly favorable reaction to this book of poetry as evidenced by his letter to Smith (undated but postmarked July 22, 1933), there would have been some reflection or mention of it in his correspondence if he had seen such a copy earlier.

In the charming inscription he penned on the flyleaf of the copy he sold to the younger writer, Smith addresses Howard as a brother:

> For Robert E. Howard,
> These litanies to Astarte
> and Hecate and Dagon and
> Demogorgon.
>   With fraternal good
>   wishes,
> July 4th, 1933.   Clark Ashton Smith.

(This copy, number 431, was once in the possession of the Library of Howard Payne College, Brownwood, Texas, now withdrawn.)

Howard's probable models, if he needed any, were such prose-poems by Edgar Allan Poe (one of his favorite writers whether in verse or in prose) as "Shadow—A Parable," "Silence—A Fable," and "The Masque of the Red Death." Since Aloysius Bertrand (1807–1841) had first introduced the prose-poem in French literature with *Gaspard de la Nuit* (published posthumously in 1842), the form had become a standard and favorite one with French writers. But in English, even though the form had been created in the language comparatively early in the nineteenth century by Poe (1809–1849), it had never caught on in the way it had in French. The work in this genre done by the English Decadents and Symbolists is largely ineffective and superficial, apart from a few outstanding pieces by Arthur Machen, the author of *The Hill of Dreams.* Only Clark Ashton Smith, modeling himself principally after Poe and Baudelaire and Sir Thomas Browne, has produced a body of work in English that, for both quantity and quality, equals, and occasionally surpasses the work of the French Symbolists as well as the Russian Symbolists, the most successful rivals as a group of their French progenitors.

(Smith had also studied early in his career, and with fruitful results, that rare volume *Pastels in Prose,* a selection of prose-poems translated by Stuart Merrill from the French of twenty-three authors and published by Harper & Brothers of New York in 1890.)

Just as much as Lovecraft or Smith, Howard had a remarkable sense of the cosmic-astronomic, and "Bloodstones and Ebony" is especially noteworthy for its evocation of cosmic splendors in a comparatively small compass. But all these pieces by Howard are noteworthy in one way or another, and all are beautifully strange dream-pieces, haunted and haunting. For their color, their imaginativeness, their vivid delineation, their strangeness, and their dreamlike rhythms, they are equal to some of the finest prose-poems of Clark Ashton Smith. As a succession of fantastic imageries, they would not prove unworthy of a place in George Sterling's great imaginative poem, "A Wine of Wizardry." As a prose-poet in English, Howard is second only to Smith himself. One can only regret he did not write other similar sequences of poems in prose, but at least one can be grateful for these unique *Etchings in Ivory.*

San Francisco, 17 November 1967

Afterword to "As It Is Written"

If the novelette "As It Is Written" is not the work of Clark Ashton Smith, alias De Lysle Ferrée Cass, then someone has gone to an extraordinary amount of bother to imitate him, his way of thinking, his proper and personal style of prose composition, all at a highly transitional point in his literary career, and for only sixty dollars! Even allowing for the fact that sixty dollars in 1919 amounted to far more money than it would today, still it would hardly have served any imitator to mimic Ashton Smith at that time in his life, particularly when the story was to languish in a state *beyond obscurity* for some sixty years!

Apart from the early Oriental stories contributed to the *Overland Monthly* and the *Black Cat,* the only other prose of Smith's that anyone could have imitated was that of the half dozen or less poems in prose that had appeared in the middle to latter 'teens in the San Francisco literary magazine *Bohemia* on the one hand, and the New York-based *Smart Set* on the other. Altogether, the then-published tales and prose poems scarcely formed a viable and physically sufficient foundation for anyone to imitate.

It is of direct significance to note that the British spelling preferences and grammatical usage—which we find on occasion in Smith's early work—had greater currency in the United States back then than they do today. However, in Ashton Smith's case. such undoubtedly reflect the practice favored by his British-born father, Timeus Smith, in the same way as CAS's early, purely earthly exoticism often reflects, indubitably, the globe-wide travels and experiences of his father in the tropics.

The essential case for the authorship of "As It Is Written" being authentically Ashton Smith's has been made, and very well made, by Will Murray. The story of how this novelette was rediscovered and rescued after languishing in oblivion for more than half a century is, in itself, an exciting and marvelous tale, almost as much a romance as the novelette itself. Great credit is due to Messieurs Will Murray, Daryl Herrick, and John Howard for their literary detective work and in particular for their perseverance and painstaking research. All true Ashton-Smith-ophiles (or Klarkash-tonophiles, to employ a more

Lovecraftian term) are the richer by the addition of a new hitherto-unknown story to the canon of Ashton Smith's fiction.

It is true that there are many parallels between "As It Is Written" and Smith's other fiction, both early and late. These parallels go beyond matters of mere vocabulary, style, and even favored type of hero, to the unique and ironic perspective apparent in this novelette. The ironic perspective is quite noticeable in the byline attached to the manuscript: De Lysle Ferrée Cass is not an ordinary pseudonym, even when considered vis-à-vis the few known pen names or variations of his own name used by Smith. Clérigo Gallardo, Christophe des Laurières, Timeus Gaylord, Clérigo Herrero, and C. Ashton Smith (in the manner of A. Conan Doyle)—all these are pen names that Smith employed on rare occasions; but of all these, De Lysle Ferrée Cass may be the most ingenious and bizarre. If "Cass" is "CAS" with an added "s," then "De Lysle Ferrée Cass" would mean "Clark Ashton Smith of the Island Bound (or Circled) with Iron." The at once ironic and imaginative reverberations of such a name are legion. Thus it is the pseudonym itself that is the final conclusive piece of evidence establishing the authorship of "As It Is Written" as Ashton Smith's; only the Bard of Auburn would have used such a byline!

There is a strong possibility that this novelette is one of those long Oriental adventures which Ashton Smith records himself as creating c. 1905–10, and he may very well have considerably revamped this story for the *Thrill Book*. If this is true, then "As It Is Written" indicates a direction of less lethal denouement that his later fiction did not generally take.

N.B. As it turns out, Smith did not compose "As It Is Written." D. Sidney-Fryer has written in vain that Smith did in fact create it. Still, a noble and worthy speculation!—and an interesting novel.

Emeraude Indeed

Margo Skinner is that rara avis indeed, a modern Romantic poet, with a tone and style uniquely her own, and her tone is at once one of celebration and compassion. Her mode of presentation is refreshingly clear and straightforward with a strong narrative drive and with a singularly rich vein of imagery. Her style features a curious and yet perfectly natural amalgam of traditional prosody and modern technique. But much of this volume's distinction is immediately due to her own native and carefully nurtured mixture of reality and imagination, of actuality and fantasy.

Although her particular poetic forebears do indeed include the English romantics on one hand and the Elizabethans on the other, Margo's unique modern romanticism continues that earlier and largely Northern Californian tradition (*c.* 1900 to 1930) of such full-blown Late Romantics as George Sterling, Nora May French, and Clark Ashton Smith. However, she remains (paradoxically enough) totally underivative of their work, even though she does continue their tradition. Significantly, she is no less cosmic-minded, but her tone is perhaps more immediately human as well as humane.

When the *Golden Hind* put into a "faire and good Baye" for repairs on June 17, 1579, somewhere on the Californian coast at about latitude thirty-eight degrees north, Sir Francis Drake apparently planted some "seeds" that were not to bear fruit until not quite 400 years later. *The Shepheardes Calendar,* which directly heralds the Elizabethan efflorescence of poetry and song, appeared in the same year as Drake's discovery of New Albion. Edmund Spenser, its poet-author, had finished it by April 10th. Widely circulated in manuscript for the rest of that year, it was entered in the Stationer's Register in London on December 5th, and was then published under the pseudonym of "Immerito" soon after in that same month.

Like a seed long since planted and then apparently forgotten, the Renaissance Pleasure Faire (owing much of its original inspiration to the Age of Elizabeth I) opened first of all in 1967 in Marin County (which certainly formed part of that New Albion claimed by Sir Francis Drake), and is now well past its twentieth year. Like yet another seed planted long agone, *As Green as Emeraude* symbolizes par excellence the new romanticism that came furiously to life in the late 1960s and early 1970s (which still belong after all to the Age of Elizabeth II).

Within the highly variegated contents of this collection, within its spectrum of brilliantly tropical colors, the reader finds not only a considerable poetic inspiration but also, and in abundant measure, the sapphire and aquamarine of compassion as well as the emeraude, or emerald, of hope and life.

Sacramento, 1990

Grim News from the Far Future:
Introduction to *New Tales of Zothique*

It is one of the curious paradoxes in the limitless domains of art that anything can minister to pleasure, including many things that most of us might very well go out of our way to avoid in our immediate lives. It is a further paradox in the specific universe of literature that, in abundantly describing one thing, the writer can most effectively suggest another thing, that other phenomenon or condition being the diametric opposite of the first. Of all the prose fictions by Clark Ashton Smith (1893–1961) that he devoted to celebrating one geographical area more or less, those that he wrote about Zothique as the last continent of Earth are the most numerous. It is obvious that Ashton Smith enjoyed writing about the mainland that will presumably come about only during the final cycle of the planet. At that general time a numerically dwindling and spiritually sick and senescent humankind will somehow still manage to survive before the ultimate fall of Night, when all humans will presumably perish. Smith conceived of Zothique largely as arid and semi-arid but the latter to a much lesser extent—vast deserts extending in all directions underneath a blood-red sun during the day, and unbearably brilliant stars during the night—and such a countryside relieved only by the rare or occasional oasis, or yet verdant valley, or irrigated fields. However, it is in those poetic evocations of desert landscapes with their general desiccation and/or desolation that Smith most successfully brings to mind the exact opposite: vividly lush and green fields, groves, and forests that tease and haunt us all the more compellingly because of their express absence. Amid this exhausted and near-lifeless environment Smith characteristically posits a fast-moving narrative that, although colorful and picturesque, almost invariably depicts nothing but death, decay, dissolution—or on the other hand the ironic and empty triumph over death by means of an illicit necromancy, by which people, animals, or entire landscapes are restored to a semblance or mockery of life. Only the archaic magick, or gramarye, resuscitated from the primordial cycles of the first continent inhabited by humans, Hyperborea, displays the greatest animation of vitality. As ever, in the oeuvre of Ashton Smith whether cast in verse or prose, the one supreme antidote to the horror and banality of life is love itself, and the seductive enchantment that derives from it: love that defies death, and sometimes, (albeit but rarely and briefly) triumphs over it.

Unlike the fictional output of his great colleague and correspondent H. P. Lovecraft (1890–1937), Smith's own tales have engendered relatively few sequels or imitations. Just Lovecraft's own stories that collectively make up the Cthulhu Mythos have spawned so much derivative fiction that surely this further development has now come to outnumber the stories that inspired them by quite a significant margin. What is more, we might add, much of this imitative fiction reflects considerable discredit on Lovecraft's original stories. The present volume of new stories by various authors, new stories that utilize the same fictional background or locale as created by Smith for his own tales of Zothique, represents an obviously pioneering development as instigated by editor John Pelan. The point here simply is to present a new collection, to spin some new yarns, but it is not to rewrite Smith's own stories or to imitate Smith's own proper and personal style of writing, at least not consciously. To imitate his own style, and to do so successfully, would probably prove impossible in any case. Moreover, what would be the point? Young or beginning writers in general should occupy themselves with constructing their own plots or narratives, as well as concocting their own idiosyncratic styles of writing.

However, we live at a time when otherwise perfectly capable people must invent all over again what other creative people before them have originated, and then must claim their new version, or versions, as somehow on par with the original work of art itself. Such a case is exactly analogous to that of the great ballet-master Marius Petipa (1818–1910), who served the Imperial Russian Ballet during an overall period from the latter half of 1847 until sometime in 1904, first as a dancer and then as a choreographer. During 1904 a new and not at all sympathetic head of the theatre administration in St. Petersburg forcibly retired him, or at least relegated him to the status of inactive service. Just before this de facto retirement was forced upon him, as well as after, Petipa experienced the supreme displeasure of seeing a number of his best major works (usually characterized by highly fantastic plots) deliberately refashioned by other ballet-masters into "stylized interpretations"—as though ballet were not already quite stylized as a primary condition of its existence! Petipa complained to the head of the theatre administration, Colonel Telyakovsky, but in vain. As Petipa himself expressed it with considerable bitterness and with especial pertinence: "As if people had nothing else to focus their attention," he repeated, "as if there were no new stories to tell." That is, as if people had nothing else to do, as if they had nothing of their own to relate.

Whether such a phenomenon involves Michael Bourne's radically modern version of *Swan Lake* (a product of the early to middle 1990s) or Gus Van Sant's remake (1998) of Alfred Hitchcock's original film *Psycho* (1960), it represents a genuine distortion of the original, or a needless repetition, respectively, and as such, a deliberate mockery, however well intentioned, which almost never can be considered on the same level as the original itself. How much easier to exploit an established idea, concept, plot, or whatever, as made famous through someone else's invention and hard work—to exploit a pre-existing work of art—than to come up with something new, and to do all the difficult and necessary labor to bring it into existence, and then struggle to present it in public. One thing represents genuine creativity, and the other mere embroidery after the fact.

Whoever picks up this volume will at least have an original reading adventure, and will encounter stories that, whatever else may be their merits or demerits, at least represent only themselves, and are not imitations of anybody else's previous fictional efforts. Take any single story in this collection, as for example, "Where the Past Lay Buried," by David B. Silva. The climax of this particular tale takes place amid the tombs and graves of a vast cemetery such as was so dear to the heart of someone like Lovecraft or Ashton Smith. This necropolis lies to the west of the ancient city of Cerek, and is half the size of the municipality itself, a locale that has obviously seen much better days. To this place, in pious obedience to a maternal vision that has pursued him in his slumber three nights in a row, as accompanied by his friend, the fellow academic Rhleem Skrambar, the hero Ezeck has traveled to unearth his mother as requested to do so by that estimable parent while he lay sleeping. However, in fulfilling this pious mission, he unearths much more than what he rather naively has anticipated, and such inevitably becomes a source of deep regret. Ezeck realizes too late, as most of us do, that you can escape neither the past nor your origin and essential nature. Our flights of fancy that sometimes take place high in the heavens find themselves almost invariably rooted in the earth, which represents both the beginning and the end of our physical consciousness—the earth without which we cannot survive, and from which we cannot escape. Thus while Mr. Silva may have learned a lesson or two from Ashton Smith, he nonetheless emerges with his own story to tell, and with his own resolution to the problem presented by that innocent adventure. And thus it goes with all the other stories in this collection, stories that we can certainly recommend to the attention of the brave and adventurous reader. Good or great fantasy is never just an escape to an alternative reality, but returns us instead to the rock-bottom conditions of our existence.

Westchester, Los Angeles, 1 January 1999

The Phosphor Lamps of Clark Ashton Smith

with Ron Hilger

In a small garden area outside the Auburn Library is a plaque surrounded by jasmine and wisteria vines and dedicated to the memory of Clark Ashton Smith. The plaque reads:

CLARK ASHTON SMITH

"THE BARD OF AUBURN"
JANUARY 13, 1893–AUGUST 14, 1961

I pass . . . but in this lone and crumbling tower,
Builded against the burrowing seas of chaos,
My volumes and my philtres shall abide:
Poisons more dear than any mithridate,
And spells far sweeter than the speech of love . . .
Half-shapen dooms shall slumber in my vaults
And in my volumes cryptic runes that shall
Outblast the pestilence, outgnaw the worm
When loosed by alien wizards on strange years
Under the blackened moon and paling sun.
—"The Sorcerer Departs"

Although this poem is unfinished, it remains nonetheless one of Smith's best-known and most reprinted pieces, frequently used as a prologue to a collection of his tales or included in articles about the poet/author. Indeed it is remarkable that in only ten lines Smith could conjure up such imagery and philosophical food for thought. But as well known as this fragment may be, it is generally unknown that there is a much longer, completed version of this same poem, in which Smith deals fully with the philosophical themes he only hints at in the earlier fragment. This poem is called "Soliloquy in an Ebon Tower" and was included in Smith's first poetry collection *The Dark Chateau,* published in 1951 by Arkham House.

Aficionados of weird fiction and fantastic poetry may be well acquainted with Smith as a poet, short story writer, or even as an artist; but how many are familiar with the concept of Smith as a philosopher? Of course, a certain amount of philosophy is inherent in most poetry that is not merely descriptive, but Smith's poetry is much more than this; Clark Ashton Smith was a poet who had something to say, as well as the ability to say it clearly and beautifully. Using a form of blank verse similar to that of *The Hashish-Eater,* and relying heavily upon classic mythology for its imagery, this long narrative poem explores in great detail some of the most fundamental questions in human existence: What is the purpose of Life? Or, in the specific case of Clark Ashton Smith: What does a poet achieve who struggles his entire life to create literature of superior beauty and quality, yet receives little recognition or appreciation and even less monetary reward? For Ashton Smith the privilege of experiencing his many worlds of fantasy seems to have been recompense enough as indicated in these lines "Yet, for a toll so light, by Song transported, / To sail beyond Elysium and Theleme." The very act of creation was ample reward "For all the breadless days, the unguerdoned labors."

The outstanding collection *The Dark Chateau* contained many excellent poems not included in Smith's *Selected Poems,* which was published in 1971, again by Arkham House. Although twenty years separates these two collections, *Selected Poems* is actually the older of the two with respect to the age of the material, being made up of material written prior to 1950, including most of the poems from *The Star-Treader, Ebony and Crystal,* and *Sandalwood.*

Smith worked on revising these poems and preparing the manuscript for *Selected Poems* from 1944 until the manuscript was delivered to Arkham House in December 1949, but publication of the book was deferred until 1971 for financial reasons. It stands to reason that if "Soliloquy in an Ebon Tower" had been completed before December 1949, it would certainly have been included in *Selected Poems,* so we can approximate the completion of this poem around 1950 through early 1951. This completion date is interesting because during the remaining ten years of his life Smith wrote very little, spending much more of his creative time sculpting little figurines out of rock. In 1958, Arkham House published *Spells and Philtres,* but only seven or eight of its sixty poems were new, the rest coming from the still unpublished *Selected Poems.* Thus, "Soliloquy in an Ebon Tower" was written at the end of Smith's final creative period and was the result of many years of sustained interest and technical polishing. This would seem to indicate that Smith had a considerably higher than average regard for this piece, and if the literary theme of the poem is also taken into account, a good case could be made for "Soliloquy in an Ebon Tower" representing a culmination of Smith's poetic production.

One of the most important research tools available to the Smith scholar (along with Donald Sidney-Fryer's excellent bibliography *Emperor of Dreams*) is *The Black Book of Clark Ashton Smith.* This book is a replica of Smith's own literary notebook, which he began using about the year 1929 and continued to use for over thirty years until his death in 1961. This notebook contains plot ideas, bits of poetry in various states of completion, lists of fantastic names and titles of stories, both used and unused. The items in the Black Book have been carefully reproduced in the exact order in which they appeared in Smith's original notebook and each item has been numbered to aid in location and comparison. By comparing plot ideas with their corresponding finished tales, or first drafts of poems against the final versions, it is possible to gain insights into the creative process demonstrated by Smith. For example, following the unfinished poem "The Sorcerer Departs" [item 71] the editor has written "Compare this poem to the later and much longer poem 'Soliloquy in an Ebon Tower,' of which it may be a first version." This longer poem is included in the Appendix of Finished Poems, and also as an incomplete, working version [item 159]. Scattered here and there throughout the book are many other lines that are easily identified with "Soliloquy." It is apparent that Smith worked on this poem over a period of many years.

I wrote to Donald Sidney-Fryer, the editor of *The Black Book,* and asked him about his feelings regarding the significance of this poem. I have included here a quotation from his response: "Thank you for calling attention to this remarkable poem. It is readily apparent that this poem was very important to CAS because he worked on it for many years and wrote several drafts. In my opinion this poem represents Smith's *intellectual* poetic testament, philosophically and imaginatively expressed. In much the same way, 'O Golden-Tongued Romance' represents his *romantic* poetic testament, aesthetically and emotionally expressed."

At first glance the main theme of both poems compares favorably; the sorcerer (or poet) passes on, leaving behind his literary works to posterity, thus ensuring his legacy will survive.

Compare these lines in "The Sorcerer Departs," "My volumes and my philtres shall abide" and "When loosed by alien wizards on strange years," to these lines from "Soliloquy in an Ebon Tower": "Wherein our thoughts are twi-shaped Minotaurs / The ages shall not slay. Our ironies / Like marbled adders creeping on through time, / Shall fang the brains of poets yet to be." (It should be pointed out that throughout the poem when Smith speaks in the plural sense, he is also speaking for Baudelaire, and in a sense for all poets who embrace the high ideals of pure literature.)

I must confess to receiving a strange and wonderful thrill the first time I read these lines, which Smith obviously intended to be read and appreciated by future poets and scholars. I hope that your brains will be fanged as well and that you too will follow the phosphor lamps of Clark Ashton Smith as he guides you along dim paths of myth and conjecture.

Imagine, if you will, a hot summer night in the foothills of the northern Sierra Nevada as the clock approaches midnight. The Bard of Auburn muses alone in his cabin, considering the many loved ones he has lost; both of his parents, as well as his good friend and fellow writer H. P. Lovecraft, have all passed away in the short space of a few years. He also reflects upon the literary fame and fortune for which he has faithfully struggled all his life, but which has earned him little more than a slight reputation among a select group of writers and readers of weird fiction. At last he finds solace in the contemplation of the French poet Baudelaire, a fellow poet in whose writings he has found a special affinity. In admiration he raises his glass in a silent toast to the picture of his French counterpart that stands upon a bookcase . . .

Soliloquy in an Ebon Tower

The poet speaks, addressing a framed picture of Baudelaire upon a bookcase:

The lamp burns stilly in the standing air,
As in some ventless cavern. Through wide windows
The midnight brings a silence from the stars,
And perfumes that the planet dreams in sleep.

5   The hounds have ceased to bay; and the cicadas
To ply their goblin harps. The owl that whilom
Hooted his famine to a full-chapped moon,
Has pounced upon his gopher, or has gone
To fresher woods behind a farther hill;

10   And Hecate has grounded all the witches
For some glade-hidden Sabbat.

                In my room
The quick, malign, relentless clock ticks on,
Firm as a demon's undecaying pulse,
Or creak of Charon's oar-locks as he plies

15   Between the shadow-crowded shores. Evoked
Within the vaults of my funereal brain,
Voices awaken, sibilant and restless—
Tongues of the viper's charnel-fostered brood,
Half-grown, amid the shreds of winding-sheets

20   And crumbling wicker of old bones. They sing,
Those little voices, all the poisonous,
Importunate melodies you too have heard,
O Baudelaire, in midnights when the moon
Sank, followed by some cloudy hearse of dreams,

25   Into the skyless nadir of despond.
Black-flickering, cloven tongues! Though we distill
Quintessences of hemlock or nepenthe,
We cannot slay the small, the subtle serpents,
Whose mother is the lamia Melancholy

30   That feeds upon our breath and sucks our veins,
Stifling us with her velvet volumes.

                                                Now
     My thoughts pursue the santal and sad myrrh
     Sighed by the shrouds of all hesternal sorrows.
     Busied with old regrets, they carry on
35   Such commerce as the burrowing necrophores
     Conduct from grave to grave; or pause to mumble
     Snatches of ancient amorous elegies,
     Deploring still some splendid, stately love—
     Gone like the pomps of void Ecbatana—
40   That only lives in epodes, but will rise
     To ghost the goldless morrows, clothed about
     With hues of suns declining and decayed,
     And crowned with ruinous autumn.

                                      Other thoughts
     Exhume the withered wing-shards of ideals
45   Brittle and light as perished moths, or bring
     To sight the mummied bats of blear mischance,
     By dismal eves and moons disastrous flying,
     But fallen now, and dead as are the heavens
     Their vans have darkened. On beloved deaths
50   I muse, and through my twice-wept tears re-gather
     The threads that Clotho and Lachesis have spun
     And Atropos has cut; and see the bleak
     Sinister gleaming of the steely shears
     Behind the riven arrasses of time. . . .

55   What weapon can we arm us with? What bulwark
     Build against grief and time? What moat renewed
     With waters mortal as those that shroud Gomorrah,
     Will the sea-going termite never ferry
     To gnaw the ebon tower, the ebon ark
60   Holding the Muses' covenant? Splendor-brimmed,
     What grail of God or Satan will suffice
     For all the breadless days, the unguerdoned labors?

     Yet, for a toll so light, by Song transported,
     To sail beyond Elysium and Theleme,

65   And see, from oblivion looming, balmier shores
      Of fables infinite! To light our dreams
      At rose Aldebaran or sky-huge Antares,
      Then quench their heat, or temper Damascus thought
      In cold aphelions and apastrons far!
70   To pace the sun's Typhoean ramparts vast!
      To couch on Saturn's outmost ring, or roll
      With Pluto through his orb of eventide
      Whose Hesper is the dwindled sun! To flaunt
      Before the blind an immarcescible purple
75   Won from the murex of Uranian seas,
      And fire-plucked vermeil of Vulcan, worn against
      These aguish mists and wintry shadows! Thus
      We triumph; thus the laurel overtops
      The upas and the yew; and we decline
80   No toil, no dolor of our votive doom.

      High-housed within the Alchemic Citadel,
      We are served by Azoth and by Alkahest.
      Out of the gleamless mire and sand we make
      Pactolian metal. Fumed from our alembics,
85   The world dissolves like vapors opium-wrought,
      Or drips, condensed, to philtres and to venoms
      That Circe nor Simaetha dreamed. We build,
      Daedalus-like, a labyrinth of words
      Wherein our thoughts are twi-shaped Minotaurs
90   The ages shall not slay. Our ironies,
      Like marbled adders creeping on through time,
      Shall fang the brains of poets yet to be.
      Our nacred moons and corposants of beauty
      Shall float on ever-mootful lands retained
95   By Lar and Lemur; where Chimera flies,
      And still the Sphinx unanswerably rules;
      Where the red phantoms we have loosed from Dis
      Still haunt the thickets and the cities; where
      Our phosphor lamps may serve as well as any
100   Along the rutted way to Charon's wharf.

Appendix of Related Material from *The Black Book*

Item 159   Soliloquy in an Ebon Tower

The lamp burns stilly in the standing air,
As in some ((sunless)) breathless antre. Through wide windows
The night ((brings in)) has brought a silence from the stars,
And perfume that the planet dreams in sleep.
The hounds have ceased to bay. The owl that whilom
Hooted his famine to a hollow moon,
Has pounce upon his gopher, or has gone
To ((fresher)) farther wood ((lands))s unhunted past the hill . . . .

                                        Within my room
Only the quick, relentless clock ticks on,
Firm as a demon's ((unsuspending)) undecaying pulse:
Or creak of Charon's oar-locks ((. In my brain)) as he plies
                        Evoked thus
((And in my vaulted brain, ((as if to answer it,)) evoked thereby,))
((Eloigned in ecstasy that is not of delight))

Within the vaults of my funereal brain,
Voices awaken, sibilant and restless,
Like to the viper's charnel-nurtured brood
Half-grown, amid the shreds of winding-sheets
And crumbling wicker of old bones.

Busied with old regrets, they carry on
Such commerce as the burrowing necrophores
Conduct ((between the)) from grave to grave,

            My alembics have distilled
Quintessences of hemlock and nepenthe

Beneath a fierier Zodiac I have launched
Tall carvels, zanthic-sailed and oriflammed,
By compasses that point to poles occult.

Item 123   O splendid, stately love,
        Gone like the pomps of void Ectabana! [see lines 38–39]

Item 151   O (perennial) Beauty, clothe thyself
        With hues of suns declining and decayed. (see lines 41–42)

Item 162   The tale of long,
        Unguerdoned labours and of breadless days. (see line 62)

Item 125   Strange pleasures are known to him who flaunts the im-
        marcesible purple of poetry before the color-blind. (see
        lines 73–74)

Item 153   I build,
        Daedalus-like, a labyrinth of words
        Wherein my thoughts are hidden Minotaurs. (see lines
        87–89)

Item 126   Mine ironies
        Like marbled adders creeping on through time
        Shall fang the brains of the unborn. (see lines 90–92)

Rejected readings?

Item 122   Zoned with green zircon and with palest gold.

Item 127   The marbled viper crawls where crawled the melon-vine.

Item 128   Taught by me, they will,
        Reject the fading phantoms called the Real,
        And chose in place of them those other phantoms
        That fade not, being immaterial.

Item 147   Seek the fabulous mountain-crag where roosts the roc.

Item 152   Say, wouldst thou have
        Wisdom, or love, or empire? Let each man
        Follow (his) some chosen phantom into death.

Item 158   Knowledge is often most concealed when most divulged;
                  And haply none will harken if I whisper
                  The secrets wooed from lipless mystery,
                  Or cry aloud a tomb-extorted lore.

Item 191   Disburse a thin and phantom opulence.

Item 219   Through (telic) ultimate cycles, as in cycles old,
                  Phantoms, and apparitions manifold,
                  Shall pass before the spectral eyes of man
                  In whom illusion doth itself behold.

Item 222   To sleep, assured of Devachanic dreams.

Glossary of Unusual Words and Names

Line

6   Whilom. Formerly; before.

27   Nepenthe. A potion or drug used by the ancients to drown pain and sorrow.

32   Santal. A variation of the incense Sandalwood.

33   Hesternal. Pertaining to yesterday.

35   Necrophore. One that bears or carries the dead, as in worms, etc.

37   Elegies. A lyric poem. Especially a lament for the dead, or a lost love.

39   Ecbatana. Capital of ancient Media, later conquered by Persia.

40   Epodes. A lyric poem in which a longer verse is followed by a shorter one

51   Clotho. The spinner; one of the three fates of Greek mythology.

51   Lachesis. Disposer of lots. One of the three fates of Greek mythology.

52   Atropos. She who cuts the threads. The third Fate of Greek mythology.

62   Unguerdoned. Unrewarded.

64   Elysium. The mythical paradise of the Greeks.

64   Theleme. The Abbey of Theleme, a utopia invented by Rabelais.

69   Aphelions. The point of a planet's orbit which is farthest from the sun.

69 Apastrons. The point in the Moon's orbit when it is farthest from the Earth.

70 Typhoean. A mythical monster who belched flames from a hundred mouths.

73 Hesper. The Evening Star; Venus.

74 Immarcescible. Unfading, endurable.

75 Murex. A secretion of certain mollusks which is used as a purple dye.

76 Vermeil. Vermilion; a bright red color.

77 Aguish. Pertaining to the ailment known as "Ague."

79 Upas. A tree native to Indonesia whose sap is poisonous.

82 Azoth. A name given by alchemists to the metal mercury.

82 Alkahest. A fabled universal solvent of Arabian myth.

84 Pactolian. A legendary river of gold in Asia Minor.

84 Alembics. A still or cup used by an apothecary.

87 Circe. A sorceress who held Odysseus captive in "The Odyssey."

87 Simaetha. An alluring sorceress from the 2nd Idyll of Theocratis.

88 Daedalus. The builder of the labyrinth of Greek myth.

93 Nacred. Mother of Pearl.

93 Corposants. Pertaining to a thing of sacred beauty, such as Saint Elmo's fire.

95 Lar. A tutelary god or spirit of a particular household.

95 Lemur. Nocturnal spirits or ghosts.

97 Dis. Roman god of the underworld.

Afterword

Donald Sidney-Fryer

Reading and pondering again this outstanding poem by Ashton Smith, thus many years after I first encountered it in the mid-1950s, and now some forty-five years later, I am once more impressed not only by the substance of what the poet is actually stating (in the course of the precisely one hundred lines that constitute the corpus of the poem, arranged significantly into seven sections, that number of supreme importance in the occult science of numerology), but I am struck even more by the exceptional clarity and elegance of his modus operandi. The poet's thought or thinking, as it evolves in the course of the poem, remains remarkably lucid, that is, as it is presented in successive stages from one verse paragraph to the next. This extended piece of blank verse, although certainly not without genuine intellectual depth and resonance, stands out by the express absence of that deliberate obscurity or obfuscation such as appears to distinguish so much other modern poetry. Re-reading this poem, I am especially struck by the prominent reference to Charon at the end, no less than at the virtual beginning, of the soliloquy: Charon, he who ferries the souls of the dead over the river Styx from the land of the living to the land of the dead.

The concomitant reference to the phosphor lamps obligingly lit by Baudelaire and Ashton Smith not only serves as a particularly apt metaphor by one who illuminates the darkness so that others may see), but is also deliberately ironic. A phosphor lamp, here employed presumably to indicate any illumination from something phosphorescent, gives off only enough light to permit an approximate identification of an object or a text, for example, but is infinitely more difficult, if not impossible, to use for studying or even desultory reading than the light from the often single candle flame that our ancestors once utilized (Abraham Lincoln, for example) or the flickering light from a pile of logs on the hearth of an old-fashioned fireplace. (The reader should attempt to read by a single candle or by the light from a blazing fireplace in order to see just how less than satisfactory such illumination actually is in all truth!)

In terms of the poem's overall meaning, phosphor lamps as an actual guide are so dim that they can only confirm the essential and enduring mystery surrounding, and inhering in, all existence. The point that Ashton Smith makes is thus both ironic and no less poignant. Yet, although bound at both ends of existence by death and the unknown, the one superlative talent or gift that humans have developed over thousands or millions of years remains the capacity to dream or to imagine, a capacity worth any labor, tedium, or sacrifice. The human imagination is in and of itself the supreme blessing, the ultimate magic of all . . . at least for human creatures.

(N.B. A faithful correspondent, a friend who regularly monitors the popular mail-order catalogues available in the U.S., has informed me that conventional phosphor lamps after a period of absence for many years are once more available from L. L. Bean & Company, the well-known purveyors of hunting gear by mail and telephone order.)

Captain Volmar and Crew: An Afterword

Between 1928 and 1938, the longest and most productive in his fiction-writing career—as perceived vis-à-vis his other major career, that is, as a poet—Clark Ashton Smith created the bulk of his approximately 140 extant stories. He began small with the little philosophical thriller "The Ninth Skeleton" in 1928, and 1938 witnessed the end of this amazing flood of prose fictions, when for a complex of reasons during 1939–41 the poet-author did more living than writing, and much of this living quite away from his home town Auburn, but in other areas of Northern California not overly distant. It was not until 1930 that Smith began creating stories in noticeable abundance, including his earliest attempts at science fiction written for Hugo Gernsback's magazine *Wonder Stories,* one of the earliest of the specialist "scienctifiction" markets.

Out of his overall output of about 140 stories, Smith's achievement of artistically realized prose fictions remains very high, ranging all the way from novelettes to short shorts. We would estimate this at perhaps between sixty to eighty percent. Although the tales that he wrote for *Wonder Stories* include some of his very best work—such as "The City of the Singing Flame," "The Eternal World," and "A Star-Change"—it also includes a certain amount of problematical stuff, stories that are obviously less than first-class, whether stylistically or otherwise, but still provocative and at least worth reading and experiencing. The three Volmar stories represent a case in point. Written over an arc of time starting in the spring of 1930, continuing through that summer, and ending in the late autumn of the same year, or in the early winter of 1930–31, these three or four stories include "Marooned in Andromeda," "The Red World of Polaris," "The Amazing Planet," and possibly "The Ocean World of Alioth," which is extant only in the form of a synopsis, accompanied by the beginning of what appears to be the first draft, and that is all. Smith may or may not have completed this last narrative, but we have only the synopsis and a fragmentary draft, and these thanks only to the literary researches of particle physicist Steve Behrends.

"Marooned in Andromeda" first found publication in *Wonder*

Stories for October 1930, and "The Amazing Planet" in *Wonder Stories Quarterly* for Summer 1931. Oddly enough, "The Red World of Polaris" as the most original of the three extant Volmar tales found only repeated rejection until 1950, when along with another much-rejected story Smith sold it to Michael DeAngelis for publication in his semiprozine *Asmodeus.* DeAngelis had planned, and had apparently worked up, a special issue of his magazine dedicated to Clark Ashton Smith, but unfortunately it never made its appearance. However, Ronald Scott Hilger, the Smith devotee, located by no later than the spring of 2003 the only copy of the story extant through DeAngelis's former co-editor of *Asmodeus,* who made a photocopy for Hilger, who then had it in hand by the early summer of the same year. It is this photocopy that has enabled us to read "The Red World of Polaris" in its current publication.

Although none of these three extant stories about Captain Volmar and his crew of Jasper, Roverton, and Deming are masterpieces, indeed far from it, including "The Red World of Polaris" as the most interesting and most imaginative of them all, these earliest "scientifictions" that Smith wrote for Hugo Gernsback have a real significance for other but closely related reasons. These tales exhibit Smith at quite an experimental stage in his development as a fictioneer, and actively figuring out just what kind of fiction he should write for *Wonder Stories.* "The Face by the River," the tale of a haunting, completed after "The Red World of Polaris," very much exhibits the same quality of experimentation. It is axiomatic that one must grant any writer or any kind of creative person the right to experiment, and to find his bearings in a given genre of writing, especially the one of magazine science fiction, which was just beginning at that time, and at that time obviously pioneering, at least in terms of the U.S. Smith soon found his bearings and went on to write his most memorable tales for the Gernsback publications, even if the editor-publisher did not always pay his authors until forced to do so through one or more lawsuits.

Just as one can read now some of Smith's better juvenile fiction at last in published form, so can one also read, or read again, these three Volmar stories—and for the very same reasons: for what they prefigure or anticipate of the later magisterial teller of outré narratives. However uneven they may be, what redeems these early science fiction tales are the otherworldly descriptions replete with Smith's powerfully delineated cosmicism: the fanatical Captain Volmar and his indomitable ambition to circumnavigate the known universe; the vast and labyrinthine alien cities with their sky-high towers; the curious and often frightening alien entities who sometimes are masters of strange and highly advanced sciences. These descriptions are of a piece with the same in Smith's best narratives in prose, whether weird, whimsical, fantastical, or science fictional. These can still rivet the attention and compel our imagination into new and startling directions. They still retain the power to move and fascinate us.

The following experience, as described and recalled from his early adolescence by Ray Bradbury in a brief but unusually choice appreciation, is perhaps the one that best summarizes the effect of Smith's own type of science fiction on sensitive readers. "He filled my mind with incredible worlds, impossibly beautiful cities, and still more fantastic creatures on those worlds and in those cities." Whether instigated by his best or by his least remarkable science fiction, the effect nevertheless holds true for all of it. It still makes for a uniquely rewarding experience to read, or yet to re-read, the Captain Volmar series as gathered in the present volume.

Los Angeles, 7 August 2003

In Defense of "Little Boys"

I yield to no one in my profound admiration for Howard's best stories of whatever type that I have had the pleasure to read and re-read, whether pure adventure, overtly fantastic, or marvelously comic. Therefore it has been a pleasure to witness the *Cimmerian* establishing itself. Not since the now-primordial run of the *Howard Collector* have I so much enjoyed a specialist magazine devoted to one writer.

Amid such an embarrassment of riches there is no lack of interesting, or even fascinating, items to discuss. What I would like to mention in this instance are the two reviews accorded *The Barbaric Triumph* (2004) that appeared in the issue for June 2004 (Vol. 1, No. 2)—in reaction to what is the second book of serious essays about Howard as edited by Don Herron, following the first such book, *The Dark Barbarian*, first published in 1984 and republished in 2000.

One review, "Small Poets Sing," bears the name of the eminent and respected REHophile Robert Weinberg and need not detain us. It is well and aptly "schizophrenic," presenting two rather divergent perspectives on what Don Herron has achieved in the volume under discussion. For me Weinberg's account is invalidated, or vitiated, by his pointed question concerning the issues and concerns raised by the various authors of the individual essays: "Who cares?" Evidently *he* does not care, and therefore I need not care either!

The other review, "Dog in the Manger," is by Richard Lupoff, and a fine, all-inclusive, and appreciative account it is of *The Barbaric Triumph*. Lupoff does quite a good job not only dealing with the overall volume itself, but also appraising the general times and conditions when the American pulp magazines flourished in the 1920s and 1930s but then less so in the 1940s. In general I could not, and would not, argue with most of Lupoff's remarks, conclusions, and summaries. I must agree that the magazine *Weird Tales* managed to publish, along with a lot of junk, a great many stories of genuine literary merit by a wide variety of authors.

But several statements made by Lupoff stop me dead in my tracks every time I read them. Let me present them here, en masse; and even though I am taking them out of their context, I shall do my best not to

misrepresent Lupoff's carefully marshaled arguments. I am only concerned with indicating an alternative viewpoint, and—I hope—a valid one.

1. "None of the three [writers—i.e., Lovecraft, Howard, and Clark
Ashton Smith] lived what would be considered a normal life."

2. "I think that it would not be stretching a point to suggest that none
of the three ever grew up. Each remained a little boy within himself most
of his life. Each remained attached to his Mommy or to a Mommy surrogate whether aunt or wife, for all of his days."

3. "Like little boys in every era, HPL, REH, and CAS lived rich and
vivid fantasy lives."

4. "None of the Three Titans ever knew the richly rewarding yet
tempering experiences that go with becoming a young bridegroom, establishing a 'starter home,' learning to be a husband, nor yet becoming a father and raising a child."

5. "There is clearly an Oedipal element in the lives and works of the
Three Titans."

Reading, re-reading, and pondering what Lupoff has written here
makes me wonder if today we don't define rather too narrowly what
might be considered a *normal* life. I was born in the mid-1930s, and
as I recall the situation from the later 1930s when I was growing up,
even then people were a little more elastic when defining a normal
life than they are today—never mind *after* the standards that obtained
when Lovecraft was born (1890), or Smith (1893), or Howard (1906).
Young people often continued living in the family home even after
attaining adulthood, even after *marriage,* for a variety of perfectly
good reasons. This was true particularly of people living in rural areas. Families lived much closer, and the presumed ideal of living independently—that is, away from the ancestral or family home—had not
yet achieved universal recognition as the desired standard (I am
speaking here of conditions throughout the U.S.). This is all quite
apart from the fact that many people, then and now, do not wish to
marry and/or have children. That does not mean that they must necessarily deny themselves the pleasures of intimate companionship or
normal sexuality, which as we now recognize may take shape from a
wide range of possible behaviors.

The main reason that our three writers continued living at home
with parents or parent surrogates was probably financial—also, the
children and the parents could then continue to enjoy each other's

company. In addition, as the parents aged and became ill or frail—or both, as is often the case—one or more offspring, now become adults, could then conveniently take care of them, not only out of filial duty but just as much out of genuine love. Of course, circumstances may not be quite the same in the case of the three writers under discussion, because they were obviously quite exceptional people. However, I think that the general family situation just presented holds just as true for them as for other people, perhaps even more so.

Even when the Church in Europe during centuries past put much more pressure on the individual to marry and beget children—back when the world was much less populated than it is today, say for example during the Renaissance of the 1300s through the 1500s—not every person, whether physically or financially, decided to get married or cared to get married. Such people were not necessarily considered any the less normal for all that. Given the manner in which inheritance functioned, with the eldest son usually inheriting the bulk of the parents' estate, the younger sons were often tonsured—that is, they often took minor ecclesiastical orders, a step that often helped them a lot much later in a variety of possible career decisions. That did not mean that they might not marry at some point in their later lives, or that they denied themselves female or male intimacy in a variety of ways. A quick chronological survey of, for instance, the major poets of the French Renaissance—Marot, Scève, Labé, du Bellay, de Ronsard, de Baïf, de Belleau, de Tyard, Desportes, du Barras, d'Aubigné, La Ceppède, de Sponde, Régnier—indicates a startling variety of backgrounds, lifespans, and lifestyles, both married and not, tonsured and not, and with many ancillary relationships and affairs that fail to adhere to modern standards of normalcy, to the degree that such a thing can ever be adequately defined. The work of these poets, especially the last three—La Ceppède, de Sponde, and Régnier—as well as others like them, helped lay the foundation for the deliberately classical development of drama and poetry during the reigns of Louis XIII and Louis XIV. Given the often tumultuous times through which circumstances forced many of these poets to live often precarious lives—all the way from Clément Marot through d'Aubigné, thus from the late 1400s on into the early 1600s—the concept of what might have passed for a normal life would probably have appeared to the people back then as an issue that was quite beside the point. Simply to have survived for varying periods throughout the overall span of more than an entire century, simply to have been able to live at all for any reasonable length of time, would have seemed an achievement, quite apart from any discussion of these writers as children who never grew up, never mind as poets undergoing some vague Oedipus Complex.

The preceding cavalcade of poets—and literally thousands of similarly eclectic examples throughout history—afford us a better and better-balanced perspective from which to perceive the lives and careers of the Three Musketeers of *Weird Tales* (four if we include Henry S. Whitehead, a writer often left out of the discussion, but one whom the three others would have considered equal to themselves), moreover as perfectly normal given the conditions peculiar to them as individuals born into a certain place at a certain time.

Unlike the situation in medieval France, a period marked intermittently by considerable turmoil politically and otherwise, the U.S. of the settled or long-settled areas (in what later became known as the lower forty-eight states in North America) has enjoyed an extended interlude of generally peaceful conditions, remarkably free from direct attack, armed warfare, and other forms of destabilizing strife, even when all-out war was raging elsewhere, that is, since the end of the Civil War in 1865, and until the recent terrorist attack on the World Trade Center in New York City on 11 September 2001. In fact, we acknowledge that such a long-lasting state of peace in such an overall remarkably large territory is distinctly unusual, if not abnormal, if we compare the situation to most other periods of recorded history.

This then was the world in which our Three Musketeers lived out their lives: indeed, a singularly protected or buffered existence overall in terms of external threats, not just for them personally but for an enormous number of people. This was the period, moreover, during which they created their writings—poetry, prose fictions, essays—literary arts that they in fact took quite seriously as the doubtlessly serious artists that they were. It is notable and curious that all three proved themselves as poets, and as independently minded poets, at a time when poetry was going through a period of great change, during which the traditional forms in which they all excelled found themselves attacked, abandoned, and ridiculed as irrelevant or obsolete.

(However, the recent emergence of a new school or group of poets, the so-called New Formalists, has once again made the traditional prosody relevant and meaningful.)

We now refer the reader's attention back to the five citations from Lupoff's review presented earlier. Citations 2 and 3 allude implicitly to the rare continuity of creative writing in the lives of REH, CAS, and HPL, from childhood and/or adolescence on into adulthood, but without Lupoff evidently appreciating how rare and beneficial such continuity proved in the case of each of these writers. In each case, as has often happened in similar mother-son relationships, it was primarily the mother who encouraged the son to create, to write, to invent.

In regard to citation 4, two of the three writers did get married, even if not on the terms laid out by Lupoff, and the third probably would have if he had lived longer, and if circumstances—meaning income, whether from wife or husband or both—had proven favorable. We should mention that some people simply do not want to get married, to produce children; and some people even actively, intensely, dislike the concept, that is, as it would apply to them. For such people non-marriage and non-reproduction is the natural or normal mode.

As for citation 5, "the Oedipal element in the lives and work of the Three Titans," that is admittedly a more troublesome and complex issue. Let us examine it briefly with regard to our three writers, but in general terms. The one writer who might seem the perfect candidate to fulfill the Oedipal agenda proposed by Lupoff is Lovecraft. Apart from a year or so passed in the Boston area when he was quite a young child, and then his residence in New York City during several years of his marriage to Sonia Greene during the 1920s, not to mention several extended sojourns that he took to places like Quebec and New Orleans, HPL spent his entire life in and around Providence, Rhode Island, and in a very small number of different residences. Although he never knew his father, his grandfather seemed to have acted as a kind of father surrogate and encouraged Lovecraft's reading in the grandfather's library of the works of Edgar Allan Poe, the one writer who exercised the greatest and best influence on Lovecraft's own writing.

Lovecraft's mother's family was wealthy, or at least quite comfortable during a substantial period. He never attended regular public school, but his family taught him at home. In a larger sense he was an autodidact, and he taught himself much better than what the local schools might have done. He did not serve in the military, but gained exemption because of his poor physical condition. He never held a regular job, but in addition to his commercial fiction he did revision work, ghostwriting, etc. After his grandfather's death and the consequent breakup of his estate, mother and son continued living together, but in different quarters, HPL being still quite young.

After the death of his mother, and apart from the years of his marriage passed elsewhere, Lovecraft resided with one or both of the aunts on his mother's side. In fact, it was the rare period in his life when he did *not* live with women in one condition or another, whether or not such involved sexual expression. In other words, he spent most of his life living with women. None of his closest relatives ever questioned his predilection for constant reading and writing, which in his case began quite early in his childhood. Moreover, they all seem to have encouraged him in his writing of whatever description, and acted extraordinarily protective of him both as writer and person,

But is all that necessarily a sign of an Oedipal element? Lovecraft could count himself more than usually fortunate in that he never had to hold a regular job but was able to devote his main time and energy to writing, whether fiction or essays or distinctive epistles. In general HPL did not have to care for his mother in terms of intense physical attention, as did both Smith and Howard. However, had it proven essential that he should have done so, we can be sure that he would have done his best. Filial duty and affection rank high in most people's lives. If Lovecraft was a product of his own unique environment, then he was that but only in a highly selective way.

In spite of the relative poverty in which his family lived, and in spite of which they managed to enjoy an adequate but frugal existence, Ashton Smith had the advantage of being born into a region of great natural beauty at a time (the 1890s) when California would seem to us today (the early 2000s) almost *un*populated, never mind just *under*-populated. This was the general region of Auburn and Long Valley up in the first notable foothills, an area that lies at a general altitude of a thousand feet above sea level. Father, mother, son resided at first with the mother's family, the Gaylords, members of the local gentry, in their house that stood in Long Valley about six miles south of Auburn—the building, somewhat modified, still stands, harboring other people. When Smith was about nine years old, his nuclear family moved to a small but adequate cabin that father and son had built about a mile south of Auburn, and where they had also dug an essential well for water.

Auburn at that time was only a small city, albeit the seat of Placer County, and the community's lights at night did not impinge on an astronomer's ability to survey the nocturnal heavens with remarkable clarity, never mind the very few neighbors who did not live at all in close proximity. Here in this cabin Smith resided almost exclusively until 1954, apart from visits to Sacramento, San Francisco, selected places in the San Francisco Bay Area (e.g., Oakland, Berkeley, and San Rafael), Monterey and the general area south of there, not to mention selected places in the High Sierras and in westernmost Nevada. In late 1954 Smith married Carol Jones Dorman and moved from the family cabin on Boulder, or Indian, Ridge not far from Auburn, to live with his wife in her home at Pacific Grove next to Monterey, where he lived until his death in 1961. He attended elementary school in Long Valley and Auburn, but with his parents' approval he did not attend high school or college, conducting instead his own education (among other ways) by reading all the books, or almost all, contained in the local Auburn Public Library, the gift (in 1908) of Andrew Carnegie, the Scots-American industrialist and philanthropist.

Thus like Lovecraft, but starting much later in life, Smith became an autodidact, that is, in terms of high school and college. Like Lovecraft he did not serve in the military, but gained exemption apparently because of the nervous breakdown and incipient tuberculosis that he suffered, evidently somewhat before the American involvement (1917–18) in World War I. But reportedly he suffered often from divers childhood illnesses during the years that he went to elementary school, forcing him often to miss attendance. Like Lovecraft, he never held a regular job—when he did, it did not last long—but only or chiefly worked at seasonal or sporadic jobs. Although he claimed to have started writing only in his early teens, Smith actually began writing at least poetry when he was rather young, that is, as a child. Although he began sexual experimentation with girls, again rather young,

Smith apparently never got any of these or later girls pregnant. More-over, he lived exclusively with his parents from his birth until their deaths in 1935 (mother) and 1937 (father).

It was the mother who had always encouraged the son in his crea-tive writing, even if (evidently) the father must have taken some real interest in it as well. Certainly it was the father who related many amazing and amusing anecdotes to the son about the travels that he had taken all over the world after coming into a large inheritance as a young adult, and when he met all manner of people existing at all economic levels. The family had always been extraordinarily close, the mother being especially cheerful and demonstrative in her affec-tion, and the father, while retiring and not demonstrative, making his affection felt in other ways. It was Smith, and Smith only, who cared first for his mother through her terminal illness or decline, and then for his father through a similar period, none of which could have proven easy in any way.

I wonder how many people reading this have ever given intense physical care to older persons, never mind their own parents. It is awkward, it is hard, it is messy—what with bedpans and such—it is ex-hausting, and sometimes it lasts over quite a long period. It takes real grit and real character to give such care, and—I might add—a great amount of love. Given the lack of money with which to pay someone else to do it, Smith himself had no choice but to take it in hand. However, he would not have shirked this duty, even if it interfered with his literary creation. I seriously doubt that any Oedipal element played any role in Smith's enduring affection for his parents while they lived or any role in his care for them as they declined and then died. If Smith was as much a product of his own environment as Lovecraft was of his, then we must understand Smith's environment as very special indeed, and in a very liberated and "extrapolated" sense.

Whereas HPL was the product of a long-settled ambiance that had existed for over two full centuries (Providence, R.I.), and similar-ly, whereas CAS was the product of an unique rural ambiance not for from a town that came into existence almost overnight because of the Gold Rush of 1849 (Auburn, Cal.)—then Robert Ervin Howard was the product of a world vastly different from the cultured purlieus of Providence on the one hand or the idyllic loveliness of the more recently established Auburn and Long Valley. Howard was very much the product of the wild and wooly Republic of Texas—the one and only Lone Star State—altogether as different an environment from the rest of the U.S. as the continent of Antarctica is from the rest of our planet—well, almost. Because he was born in the small town of Peaster as the son of a pioneer physician, REH participated as a child and adolescent in several distinct changes of residence, as his family moved from place to place in East, West, and South Texas, as well as in western Oklahoma, before they settled in Cross Plains, near Brownwood, in an overall region that constitutes the center of the state.

Thus, while he went to elementary or grammar school in a variety of locales, Howard attended high school in Brownwood, and then Howard Payne College in the same town, even if apparently he did not get his baccalaureate. However, like HPL and CAS, he basically gave himself his own best education by reading and then by writing: he was as much of an autodidact as they, but in a different sense. In Howard's case, as in Lovecraft's or Smith's, it was his mother who encouraged the son to write. Like Smith, he began writing in earnest during his adolescence and had his first professional story published in *Weird Tales* in mid-1925. However, even his pre-professional— that is, his earliest—stories already exhibit the vivid, exuberant, and yet sensitive characteristics of his later fiction, by which he became one of the leading writers not only for *Weird Tales* but for many other pulp magazines.

Whether before or immediately after his death on 11 June 1936, Howard easily had more than eighty appearances with his prose fictions, long or short—not to mention almost forty appearances with his variegated poems—in *Weird Tales* and related magazines. Along with Lovecraft and Smith, Howard was clearly one of the Unique Magazine's most prolific fictioneers and poets. His unique and humorous "tall tales" of Western Americana, no less than his boxing stories (the author had become a notable amateur boxer during the decade before his death) stand in a class by themselves. His Western tales in particular exhibit Howard's wild and wacky sense of fun and outrageous humor (as outlandish as that of Rabelais or the Baron Munchausen), as well as his historical and regional researches in Texas pioneer lore. His prose fictions, in whatever genre he wrote, betray great imaginative power as well as unimpeachable integrity and authenticity.

Whether or not his mother's death and his own reflect an Oedipal element, they do reflect well on Howard's concern for not only his mother but paradoxically just as much for his father. My friend E. Hoffmann Price felt that, although Howard might have left home to go a-traveling and adventuring, it was his concern for his parents that kept him living at home and in Cross Plains. Certainly, once his mother's long-term tuberculosis came to the fore, that and that only kept him tied almost literally to their shared homestead. In his brief but pithy summing up, the article "Heart's Blood," appearing in the *Cimmerian* for October of 2004, editor Leo Grin has unequivocally laid out, in an intense physical sense, what was involved in Howard's caregiving to his mother, as she lay dying of tuberculosis over a period of years. It is not a pretty picture, and emotionally it is nothing less than harrowing. This caregiving evolved into quite a demanding regimen for the son: a sustained nightmare of pain, despair, and horror illuminated only by the undoubted love shared between son and mother—given that his father, because of his professional duties as a country doctor who visited his patients in the once time-honored fashion, could not dance medical attention on his wife. Despite a succession of hired nurses or caregivers, there was really no one else but Howard to give care to his mother on a sustained basis.

Howard clearly became despondent because of a variety of things: first, the lengthy decline and impending death of his mother (the chief person to have encouraged him in his literary creation and to have awakened in him as a child a great love of great literature by reading to him); then his inability to do any sustained writing because of the attention that perforce he had to lavish on his mother (not that he would have begrudged it to her!); and—not at all insignificant—Farnsworth Wright owed Howard over $2000 for stories published in *Weird Tales.* We need not emphasize what a large sum $2000 represented in the mid-1930s, almost a small fortune. These factors and others would all have played their part in contributing to Howard's despondency. However, this despondency sounds much more like clinical depression, such as is described by William Styron in the book that he wrote about his own very deep depression, *Darkness Visible.* If as we suspect Howard was suffering from clinical depression—like gut fear or panic, clinical depression is intolerable to endure at full force for very long—and given that he knew that his mother was dying, it is not surprising that under the circumstances he committed suicide. I personally doubt that any Oedipal element had anything to do with it.

My dictionary defines the Oedipal Complex as "a complex involving an early and primary attachment to the parent of opposite sex, with hostility to the other (often restricted to its appearance in males)." Lovecraft never knew his father, but never had anything but love for his grandfather, who played the role of father surrogate to him until the grandfather's own death. Smith knew, and lived with, his father from 1893, when he was born, through 1937, when the father died but only after the son had managed to keep him alive through infusions of spirits, or hard liquor, somewhat longer than what he would have lived otherwise. Insofar as we know, Smith never had anything but profound respect and affection for his father, whom he resembled in many aspects, physically, temperamentally, and emotionally. In a similar fashion Howard and his doctor father were apparently very close and profoundly loved each other as father and son. I consider that in the case of each of the Three Musketeers of *Weird Tales* that neither Oedipus Complex nor any Oedipal element was in operation or at the basis of things emotional or otherwise.

All this discussion of these three writers as little boys who never grew up because of some debilitating attachment to a mother or a mother surrogate, each writer implicated in some family situation that may or may not have involved some Oedipal element, is quite frankly beside the point. It fails to address the real issue, and to give proper emphasis to the dominant fact: to wit, the Three Musketeers of *Weird Tales* were utterly serious artists, as serious in the case of each and every one of them as Poe or Baudelaire. Despite whatever problems or difficulties they may have encountered in the course of their lives or careers, the dominant fact is that they each achieved an extraordinary and highly individual corpus of literary work. It is their *artistry,* individual or collective, that should absorb our attention.

Unlike the major poets of the French Renaissance, most of whom could not devote their full time or attention to their writing whether poetry or prose, circumstances external and internal permitted our three writers to give as much of their time and energy to theirs as possible. They each managed to produce a considerable output in terms of both quantity and quality. Biographical details prove useful in understanding creative genius, but they should not determine or dictate our final assessment of the artistic accomplishment of any specific writer or artist of exceptional gifts. As in the famous French farce of the Middle Ages, *Pathelin,* to quote the celebrated refrain, *"Revenons à nos moutons."* Only instead of returning to our sheep (that is, to the subject of discourse), let us focus our attention on the works of art, the literary texts, and not overmuch or hypercritically on the lives of their authors, and the often pitiful or pathetic details of their private lives.

James Blish versus
Clark Ashton Smith;
to Wit, the Young Turk Syndrome

A RIPOSTE

By an odd coincidence—and it surely must remain as no more than that—two of the strongest negative criticisms of Clark Ashton Smith and his writing appeared at almost the exact same time during the mid-1940s. These criticisms came to light in two different fanzines, or perhaps more accurately, perzines, or personal magazines. The first one appeared in the May 1945 issue of *Diablerie,* "Of Corsets and Flea-Traps," by one "Maliano" (otherwise unidentified). Of the two criticisms this is the less interesting, despite its piquant appellation. Its main item of attention remains the illustration chosen to accompany it: a rather charming caricature-portrait of Smith by Virgil Partch, of all people. No, Smith and Partch never met; instead, the artist worked from a photograph of Smith supplied him by Forrest J Ackerman around 1945. At that time Ackerman was the editor of the camp newspaper at the U.S. Army induction center Fort MacArthur near San Pedro (the port of Los Angeles located between Rancho Palo Verde to the northwest and Long Beach to the northeast). Partch was one of the staff artists on the newspaper and was officially assigned to do caricatures of the officers at that military base. However, between his official assignments, Ackerman would furnish him with photos of various fantasy and science fiction authors, from which Partch would create his caricatures. This was how the cartoonist-artist happened to make his caricature-portrait of Ashton Smith, who is observed winking at us with his left, or sinister, eye!

But it is the second of these two rare negative criticisms that will detain us here, and at some length. Oddly enough (again), this made its appearance just one month after the one in *Diablerie,* and in the second issue of *Tumbrils,* rather well named as it turns out, thus dated June 1945. This overall unfavorable essay concerning Smith and his writing took the form of a brief but penetrating censure entitled "Eblis in Bakelite," by James Blish, a title referring to the Mohammedan concept or image of Satan as physically realized in bakelite, an early form of plastic, or in this case, a synthetic resin, whose uses were like those of celluloid or hard rubber. "Eblis in Bakelite"—it makes an arresting and memorable title, in the same way as is this uncommon piece itself. *Tumbrils* was Blish's own perzine and remains an excellent example of this type of magazine, such as flourished from the middle to later 1930s to the 1940s. Other writers of the same period, who later became famous like Blish, also put out similar publications, sometime regularly, often irregularly, usually mimeographed or hectographed. For example, Fritz and Jonquil Leiber published on a regular basis for half a year or so their own perzine under the title *New Directions*.

In Blish's case, as the title (in the plural) indicates, it provided the writer-editor the opportunity to express critical opinions, if not Olympian judgments, and, it would seem in his case, more unfavorable criticisms than any other type. Tumbrel or tumbril generally refers to the farmer's cart or wagon that during the French Revolution was employed to transport to the guillotine the people condemned to death. In this particular essay, rather unusually for a fantasy and science fiction critic and writer of that general period, Blish concerns himself not just with Smith's prose fictions (as we might expect) but also with some of his best poetry. It remains to this day one of the most vivid and incisive of the very few negative criticisms ever written about Clark Ashton Smith as an overall artist and creative scholar. Let us examine the essay's major points or issues in their order of appearance.

A word of caution. We are not disputing either the opinions held by Blish relative to Smith and his output, or his right to these opinions. To quote the ancient saying: *De gustibus non disputandum est.* There is no disputing in regard to (individual) tastes, or expressed otherwise, there is no arguing about opinions. Nevertheless, it is possible and permissible to suggest other, and possibly more fruitful, approaches to Smith and his oeuvre, and this is that we shall do, using Blish's essay as our criterion of reference.

Surely, if people as diverse as Ambrose Bierce, George Sterling, Edwin Markham, Samuel Loveman, Arthur Machen, Donald Wandrei, H. P. Lovecraft, David Warren Ryder, Benjamin De Casseres, Vachel Lindsay, George Work, David Starr Jordan, and yet still others of similar stature considered Smith "the greatest American poet," or simply a true genius and a great poet, they all must have had excellent reasons for believing as they did, contrary to what Blish somehow suggests, that these folk obviously erred in holding such elevated opinions of Smith just as a poet. Blish patently overstates the case when he declares that, apart from a very few brief articles he managed to find, no true criticism of Smith, especially as poet, has ever made its appearance in print. The official discovery of Smith by the San Francisco press, no less than the reviews accorded to Smith's first three major poetry collections, contain much excellent criticism of Smith, not all of it positive and admiring, and firmly locate him in the poetico-cultural climate and landscape of 1910/11–1925/26. Blish evidently, and not surprisingly, knew nothing of this early critical reaction and acclaim, but even then, had he known of it, he would probably not have reacted positively to the laudatory tone that still is the prevailing one overall.

Personally the present writer feels that, in the case of a little-known but quite exceptional author, it is better to overpraise than to underestimate. At least the former calls attention to itself and the author in question. Some critics will never like or admire certain works of unusual value, no matter what. Today, compared to Smith's period, the cultural scene abounds in excellent poets of every and all schools, whether working in traditional prosody or in free but carefully structured prose. Gifted poets today seem to gain recognition early, receive the benefit of scholarships and fellowships, become teachers and professors, have their collections issued by prestigious publishers in New York City, etc. Almost none of this apparatus existed in the early part of Smith's literary career, and it is unlikely that he could or would have taken advantage of it, given his independent nature. Ironically, and quite contrary to the statement made in "From the Persian," one of Smith's juvenile couplets, Smith as poet received, apart from recognition in California and Great Britain, nothing less than dross for all the gold that he so lavishly purveyed. This early couplet reads: "I read upon a gate in letters bold: Let him that giveth dross expect not gold." In Smith's case this must be emended as follows: "I read upon a gate in letters bold: Let him that giveth gold expect but dross."

Contrary to Blish's assertion that "nor did any general anthology include a line of his much-lauded poetry," almost three dozen different poems of Smith's made their appearance in some two dozen anthologies of diverse types in the period between 1914 and 1945 alone, and our list is probably not complete. Also, contrary to Blish's assertion that until 1942 "there was no anthology of Smith's work (i.e., in fiction)," Smith himself had issued six of his best but up-to-then unsalable stories in a single collection during mid-1933 after the press of the *Auburn Journal* had printed some 1000 copies of *The Double Shadow and Other Fantasies.* Although not noted in our reconstituted bibliography following Blish's essay, it is quite possible that Blish may have bought a copy of this now rare first collection for 25¢ and at the same time a copy of *Ebony and Crystal* for $1.00. Smith still had a small remainder of the latter collection from the early 1920s, and he was advertising and selling both books from the early to mid-1930s, and probably later. However, *Out of Space and Time* in 1942 and then *Lost Worlds* in 1944 do represent in fact Smith's first two *major* prose collections, and are now, contrary to Blish's negative assessment about *Out of Space and Time,* generally considered excellent collections made from among Smith's best fiction in short-story form.

Blish's original suggestion about assembling a register of typical paragraphs from some of the *best* articles about Smith "with comments appended in the style of the Institute of Propaganda Analysis" is actually quite witty and profitable, and has much to recommend it, inasmuch as it would form an idiosyncratic method for analyzing literature written in praise on behalf of little-known but worthwhile authors. "Does Smith deserve the damnation that his admirers have visited upon him?" Well, a littérateur can react to what seems excessive praise about something unknown but artistic in at least one of two ways: either negatively, if a few typical examples fail to live up to the high praise; or positively, if the characteristic samples more than justify the laudation, thus opening the way to further discovery and exploration.

However, it is anomalous that, after admitting that "Smith at his best is a fine creative scholar," Blish then cites "The Kingdom of the Worm," no less than the special conclusion that Smith provided for "The Third Episode of Vathek," as prime examples of Smith at his best. True, both are worthwhile pieces of (short) prose fiction, perfectly at home in the styles of their respective centuries, the 1400s and the 1700s. Nevertheless, they are not the major efforts represented by "The City of the Singing Flame," "The Dark Eidolon," "The Colossus of Ylourgne," "The Ice-Demon," and "The Voyage of King Euvoran," among others.

As for Smith's poetry being "the product of a pyramid of influences"—such as from Poe, Wilde, Shelley, Milton, James Thomson, no less than other poets but to a lesser extent—S. J. Sackett has already answered this issue. We can do no better than repeat what he states: "It is dangerous to try to find a source for all of Smith; his affinity to certain writers has occasionally led critics to assign to him influences in [i.e., from] other poets whom he has never read."[1] Like other poets before and after him, Smith for profound personal and poetic reasons of his own sometimes treats with all due seriousness certain universal themes first handled in depth by his predecessors. Just as Shakespeare in *The Tempest* and Milton in *Paradise Lost* and *Paradise Regain'd* derived in part out of Spenser and his epic-romance-allegory *The Faerie Queene* (1590-96), and above all out of the *Mutabilitie Cantos* (1609), so did Smith in such pieces of blank verse as "Satan Unrepentant" derive from Milton and his two great epics.

However, in "Satan Unrepentant" and the sonnet "A Vision of Lucifer" Smith introduces a viewpoint strongly opposite to Milton's (at least in a personal sense for the elder poet), and remarkably sympathetic to Satan-Lucifer, no less than undeniably hostile to the usual portrait of the God limned in the Old Testament of the Bible, whom Smith perceives in terms of some Oriental despot or tyrant-king. In these two poems the Californian poet is clearly continuing, and extrapolating from, selected aspects of the discourse begun by Milton in *Paradise Lost*. With Poe and Wilde, Smith has a genuine personal and poetic affinity, but his "Requiescat" is not just a mere derivative of Wilde's poem of the same name. If Smith uses a concept or theme employed by some predecessor, it is to express something, a creative comment or feeling, of his very own. This brings up the related issue of conscious or unconscious plagiarism, but possibly quotation is the better word. There exists little such in Smith, except what may be perceived as "enrichment," in the sense of the practice favored by Renaissance poets deliberately "imitating" the poets of Greco-Roman antiquity. The present writer would venture the guess that almost all of Smith's poetry is

---

1. S. J. Sackett, "The Last Romantic" (1956), *Nyctalops* No. 7 (August 1972): 23.

his own, and that it is technically quite original and not a direct copy of some other poet's lines, despite all the inspiration that Smith may have derived from an intensive study of the work of other poets.

George Sterling, probably more than any other poet, had the greatest influence on Smith, inasmuch as the two poets were contemporaries and particularly close friends during 1911–26. Sterling acted as mentor to the younger poet and encouraged and inspired him. For example, "The Ministers of Law" has nothing to do with "The Massacre at Piedmont," and the title that Blish uses to identify Smith's own sonnet derives from line 13, i.e., "The Constellations of the Law." "The Ministers of Law" derives indeed from Sterling's epic "rumination" *The Testimony of the Suns* (line 258). The phrase comes from quatrain 65 (lines 257–60), which reads in full:

> What powers throng the pregnant gloom!
>   Unseen, the ministers of Law
>   Reach from eternity to draw
> The suns to predetermined doom.

Blish apparently knew Smith's poetry only, or primarily, from *Ebony and Crystal* (1922) and *Nero and Other Poems* (1937), in addition to the poems published in *Weird Tales,* but had no knowledge in depth of *The Star-Treader* (1912) and *Sandalwood* (1925). The poetry of Poe and Sterling (e.g., "A Wine of Wizardry"), first experienced and selectively memorized by Smith when he was thirteen and fifteen, respectively, exercised with no doubt about it the greatest influence on Smith and his own subsequent work; but Blish—by not knowing the full range of Smith's early poetry as laid out chronologically in his three major collections—could not thus follow the logical progression of Smith's development first as poet and then as prosateur, and how each major volume of poems led to the next, and then how the prose-poems in *Ebony and Crystal* led to his major (mature) prose fictions, as well as his extended poems in prose, c. 1925/28–1938.

Also, it is perhaps too facile to see Baudelaire's influence on Smith in the genre of the *poème en prose* as greater than what it actually was. The influence of (selected) very short pieces by Poe (such as "Shadow—A Parable," "Silence—A Fable," "Eleanora," and "The Masque of the Red Death") proved undoubtedly greater, inasmuch as it came into operation earlier in Smith's life, and moreover in the English language that perforce both Poe and Smith shared. As far as we are able to discover, Smith first underwent the influence of Baudelaire, his poems both in verse and in prose, thanks to George Sterling and his copy of some translations by Arthur Symons, in the course of his month-long visit with Sterling in Carmel in June 1912. On the other hand, the earliest and possibly strongest influence from the French genre of the poem in prose upon Smith came c. 1910–11, or possibly even earlier, when he first read and studied that rare collection *Pastels in Prose,* translated by Stuart Merrill from the French of thirty-two poet-authors (including Louis Bertrand and Baudelaire, among many others), and published in 1890 by Harper & Brothers. Smith retained a remarkable affection for the book in question all his life, when he would often read and reread this extraordinary anthology. He continued studying the book up to the last years of his life.

Despite Smith's affinities with Poe and Baudelaire among other poets, the mood or effect of the Californian's most serious prose-poems, as for example "The Shadows" and "From the Crypts of Memory," or "The Black Lake" and "The Memnons of the Night," or "The Crystals" and "The Passing of Aphrodite," turns out to be more often than not much more "terrific" or Miltonic than anything else, much of the portentousness of the tone deriving from the strong emphasis not only on fate or destiny but especially on the succinct and vivid cosmic-astronomic element. There is another curious result of Blish's ignorance of the overall corpus of Smith's early (mature) poetry, curious inasmuch as Blish was primarily a science fiction writer, and one might think that he would have made a point of overtly noting this. He not only fails to emphasize the paramount importance of the cosmic-astronomic element or subject matter in Smith's oeuvre, whether positively or negatively (in an artistic sense), but he does not even directly *mention* it in any way—a curious oversight.

Why Blish especially singles out "Medusa," "In November," and "Chant of Autumn," from among so many others, is puzzling because they are not any more noteworthy than most of the other lyrical poems, or pieces in blank verse, but instead are *equally* remarkable. "In November" is only one of not quite a dozen lyrics cast in alexandrines, that is, in iambic hexameter. The alexandrine does not work quite the same in English as in French, and must be handled with great care to avoid the heaviness and monotony often inherent from its use in such a strongly accented language as English, at least for the purposes of the traditional prosody. However, for his greatest and most extended poem cast in non-rhyming verse, Smith chose the traditional iambic pentameter, or expressed otherwise quite genuinely, it chose him. Contrary to his usual practice of slow and careful workmanship, Smith created the roughly 600 lines of blank verse making up *The Hashish-Eater* in about a month and a half, or even somewhat less, literally a fantastic or astonishing achievement. This enormous poem literally came exploding out of his subconscious and remains his most ambitious and exhilarating composition. Most critics or commentators have assessed this amazing exercise in cosmic-astronomic imagination at a high level of accomplishment. Blish stands alone in characterizing this imagery-fraught narrative as "merely the sewage of a plastic-and-chromium Eblis." It is not clear what he means by the phrase "mashed-potato language" whether written by Lovecraft or De Casseres, unless what he purposes by this usage is just "muddled language." Blish's own language is less clear than the phrase that he castigates while criticizing Smith's magnum opus even more severely.

Again, Blish stands alone in his extremely negative stance not only in regard to the carefully cultivated style of Smith's mature prose fictions, c. 1928–38, immediately derived from that of the prose-poems of c. 1914–22 (as gathered into *Ebony and Crystal*), and also from that of those of c. 1925–29—but above all in referring to the style of Sir Thomas Browne in *Hydriotaphia,* or *Urne Buriall,* as "glaucous logorrhea"—although just what Blish means by "yellow-green talkativeness" (or verbosity) is not very clear. *Hydriotaphia, The Garden of Cyrus,* and other masterpieces of baroque prose by the same author are probably the closest things to poetry created in prose before the later experiments in prose style of Thomas De Quincey, Edgar Allan Poe, and others in English, not to mention those of the French poets of the nineteenth century, beginning with Louis Bertrand and continuing through Mallarmé. We would be singularly impoverished if our ultimate preferences in prose style would shrink down only to those favored by admirers of Ernest Hemingway as well as other well-known but serious writers of the twentieth century just past.

While certainly not a novice writer at that time, by mid-1945 James Blish had not yet established himself as one of the leading masters of imaginative narratives or of a rigorously extrapolated scientifiction, such as would later gain for him a richly deserved celebrity. Why then at that stage in his career did he attack an elder scrivener, of little or no wealth, who had no great fame for the most part except among the readers of *Weird Tales* and similar pulp magazines, except among specialists of poetica Californiana, and surely not among the mainstream academic and intellectual communities at large? Such a question might elicit an explanation like the one that follows. There are at least two courses open to an unestablished writer on his way up. He can be pious and reverent in regard to one or more eminent writers in the genre to which he aspires, and he can attach himself to that same writer in some accommodating capacity; or he can call attention to himself by attacking some eminent scrivener in that same genre, and thus make a name for himself by writing one or more stringently critical essays of quite a negative type attacking that established scrivener. Such an individual on the attack can be called or considered a Turk, either a cruel or tyrannical person, or a young Turk, that is, a young dynamic person eager for change, and attempting to bring it about, if necessary, by attacking somebody conspicuous.

Was James Blish during the early to middle 1940s infected or influenced by such a syndrome, the young Turk syndrome? Or was he only expressing some legitimate gripes about a writer whom he sincerely thought was overpraised? Well, possibly both, but there can be no doubt that he was absolutely serious in his intention, positive or negative, especially when he states that "the sheer wordage concerning [Ashton Smith] nearly equals that written about Branch Cabell, a truly fantastic numeral if one attempts, as I have, to run most of it down." Although this attempt did not apparently extend to the earliest reviews and critical pieces about Smith, those for the period c. 1911–26, just discovering those for the period c. 1930–43 would have represented a real task. Anyone who goes to such lengths to discover such rare materials must be adjudged utterly sincere and serious. Still, it seems like a great amount of bother to undergo merely to attack a writer at that time but obscurely known, if at all, to the mainstream audience or public.

Blish's no-nonsense condemnation of Smith's prose, with which he concludes his essay "Eblis in Bakelite," came to Smith's attention at some point, as well it might, and it is obvious that he reacted to it. Specifically, noting the challenge implicit in Blish's statement that Smith "has demonstrated conclusively that he has the sensibilities and the sensitivity to handle nearly any prose style that happens to appeal to him, excepting only the very tightest and sparest of modern idioms," he responded by writing one of his briefest stories expressed in some of his sparest prose, "Monsters in the Night," which he composed or finished on 11 April 1953. It first appeared in print as "A Prophecy of Monsters" in the *Magazine of Fantasy and Science Fiction* for October 1954, the only such tale that he ever contributed to that periodical. However, Smith had already responded in general to Blish's austere attack on his characteristic prose, but somewhat earlier, that is, by mid-1950. A gentleman to the last, Smith answered this overt condemnation with his characteristic graciousness, and we shall therefore allow him to have the final word in this debate.

In explanation of the elaborate style characteristic of his poems in prose and of his tales and extended poems in prose—as well as in explanation of his use of rare and exotic words and of word-coinages—Smith commented as follows, in his letter to S. J. Sackett dated 11 July 1950. He also defended, but indirectly, *The Hashish-Eater* and his modus operandi in that epic poem:

> As to my employment of an ornate style, using many words of classic origin and exotic color, I can only say that it is designed to produce effects of language and rhythm which could not possibly be achieved by a vocabulary restricted to what is known as "basic English." As [Lytton] Strachey points out [in his essay on Sir Thomas Browne], a style composed largely of words of Anglo-Saxon origin tends to a spondaic rhythm, "which by some mysterious law, reproduces the atmosphere of ordinary life."[2] An atmosphere of remoteness, vastness, mystery and exoticism is more naturally evoked by a style with an admixture of Latinity, lending itself to more varied and sonorous rhythms, as well as to subtler shades, tints and nuances of meaning—all of which, of course, are wasted or worse than wasted on the average reader, even if presumably literate. [. . .]

---

2. In Strachey's essay, the original wording reads: "which seems to produce (by some mysterious rhythmic law) an atmosphere of ordinary life."

As to coinages, I have really made few such, apart from proper names of personages, cities, countries, deities, etc., in realms lying "east of the sun and west of the moon." I have used a few words, names of fabulous monsters, etc., drawn from Herodotus, Mandeville, and Flaubert, which I have not been able to find in dictionaries or other works of reference. Some of these occur in "The Hashish-Eater," a much-misunderstood poem, which was intended as a study in the possibilities of cosmic consciousness, drawing heavily on myth and fable for its imagery. It is my own theory that, if the infinite worlds of the cosmos were opened to human vision, the visionary would be overwhelmed by horror in the end, like the hero of this poem.

I hope that I have made it plain that my use of rare and exotic words has been solely in accord with an esthetic theory, or, one might say, a technical theory. (*SL* 365–66)

Note

Quite apart from any real critical or literary value that Blish's essay may possess intrinsically, it may also serve as a pertinent illustration of the difficulties involved in conducting research, bibliographical and otherwise, among materials not collected by, or easily accessible in, academic or other libraries associated with institutions, usually the best homes for uncommon materials. Fanzines, perzines, and semi-prozines (i.e., semi-professional magazines) by their very nature did not or do not lend themselves easily to the status of conventional printed collectibles. Although a few college or university libraries may now possess random and meager holdings of the fanzines from the 1930s and 1940s, researchers academic and otherwise have had to rely for the most part on individual collectors for any kind of access to such idiosyncratic publications.

The present writer states this directly from personal experience. While conducting the research for his Clark Ashton Smith bio-bibliography *Emperor of Dreams* (1978), he was fortunate enough to have access to Forrest J Ackerman's unparalleled collection of all types of books and magazines dealing with fantasy and science fiction, including what must have amounted (if piled one item on top of another) to a twenty-five- or thirty-foot stack of fanzines of every description, as faithfully amassed by Ackerman from the 1930s on into the early or middle 1960s. This overall collection proved an invaluable resource, even if (as it turned out) Ackerman did not have any copies of *Tumbrils,* and even if we had thought to ask at the time. (We could not have done so because we did not yet know that *Tumbrils* had existed.) It was Fritz Leiber who, following our principal search among Ackerman's archives, let us know of the existence of Blish's essay, of which otherwise we would not have known anything at all. We wrote at once to James Blish himself (address courtesy of Fritz again), then living somewhere on the East Coast, requesting of him a copy of his own essay as politely as we could. What better strategy could there be to get a copy than applying directly to the very source himself?

Alas, as the essay's author kindly replied almost at once, his own file of *Tumbrils,* along with many other valuable papers, had undergone such damage in a flood at a previous place of residence near a river that they had emerged from this disaster in a state beyond repair or any further usage. He had no choice except to throw most of them away. Since we had no other clue as to where else to search (nor did Blish himself), we gave up any further quest for the elusive piece, and nobody else appeared to know either.

Many years later, acting on this datum about Blish's essay as reported in our bio-bibliography, Don Herron finally discovered a copy and bought it at great expense, later sharing it quite generously with others, including Scott Connors, Ronald Scott Hilger, and myself. Otherwise we could not have reproduced Blish's essay here, nor could we deliver our present riposte.

Eblis in Bakelite
James Blish
with an addendum by Donald Sidney-Fryer

> The shaddow of that Body heer you find
> Which serves but as a case to hold his mind,
> His intellectual part be pleas'd to look
> In lively lines described in the Booke.
>   —Thomas Cross: "In Effigem Nicholai
> Culpeper Equitis" (*A Physical Directory,* 1649)

Clark Ashton Smith has been called "the greatest American poet" by Edwin Markham, and while it is obvious from internal evidence that "The Man with the Hoe" was a fluke, it is possible for a man to be right twice in his life. Benjamin De Casseres, once a considerable figure in American letters before he took a job with one of Hearst's brothels, spoke for Smith in glowing terms; David Warren Ryder and George Sterling, as well as Samuel Loveman, may be added to the list of discerning people who have found things in Smith's work to admire. If one adds to this list the nearly endless columns written about Smith by fantasy fans from Lovecraft on down, it becomes evident that this one man has been one of the most extravagantly eulogized figures in American literary history—the sheer wordage concerning him nearly equals that written about Branch Cabell, a truly fantastic numeral if one attempts, as I have, to run most of it down.

In the attempt another fact soon becomes evident: except for one or two short articles, totaling perhaps 2000 words, no true criticism of Smith ever has appeared in professional or amateur print. I have sought nearly fruitlessly for paragraphs about the man which set forth a clear perception of the kind of work he does, its relationship to the rest of literature past and present, its antecedents and progeny; for any paragraph about him not crammed with sweeping dogmatic statements, false associations, bases of judgement that shift at the whim of the writer sometimes in the course of a line, report of estimates without documentation or demonstration, and emotional assessments which clearly indicate nothing save that their author likes fantasy no matter who writes it, or how badly. More: until last year, despite the fact that Smith has been active for more years than most fans can remember, there was no anthology of Smith's work, nor did any general anthology include a line of his much-lauded poetry—nor are any of the latter ever likely to do so now, since the Arkham bookbinders in their expected way have crammed every turkey egg Smith ever laid into print without the slightest discrimination, so that Smith in book form actually means less than Smith hidden from sight in pulp, amateur and private publications.

It would be interesting to compile a list of representative paragraphs from some of the best articles about this man with comments appended in the style of the Institute of Propaganda Analysis, but the space limitations of *Tumbrils* being what they are, a bibliography must serve. In the meantime, the pertinent question is: Does Smith deserve the damnation his admirers have visited upon him? And the business with which I concern myself is to answer this question in a milieu as remote as possible from the unselective happiness with which the average *Weird Tales* reader has greeted every tale of Zothique or Averoigne, upon the premise that such an estimate is grossly unfair to the poet and scholar which is Smith at his best.

For Smith at his best is a fine creative scholar. I know of no more impressive way to introduce Smith to a stranger than with "The Kingdom of the Worm," which was published in *The Fantasy Fan* many years ago. The episode was perfectly in the style of its ostensible period; it could have been slipped into *The Voyage and Travel of Sir John Mandeville, Knight* without the unwary reader's detecting it in his perusal of that recondite volume; as an entity in itself it held together beautifully, and preserved throughout that atmosphere of naive wonder mixed with uneasiness which is the literary signature of the great French liar—and a far more difficult thing to achieve than a mere parroting of stylistic tricks. Some time later, in R. H. Barlow's excellent mimeographed magazine *Leaves,* Smith addressed himself to the fragmentary narratives of the prisoners of Eblis which Beckford had planned for *Vathek* but never included. If anything, this performance was the more exacting of the two; *Vathek* anticipated the main course of literary development by a century in several ways, but in general Mandeville's way of doing things is much closer to what we know as the "Smith style" than Beckford's, since the last-named remained always an undoubted child of the Eighteenth Century, wherein neither Smith nor Lovecraft, despite the propaganda, could reasonably be expected to feel at home; but Smith carried it off with manifest ease and pleasure.

One of the consequences of these observations is to separate his poetry rather sharply from his prose, in a manner which will become clear in a moment. A study of the poetry will convince anyone seriously interested that its idiom is the product of a pyramid of influences—Poe and Wilde particularly, and then Shelley, Milton, James Thomson and a lengthening list of stragglers, who exert their effects not in concert but one at a time in the most marked fashion. "The Constellations of the

Law,"[3] for instance, is "The Massacre at Piedmont" to the life; "Satan Unrepentant" advertises its parentage too loudly for me even to bother naming it; "Requiescat" is Wilde's, well-thumbed; and so on. It is not so easy to attach single names to individual prose stories of Smith's, though the influences are plain enough. (I am not counting, naturally, the prose-poems, though even there Lanier occasionally nibbles at the edge of the Baudelaire.) One expects poets, however, to be an ancestor-worshiping race, and if Smith appears to be more than a little overly sensitive to the decadent-Romantic universe of discourse, still and all such a pressure is not lightly to be shrugged off. In addition, the synthesis of the best of bygone poems, up to and including direct quotation, has become through "The Waste Land" and the "Cantos" a nearly standard Twentieth Century technique; and Smith has occasionally achieved some really moving effects with such eclectic material—witness the ending of "Medusa," or "In November," or even more markedly, in "Chant of Autumn" where the intoxication is no less magical for being the heritage of Swinburne. Occasionally the results are more unfortunate and Smith gushes forth a "Hashish-Eater"—"perilous nightmares of superterrestrial fairylands accursed," in Lovecraft's mashed-potato language, but to the sober reader merely the sewage of a plastic-and-chromium Eblis.... The matter, it appears, is not entirely under Smith's control, and until he decides just *who* he is, we must be content to spear the effective poems like fishes as they float by.

In prose the matter *is* entirely under Smith's control. In the two works I have named above, and in one or two others, he has demonstrated conclusively that he has the sensibilities and the sensitivity to handle nearly any prose style that happens to appeal to him, excepting only the very tightest and sparest of modern idioms. The inevitable conclusion is that his characteristic prose manner, with its material drawn exclusively from the Poe horror story and the Wilde fairy tale, and its style from the glaucous logorrhea of Sir Thomas Browne's *Hydriotaphia,* is a conscious choice. And from almost any angle it is a bad one. It is incomprehensible and boring to the pulp readers whom he has—perhaps perforce—addressed most often. It is moribund and intolerably "arty" to a literate reader. The best he can hope from it is

---

3. I.e., "The Ministers of the Law" in *Ebony and Crystal.*

that it will please the very tiny segment of the reading public which is made up of men like Derleth and Lovecraft, who, incapable of distinguishing the artistic from the arty, can pass it through their digestive tracts and absorb from it the little nourishment that it contains.

As a product of irresistible influences and inclinations it might have been forgivable. As the conscious choice of a man who has shown that he can do better, it is funny. And tragic? Yes; if you think Smith could do *that* much better. When the laughter is over, it might also be counted as evidence for damnation, however; and probably it is better, in the long run, to let his admirers attend to that.

(Bibliography upon request.)

N.B. Because there is evidently no way to discover or obtain the "Bibliography upon request" mentioned at the end of Blish's essay, we have attempted here to reconstitute what may have been this listing of books and articles, at least relative to Smith's own life and career, or output, in the present addendum, but only in the order of appearance for the said books and articles as discussed by Blish in his critique. In this reconstitution we have used our own Clark Ashton Smith bio-bibliography *Emperor of Dreams* (West Kingston, RI: Donald M. Grant, 1978). We have also appended here and there any relevant comment where such appears to warrant it. A strategic detail concerning the general date of composition for "Eblis in Bakelite": although his essay appeared in June 1945, it is clear that Blish apparently wrote it sometime in 1943, a fact that we deduce from the reference to what must be Smith's collection *Out of Space and Time,* published in August of 1942. The reference reads in part: "until last year . . . there was no anthology of Smith's work," and thus the statement cannot refer to the second Arkham House collection by Smith, *Lost Worlds,* published in October of 1944.

Benjamin De Casseres, "Clark Ashton Smith: Emperor of Shadows," a brief but incisive appreciation written c. August 1937 and published by The Futile Press (Lakeport, California), c. November 1937 (70 copies), evidently at Smith's own request, and evidently included with some copies of Smith's collection *Nero and Other Poems,* published by The Futile Press in May 1937 (c. 250 copies), along with the separate article "The Price of Poetry," by David Warren Ryder, published by the same press in June 1937 (reprinted from *Controversy* for 7 December 1934).

George Sterling, prefaces to Smith's two poetry collections *Odes and Sonnets* (published June 1918) and *Ebony and Crystal* (published December 1922).

Samuel Loveman, no known published source, but Smith dedicated *Ebony and Crystal* to this fine lyrical poet, who was also a friend to H. P. Lovecraft. Loveman's one and only major collection is *The Hermaphrodite and Other Poems,* published by The Caxton Printers (Caldwell, Idaho), 1936.

Clark Ashton Smith, *Out of Space and Time* (Sauk City, WI: Arkham House, August 1942), with an introduction by August Derleth and Donald Wandrei. The curious phrase "the Arkham bookbinders" undoubtedly refers to Derleth and Wandrei as the then owner-editors of Arkham House.

Smith, "The Kingdom of the Worm," first published in the *Fantasy Fan,* October 1933, and included in Smith's collection *Other Dimensions* (Arkham House, April 1970), but under his preferred and final title "A Tale of Sir John Maundeville."

Smith, "The Third Episode of Vathek: The Story of the Princess Zulkais and the Prince Kalilah," by William Beckford, first published in *Leaves,* issue "1" (Summer 1937). Conclusion only (c. 4000 words) written by Smith to this final episode deliberately left unfinished by the original author. Included in Smith's collection *The Abominations of Yondo* (published by Arkham House, February 1960), wherein the completed episode occupies pp. 177–222; Smith's conclusion occupies pp. 212–22.

Smith, *Ebony and Crystal: Poems in Verse and Prose,* published by Smith himself but printed by the press of the *Auburn Journal* (Auburn, CA, December 1922). This collection contains nearly all the poems mentioned by Blish in his text. "Medusa" is either the sonnet "The Medusa of Despair" or the ode "Medusa" (first published in Smith's first collection *The Star-Treader and Other Poems,* November 1912, later republished in *Nero and Other Poems*).

Smith, *The Star-Treader and Other Poems,* A. M. Robertson (San Francisco); *Odes and Sonnets,* The Book Club of California (San Francisco); *Nero and Other Poems,* The Futile Press (Lakeport,

California). For dates of publication and other data, see the entry above and also the entries under De Casseres and George Sterling. Blish may or may not have had copies of these three collections.

"Eblis in Bakelite" first appeared in *Tumbrils* 2 (June 1945).

Shadows and Light

A brief review of—and thoughts inspired by—
Echos de Cimmérie

It is always a pleasure to read a book (in this instance, galley proofs—the book itself is still forthcoming) that is essentially an extended homage to a writer who was little known to, and surely underappreciated by, the mainstream of his own time, moreover a writer born to the same language as the reader himself. But it is an equal, and perhaps even greater, pleasure to read such a book in another language reflecting a different culture and civilization, another language that the same reader has learned spoken formally later in life (even if he has heard it from babyhood onward), starting in that same reader's adolescence. Such is the case with *Echos de Cimmérie,* as edited and partly written by Fabrice Tortey, a French pharmacist living in Saint-Maur-des-Fosses (east of Paris) and writing for Francophone readers wherever they might find themselves. This large volume is a heartfelt piece of tribute to the Texan poet and storyteller Robert Ervin Howard, one that reflects very well indeed nor just on the individual writers whose essays appear in it (some of them translated from American English), but above all on the editor who conceived and put it together.

The volume opens with a brief but cogent introduction by the editor, which is essentially a kind of balance sheet on the state of publishing relative to REH, whether it involves materials by him or materials about him and his work, whether in the U.S. or in France. The introduction ends with gracious acknowledgment to all the people who aided and encouraged Tortey in his arduous task, which represents a considerable investment of time, thought, and energy. The editor's preface then leads effortlessly into the careful, conscientious, and even-handed account of Howard's life and career by the same editor, "Robert Ervin Howard: De l'ombre vers le jour" ("From the shadow into day"). This lengthy but always intelligent and interesting report is a major piece of writing, a real prize.

Although the present critic read the pioneering biography of

REH by Sprague and Catherine de Camp with Jane Griffin, *Dark Valley Destiny,* soon after it appeared in 1983 (courtesy of Fritz Leiber, who read and reviewed it favorably and then passed his copy on loan to the present writer), it is salutary to read Tortey's account—especially minus Sprague de Camp's biases and animadversions as a professional writer in disfavor of the Texan author—and to reacquaint oneself with the basic facts through a better balanced presentation and appraisal.

Inter alia Tortey handles the details of Texas life, geography, and history more than competently, in fact surprisingly well, with charming touches of wit and humor. Readers in France (the main market for the book) should consider themselves fortunate to have at their disposal this lively, well-written, and well-balanced biography-cum-literary assessment. The present critic would buy this book just for the editor's opening article, which sets the record straight on the misinformation and misconceptions about REH that have been circulating for far too long. Tortey's even-handed approach lets the reader make up his own mind about certain salient problems and difficulties in Howard's life.

His mother's tuberculosis had essentially created quite an awkward—if not near-impossible—situation in which everyone involved came to suffer, and not just Hester Howard the mother, but Dr. Isaac Howard, whose rural practice kept him absent from home for long periods of time (so he could perform the indispensable work that supported his family), and above all REH the son, who took over the principal care of Hester for the last few years of her life, with devastating consequences for his creativity.

The miracle is that the son managed to create as much as he did, not only during that awkward period but during the short span of his creative life. While reading Tortey's account, the present critic even felt much sympathy for Novalyne Price and her desire for a normal life with Robert, which was not to be. Without her testimony there is so much that we would never know concerning the last years of his life. Price evidently did not fully grasp the depths of REH's despair and pessimism. He had become suicidal from at least his latter adolescence onward, as his letters reveal. But Price denied Howard any real sympathy when he needed it most, a sympathy that might have made the difference in preventing his suicide, which still represents a tragic loss to American literature.

Before we leave the subject of biographies good, bad, and indifferent, I wish to render some justice to Sprague de Camp. Although not temperamentally suited to handle authors like Lovecraft and Howard (in short, he blames them for not being de Camp himself as an exemplary professional writer and well-equilibrated individual), he deserves considerable credit for publishing the first major biographies of Howard and Lovecraft (however wrongheaded he may seem at times to some critics). He did much valuable firsthand research, interviewing people who had known Howard and his family, and thus preserving much oral material that would otherwise be lost.

One other strategic point, which neither Tortey nor any of the other scriveners in the volume at hand appear to mention. The de Camps included Jane Griffin, a competent academic and native Texan, as their chief Texas collaborator for the insights that only a native could make about the Lone Star State. Otherwise Griffin was, alas, the completely wrong collaborator, since she had no understanding or appreciation of Howard as an original fictioneer, and in particular she could not abide the Conan saga. When at a fantasy convention years ago the present critic met both the de Camps, who then introduced him to Griffin—all three were gathered at one spot—Jane confessed to me her inability to read much of Howard's fiction with anything other than distaste. His Conan stories apparently made her feel rather ill. She felt bad about this, but felt she had to be honest. Nevertheless, Jane was not confessing her distaste for Howard's work to just anybody at all. De Camp, a perfect gentleman, had introduced me to Jane in a very flattering way, and she felt she could trust me, which was true.

In the first chapter of *Dark Valley Destiny* certain things concerning Texas are mentioned (I'm guessing courtesy of Griffin) that only a sensitive native would know. The state not only possesses violent contrasts in terrain and weather from one region to another—Texas is immense, and the same size as France—but often violent contrasts in the same area. There is the arboreal beauty and greenery of eastern Texas continuing that of Louisiana, the arid and stark desert around El Paso that continues on into New Mexico and Arizona, the individual climate of the Panhandle, the more moderate weather and often remarkable beauty of Austin, San Antonio, and Corpus Christi. The geographical scope and variety of Texas are nothing less than astonishing, not to mention tornadoes and hurricanes! And almost everywhere in the state there is the extreme heat, extreme drought, or extreme humidity of summer, no less than the genuine and surprising cold of winter. Just as the winters in Russia have certainly affected and shaped the overall character of the Russian people, so too have the violently contrasting weather and climate of Texas worked to fashion the character of her native modern population. With no doubt about it, Howard's writings in their own turn reflect the variety, violence, and volatility of the Texan weather and climate.

One final consideration about an issue that many have underestimated. Without overemphasis Tortey consistently weaves into his text, once Howard becomes a full-fledged professional fictioneer and poet, what he would earn in a given year. We know that he prided himself on being a professional writer, and that he accomplished some of his best work for *Weird Tales* (although his humorous westerns and his boxing stories contain some of his most compelling work as well). Therefore the large sum (c. $1000–1400, especially by Depression standards) that "Satrap Pharnabazus" (Farnsworth Wright) as editor of *Weird Tales* owed him weighed with an especial heaviness on Howard during the last years of his life, as he struggled with his pride, and as he struggled to meet his obligations, and had to beg or demand that Wright pay him something of what was owed.

Don Herron has hit the nail on the head in his justified attacks on Wright's inadequacy as editor for treating Howard and Lovecraft, two of his most popular contributors, in the offhand way that he did. If Howard did in fact consider himself a failure because of Wright's failure to pay him on publication (when he had to work so damn hard to earn that money), it is easy to see how the lack of this money might have helped to drive him to suicide, to push him over the edge, especially when coupled with the lack of understanding and sympathy from Novalyne Price when he most needed that support. REH truly must have felt as if he were struggling for his very existence in that last year or so of his life and career.

The remainder of *Echos de Cimmérie,* that is, the major part of this volume, comprises quite a grand mixture of materials—some by Howard but most of them by other writers, and where necessary translated by quite a few capable translators into French—but it is all of direct moment to anyone seriously interested in REH. I cannot do adequate critical justice to it all, but shall make pertinent critical comment here and there where it seems apropos, paying especial attention to the articles by French writers (under the assumption that those written by Americans will be duly published in English).

The Junto was a magazine published by members of Howard's circle that appeared from April 1928 through February 1930 at least. During 1923–29 Howard corresponded with five Texans of literary inclination, and Herbert C. Klatt has remained the least well-known until Glenn Lord's article, reprinted here from various American appearances, devoted to this "fourth musketeer." Christopher Gruber's article details the ruins that remain of the old Cross Plains ice house, where REH himself appeared as a boxer on a number of occasions.

In "Le Sens du récit chez Robert Ervin Howard," ("The Narrative Sense of Robert E. Howard") Simon Sanahujas discusses the sense or meaning of the narrative in Howard's practice of it, how he as fictioneer opens, develops, and ends a typical narrative, and how his modus operandi descends less directly from his reading but far more from the oral tradition that he as a child experienced from listening, mostly to four women reading aloud to him or telling him folk stories of varying types.

"Bob Howard ou le pouvoir du regard intérieur" ("Bob Howard or the power of the inner look") is parallel to the previous essay. Argentium Thri'ile develops his thesis concerning the power of the interior gaze, as subsumed under the different powers of negation, of meaning. of absence, of archetypes, of action, and of efficacy.

In the major essay "Kull, Bran Mak Morn et Conan," Patrice Louinet explores Howard's concepts of kingship and authority, whereas in another piece Pierre Favier perceives a Shakespearian allegory in the short story "Kings of the Night." Rodolphe Massé, in his essay concerning "'The Phoenix on the Sword' and other fulgurances or lightning-like illuminations," explores how the works of REH are all compact of the sovereign faculty of imagination, and then presents his thesis under three rubrics: the landscapes of the soul, allegories of the quest, and seven flames for Conan.

A pair of Solomon Kane articles by Patrice Allart and Oliver Legrand illuminate one of the most important but probably most neglected of Howard's major characters. The Legrand essay in particular proposes the notion that, while REH partakes of the typical racism of his period, this became modified in his socializing in accordance to the individual with whom he was dealing whether personally or as projected through a character like Solomon Kane in his fiction.

Two essays in this collection appeared in English in the *Cimmerian*. In the first, Michel Meurger demonstrates how the imaginative concept or "dream" (actually "awakening") that HPL and REH entertained concerning the archaic world was also experienced by Captain Vere Shortt as demonstrated in his posthumously published novel *The Rod of The Snake* (1917). The other concerns Jacques Bergier, best known for his monograph *Le Matin des magiciens* (written with Louis Pauwels), or *The Morning of the Magicians,* but also for other influential books. Joseph Altairac recalls the important role played by Bergier in the initial discovery and subsequent vogue in France of H. P. Lovecraft, J. R. R. Tolkien, and R. E. Howard among other important modern writers of imaginative fiction.

"Face à Cthulhu" is Patrice Allart's examination of how REH is as much of a master of the uncanny tale as he is of heroic fantasy, vis-à-vis a certain cosmic influence from Lovecraft. In "Entretien avec François Truchaud," *Madame* Parente and *Monsieur* Tortey conduct a notable "conversation" (in the traditional form of the interview, that is, brief questions or comments followed by extended responses) with the man who ranks as the chief translator of Howard's fiction into French.

This major volume concludes with quite a long and useful register of the writings of REH published in France up to 30 November 2008, "Bibliographie des oeuvres de Robert E. Howard traduites et publiées en France," compiled by Simon Sanahujas. This listing divides into five sections, as follows: 1. Novels; 2. Short stories, fragments, and rough drafts; 3. Fragments completed and texts rehandled; 4. Poems; and 5. Chronological list of books or periodicals in which have appeared the texts of REH. A presentation of the authors and artists involved in the preparation of this volume follows the bibliography, and "Pour aller plus loin . . ." (in order to go farther on . . .) in turn follows the list of contributors, and presents for the serious collector of Howard a condensed bibliography of guide books in the English language, specialist magazines, computer websites accessible on the Internet, special organizations and annual events in the USA and France featuring REH, his life and letters.

Following the lead of Tortey in his own major piece "De l'ombre vers le jour," these diverse French writers treat REH and his works with an altogether admirable seriousness and perspicacity. From this incomplete and inadequate account that I have attempted, the reader can still perceive that what we have here in Tortey's major volume is a magnificent feast of analysis, discussion, comment, and bibliography.

Foreword to *Not Quite Atlantis*

When the omnibus collection *The Atlantis Fragments,* containing the three presumably miscellaneous series (1971, 2003, and 2005) of *Songs and Sonnets Atlantean,* appeared in the latter half of 2008, the author-poet realized that he had unintentionally created a kind of allegory, or extended metaphor, in mythopoeic guise. He had built it around the planet Earth, around the natural world, or if you will, around Mother Nature, the mother of our nature and all the other nature evolving over a sizeable expanse of Terran geography. He had accomplished this allegory by means of Plato's Atlantis Mythos, through the latter's postulation of a great and otherwise unknown Empire of Atlantis, but out in the Atlantic Ocean, ranging from the Arctic to the equator, from the Americas to Europe and Africa.

Does the same author-poet need to point out, to emphasize, the direct correlation of the Atlantis Mythos—of a world infinitely remote in time but overwhelmed by a Great Cataclysm—with our own world of today threatened by a similar cataclysm but of a different kind? Consciously the author-poet had achieved his own mythopoeic objective not just through his own original poems, as well as his translations from the French, but above all by translating into English the largest group of poems (whether in verse or in prose) ever made available from the ancient language of Atlantis—by many twists and turns—over a very long period of time, and through the unique recension of these poems by the French Renaissance poet Michel de Labretagne. Moreover, the present author had also created a kind of myth, or allegory, about poetry itself, traditional versus non-traditional, an adversarial position far more noticeable in the U.S. than in the British Commonwealth, if at all in the latter.

Many threads and strands have gone into the tapestry making up *The Atlantis Fragments,* not all of them overtly Atlantean. These threads concern the immediate origin of the poems as modem creations, but as conceived in the tradition of selected other poets of both the French and English Renaissance, no less than those of the nineteenth century, as well as those constituting the California Romantics, primarily Ambrose Bierce, George Sterling, Nora May French, and

Clark Ashton Smith, a group that flourished approximately during 1890 to 1930. The present selection *Not Quite Atlantis* emphasizes those poets, other than Michel de Labretagne, in whose tradition the author-poet has written, to produce an omnibus collection of poetry comparable in size and scope, but not in fame or merit, with *Les Fleurs du mal* by Baudelaire.

Westchester, Los Angeles,
15 November 2009

Klarkash-Ton, High Priest of Atlantis

Apparently H. P. Lovecraft (1890–1937) in his letters and prose fictions (during the 1920s and 1930s) became the first writer in modern times to identify Clark Ashton Smith (1893–1961) correctly as Klarkash-Ton in the latter's evidently prime incarnation as High Priest of Atlantis.

Smith's later, non-Atlantean incarnations remain relatively obscure, apart from the one most recently manifested (see his dates above), even if not yet recognized by the literary mainstream. In this last but publicly acknowledged manifestation he lived the life of a freelance but fiercely independent poet, fictioneer, essayist, epigrammatist and aphorist, sculptor, painter, and so forth.

But Smith also conducted a parallel but separate mundane work-life on and off during much of his literary career. He also worked as a journalist, a fruit-picker, a fruit-packer, a woodchopper, a typist, a gardener (and not just as a landscape-maintenance worker), and a hard-rock miner, mucker, and windlasser.

These occupations he pursued either full-time but just seasonally, or on a part-time basis whenever circumstances demanded, in order to support his ageing parents and /or himself while creating his inimitable poetry and prose.

But from all appearances Ashton Smith never forgot that prime incarnation as High Priest of Atlantis. From that lifetime he projected the poems, the poems in prose, and the stories that in his most recent incarnation make up the different cycles of what he could still recollect from his other past lives.

These other lives he recorded as they presumably took place in Hyperborea, Averoigne, Xiccarph, Zothique, and especially Atlantis, or as in his remembrance of it as Poseidonis, the last major fragment of that antediluvian island continent. The precise and separate identity of Poseidonis, the Theosophists as headed by Yelena Blavatsky (or Blavatskaya) rediscovered and kept alive during the later 1800s and early 1900s. However, only Smith's Atlantis or Poseidonis fragments, whether poetry or prose, need occupy us here.

Like Francis Melchior, as veraciously chronicled in that incomparable (extended) poem in prose "The Planet of the Dead," Smith obviously "was one of those who are born with an immedicable distaste for all that is present or near at hand: one of those who have drunk too lightly of oblivion and have not wholly forgotten the transcendent glories of other eons, and the worlds from which they were exiled into human birth so that their furtive, restless thoughts and dim, unquenchable longings return obscurely toward the vanishing shores of a lost heritage. The earth is too narrow for such, and the compass of mortal time is too brief, and paucity and barrenness are everywhere; and in all places their lot is a never-ending weariness."

Smith's usual emotional condition patently claims kinship to that limned in the poem "The Infinite Quest":

> For each horizon straitly sought,
>   With fealty to the stars,
> What death or weariness was bought,
>   What bitterness, what bars!

It also bears a close relation to the imagery even more poignantly presented at the end of another poem "Mirage":

> For ever lost—
> Like sunset on a land of old romance—
> The splendour fails, and leaves the traveler
>   In endless deserts flaming to the day.

Or indeed, much more appositely, Smith's usual emotional condition seems to echo the state pictured at the end of another (extended) poem in prose "The Last Incantation." In this conclusion, after fruitlessly invoking the past, Malygris the magician discovers that "There was nothing left but shadow and grayness and dust, nothing but the empty dark and the cold, and a clutching weight of insufferable weariness, of immedicable anguish."

Despite the anterior spell of "The Last Incantation," and although somehow still alive just after having died, Malygris yet manages one final spell by means of one final incantation, a supreme anathema or malediction, in yet another (extended) poem in prose "The Death of Malygris." Or was Malygris just another one of Smith's Atlantean or Poseidonean incarnations after that as High Priest of Atlantis?

Sacramento, 30 December 2013

Crimson Pages from the Future Perfect Past

Once upon a time a certain remarkable pulp magazine existed by the name of *Weird Tales,* and sustained that existence from 1923 to 1954. Certain writers and poets contributed to "The Unique Magazine" (as the subtitle ran). Although similar as well as dissimilar in background and education, as observed in the fantastic, often macabre stories that they had published in it, they had enough similarities to merit the term of a "*Weird Tales* School." The late L. Sprague de Camp, fictioneer, popularizer, and critic, rightfully considered them "the Three [or four] Musketeers of *Weird Tales*": Henry S. Whitehead, H. P. Lovecraft, Robert E. Howard, and Clark Ashton Smith. Other scriveners came along somewhat later to add their own distinction to the periodical: E. Hoffmann Price, August Derleth, Manly Wade Wellman, Seabury Quinn, Ray Bradbury, etc.

Arkham House under August Derleth later gathered many of their stories into a series of handsome hardcover books, either anthologies or collections devoted to one author or another. These books in turn gave entertainment and inspiration to new generations of readers and budding authors. Thus, despite the initial inattention or even disdain meted out to the magazine by the literary mainstream, the best stories by these authors have obviously survived to become canonical classics. However, the poets inspired by them, especially those working in traditional forms, have appeared but few and far between.

A new poet, and a traditionalist (albeit innovative), has now made his appearance to augment the limited register of these poets' names. He is K. A. Opperman, and he makes his debut with the volume in hand [*The Crimson Tome*]. Given the almost relentless pageant of doom and gloom, of death and blood, invoked herein, one would never guess that the author of this poetry is not some cynical, world-weary, and pessimistic older man, but instead a bright and agreeable young adult in his mid-twenties.

And just what has Opperman presented in his first collection to the aficionado of fantastic and/or macabre poetry? Overall *The Crimson Tome* contains six sections, or more properly, six collections. His first auctorial offering is a collection of collections. In the order of presentation these include: *The Nightmare Muse, Unpleasant Dreams, Nocturnal Lovers: I, Nocturnal Lovers: II, The Palace of Phantasies,* and *Twilight Sorrows.* The reader will notice that the poems often feature much beautiful and unusual (sometimes archaic) language, most of it long since abandoned, if not forbidden, by the American, but not the British, poetic mainstream.

The table of contents dutifully lists the given selections, whose titles the poet has chosen with care and cunning, titles that beguilingly invite the aficionado into their usually very dark locales, into places or situations of very grim contemplation or action. Nor does the poet fear the use of unfashionable inversions here and there; adroitly handled in general, they impart a needed elegance, emphasis, and variety. Opperman clearly knows his rhetoric, and deploys it to good effect.

Let us take a look at what the poet has offered us in this generous volume. Opperman wisely opens with a strong sonnet sequence, titled "The Land of Darkest Dreams," to some extent but not overmuch in the tradition of the *Fungi from Yuggoth* by H. P. Lovecraft, or of the *Sonnets of the Midnight Hours* by Donald Wandrei. For his own sequence Opperman has ingeniously created an unconventional sonnet slightly expanded into fifteen lines. A sonnet form in fifteen lines, what? Yes!

Before the petrifaction of the sonnet into fourteen lines, the term sonnet simply meant a "little song," its literal meaning, and could include rondeau, rondel, and other short lyric forms. An unusual and innovative rhyme arrangement—featuring an octave followed by a septet (rather than the traditional sestet)—the basic rhyme scheme appears to be, more often than not, as follows:

> a b b a c b a c (octave)
> d c e d e d e (septet)

Reader, have no fear! This new sonnet form works as well as any other, and surely functions quite well for Opperman. A few sonnets intriguingly mention a certain rather Lovecraftian town called Yorehaven, an apt and attractive name coined by the poet.

The next section or collection, *Unpleasant Dreams,* continues the same dark imagery and episodes, in varied forms and in length of line, such as fourteeners and alexandrines, the latter distinctly uncommon in English (apart from their use by Clark Ashton Smith and the poets of the English Symbolist school). For example, each of the seven quatrains making up "Nocturnal Poet" skillfully alternates decasyllabics with alexandrines. The poet casts "The Thirst of Count Aster" in these iambic hexameters and cleverly varies them to strong dramatic effect. Another innovation: the author has narrated "A Vampire Fear" and "Bathory" (Countess Erzsebet Bathory) in patently Swinburnian metrics, and effectively. But he also sagely avoids the diffuse indirection that can baffle and defeat the would-be reader of Swinburne's curious but individual Muse.

The two cycles of love poems constituting *Nocturnal Lovers* make an immediate impact. Despite or because of their strange mixture of the macabre with the erotic—an exceptional combination—they strike the present writer as pretty hot stuff. One admires the poet's versatility in these two notable sequences. The book's two last sections or collections, *The Palace of Phantasies* and *Twilight Sorrows,* appear as notable in their own fashion as the two connected cycles of love poems. *The Palace of Phantasies* contains among much else a powerful ballad, "Duel with the Dark Double," in which the poet combats, and vanquishes, the dark side of his own personal nature—a narrative that bears worthy comparison with some of the poetry by Robert E. Howard, that master chronicler of "sanguinary conflict" (in Lovecraft's accurate phrase), as exemplified in "The King and the Oak."

A word of warning: this volume is not for the squeamish reader. In his imagery and narrative episodes Opperman seems to delight in a crimson tide of blood (hence the Crimson Tome), not to mention an occasional flood of other precious bodily fluids. Caveat lector: let the reader beware!

Mingling metaphysical, spiritual, and physical horror, Opperman patently derives from, and meritoriously continues, the macabre heritage of the modern poetic masters in the genre (that is, of fantasy and science fiction), H. P. Lovecraft, Clark Ashton Smith, and Robert E. Howard. (Rather interestingly, all these poets worked in traditional forms.) But make no mistake about it, Opperman remains very much in his own poetic persona, despite whatever he may have derived from "The Three Musketeers of *Weird Tales*." A native Californian, he claims prominence as one of the few authors who have deliberately followed in the poetic footsteps of such Californians as Ambrose Bierce, George Sterling, and Clark Ashton Smith. As a Golden State Phantastick, K. A. Opperman in this volume becomes another original figure in the line or lineage of those unique California Romantics.

Sacramento, 9 November 2013

Averoigne: An Afterword

By putting *The Averoigne Chronicles* together, Ronald Hilger in the immediate editorial tradition of Lin Carter has rendered a genuine and singularly creative service not only to the Klarkash-Tonophiles, the solid core of Clark Ashton Smith aficionados here and abroad, as well as to the specialist audience consisting of the devotees of fantasy and science fiction, but just as much to the general reading public, especially those individuals who value modern imaginative fiction in some of its more intense manifestations. Quite unintentionally, by gathering these more or less related materials into the overall form exhibited here, Ronald Hilger has come up with something that is very much like a novel or a romance, a development that neither he nor his editorial precursor could have anticipated. Such an historic achievement as this collection represents deserves not only to be generally noticed but also to be signalized and even celebrated.

The late Lin Carter certainly takes an eminent rank among the other notable Klarkash-Tonophile connoisseurs of the latter half of the twentieth century, as witness the series of four Ballantine paperbacks made up of the writings of Clark Ashton Smith that he compiled and edited. During his extensive and fruitful career as a poet, a writer, a general man of letters, and above all else as an editor, Carter often expressed a certain enthusiastic desire in person, and at least a number of times in print while he was editor-in-chief of the Adult Fantasy Series published by Ballantine Books. Although he expressed it in a slightly different way, the essence of this desire was that he very much wanted to read an authentic novel by Ashton Smith as a master of perfervid imagination and polyphonic prose, that is, as a master of certain unique gifts in prose fiction, especially as exemplified in the genre(s) of the short story and the novelette. Moreover, Lin Carter astutely reckoned that, had Ashton Smith written (and finished, we should probably add) such a novel worthy of his best abilities in prose, something rare and choice might very well have resulted—something quaint and curious that at least would have united grand melodramatics and magnificent outré pageantry with pungent grotesquery—and thus, in rarity and choiceness, something comparable to

196

the definitely unorthodox *History of the Caliph Vathek* by William Beckford, or the historical romance *Salammbô* by Gustave Flaubert.

Sometime between his early and late adolescence, Smith did in fact write and apparently complete a number of long novels laid in that particular Orient (at once real and mythical) revealed by, and extrapolated from, *The Thousand and One Nights,* one of the pivotal texts that had enchanted his childhood and early adolescence. Smith once described these extensive narratives of his as "long adventure novels dealing with Oriental life." In such experimental fiction as these very long and evidently rambling stories, as well as in his imitations of European fairy tales, Smith was directly learning for the first time his craft as a concoctor of make-believe, that is, as a fictioneer. Apparently only two of the early novels have survived, *The Black Diamonds,* (almost 250 pp in all) and *The Sword of Zagan,* (much shorter at just over 100 pp). Technically, however, such early work ranks, of course, as juvenilia, and apart from such overt as well as latent tendencies as they may disclose in anticipation of those of the adult fictioneer, this early work has no particular importance or interest except for specialist scholars. Certainly, upon attaining his maturity as an active fictioneer during the early and middle 1930s, their author never wanted or anticipated their serious publication!

In a different class from his acknowledged juvenilia are such novelettes as he produced in the 1930s as "The City of the Singing Flame," "The Ice-Demon," "The Dark Eidolon," "The Letter from Mohaun Los," "The Monster of the Prophecy," and many others, including as well "The Colossus of Ylourgne," collected herein as the single longest of *The Averoigne Chronicles.* These are not only some of his longest and most characteristic adult fiction, but they are also some of his best and most original work. Still, these and other similarly long tales are only novelettes, and still are not full-length novels. However, Smith did leave behind him at his death one unpublished and unfinished novel that emerged, like the stories just cited, as a product of the 1930s, his busiest and most creative period as a fictioneer. This fragment was *The Infernal Star,* comprising about 12,000 words (Smith's own estimate), begun and completed in February 1933. Its author had originally conceived it as a book-length fantasy novel, and he once reckoned that he had at least achieved one-third or one-half of the overall work. He had first planned the novel as a serial for *Weird Tales,* but when the magazine's editor Farnsworth Wright discouraged him in this plan, he then put it aside indefinitely. Much later, Smith considered finishing it; this was during the late 1950s. Apparently by means of the regular postal service, he showed it as it was to August Derleth in February 1958 in the hope of its eventual publication by Arkham House, which had become Smith's book publisher starting in 1942. It would have thus appeared either as a separate book or as part of the ongoing series of Smith's hardcover collections. However, these tentative plans also came to nothing, and by the time of Smith's death in August 1961 the fragment remained unpublished, and apparently more or less as the author had left it almost thirty years before.

When the unfinished novel was finally gathered into *Strange Shadows* (Greenwood Press, 1989), a final collection of hitherto unpublished fiction and miscellanea by Smith, editor Steve Behrends well summed it up as "an unfinished novelette [*sic*] that expertly mingles elements of fantasy, horror, and science fiction." Even though the work is in fact a novel, albeit in fragmentary form, and even though it does have a certain originality about it, *The Infernal Star* would still not answer, any more than would his juvenile novels, to Lin Carter's desire or expectation of an exotic and idiosyncratic novel by Smith of the type either of *Vathek* or of *Salammbô.* However, the present volume might possibly have satisfied Carter's wish. As gathered and arranged by Ronald Hilger more or less chronologically (that is, according to the inner chronology of the individual tales), *The Averoigne Chronicles* in its present embodiment does indeed shape up into what is possibly the closest thing that we shall ever have to an authentic novel by Ashton Smith. Explicitly, by including, and even having the stories open with, the virtual prose-poem "A Night in Malnéant"—a tale closely related in theme, atmosphere, and mood (and apparently even geography) to the narratives concerning Averoigne—Ronald Hilger has greatly enriched and extended the tone, concept, and feeling of this collection, and has heightened even further its resemblance to a novel or a romance, especially as interspersed with poems in verse or in prose, most of them by Smith—poems chiefly of a medieval flavor or imagery—carefully selected to echo, reflect, or comment upon, sometimes ironically, the stories in whose proximity they appear.

Even if it does nothing else, the present compilation—with its more or less alternating sections of verse and prose, its narratives long, short, or middling, as well as major or minor—does at least rather strongly resemble one of those multifarious bodies of lore favored for narrative use during the Middle Ages. Medieval storytellers were accustomed to utilize subjects or themes from three principal bodies of narrative material. The *Matière de Rome,* or *Matter of Rome,* included subjects from Roman and Greek history, as well as mythology, embracing (among other things) Thebes in Greece, the Trojan War, and Alexander the Great, especially his presumed fantastic adventures in India. The *Matière de France,* or *Matter of France,* concerned itself mainly with Charlemagne and those of his knights, such as Roland, revolving around the court of that monarch, first as King of the Franks and later as the first Holy Roman Emperor. The *Matière de Bretagne,* or *Matter of Britain,* involved itself, of course, with King Arthur and his Knights of the Round Table, Arthur having been transformed by this time into another Charlemagne thanks to Geoffrey of Monmouth's monumental *Historia Regum Britanniae.* However, as this last body of lore developed into its most characteristic form, it concerned itself above all with the machinations and amours of Lancelot and Guinevere, Tristan and Yseult, and other lovers. Indeed, it was primarily from such stories as these last ones, as well as from the poetic activity of the troubadours and trouvères, that our modern concept of romance first emerged and crystallized. The present *Chroniques d'Averoigne* seems to hint at an apparently otherwise unknown, forgotten, or overlooked *Matière d'Averonne,* or *Matter of Averoigne.*

But can this compilation indeed technically qualify as a novel? That would obviously depend on how we define the form. First, we must peremptorily dismiss from our minds the concept of the evolved modern literary novel of the twentieth century; such has absolutely no relevance or application here. We must return instead either to the ancient Mediterranean world or, more appositely, to the Middle Ages for the more appropriate models that might have influenced Ashton Smith, however vaguely, and even if he himself might not have been consciously thinking of them in quite the same terms as indicated by our present discussion. If we define the novel in terms of its original and historically most fundamental form—which in brief is simply that of a genuinely long piece of fiction, whether in verse or in prose—then, yes, this collection can qualify in some sense as a kind of novel, not so much a novel of one person or of several persons, but rather a novel of a specific place or an overall region. We must not forget that, whether cast in verse or in prose, the mediaeval epics and romances, as well as the epics and romances of the Renaissance which succeeded them, were in fact the direct precursors of the modern novel, overtly literary or not.

Unexpectedly, and almost paradoxically, *The Averoigne Chronicles* as a concept emerges with a greater degree of cohesion than what the original author himself may have consciously thought possible, or than what the material itself may have promised or may have seemed inherently to possess before being put into this more coherent form, even if that very, and more ample, cohesion may seem, at least at first consideration, to be the result of mere happenstance. After all, one form or shape or arrangement of the material is as good as another, and surely it is the substance that is important, at least more so than the form—or are they?! Considered as a novel—in the present case as an explicit or implicit overall narrative frame or structure as embodied and developed in a series of highly diverting and original tales or episodes taking place over a long historical period—*The Averoigne Chronicles* thus becomes the story or history of a French province apparently otherwise unknown to orthodox culture and chronology.

Undeniably, even if perceived as the result of seeming happenstance, the present arrangement of *The Averoigne Chronicles* still possesses a greater cohesion and, equally important, a greater variety than those possessed by Lin Carter's own editions of Smith's prose tales of a similar nature, that is, *Zothique* (1970), *Hyperborea* (1971), *Xiccarph* (1972), and *Poseidonis* (1973). We may well ask why this should be so, and why *The Averoigne Chronicles* should succeed in this way to a greater degree than what those previous volumes have done.

We know from his letters to his fellow scriveners of the 1930s, as well as from *The Black Book,* the notebook that he used from the late 1920s until his death in 1961, that Ashton Smith obviously intended at one time to gather in an appropriate manner his various series of tales laid in certain general ambiances. In *The Black Book* we find these titles with attendant lists of stories for such seriously proposed collections as *The Book of Hyperborea, Tales of Zothique, Tales of Atlantis,* and *Averoigne Chronicles.* This original intention he never did accomplish, but had he done so, we may be sure that there would have been yet a further and final stage of shaping and filling in. It is quite evident that the various series of tales as now collected in various forms lack here and there obviously needed echoes as well as entire sequels to previous and often monstrous events, something that probably would only have become apparent once Ashton Smith had gotten the various series up to this final stage. Also, at the same time, he might then have perceived the equally obvious need of an even greater variety of theme and content than what the divers materials already possessed, and might then have supplied such an evident deficiency. We may regret that for whatever reason he never did thus gather the relevant stories and shape them into the appropriate forms that he might have done. We can only speculate as to what he might have made of them in an overall sense, and furthermore, in the case of *The Averoigne Chronicles,* exactly into what kind of potentially glamorous composite he might well have transformed them.

Why then does an Averoigne volume possess at once a greater cohesion and a greater variety than those put together by Lin Carter? Why is it that, in the specific case of *The Averoigne Chronicles,* the concept seems to function more effectively than in the case of Zothique, Hyperborea, Xiccarph, and Poseidonis? In asking such questions, we are not belittling in any way Carter's achievement with the original four paperbacks. First, there is the primary and determining nature of the geography involved. Zothique and Hyperborea are large and far-ranging continents with considerable geographical variation within the margins formed by their coastlines. Xiccarph is an entire planet (and about which Smith wrote only two stories), and Poseidonis is the last and considerable remnant of Atlantis (and about which he completed only a handful of extant stories)—a continent that, it is obvious, had originally no less geographical variation than Zothique and Hyperborea. Similarly to the present collection, the volumes Zothique and Hyperborea are presented as interconnected series according to the inner chronology of the stories involved. However, in the case of these two volumes, the tales themselves deal almost unrelentingly with doom, death, and necromancy, and when assimilated en masse, one right after the other, the overall impression is one of considerably less variety of theme, content, and mood than what at first we might expect from the variegated backgrounds against which they are set. Apart from this one caveat, many of the stories are nevertheless individually outstanding, often outrageous, and startlingly original. Conversely, although not without their own structural logic, the volumes *Xiccarph* and *Poseidonis* offer for the most part an obvious variety of stories and poems to fill the collections out, and clearly have no pretension of being other than overt miscellanies of prose and verse.

As developed and presented by Ashton Smith (in manifest imitation of Auvergne), Averoigne by contrast, while still exhibiting some variety of form and feature, is nevertheless geographically, as the former Roman province of Averonia, a patently cohesive area, representing the Massif Central, the mountainous and forested heartland not only of southern France but also of France as a whole. Culturally the people living there are predominantly auvergnat, or (more properly) averoïgnat, speaking more or less the same dialect of French. But beyond the common geography, and in addition to Smith's omnipresent themes of death, loss, and necromancy, the Averoigne stories are super-romantic, patently more so than any other connected group of tales by this author, and feature love and romance in a variety of forms and appearances. Furthermore, in the instance of these especial tales, the women characters, many of whom literally are enchantresses, have obvious charm, fascination, savoir-faire, and that undeniable glamour which, in the perspective of the chief male character, the paramour, transforms the chief woman character, the enchantress, into a manifestation of the supernal and the ideal. Moreover, with all the attendant picturesqueness and grotesquery of those times, most of the extant stories take place during the long cavalcade of the Middle Ages, which is, of course, exactly when our modern, now rather generic, and curiously enduring concepts of romance and romanticism first came historically into being in all their outrageous efflorescence.

The note of supreme and uncompromising romance is struck at once by "A Night in Malnéant" as the opening story, which apparently occurs in a realm immediately contiguous to Averoigne. But beyond love and romance, and contained within the shared topography, inhering as a constant and ineluctable presence, there looms the vast and all-embracing Forest of Averoigne, concealing, revealing, interconnecting almost everything, or so it would seem, and extending from the mountains and woodlands on the north, south, east, and west all the way down to the marshes on the southeast where the now meandering Isoile, the chief river of the province, after leaving the great forest and passing through the extensive marshland, changes to the yet Lower Isoile and ultimately flows into the yet greater Rhône.

It is perhaps incumbent on us to continue this Festschrift in that spirit of exploration, discovery, and invention so characteristic of those various "matters," or bodies of material, favored for narrative use by medieval storytellers. In the essence of that very spirit we should consider some of the ramifications of known French history vis-à-vis this little-known French province. Due to a variety of reasons, by a miracle of historical accident, Averoigne like Auvergne was evidently spared the worst excesses of the Albigensian Crusade, which—conducted in Toulouse and Provence, among other areas, with such ferocity during the first half of the thirteenth century under the direction of Simon de Montfort—virtually destroyed not only the Albigensian heresy that had previously flourished during the eleventh, twelfth, and thirteenth centuries primarily in southern France, but also ruined the brilliant Provençal culture and lifestyle of the Middle Ages. The principal reason why Averoigne like Auvergne evaded the terrible fate meted out to Toulouse and Provence was elementary: richer and more easily accessible prizes existed elsewhere. What had started out as a religious war soon degenerated into an excuse for the princes of northern France to massacre and plunder at will, and thus to aggrandize and enrich themselves with goods and lands at the expense of the princes of southern France.

Some five hundred years or so later, again by a miracle of historical accident, Averoigne was also patently spared the worst excesses of the French Revolution during the 1790s. Likewise, it would seem, the province's great forest escaped, almost unscathed, the direst effects of the Industrial Revolution which followed. The ancient forest survived thus more or less intact into the nineteenth century, just as it does into

our own time in the twentieth. Now, thanks to some enlightened legislation emanating from Paris, the major portion of the extensive forest
enjoys virtual immunity as an enormous nature preserve as well as a
national treasure, unique in France.

The fact and effect of this fortunate preservation vis-à-vis certain
selected temperaments during the 1800s were sensitively recorded in
the latter part of that century by the poet and general man of letters
Gabriel d'Ysère, among other writings, in his picturesque itinerary *A
Walking-Tour of Averoigne* (*Un Tour à pied d'Averoigne,* first published in Lyon, 1881; translated into English by Sir Frank T. Marzials,
and published in London, 1912). A native of the town of Tournon on
the west bank of the Rhône but north of the Lower Isoile, d'Ysère
became fascinated with the idiosyncratic area of Averoigne to the west
and northwest early on in his childhood and adolescence. As a young
adult, he began recording the curious traditions and legends from
Greco-Roman antiquity and from the Middle Ages that had survived
among the peasantry of Averoigne.

A Walking-Tour of Averoigne details the route followed by two
youths in 1851 during the middle part of summer. They both came
from the same extended family of Néanvair but, oddly enough, each
from one of its two principal branches, the older and major one being
centered in Lyon east of the northernmost section of Averoigne, the
younger and minor one in Moulins north of the same geographic area. The story of the itinerary taken by the two youths and its aftermath passed down to d'Ysère, among other reasons, by virtue of his
own family's distant but longstanding relationship with the Néanvair
branch in Lyon. The account by d'Ysère not only includes some unusually lyrical descriptions of the ancient forest, but can still serve to
this day as a practical guide to the chief legendary as well as historical
sites of the old province.

To what extent—if indeed any—Ashton Smith was influenced in
his depiction of Averoigne by the preceding account and other writings of d'Ysère, as well as by those of other writers, has not yet been
completely or even partially determined. Certainly, in regard to the
overall geography as well as the flora and fauna peculiar to the area,
Smith developed and presented his conception of Averoigne in manifest imitation of Auvergne. In "The Maker of Gargoyles," the earliest

extant completed story that we have in terms of the (revealed) inner chronology of the over-all cycle of tales, the poet-author adumbrates the entire locale of Averoigne in a concise but sufficient style while overtly describing just the general situation of Vyônes.

> At that time, in the year of our Lord, 1138, Vyônes was the principal town of the province of Averoigne. On two sides the great, shadow-haunted forest, a place of equivocal legends, of loup-garous and phantoms, approached to the very walls and flung its umbrage upon them at early forenoon and evening. On the other sides there lay cultivated fields, and gentle streams that meandered among willows or poplars, and roads that ran through an open plain to the high châteaux of noble lords and to regions beyond Averoigne.

This description correlates well enough with Auvergne in a general way. As borne out by other chronicles in the same series, Averoigne is quite well forested and semi-mountainous in the same fashion more or less as Auvergne is both well forested and genuinely mountainous, rather than just semi-mountainous. Both Averoigne and Auvergne obviously have oak and beech forests, usually at the lower levels, together with stands of evergreen trees, including larches and pines, usually at the higher ones. Pursuing our imaginative equation of the two areas, we should note that, apparently in the same way as Averoigne, Auvergne is rich in lakes, ponds, pools, streams, and mineral springs. Rugged mountains alternate with rolling farmlands, stark summits contrast with sprawling forests of great oaks and beeches.

We know for a fact that Ashton Smith also definitely identified, in certain respects both actual and imaginative, his own native area with Averoigne. This native area included both Long Valley and Auburn, California, together with their general surroundings, located in the lower foothills of the Sierras. The Klarkash-Tonian identification of the general Auburn area with Averoigne is confirmed by external evidence such as that stemming from the visits to Smith by Rah Hoffman in the early 1940s, and as recorded by the same and other visitors in various memoirs. But the identification is also corroborated by the direct textual evidence preserved in Smith's own writings (including his personal letters), and especially (for one salient example) in such a poem as "To Howard Phillips Lovecraft," dated March

31st, 1937, and created almost immediately after H.P.L.'s death on March 15th of the same year.

> And yet thou art not gone
> Nor given wholly unto dream and dust:
> For, even upon
> This lonely western hill of Averoigne
> Thy flesh had never visited,
> I meet some wise and sentient wraith of thee,
> Some undeparting presence, gracious and august.

The imaginative equation of the Auburn area with Averoigne is also clearly borne out to some extent geographically. As regards the Auburn area's general topographical situation, rolling parklike expanses alternate with yet higher hills, fruit ranches or farms of fruit orchards alternate with stands of oaks and forests of pines. While Northern California gradually dries up during the summer and autumn until the rains arrive in the latter autumn, the weather is cool or cold and wet throughout the winter. During the rainy season and after, the land actually becomes green and lush, and while it still remains in this condition, the area could sustain a generic resemblance to Averoigne. However, unlike the mountains of Auvergne and the semi-mountains of Averoigne, the high Sierras of Northern California are still some considerable distance away, even though distinctly visible on a clear day. In a similar manner, Smith's native Auburn area has pines, larches, oaks, willows, and poplars, among other species of trees, but relatively few beeches.

In the corpus of Smith's works whether in verse or in prose—to pursue our imaginative equation of Auburn with Averoigne as a kind of generic principle of locale—Cocaigne also becomes, as does Amithaine, the imaginative equivalent of Averoigne. The landscape presented in the prose-poem "In Cocaigne" is an imaginative projection of Smith's native Auburn area. Two lovers, the poet and his sweetheart, go forth into the vertumnal forest. They pass first through a parklike area of oaks alternating with zones of vernal flowers, and then they enter the lonely woods of pine trees. There they find Cocaigne at last in each other's kiss and embrace.

In our imaginative equation of Auburn with Averoigne and other similar places, we have put considerable emphasis on woods and forest, because such locations loom large in both Smith's literary and artistic output whether as physical realities or as imaginative projections or as both, whether they are Smith's own native Californian forests, the dangerous and often lethal jungles featured in Smith's own concept of Hyperborea, or the gorgeous but patently lethal woodland that overcomes the child Natha in Smith's prose-poem "The Forbidden Forest," among many other examples that we could cite. Many, if not indeed most of, Smith's extant Averoigne stories take place completely or partially in the forest or ineluctably close to it. Two of the three unwritten chronicles that now survive only in the form of plot-sketches—these two being "The Oracle of Sadoqua" and "The Sorceress of Averoigne"—also take place almost completely in the forest.

Like the mountains, the desert, or the ocean, the forest from time immemorial has almost always functioned as a prime and primordial place of adventure, whether it is perceived or presented as mercilessly forbidding or miraculously beautiful. Like Longfellow's forest primeval in *Evangeline,* or like Dante's dark forest, or *selva oscura* (as described in the first canto of *The Divine Comedy*), the ancient Forest of Averoigne is a place not only of "equivocal legends" but of an ambiguous reality as well, whether sometimes grimly threatening, or at other times gorgeously inviting, or merely curiously affording consolation. The great forest allures us with its beauty and mystery as much as it can repel or deter us with its darkness and peril, as well as with its adumbration of the unknown and the otherworldly.

As for the writer of this afterword, he is himself actively planning, as a future tourist, an imminent vacation in Averoigne, aided not only by Ronald Hilger's useful map as well as by d'Ysère's walking-tour of the same area, but also, and especially, by the immediate advice of a close local friend whose profession is that of travel agent. The present writer must allow at least a month for his trip, or possibly even much more than that, since there is so much to see and to do in that ancient province. He has long desired to linger among the hallowed stones making up the imposing pile, half Romanesque, half Gothic, that is the Cathedral of Vyônes. He wishes to loiter among the no less hallowed stones of the venerable Abbaye de Périgon rising not very far from Vyônes. Perhaps he will visit the village of Ste. Zénobie, or further afield, the unhallowed ruins of the Château des Faussesflammes where it dominates the level area at the top of its own hill.

Or traveling much further afield, going eastward, he might spend the day (but certainly not the night!) at the grim and ruinous mass of the Château d'Ylourgne where it still lifts up from its semimountainous eminence. Or crossing the valley that gives birth to the river Isoile in the form of a small stream, he might pass to the other side and visit the Cistercian Monastery, about a mile distant from the castle. The monastery sits more or less midmost on the western slope of the valley. Here he might pause awhile and possibly say a silent prayer or two in the austere quiet of the monastery chapel, where the depredations wrought by the Colossus of Ylourgne have long since been repaired. The new stained-glass windows installed around the middle of the nineteenth century have been recently restored, and indeed look magnificent, especially at sunset and sunrise, when the light passing through them creates a kaleidoscope of shifting colors.

Then, rambling further south, along the banks of the Isoile, he will come eventually to the estate surrounding the still inhabited and superbly maintained Château de La Frênaie, and from there pass on by the Tomb of Malinbois. Perhaps he will wander on further until he reaches that inn once called the Auberge de la Bonne Jouissance, and then later the Auberge de la Haute Espérance, where he might spend the night after consuming a gourmet dinner in the excellent restaurant kept up there, accompanied by the still exceptional wines of Averoigne, especially those produced in the wine cellars of La Frênaie. Or later, the next morning, crossing the main road that leads from Vyônes to Ximes, he will visit the lonely but still somehow extant Tower of Moriamis where it rises amid the dense woods of the ancient forest. Or strolling back across the road, perhaps he will ford the Isoile where it flows not far away, and then climbing some high hill, he might catch a rare glimpse of the other-dimensional Tower of Séphora sitting somewhere near the top of her demesne of Sylaire.

At last he will arrive in Ximes, where he will visit that town's very own cathedral, perhaps not as large as that of Vyônes, but surely a magnificent example of Gothic Flamboyant. Built between 1450 and 1530, it replaced the earlier Romanesque structure destroyed by fire in

1445. From there it is only a few steps to the grandiose Bishop's Palace, brought to its height of architectural splendor in the latter part of the twelfth century through the efforts of the thrice-blessèd Bishop Azédarac. Linking the palace and the cathedral is the huge mausoleum reared for the selfsame St. Azédarac, duly canonized after his death in or around 1198. Evidently it never contained his body; the local legends hint that, like the Virgin Mary, he was transported to heaven alive.

Perchance next the traveler will move on from there to spend a few days in the charming and unpretentious village of Les Hiboux, located some real distance away to the south and west of Ximes. The village presently sits in the midst of dairy farms, and north of the extensive marshland formed by the now meandering Isoile. Then wandering north along the banks of the river, the traveler will come again to the main road that leads from Ximes to Vyônes, and following this westward, he will arrive at the ancient Auberge de l'Oracle, where he will put up for the night. Then he might very well spend the better part of the next day visiting the subterranean Caverne de St. Sodagui, once the dread Oraculum Sadoquae, and a favorite spot for tourists since the days of the Romans. The entrance to the cavern lies amid the deeper woods that extend towards the mountains of southwest Averoigne, an area still relatively uninhabited.

However, most of all the present writer wishes to pass as much time as possible taking long, long walks through whatever part of the great Forest of Averoigne that he happens to find himself near.

In the vertumnal season the forest becomes a riot of burgeoning verdure and vernal color as the trees and flowers unfold or unfurl into blossom. In the autumnal season the infinitely variegated green of the forest becomes a blaze of kaleidoscopic red, orange, yellow, brown, purple, and rust. But whatever the season, the forest is ever supernally beautiful, and forms a welcome retreat away from the bustling towns.

Nevertheless, for those readers who cannot at this time actually travel to Averoigne, the present volume—whether chronicle, romance, or novel—can suffice as a source of equivalent experience. To such readers the present writer can only say: Bon voyage! He can but envy those who have picked up this volume for the first time. In the venerable tradition of the best medieval storytellers, Ashton Smith serves indeed as an exemplary guide to the old province of Averoigne.

Thibaut di Castries, Revenant

Re-reading the modern classic novel of supernatural terror *Our Lady of Darkness* in its original form as *The Pale Brown Thing*—published in two parts in the January and February 1977 issues of the *Magazine of Fantasy and Science Fiction*—the student of its author receives ample proof of not just his innate superiority as a veteran fictioneer but, what is more, of how much Fritz Leiber wrote as a realist, albeit always with imaginative overtones.

A case in point, *The Pale Brown Thing* furnishes us with a perfect example of both his imaginative realism and the manner to which he extrapolated fiction out of his immediate life and environment, such as it was at that time, in this instance, the San Francisco of the late 1960s through the early 1990s, until his death on 5 September 1992 at almost a full eighty-two years (he had been born on 24 December 1910). The novel in question very much reflects, and amiably so, the Hippie Period that flourished in "the City" during 1965 through 1975, and then lingered in some form or fashion for some yet further time.

Shortly after the death of Jonquil, his wife of many years, Fritz moved to San Francisco during the Christmas season of 1969, with the assistance of a few close friends, including Margo Skinner, Gloria Kathleen Braly, and myself, Donald Sidney-Fryer (the latter two had just married), driving north from Los Angeles (from Venice to the south of Santa Monica) and its western littoral on the Pacific Ocean. Later Fritz retrieved his possessions from his former coastal residence near the so-called Boardwalk.

At first Fritz stayed for a while with friends, but as soon as he recovered from his prolonged grief over Jonquil's death (and concomitant alcoholic daze), he found his own residence. He settled in a small apartment in the same building and on the same floor as Margo Skinner, who for years typed up the final versions of his manuscripts. The small apartment in question was located in downtown San Francisco, at 811 Geary Avenue (the former Rhodes Hotel), just as described in *The Pale Brown Thing*. This building and its neighborhood figure with especial flair in both that short novel and its final incarnation, the

210

somewhat revised and expanded *Our Lady of Darkness.*

Our Lady of Darkness, Mater Tenebrarum, the mother of utter gloom and profoundest night, the manifestation of the utter lack of light, indeed!—who makes a terrifying and unforgettable appearance in the course of the novel.

Without exactly being a *roman à clef,* both versions of this hypernatural or "paranormal" story closely reflect real people and real places: downtown San Francisco and Corona Heights, with the Junior Museum nearby, to the northwest of the major intersection of Market and Castro Streets.

Fritz has assuredly rounded up a grand and fascinating cast of characters for his at first contemplative and then fast-moving narrative. He adumbrates himself as the writer of supernatural-horror fiction, Franz Westen; and, although deceased, Jonquil is also present in the story as Daisy, Westen's late wife. He based sister and brother Dorotea and Fernando Luque, both from Peru, on the then-manager of 811 Geary Avenue and her sibling. However, the young harpsichordist Calpurnia is not the shadow of Fritz's close friend Margo Skinner, as might be supposed; instead, he based Cal on some other person, a musician who had lived in the same building. Finally, the essential or quintessential books that Franz has piled along the inner edge of his bed (flush with the wall), which he dubs the "Scholar's Mistress," becomes a real person (however briefly) in the course of the narrative.

These people become the *dramatis personae* that animate the overarching narrative, that of the author's San Francisco of the early and mid-1970s. Meanwhile, in counterpoint to this plot, Fritz has another narrative happening in the background, an historical one involving Ambrose Bierce, George Sterling, Jack London, Nora May French, and Clark Ashton Smith.

Clark Ashton Smith was living near Auburn during the late 1920s, but sojourned on occasion in "the City" following the death of George Sterling, his great mentor, in November 1926. Between then and 1930, graduating from his poems in prose composed between 1912 and 1929, Smith began writing more mature short stories, whether fantasy or science fiction, and finished a dozen or more by 1930. Fritz cleverly and implicitly suggests that during one of these trips to San Francisco Smith had an encounter that may have inspired much of his later fiction. Who knows? But it is a wonderful and creative gambit!

The main and most mysterious character in the historical counter-narrative is a certain Thibaut de Castries. An intriguing name, de Castries was possibly based in part on Adolphe de Castro, otherwise known as Gustav Adolf Danziger (1859–1959). With this gentleman Ambrose Bierce collaborated on the short novel *The Monk and the Hangman's Daughter,* first published in the *San Francisco Examiner* in September 1891. Some data concerning this novel are in order here.

Bierce was first introduced to de Castro in 1886 by their mutual acquaintance Petey Bigelow. De Castro, then a twenty-three-year-old German Jew, formerly a rabbi, a lawyer, and then a dentist, is described as a "buzzing little gadfly" in Paul Fatout's excellent 1951 biography of Bierce. De Castro had made a rough translation of Richard Voss's *Der Mönch von Berchtesgaden,* first published in the German monthly magazine *Vom Fels zum Meer* (1890–91), which Bierce rewrote into much better English, also reshaping the narrative and adding the surprise ending.

The Monk and the Hangman's Daughter tells the story of the monk Ambrosius, who murders his loved one to prevent her from marrying someone else, the plot thus another variant of the Eternal Triangle. Although critic Clifton Fadiman thought that it lacked Bierce's characteristic voice, the translated novel remains a vivid, effective, and colorful opus; and also a rather grim one, like so much of everyday life during the Middle Ages in Europe. While all this may not seem immediately germane to *The Pale Brown Thing,* Fritz had read much of Bierce's output in depth, including this unique novel spawned between de Castro and "old man" Bierce. Something of the narrative might very well have entered into Thibaut de Castries's dangerous and enigmatic personality—especially the black magick secreted somehow into his published monograph, *Megapolisomancy,* and the curious journal probably written by Smith, inspired by his brief but close acquaintance with Thibaut.

Thanks to the certain black magick set in place by Thibaut before he died, embittered somehow by his encounter with the Auburn poet and fictioneer, a subtle curse against Smith also goes into operation against Franz Westen when he by chance activates the dormant sorcery. Once things get started in *The Pale Brown Thing*'s chief narrative, they happen with exemplary speed, as they do in Fritz's earlier, and now classic, supernatural novel *Conjure Wife,* the latter taking place in the late 1930s or early 1940s. Even though his entire career is marked by exceptional books—from his first collection of stories, *Night's Black Agents* (Arkham House, 1947), to his monumental science fiction novel *The Wanderer* in 1964—it is easy to overlook just what an outstanding writer Fritz Leiber had become by the late 1970s.

In any of the fictional narratives that he develops, Fritz describes his major or minor characters with great care and cunning, and plants his clues and portents with no less expertise. We have not yet mentioned one of the most notable characters in *The Pale Brown Thing,* as notable as Franz Westen in the present or Thibaut de Castries in the past. This character is Jaime Donaldus Byers, who serves as the major bridge between the modern narrative and the historical plot of the late 1890s.

Fritz based this character on selected aspects of the present writer, Donald Sidney-Fryer. And Fritz does very nicely by him! Donaldus Byers, a bisexual, resides with a female companion, an exotic Chinese, a live-in partner and mistress, in a restored two-story Victorian house on Beaver Street, going west upward to Buena Vista Park on one of the minor side streets off Castro Street, not far from the major intersection at Haight Street and Castro. Byers is apparently well-off in a financial sense and exists in the story as a dilettante and connoisseur—one who has an insider's knowledge of Thibaut. He does not share this information at once with Franz, and not until the latter becomes more deeply involved in *l'affaire* Thibaut as associated with Smith does Byers become more forthcoming.

It is true that Sidney-Fryer lived in San Francisco during the Hippie Period (again, at its most flourishing, basically the years 1965–75) and was a practicing bisexual or rather trisexual—that is, try anything sexual with human beings. And it is true that he had friends living in a Victorian house on the south side of Beaver Street, where he entertained lovers on various occasions. During the late 1960s and the early 1970s he was married to Gloria Kathleen Braly, and after several years of domestic bliss they divorced, but remained friends. He was also an artist-writer-poet-performer. Far from being well-off, he worked at and maintained a part-time business, lived simply and frugally, and, after ten years' labor, completed the first series of *Songs and Sonnets Atlantean* (published by Arkham House in 1971), shortly after which the owner-editor of Arkham House, August Derleth, passed on.

The historical narrative involving Thibaut de Castries, and other characters less fictional from *fin-de-siècle* San Francisco, does in fact reflect Fritz's own long-term fascination with Bierce, George Sterling, Jack London, Nora May French, Herman Scheffauer, and (last but not least) Clark Ashton Smith, as he became associated, albeit marginally, with the group via his mentor Sterling. But *The Pale Brown Thing* also reflects Fritz's long-term friendship with Sidney-Fryer, and the latter's insistent and persistent interest in the same group of writers, Clark Ashton Smith above all.

Sidney-Fryer began his own writing career as a scholar expounding in a series of essays on Smith as well as others in this group, subsequently identified as the California Romantics. These pieces were collected much later (along with others) in the volume *The Golden State Phantasticks* (2012). All during the composition of these essays, beginning in the early 1960s, Fritz and Sidney-Fryer had many intensive discussions concerning the California Romantics, their world, and their diverse literary productions.

It is indeed uncanny to what extent all, or most of, the characters and locations in this early version of *Our Lady of Darkness* parallel or echo real people and real places without becoming fictional stand-ins or substitutes—so close they are to the real things! However, more than this, *The Pale Brown Thing* does capture to perfection the atmosphere of San Francisco during the Hippie Period. But, as he did so in life, Fritz handles the hippies with respect, gentleness, and love, recognizing in them free spirits akin to his own.

We may doubt whether Fritz and Margo would recognize today the overall downtown district of San Francisco, so many and so lofty have the high-rise edifices become, dwarfing as they do most of the older, more modest and less pretentious buildings. The neighborhoods outside the downtown area remain extant and intact, more or less, as they have always maintained themselves. Along with the Junior Museum, the eminence of Corona Heights, which figures so prominently in *The Pale Brown Thing*, still survives and rises above the surrounding terrain. And still, despite all the new skyscrapers, the City has somehow—by some real miracle—retained much, if not most, of her old-time charm and fascination.

In a somewhat analogous way, *The Pale Brown Thing* has also retained its genuine and eerie enchantment, evoking as it does a rare and magical period in history that will never return, any more than will Fritz himself—alas! For those fortunate enough to have known him as a close friend, Fritz will always stand out as a rare and magical individual, and as I have stated many times over the years, Fritz remains, through his multifarious writings, a great thinker, a great writer, a great mentor and—above all else—a prince among friends, a friend of friends.

Auburn, California, 12 October 2015

Introduction to *Diary of a Sorceress*

In *Diary of a Sorceress* we possess a remarkable new collection, as well as an exceptional first book, by Ashley Dioses. In this debut gathering of macabre lyrics and longer poems, the Lady Ashiel has assembled almost one hundred offerings under four headings (or "entries"): "Atop the Crystal Moon," "Kiss the Stars," "Star Lighting," and "On a Dreamland's Moon."

These lapidary selections reveal a practiced auctorial hand and a keen and enshadowed imagination. The poet-author has already gained an enviable and hard-earned reputation for herself via the many appearances of her poems in various magazines especially devoted to fantasy and the macabre, whether in prose or in verse. A close poet-friend has aptly dubbed her the Lady Ashiel in the style of the Lady Mariel featured in the narrative "A Night in Malnéant," by Clark Ashton Smith. It makes a worthy appellation and brand-new name.

Ashley's many admirers will surely rejoice at having her well-honed poems (as extant up to now) all gathered in this notable assemblage, proffered under the title *Diary of a Sorceress.* From the first selection to the last, the poet conducts us on a wild and innovative tour of beauty and horror. Many of the shorter pieces in particular showcase her sense of all-pervasive but often fearsome beauty. The "Prelude: My Dark Diary" establishes at once the tone, the voice, that she maintains throughout the entire collection.

The title poem in the first section—dedicated significantly to George Sterling and Clark Ashton Smith, and often drawing upon their oeuvre—captures much of the breadth and height of the Lady Ashiel's vision. It is a vision steeped on the one hand in the poetry and lore of such California Romantics as Bierce, Sterling, Ashton Smith, and Nora May French among others, and equally steeped on the other hand in the poetry and lore of the magazine *Weird Tales,* but especially as preserved in book form by Arkham House under the astute direction of August Derleth, its owner-editor-author.

If the members of this group or school of writers enjoyed relatively little réclame during their lifetime, they have achieved posthumously a solid fame and reputation. And if they did not establish a particular school while alive, they certainly have done so half a century or more following their individual deaths. Today there is hardly a poet working in the tradition of fantasy and the macabre who does not claim an inheritance of one kind or another from one or more of these elder poets, whose work appears to have assumed the status of Holy Writ, all proportions guarded. We cite at random such representative contemporary figures as Richard L. Tierney, Ann K. Schwader, and Wade German, among many other names.

Into the notable company of these past and present poets, let us cordially welcome Ashley Dioses with her *Diary of a Sorceress.*

Auburn, California, 9 October 2016

H. P. Lovecraft—Beacon and Gateway

During the recent NecronomiCon III held in Providence, Rhode Island, at the Biltmore and Omni Hotels, during 17–20 August 2017, Thursday through Sunday, I could not fail to note several salient phenomena concerning certain things and events Lovecraftian. Along with quite a few others, I had been invited to function as one of the guests of honor, a distinction rarely given me and one to be cherished. Thanks to Derrick Hussey and Niels Hobbs, I appeared at the convention as poet laureate, a post created in accordance with the cultivated literary standards of poet and fictioneer Howard Phillips Lovecraft. I must say that the people who put on the convention had certainly provided a very rich smorgasbord of lectures, panel discussions, and other presentations concerning a wide range of subject and activity involving poetry, storytelling and other prose, as well as film. It resulted in a genuine *embarras de richesses.*

The earnest conventioneer would have had a hard choice to select what to attend when the options included multiple events of equal interest scheduled for the same hour. The convention people had surely arranged a splendid series of fascinating programs and afforded the paying customers a helluva lot for their money, besides assuring the smooth functioning and management of the convention itself, all possible praise to those behind (and before) the scenes. As ever, the vendor rooms with their many books as produced by a variety of publishers, not to mention T-shirts and other novelties, proved eminently stimulating.

I myself had the great good fortune to appear on a number of panels where I had enough ease and expertise that I could make intelligent and intelligible statements about the authors or literature being featured: Ambrose Bierce, Arthur Machen, modern imaginative poetry of the weird and fantastic, et alia. I also discovered or met people who admire some of my own writings, and for whom I signed their copies of my own books—always a gratifying experience, particularly for a relatively esoteric poet and author like myself. But, as always, or as often occurs at conventions, the principal gratification happens while encountering people in the halls and corridors and spontaneously striking up an earnest conversation. Meeting like-minded people fervently interested in the same subjects can often result in considerable pleasure, no less than in beginning new friendships.

Thus H.P.L. (may Cthulhu bless him as a fellow New Englander) had once again provided a wide umbrella to encompass a huge assortment of topics, readers, authors, poets, and what have you. I need not rehearse in any extensive detail, at least not to Lovecraftians, the now well-known known saga of how August Derleth and Donald Wandrei founded Arkham House to give greater permanence to Lovecraft's remarkable stories, poetry, and essays of the fantastic and supernatural by publishing a hardcover series of his collections beginning in the late 1930s and early 1940s. Through Derleth and Arkham House, H.P.L. posthumously came to provide a wide umbrella indeed for publishing many other authors and collections, which otherwise might never have found the dignity of hardcover book publication.

In the same way the different conventions honoring Lovecraft, starting at least with the first World Fantasy Convention in 1975 (and in the same Providence), as founded by Kirby McCauley, have come to provide a wide umbrella for many other authors and many other books. All this, done posthumously in Lovecraft's name, appears to myself, among many other authors who have benefited by the same big umbrella, as an extraordinary legacy. As a fellow New Englander I take great pride in that achievement. Lovecraft's name and fame have now spread throughout much of the far-reaching Anglophone world covering much of planet earth; and where unknown in English, he is known in accomplished translation in quite a few languages.

During NecronomiCon III I could not help but reflect on how Lovecraft through his own writings, and through his influence by way of Derleth and Arkham House, as well as the ensuing propagandizing, has become, almost more than metaphorically, a beacon and a gateway not only for critics, readers, and literary connoisseurs, but thus also a beacon and a gateway for many other authors and other types of creators (pictorial artists, sculptors, makers of films and television features). Thus dear H.P.L. has achieved not just cult status but near universal promulgation. For an unassuming antiquarian and (at one time) an obscure mythographer, that represents a deed at once exceptional and colossal, something tremendous. In that sense the pen is mightier than the sword. I venture to say that the more ample opportunity he has created for other and lesser-known authors would give H.P.L. a huge amount of delight and satisfaction. May no negative reaction to this statement emanate from any committed Lovecraftian!

Recently there has come into my hands a fine journal-review, *Dead Reckonings,* the issue for Fall 2017, as ably edited by Alex Houstoun and Michael J. Abolafia, and published by the ever innovative and enterprising Hippocampus Press, as directed by the enlightened owner-editor Derrick Hussey. I have perused this issue deliberately and with great care, not only in regard to the excellent notices given to a variety of books and other materials (unusually extended and sensitive to the authors under review, their intentions and nuances), but especially to the reminiscences by diverse writers apropos of the recent NecronomiCon III. I can only regret that Kirby McCauley can no longer see the later result of what he started in 1975, by having the first World Fantasy Convention take place in the same town, H.P.L.'s own city par excellence.

We can merely mention in passing such extraordinary notices as those by James Machin à propos Joachim Kalka's *Gaslight;* by Jim Rockhill à propos Zoe Lehmann Imfield's *The Victorian Ghost Story and Theology;* and by Daniel Pietersen à propos Jeffrey Thomas's *Haunted Worlds.* And I don't envy S. T. Joshi having to review an anthology of contemporary weird stories that would seem to be a very mixed bag indeed.

I find myself particularly indebted to the reminiscences of NecronomiCon III by writers other than myself: "A Few Reflections" by Martin Andersson; "Curating Ars Necronomica 2017" by Brian L. Mullen III; "Musings: NecronomiCon 2017" by Dean Kuhta; "Vibrant and Vivid: Necronomicon 2017" by Elena Tchougounova-Paulson; "A Reflection: Necronomicon 2017" by Dr. Géza A. G. Reilly. These relate to events or phenomena that I could not attend (for whatever reason) in spite of my keen interest. I find fascinating what I discover about the artists John Jude Palencar and Sarah Horrocks, whose art I did not get to see, but which I can glean from the articles on, or interviews with, these artists with accompanying illustrations.

All the above puts me in a better position to continue reflecting on NecronomiCon III, not only as aided and abetted by other writers in attendance thereat, but also as inspired by the general tone and direction of the overall journal relative to H.P.L. himself. As invariably the odd man out (for much of my life, but less these days as a respected senile citizen), my reflections or observations may have some value for other readers.

I notice in many of the articles the near constant reference to the horrors created or inspired by Lovecraft and his tales of *supernatural* horror. I rarely note the use of *supernatural* relative to this horror, but it differs significantly from other kinds of horror such as those enumerated by history in general, so much of which remains a catalogue of horrors and atrocities that actually occurred: the destruction of Bagdad by the Mongols; the destruction of the Roman city of Cremona by a Roman legion; the organized pogroms of the Jews under the latter Tsarist regime; the death camps operated by the Nazis; and, at the end of 2017, the ethnic cleansing of the Rohingya Muslims out of the otherwise eminently Buddhist country of Myanmar, the former Burma.

Obviously Lovecraft in his fiction is dealing with quite a different kind of horror, rather than with pure grue, which did not interest him as a fictioneer. He had a strong sense of aesthetics that guided him in his fictional but serious revelations, no less chilling than pure grue, but infinitely more artistic.

Rather than regarding his novels and short stories as horror stories, albeit of supernatural horror—such a simplification does an artist of his high calibre a grave injustice—I prefer to regard his prose fictions, particularly the longer tales, that is, *At the Mountains of Madness,* "The Shadow out of Time," "The Shadow over Innsmouth," and so forth, as existential parables, or parables of existential unease, to remind us modern rationalists that the scheme of things might be darker, much darker, than what we care to entertain all alone by ourselves. Enlightenment through a glass darkly, as it were!

A Poetic Original

G. SUTTON BREIDING. *Ill Desperado, 2013/2014.* A collection of ten free-verse and/or free form poems. A booklet 8½ × 11 inches, 12 pages, glossy black cover (some kind of card material), poems photocopied from elegantly hand printed sheets. An edition de luxe as a privately printed or published book or booklet. Issued only to friends and fellow poets. August 2018.

In its own way *Ill Desperado*—the title is a clever take on Gérard de Nerval's melancholic sonnet "El Desdichado"—is almost as exceptional (although much smaller and with different proportions) as Frank Coffman's tome *The Coven's Handbook* (2018/19).

On the dedication page of his *Selected Poems,* Clark Ashton Smith quotes what seems his own translation of the first four lines of Nerval's lyrical poem "El Desdichado." Nerval is that unique precursor as a great poet to Baudelaire with *Les Fleurs du mal,* just as Aloysius Bertrand with his *Gaspard de la Nuit* is the unique precursor to Baudelaire with his *Poèmes en prose.*

> I am that dark, that disinherited,
> That all-dishonored prince of Aquitaine.
> The star upon my scutcheon long hath fled,
> A black sun on my lute doth yet remain.

Actually the translation stems from the pen of Andrew Lang. Whether in English or in French, it has very strong affinities with the final poem in Sutton Breiding's most recent collection. We quote this final poem in full to demonstrate him as a full-fledged legatee of Nerval, Baudelaire, and Rimbaud, albeit an original and considerable figure in his own right, and one who mines his own vein of melancholy and the beautiful, no less his disaffection or discontent with his own era.

> I am that wasted
> that dysfunctional troubadour
> hanging in a noose of silk stockings
> from the overburdened lamp post of hopes

above the Stygian gutters
where my diamond sonnets putrefy
I snap my lute strings one by one
disconsolate as a neutron sun
in the toxic void of that birth canal where Death was waiting
with the charred escutcheon of my inheritance
smeared all over in the blackest of lipsticks
of all the kisses I dishonored with a poem

I have long followed the life and career of Sutton Breiding, probably since the later 1960s in San Francisco, where I lived during 1965–75, in fact through the whole hippie period. We most likely met through the auspices of Don Herron, himself a recent arrival from Tennessee, just as Sutton and his family, mother and siblings, hailed from Morgantown, West Virginia. They resided at that time in a several-storied family house in the Haight-Ashbury district. I myself resided in a big flat in a similar but larger building not far from where Haight and Ashbury intersect.

Soon Sutton began issuing the notable series of his handmade and homemade booklets containing his poetry, at once free verse and free form, remarkable for its depth and the great variety of its wide-ranging imagery. We often visited back and forth between our respective domiciles, and I even stayed overnight at the Breiding abode several times, in addition to sharing their regular meals. They made a lively and enjoyable household. We passed many pleasant evenings together, and I cherish the memories that I still have of those happy times.

Of course, we had all become united through our fervid interest in modern imaginative literature as purveyed not only by Lovecraft, Smith, Robert E. Howard, etc., but also by *Weird Tales* and Arkham House, i.e., August Derleth. And here we wish to pay tribute, a big tribute, to a veteran and fellow poet, one G. Sutton Breiding, on the basis of his last booklet, in case we have not so done before.

Sutton has assuredly stayed the course, whether receiving laudation or brickbats. He has followed his own star, his own Muse, forthrightly. That says a lot for a poet in America who does not receive mainstream recognition. At his age Sutton should have a volume of his collected poems published in his honor by some acolyte in conjunction with a small press other than the poet's own. Let us quote some random lines from his latest booklet to give the reader an idea of Sutton's range and characteristic imagery. Let us grant the poet himself the last significant word or phrase.

chewing on air
I chase my manias in shrinking circles
hypnotized by the psychedelic monitors
in the hospital of words

it's the tragedy of the mystic impulse
bejeweled staircases going nowhere
magical toys that broke long ago

I medicate
with words and walks
gaze at the river in supernatural dawns

what is all this starry-eyed nonsense
the smeared snot of dreams all over the place

I ride my skeleton horse to Death
the beggar king of fog and off ramps
out among the powerlines and derelict toilets

the past was once a Goth chanteuse
crooning in the dead city of my heart

I am haunted unto madness
by the strangeness of this world

from the slimy troughs of verse
I dig my way to another unrequited day

I croak and stutter over stacks of paper
my hands hardening into the luminous mud of language

I'm on my way there down that dark lane

with my solid gold jetpack strapped on tightly

in the meantime my rotting head
screams out its erotic dirges

and terminally ill chimaeras lick at me
with the barbed and merciless piercings
of their long and golden tongues

No doubt about it, G. Sutton Breiding remains one of the great poetic originals of our time and still abides with us!

Dark Oracles Indeed

D. L. MYERS. *Oracles from the Black Pool.* New York: Hippocampus Press, 2019. 136 pp. Cover art and 21 illustrations by Daniel V. Sauer. $15.00 tpb.

This is a magnificent little volume remarkable not only for its contents—its raison d'être, the original poetry—but for the striking and original art as manifested on its front cover, no less than the nearly two dozen illustrations inside the book. Even if only a slender volume at 136 pages, it packs a wallop with its substantial main text. Myers here presents himself (thanks to Derrick Hussey's ongoing crusade on behalf of new poetry through Hippocampus Press) as an exceptional poet, strong and intense, even if cloaked outwardly as a calm and moderate-seeming individual in the everyday social milieu. The book itself arrives very well recommended and judiciously so, preceded by a notable preface of appreciation by K. A. Opperman, and succeeded after the main text by four deserved tributes from his siblinghood of poet-friends, Opperman, Ashley Dioses, and the irrepressible balladeer par excellence, Adam Bolivar. We had thought that dark fantasy as expressed in verse had exhausted itself, but no, this magisterial small volume proves the present critic wrong. The three poets along with Myers himself make up a special cénacle (connected in person or electronically by the Internet) that calls itself the Crimson Circle; the crimson requires no gloss.

Myers is a strong and inventive traditionalist, working within older forms, meters, and rime, and performing very well, no less than in free verse and prose-poetry. Whether experienced as presented here front to back, or merely sampled casually here and there, these poems, these oracles, prove a constant revelation, especially as punctuated by small pieces of verse, such as these four haiku, which we quote as our first citations, as evidence of Myers's invention and imagination.

Haiku One

Longing for snowflakes
In hot California sun
Tree waits for kisses.

Haiku Two

Undulating leaf
Restlessly waiting for wind
To take flight again.

Haiku Three

Ice-cold, grey rain clouds
Lie broken a cross blue sky
While I sit gazing.

Haiku Four

Her profile flutters
Among stray strands of brown flax
Tempest waves as silk.

Myers has created an exceptional ambiance for his macabre visions, a new town creatively and beautifully called Yorehaven (a memorable name), to be found somewhere not far away from Lovecraft's Arkham or Innsmouth or his own Providence, Rhode Island, as reimagined by that master in his darkling fictions major or minor, in verse and in prose. We might personally hesitate to visit Yorehaven ourselves unless escorted by a goodly company of sibling aficionados possibly armed with clubs, spears, guns, and pistols. The ambiance to which Myers introduces us appears to teem with a variety of monsters including vampires, werewolves, and more intimidating prodigies of terror or even horror as spawned from the author's ever prodigal imagination—eek! (Let us hide under the covers or under the bed.) Never mind bizarre specimens from the plant kingdom!

The Phosphorescent Fungi

A crawling darkness pressed upon my eyes
In which a moiling sea of phantoms swam,
And crazed, I hungered for a numbing dram
To send my mind to where all reason flies,
Until before me rose a fitful fire,
A corpse-light foul and bruised that chilled my soul,
Yet drew me onward toward a ghastly goal—
A grotto burning like a purple pyre!

And then I saw the things that cast that glow,
Pale fungi vile and stained with rank decay ;

And bathed in icy sweat from head to toe,
I stood and quaked before that dire display.
Then evil whispers hissed about my ears,
And I broke down in horror wracked with tears.

Well, we ourselves as reader-critic might very well follow suit! We cannot resist quoting another poem, a succinct quatrain.

Autumn Moon

The gibbous moon in ruddy cowl
Rides wild in the autumnal sky
While coyotes in the cornstalks howl
And dance to see it soaring high.

But these few poems as quoted in this review can give only a tithe of the wealth of grim imagination and invention on display in this volume, not to leave unmentioned the poet's exquisite craftsmanship. The poet has arranged the more than five dozen morceaux that he presents here as follows, that is, under these inviting seven section titles: The Streets of Yorehaven, The Acolytes of Samhain, The Summons, The Star's Prisoner, The Canker Within, The Temple of the River Goddess, and O Dark Muse. The section of four tributes by his fellow poets comes at the very end of the miniature tome.

Myers find himself in excellent company, in the fine and sympathetic siblinghood of like-minded poet-bards known as the Crimson Circle. He well deserves the tributes, as well as the just and judicious recommendation (on the volume's back cover) as penned by S. T. Joshi, that doyen of connoisseur-critics and creative scholars. Warmest congratulations to poet D. L. Myers first and foremost, next artist D. V. Sauer, and then D. Hussey, Hippocampus Press personified!

Letters to "The Lion's Den"

February 2005

Dear Editor:

One of the unexpected pleasures of *The Cimmerian,* and a definite indication of what a classy publication it is—as well as of its serious intent and accomplishment—is its presentation of new poetry, if not always directly inspired by REH, at least sharing certain heroic and/or historical qualities like those found in Howard's own pulsing and imaginative poems.

Each of the five issues making up Volume 1 (2004) of the magazine features a poem that is thoughtful, well-crafted, well-sustained, and sometimes even profound. Issue Number 1 (April) ends with a fine and fierce battle hymn, "The Stain of Victory" by Richard L. Tierney, as strong an item of this type as any by Howard himself. Issue Number 2 (June) includes quite a thoughtful and incisive piece (in open form, or free verse), "Near the End of the Epic," by Darrell Schweitzer, singing the praises of all those who made battle, who made victory possible for the anointed hero/chief/king, but who died unsung and unremembered, "the thousands of lives washed away like ashes scattered on the seashore at the turning of the tide." As we know from his fine volume *Groping toward the Light* (containing "Poems for Midnight and After," Wildside Press, 2000), Darrell is an excellent poet, working with equal strength whether in open or traditional forms.

Issue Number 3 (August) features a long, well-crafted, and well-sustained, and very moving tribute to REH and his memory by Frank Coffman. This outstanding memorial piece semi-systematically catalogues or acknowledges much of the typical subject matter so powerfully delineated by Howard whether in prose or in verse. The opening and closing stanzas in particular (i.e., stanzas 1 and 17) capture not only a real essence of Howard's epic output but also the poignancy **and** limited compass of his too-short lifespan.

> Lingering awhile, he finally up and left,
> Climbing the Texas sky that afternoon,
> Leaving a legacy for those bereft:
> Great stores of tale and song. But left how soon!

[. . .]

And looking down upon the panoply
Of all those storied lands and peoples far:
One lingering sigh, and then—a breaking free
A shout, a rush—to where the Ages are.

Issue Number 4 (October) presents quite a powerful narrative poem of eleven stanzas about Simon Magus, cast in sonorous fourteen-syllable lines, "Vengeance Quest," again by Richard L. Tierney, whose lilting cadences directly recall those by REH as highlighted, for example, in such a similar story poem as "The King and the Oak."

I particularly like the final stanza, which has an Howardian resoluteness about it.

"Oh, leave us not!" his comrades cried.
                    "Why would you seek your doom?
"Journey with us to safer lands
                    and spare your soul from gloom:"
But Simon the Mage in steely rage
                    strode off with sword in hand.
They watched him vanish in the mists
                    of that grim and god-cursed land.

Issue Number 5 (December) presents a translation by myself from the French of one from among the 117 (quite unconventional but incisive) sonnets, "To a Dead City," in the one and only collection, *Les Trophées* (1893), by Jose-Maria de Heredia (1842–1905). The city in question is Cartagena-de-las-Indias on the northwest Caribbean coast of Colombia—the major port where formerly gathered (every year from the early 1530s until about 1800) the ships making up the treasure fleet that carried its lavish cargos to Spain at the height of the Spanish Empire. Despite the pirates who swarmed to prey on this fleet, most of the treasure managed to make it through to the Iberian Peninsula. The Hispano-French poet skillfully evokes the vanished splendor of this antique metropolis with its gigantic walls.

And when the nights hang heavy
                    with their heat and calm,
Soothing your lost renown,
                    O City, how you slumber
Beneath the palms,

the long, long whispering of palm fronds.

These lines gain an added poignancy when the reader learns that it was the poet's own direct ancestor who founded Cartagena, named after the Cartagena in Spain, thus in 1532. This was none other than Pedro de Heredia, one of the original Conquistadors himself.

December 2005

Dear Sieur Leo,

Greetings and Salutations! Just a note to register my reaction(s) to the last two issues of your cooking magazine, "The Simmer-ian"! The Awards issue—great quotes!—proved as interesting as the regular one for October 2005, and in particular exemplifies the warm and generous to perfection tone of the editorship. I read with emotion and approval of the Black Circle Award going to Glenn Lord, who long before anyone else preserved, sought out, and guided REH's oeuvre when no one else did. Superbly well deserved! And I'm glad that the mag itself won an award as well, also very well deserved.

As for the October issue itself, it maintains the high quality that the magazine has consistently demonstrated. Chas. Hoffman masterfully enlightens us on Howard's last new series built around a character, a chief persona who goes or evolves from rogue to scoundrel. Leon Nielsen's article about locating the "real" Cimmeria in "Himmerland," David Hardy's "Veiled Prophet," and James Reasoner's indeed "Small World" also proved enjoyable and enlightening—and Anthony Avacato's "Bed Beneath the Stars" makes for a heartfelt and well-wrought piece of homage to REH.

"The Lion's Den" as usual made for some lively and stimulating entertainment. I do hope that we may put to rest the Don Herron/Darrell Schweitzer controversy over F. Wright as editor of *W.T.* For quite some little time I had rather sided with Darrell—I do think that Wright deserves credit as editor for keeping the Unique Magazine alive as long as he did!—but this last volley from Herron has finally convinced me that *his* assessment of Wright is the correct one overall, especially in the editor's dealings with REH and HPL both before and after their respective deaths. And I do now consider that Wright's negotiations with CAS also added quite a bit to the disgust that Smith eventually felt so strongly that he quit writing fiction—he had had it with capricious editors!

Both the October and Awards issues as physical products are a delight to handle, as ever. *Bravissimo* to you for producing such a consistently interesting and physically handsome product—you deserve all credit for your sterling work.

March 2006

Dear Leonid,

Thanks yet once again for the latest issue, that of January 2006. As ever, it is excellent! I wish you luck in having *The Cimmerian* appear every month during the current calendar year. You have set yourself quite a task, but I hope that you will indeed succeed in doing so, particularly now that you'll have some extra heads and eyes to help you. You'll need them!

This is an unusually thoughtful issue. "The Lion's Den" is its usual contentious self, and although I don't take sides, I feel that Leon Nielsen makes a very good case for Cimmeria in Denmark, given that REH was proud of his partial Danish ancestry. Quite a fine letter!

Richard L. Tierney's poetry seems better than ever—he's one of the few brave poets who are not afeared to use genuinely outmoded poeticisms like "'neath" and "n'er." *Poetic* images and *strong* meter!

The report "Disaster in Cross Plains" and the poignant obituary of Zora Mae Baum Bryant certainly give one pause, no less than food for thought and reflection. It's a miracle that the Howard House managed to survive! Big Jim's article "REH and Guns" is a good strong blast of clean air blowing in from the south of West Virginia. *The Cimmerian* can well do with more articles like this one. REH knew his guns as Big Jim does his own!

The two leading articles I perceive are your own "Birth and Death" and especially Rusty Burke's terse "The Nore." The story of REH before his death going to the typewriter and pounding out that famous couplet does indeed make quite a satisfying detail in the narrative. However, the homely alternative—finding a white slip of paper with the couplet already on it inside his billfold—I find more likely by its very homeliness and unpretentious quality. It has an everyday ring to it that I find far more likely than the usual story. But each to his own preference!

As for the famous couplet itself as authored by Viola Garvin, and as derived from the anthology of poems *Songs of Adventure* (1926)—while strangely not included in her one and only book of poems in verse, *Dedication* (1928)—her dates are instructive: born in 1898 and died in 1969. Inasmuch as her poetry is labeled a little derivative, it must be stated in all fairness that poets have been deriving from each other since time immemorial, and not necessarily out of plagiarism. Ernest Dowson remained quite popular with readers of poetry long after his own *fin-de-siècle*. His dates are also instructive (1867–1900), and it is obvious that Viola well knew the "Cynara" poem, and consciously or unconsciously quoted part of it in her own "The House of Cæsar" as revealed by Rusty in his previous article in *The Dark Man* No. 5. It whets one's appetite to seek the two volumes out in the nearest major public or university library. Incidentally, the title for Margaret Mitchell's remarkable novel *Gone with the Wind* comes from the same poem by Dowson.

Again, bravo for a splendid issue!

July 2006

Dear Leo,

Finally, but finally, I found the time to read the March and April issues, and they continue and maintain the high standards that you have created for the magazine.

David Hardy's article in the April issue is one of the best articles that I've read—ever—on REH. I don't know the El Borak character and that series, but David makes an excellent case for him.

The article on Tolkien and Howard by Steven Tompkins deserves a special mention and commendation. Thanks again for two more excellent issues!

August 2006

Dear Leo,

Just another statement of admiration and praise for the last two issues of *The Cimmerian,* those for June and July! You consistently uphold the high standards long since established for your special and specialist magazine. *Bravo,* if not *Bravissimo!* I look forward with the keenest anticipation to the remaining issues for the year 2006.

Bill Cavalier's long and fascinating memoir "How Robert E. Howard Saved My Life" easily takes pride of place in the issue for June. Despite all the good-humored tone, it remains a very moving personal piece, even quite poignant in places. I found the account of the first Howard Days in June of 1986 especially interesting and heartwarming.

Ditto for Rick Kelsey's "Celebration of the Century," the account of this year's Howard Days in the issue for July. I enjoy particularly the honor being paid to Glenn Lord both in 2005 and 2006—he deserves it! Albeit I have not corresponded with Glen in years, I well recall his pioneering efforts on behalf of REH, his specialist magazine, *The Howard Collector,* and the first ever REH bibliography, *The Last Celt.* Without Glenn an enormous amount of valuable material would have been irretrievably lost!

HPL was already well established when both Glenn and I were conducting our researches on REH and CAS respectively. Neither author had achieved any great circulation and recognition back in the 1950s and 1960s, and being pioneer scholars for authors too glibly dismissed as hacks writing for pulp magazines, we may have found it rather lonely. But both of us persevered, not knowing then that at some point in the future we would find ourselves in the company of many other aficionados such as we do today.

Incidentally, that's a great picture of Don Herron taken by Rick Kelsey on p. 20 of the July issue—with a faint smile on his face while holding forth to the onlooker two bottles of beer, one in either hand! Don's letter in the July issue covers *five* full pages! At that length it's a veritable essay. "The Lion's Den" proves consistently lively and opinionated. Insofar as I am concerned, Don could have a special department apart from "The Lion's Den" all to himself yclept "Letter to the Editor." He's the magazine's best polemicist!

However, I second Leon Nielsen's healthy and wholesome stance that the letters in general should not descend to personal attacks and incivilities—they often come awfully close to the latter. Reading the various letters in the last four issues—April, May, June, and July—and noting the divers comments on certain favorite authors of modern imaginative fiction such as Howard, Lovecraft, and Smith, I often find

myself in agreement, sometimes in disagreement, but always entertained and enlightened.

Reading also *R. H. Barlow on Lovecraft and Life,* the booklet
that you so kindly gave to Rah, I am reminded as I have never been
before just how urban HPL actually was, and how relatively helpless
he turned out to be in a rural setting, when he visited Barlow and his
family at Barlow's then-home in Florida during May and June of
1934, and when Lovecraft went berry picking with Barlow and another person. After staying behind in the woods to fill his bucket, he
them promptly lost most of its contents when he missed the board
crossing the stream to return home and fell into the cold water up to
his neck, poor guy (HPL suffered from poor eyesight). Luckily he
endured no real damage beyond that to his dignity as a gentleman of
the old school.

Still, I can't help but compare him with REH and CAS, both of
whom found themselves perfectly at home in rural or rustic settings,
REH in the wild countryside of Texas and CAS in the beloved woodland around his cabin outside old Auburn to the southeast. Although
CAS loathed cities, he knew how to take care of himself living almost
in frontier conditions with his mother and father. REH knew how to
handle himself in cities and in countryside, in polite society as well as
in environments full of pretty tough characters.

Please keep up the high quality of *The Cimmerian!*

August 2007

Dear Sieur Leo!

Thanks yet once again for another creditable issue of *The Cimmerian,* i.e., Vol. 4, No. 2, April 2007. I read this latest issue with
much less enthusiasm than usual, due not to any lack in the issue itself but more to the fact that much or most of it is devoted to negative
commentary of divers authors or editors inadequate to their chosen
task of dealing with aspects of R. E. Howard criticism. I must admit at
once that the negative commentary seems justified, and then some:
Rob Roehm on Michael Moorcock, Morgan Holmes on S. T. Joshi,
and Brian Leno on the redoubtable Ben "Zoom"!

One of the legitimate concerns of a specialist magazine such as
The Cimmerian must center not just on the triumphs of criticism on

behalf of the given or anointed writer or poet himself—in this case, REH—but on the less than brilliant (even if well-intentioned) lucubrations attempting to deal with him and his literary output. But for some reason I saved reading "Our Labor of Love" until the last, and for me it turned out to be the best piece this time in the entire issue. I had not forgotten what a good editor Leo is, but I overlooked what a good scrivener he remains.

I don't care to embroil myself in the finer points of scholarship on behalf of REH, but rather want to support, and as strongly as I can, the negative and supremely justified comments that Leo makes about book and other graphics as of now, a point also made by Dennis McHaney in his letter in "The Lion's Den" in the same issue. The fact that McHaney's professional credits are in the field of graphic design gives his remarks all the more credibility.

These comments that Leo makes find a forthright chorus in myself, *sic:*

> There's been a lot of chatter in fandom lately about the poor quality of even the most expensive books pouring into the field of late, whether they be The REH Foundation's wild margins and depressingly inappropriate covers, or Girasol's $100 price tags for enormous books lilting inside glued boards. When a real bookman—a believer in the primacy of the words and a lover of the sensual and tactile aspects of reading—pays $50-$100 for books tarnished by sophomoric aesthetics, you can't help but feel cheated.

Speaking of *Weird Tales,* Dennis makes a similar point, sic:

> What have my professional credentials got to do with how lame *Weird Tales* is? . . . my professional credentials are in the field of graphic design, something no one at the current version of *Weird Tales* seems to know anything about.

For my own taste, I can settle for a decently formatted and printed magazine or book done in the ordinary way, without illustrations or fancy graphics.

Cheers!

June 2008

Dear Leo,

Thanks for the news about the change in editorship at *Weird Tales* ("The Lion's Den," *The Cimerrian,* Vol. 4 , No. 1). Overall, Schweitzer and Scithers did a good job. But if it benefits the magazine, then the change seems justified. I will admit that I am surprised that this actually happened, but I can't say that I disapprove.

Under the Radar

As I understand the term embodied in this autobiographical essay's title, "under the radar" as a common expression means beyond or beneath ordinary surveillance or perception. As a child in New England I lived through World War II, which is when in 1941 some brilliant scientist, or scientists, invented radar as a device or system for detecting and identifying objects in motion (enemy aircraft above all). The etymology of the word reflects its logical derivation or purpose: *r*adio *d*etection *a*nd *r*anging (using radio waves). Of course, the term soon passed into the ordinary language of everyday, as in "on the radar" or "off the radar"—thus easily perceptible or observable, or not.

Perhaps because I was born in 1934, and thus grew up during 1934-45, during the first and considerable usage of radar as device or term, it impressed me. Was there no place, no refuge, away from, or against, easy detection, especially by those ever vigilant persons called adults?! However, in general at the time during 1941-45 (World War II took place during 1939-45), the invention of radar became a source of relief relative to attacks by enemy aircraft as part of the national defense mechanism. At the time it primarily registered with me that the adults were looking after us kids and our safety.

Certainly the sneak and unprovoked attack on 7 December 1941 without warning by Japanese aircraft on Pearl Harbor, Oahu, Hawaii, meaning on both the ships in that body of water and the U.S. naval air station established there, made an impression on, and registered with, the consciousness of the U.S. at that moment! I reached eleven by the end of the war in 1945, and I remember celebrating the first Pearl Harbor Days, with gratitude.

Perhaps because of growing up under the giant Nazi or Japanese threat, one in the east, the other in the west, I first became conscious of how a person might want to do something, not necessarily in a clandestine manner, but quietly and unobserved, under or off the radar, so to speak. At some point during my four years in high school (the academic years of 1949-50, 1950-51, 1951-52, and 1952-53), I realized that I did not quite conform to the stereotypical profile of the then average teenager.

I had long since discovered adolescent sex in the Boy Scouts and among the other high school students, the normal homosexual activity, no big deal. But then I realized further that guys attracted me much more. Women and girls I avoided for obvious reasons; they remained off limits. I did not want to become a father, and I did not want to get a female pregnant, surely not while I passed through my pre-adult years in high school. I would investigate women, but later, whenever, once I became an adult, once I became eighteen or twenty-one.

I had my military service to fulfill, and my college or university education to undergo, but only after I gained my honorable discharge from the military. One thing at a time, and in due course. My sex life, such as it was, I kept to myself, since I very much wanted acceptance in regular social terms, whether at school or on the job. Thus I had early learned to keep my sexual thoughts and preferences to myself, on the premise of sheer self-preservation.

However, despite my care and caution, or because of it, I did wander on occasion into some bower of bliss, of erotic desire or delight, with some other male. No big deal. It began to happen more and more often. As the reader can see, I was already operating under the radar, and had been for quite a period of time. Sex with guys was easy, always accessible and performable, despite a rare attack of lice or crabs, usually eradicated via some prescribed special lotion, or a not so rare attack of some venereal disease, typically banished via penicillin.

But these consequences of promiscuousness erotic and otherwise appeared much less expensive and elaborate than what would have developed in my life as a regular married or unmarried man!—that is, as dealing with human females. I absolutely did not want, and still do not want, to be a parent! I have mentored and nurtured other individuals (generally younger than myself) but as creative people. *That* suffices! Living among homosexual folk, as in San Francisco during 1965-75, it never came up as a problem, except among heterosexual people, who were and are always urging unmarried men to hurry up, get married, and raise a family. That option has remained anathema to me as my choice.

Without realizing it earlier in my life, I had become part and parcel of the huge army everywhere of the LGBTQ, an awkward abbreviation but too convenient not to use. When I first encountered it almost out of context, I thought that it meant some kind of exotic sandwich or pie or combination of both!—such as the "Lettuce Garbanzo Bean Tomato Quiche" special. Of course, now I know that it means "lesbian, gay, bisexual, transgender, queer (or questioning)," nothing exotic or culinary about the term at all.

As already stated, I had become habituated to operating or living under the radar, not just sexually, but simply as a private person enmeshed in private matters as, for example, those involving art, religion, or philosophy. Now this régime or regimen conducted under the radar would extend to my earliest creative efforts as an adult, such as reading, researching, scrivening, and editing.

This happened to occur during my three years in the U.S. Marine Corps. Stationed at the Marine Air Base in northwest Miami (Opalocka), I discovered the manifold riches in the base library. Thanks to some enlightened librarian(s) thereat, I found the anthologies of fantasy and science fiction edited by one August Derleth.

These anthologies introduced me to a whole new cosmos of modern literature, thanks to the considerable taste and savvy editorship of Augie, an astute and well-informed regional writer, poet, and fictioneer. Also, on the side he ran a small publishing firm, one Arkham House, out of his big house and home in Sauk City, Wisconsin. The base library also possessed quite a few titles by other authors published by Derleth and his Arkham House. This discovery changed my life and transformed me into an editor, poet, and specialist-scholar writer.

I began seriously writing at age twenty-seven, first poetry, and then (somewhat later) editing books for Arkham House by the same author whom Derleth was publishing among many others; but this author stood out, Clark Ashton Smith. Since Arkham House did not have national or international renown on a major scale, it was mere happenstance that I chanced upon Lovecraft, Arkham House, Clark Ashton Smith, and other only then little-known but fascinating writers.

Obviously I still operated under the radar, and it suited me just fine. I had the freedom to do as I pleased, or as I needed to do. And I still operate under the radar now during the summer of 2019. People speak of the American Dream, which for many means the opportunity to earn a lot of money. For me it has meant the chance to live the life that I have come to live, and to succeed more or less on my own terms.

For me personally the ideals and values that develop and evolve as they take place, with some preliminary thought, loom far more importantly in my life than just any material benefit. The latter can help a person realize his goal (not to mention a keen sense of practicality), but without the vindication that ideals and values can bring about, then it becomes meaningless.

First I began writing little essays for the so-called fanzines, the little magazines that reflected the readership of the fantasy and science fiction published in the pulp and other magazines of the 1930s and 1940s. The pulp magazines appear to have disappeared in the 1950s. Concomitantly I graduated to putting books together, editing them for Arkham House. I solicited this work, and Derleth gave me his warm approval. I also received recompense for it, but that was a secondary consideration. I wanted the experience. This represented my chance to enter the literary world.

These books that I compiled and edited into existence, all involved material by Clark Ashton Smith: *Other Dimensions, Poems in Prose,* and *Selected Poems.* In this last case I simply surveyed Smith's typescript, long since received by Derleth during 1949. I only did a tiny bit of actual editing. Smith had made it ready for the typesetter. Supervised by Roderick Meng, it appeared after Derleth's death, and in the latter part of 1971. In fact I did do the proofing for Roderick.

Meanwhile I was creating intentionally the poetry that would end up as my own first collection, innovating a new sonnet form and a new type of blank verse of 12 or 14 syllables, the last being the old ballad meter of 8 and 6 syllables done as one printed line. The 12-syllable line, the alexandrine, utilized here and there in my poems, virtually became my signature meter, as pointed out by S. T. Joshi. The collection then appeared in 1971 as the first series of *Songs and Sonnets Atlantean,* published by Arkham House just as Derleth died. All these books made their due appearance in general as part of fantasy and science fiction, and as very much beyond and away from the mainstream: thus under the radar.

Concomitantly I began writing material intentionally for Silver Scarab Press in Albuquerque, New Mexico, owned and operated under the astute direction of Harry O. Morris II, meaning above all his Lovecraft-oriented magazine *Nyctalops* (from the Greek for night vision, being able to see in darkness). This new scrivening of mine involved essays presented in his magazine as well as separate booklets published by his press. Harry was and is a printer by profession. Again we find ourselves far from the mainstream and under the radar.

Also later, and sometimes concomitantly, I began writing for the *Romantist,* the latter inspired by the novels of F. Marion Crawford—the "romantist" is his own term—and in his tradition of romantic storytelling. In this new magazine I particularly began to define romanticism in general and the specific romanticism espoused by Clark Ashton Smith. Meanwhile as part of such definition I researched and compiled a C.A.S. bibliography, ready for publication in the later 1960s but not so published by Don Grant until 1978. I must emphasize here that it was a great and good friend, John Charles Moran, of Nashville, Tennessee, who founded and edited the *Romantist.* Again all this happened somewhat away from the mainstream and under the radar.

The latest development in my literary life as poet, critic, and author (I should add historian to the list) falls under the aegis and imprint of the Lovecraft-oriented or -centered Hippocampus Press, owned and operated by Derrick Hussey. This includes some dozen or more titles as well as a handful of so-called double books, half prose and half poetry, all intentionally created for Hippocampus Press—whether I authored the books or edited them with material by other authors. Given the limelight conferred by a publisher in Manhattan, even if a specialist house, maybe I am now not so far removed from the mainstream and under the radar! I owe my latter career to Derrick Hussey.

I must also mention the several miscellaneous volumes to which I contributed or edited in whole or in part for other publishers again somewhat removed from the mainstream, such as Jerad Walters and his Centipede Press (Lakewood, Colorado), and such as Alan Gullette and Phosphor Lantern Press, now relocated in Eureka, California. All in all, this makes a consistent pattern of activity or creativity under the radar and away from the mainstream. I have recounted much or most of these personal revelations in my autobiography *Hobgoblin Apollo* (Hippocampus Press, 2016), but never before under the aspect of "under the radar" as delineated in this essay. But it bears repetition. To sum up, this procedure has given me the greatest freedom to develop as poet, critic, historian, and creative author.

ARTHUR MACHEN AND KING ARTHUR, SOVEREIGNS OF DREAM

Contents

Arthur Machen and King Arthur, Sovereigns of Dream: A Personal Interpretation

Dedicated,
with love and gratitude,
To Fritz and Jonquil Leiber,
who first showed D. S. F.
the full splendor of Arthur Machen
by letting him read their copy
of *The Hill of Dreams*

Preface

The specifically *modern* weird story, properly speaking (whether concerned with supernatural horror or not), grew out of the romance/fantasy tradition. In both the greater and the lesser aspects of this tradition, Arthur Machen (1863–1947) occupies an unique and monumental position not only by virtue of his literary works but by virtue of the aesthetic pattern and significance of his life itself.

In the following pages we attempt to define something of Machen's achievement (both as a person and as an artist) in connection with the local traditions of King Arthur in the West Country of Britain, as well as with the historical evidence (recent and mostly archaeological) supporting the reality of an actual Arthur or "Artorius" who may have lived in the late 400s A.D. to the mid-500s.

King Arthur undoubtedly ruled far longer and more magnificently during the Middle Ages than he ever did in his own historical period. His tremendous figure dominates the metrical romances (he is always there at least in the background) that flourished in the High Middle Ages; and thus his contribution (as an utmost symbol of romance) to the romance culture of the High Middle Ages must not be underestimated.

The specifically Romantic period or movement has ordinarily been conceived as embracing (more or less) the last decade of the

1700s (signalized by the French Revolution), the entirety of the 1800s, and the first 25 or 30 years of the 1900s (ending, possibly, with the Great Depression of 1929 or, at its latest, with World War II).

The last flowering of Late Romanticism (in terms of a sizable group) occurred primarily in California and included (among others) that small company of dedicated romanticists (or "Romantists," according to the usage of that magisterial romancer F. Marion Crawford) now known as the West Coast Romantics (principally Ambrose Bierce, George Sterling, Nora May French, and Clark Ashton Smith); and this last flowering more or less embraced the four decades from 1890 until 1930.

The specifically romance/Romance tradition that we propose here would cover not only the usual connotation of this Romantic period or movement but would also include the Renaissance of the 1400s and 1500s, in addition to the romance culture of the 1100s and 1200s, the beginning of romance and romanticism in our modern sense.

But in a larger and historically more inclusive sense, the romance tradition began of course with the Fall of Rome (whether 410, 455, 476, or 546/547) and the onset of the Dark Ages, and above all with the immediate sense of understandable nostalgia for the ancient Imperium Romanum on the part of the former Roman population still inhabiting the now fallen Western Roman Empire. One of the principal ingredients or "constants" of romanticism has always been the vague and ill-defined "emotion" of nostalgia, an unquenchable hankering after past magnificence, vanished beauty, and lost splendor. Thus, once the political sovereignty of Rome had become a thing of the past, we have the conditions for the first Romanticism (with emphasis on the "Roman"). Further, while we may recognize the beginning of romance and romanticism (in our modern sense) in the romance culture (and most pivotally in the medieval metrical romances) of the 1100s and 1200s (the true flowering of the Middle Ages), we should also recognize the Dark Ages as a period of "proto-romance" and as a time when the foundations of medieval romanticism were established.

Nowadays it is quite well-known that in the development of the metrical romances (as well as of the later romances in prose) of the Middle Ages, the semi-fabulous world of King Arthur, his court, and his Keltic dominions exercised the single most important influence, thanks to the *Historia Regum Britanniae* (c. 1135) by Geoffrey of Monmouth, and thanks as well to *Li Romanz de Brut* (1155), Wace's translations into the standard European languages of that time. These translations opened up for the medieval writers of romance a whole new world for their imaginative development. Among other results (and again thanks primarily to Geoffrey of Monmouth), the historical Arthur became transformed into another Charlemagne with a "glamorous" imperial court and a vast imperial domain.

The last flowering of Late Romanticism that occurred in the case of the life and the works of Arthur Machen was radically generic and reached back for its roots into the Late Roman period of Latinized Britain. Indeed, the older classicistic romanticism (common to Machen's time and of which his work is a modern extension) had just about run its course apart from some last-minute developments of great and unique artistic significance. Certainly Machen's work represents one of the finest as well as one of the most individual of these last-minute developments of classicistic romanticism.

This ROMANticism that is peculiar to Machen was able to emerge only because of the very fortunate juxtaposition of Machen and Caerleon-on-Usk ... old Caerleon, which had once been the "Castra Legionis" or "City of the Legions" and later one of the imperial camelots or capitals of King Arthur ... that same Artorius whose towering figure illumines the early Dark Ages, that very same period of "proto-romance" when Rome fell and the Western Roman Empire collapsed (into the shards and fragments of innumerable independent successor states), and when the selfsame foundations of medieval romanticism were established.

Arthur Machen—the high priest of Late Romantic prose fiction (or at least sharing that honor with Joseph Conrad)—stands virtually by himself in his profound symbolic and psychological understanding of the moral and ethical responsibilities that had become inherent in modern romance; and this latter development is actually very much in the tradition of Edmund Spenser and his great epic–romance–allegory *The Faerie Queene.*

Considerably before Hermann Hesse and the post–World War II vogue for the German poet's work, Machen had pioneered the romance of alienation, especially as crystallized by his magisterial novel *The Hill of Dreams.* He had pioneered in his own life (that is, during his early London period) by fulfilling the role of an archetypal Steppenwolf long before Hesse conceptualized the basic character pattern in *Steppenwolf* and other novels. What was to save Machen (as it was not to save later the French Existentialists), in the face of terrible circumstances and vicissitudes, was his quiet and abiding sense of self-humor. This inherent sense of self-humor was one of the few but singularly important "graces" permitted to Machen in his pilgrimage through life; and in this he was fortunate: he did not die as does Lucian Taylor (Machen's fictional alter ego) from an accidental overdose of laudanum in the final pages of *The Hill of Dreams.*

Incidentally, Machen certainly takes his own place among the great Romantic and Victorian masters of prose (and such writers would include at least Thomas Carlyle, John Ruskin, Matthew Arnold, Walter Pater, Robert Louis Stevenson, Rudyard Kipling, and Joseph Conrad). In some respects—for example, simply as a fictioneer—Machen's only serious runner-up would be Conrad, who is quite a different writer from Machen.

The present monograph seeks to honor the romance and fantasy tradition of the Western world by demonstrating just how Arthur Machen (both directly and indirectly) drew upon the particularly Late Roman and Arthurian traditions of his native Caerleon in order to define a significant and ultimate stage in the Late Romanticism developing during the late 1800s and early 1900s.

The achievement of Arthur Machen in life and letters has been notoriously difficult to define because (among others) of its Catholic quality of "ineffability" (a word and concept only recently having become acceptable again to many intellectuals). But we firmly believe that it is only in connection with the Arthurian tradition that it is possible to grasp something of the full meaning behind Machen's tremendous achievement as a "myth-maker" or *fantaisiste.* We do not mean by this a literal one-to-one parallelism between the Arthurian cycles of legendry on the one hand and Machen's fiction on the other; nor do we mean a literal usage of familiar characters and stage props directly lifted from Victorian or (for that matter) medieval fictional formulations of the Arthurian Mythos. But what we do intend here is a matter more elusive and subtle, that of an actual transference by Machen of something of the spirit of Arthurian splendor still lingering in Caerleon-on-Usk. By its very nature, such a piece of magic or artistry cannot be argued conclusively, cannot be presented in terms of incontrovertible proofs, because proofs of such a nature do not exist, and further, because the evidence for the most part does in no way warrant such a presentation.

What we proffer here then is frankly an aesthetic speculation, a construct of suggestive probability, an obvious "gallimaufry" of some historical fact, some selective aspects of fiction (or myth), and some plain and simple guesswork of the most elementary type.

In putting together the present monograph, we have drawn not only from the books mentioned in the text (and the standard encyclopedias and other reference works) but just as much upon the various Arthurian articles in that unique and invaluable compendium *Man, Myth and Magic* (subtitled the "Illustrated Encyclopaedia of the Supernatural") and of but recent publication. However, the divers conclusions and premises in regard to the Arthurian materials are for the most part strictly those of the present writer. We have also drawn upon (and here more immediately) an actual visit to the West Country of Britain during the first week of April 1972, with two English friends, Jack and Audrey Hesketh; to both of these friends we are singularly indebted for making that experience possible.

The real Arthur may or may not have been a sovereign. He does appear to have acted as *imperator atque dux bellorum* for the remnant of the Romanized Britons, and he does appear to have won a period of peace or semi-peace—the not inconsiderable respite of what seemed in retrospect a "golden age"—during the often desperate British defense against the Saxons and other Germanic invaders of what we today call England. He certainly was a paramount and paragon "sovereign of dreams" during the High Middle Ages.

Arthur Machen may have been forced by circumstances to assume the role of literary Jack-of-all-trades; but his fortitude and his quiet good humor in the face of tragedy or adversity made him his own aristocrat, his own best person, his own outstanding alchemical experiment. Despite his own creative agony, despite both popular and critical neglect and what seemed to Machen at the time as artistic failure, his fortitude and perseverance as a writer mark him out as a true Prince of Letters. In spite of the contemporary presence of such other excellent fantasy writers as C. S. Lewis, J. R. R. Tolkien, and Charles Williams in English alone, Machen's preeminence as a myth-maker (particularly in the difficult genre of self-myth as exemplified in the form of an autobiographical fiction) crowns him as a veritable "sovereign of dreams" in the opinion of many connoisseurs and, in the opinion of the present writer, no less a "sovereign of dreams" than King Arthur himself.

Sacramento, California, Thursday,
14 August 1975, the 14th anniversary of the death of Clark Ashton Smith.

I. Arthur Machen, Geoffrey of Monmouth, and Caerleon

It is altogether fitting that we embark our Late Romantic personalities-on-parade first with Arthur Llewelyn Jones-Machen, alias Arthur Machen, truly "The Last of the Arthurians." As much as any who have managed to outlast the age in which they were born—instinctively feeling as outsiders therefrom—and who have suffered singular bitterness and (on occasion) breadless days on behalf of their chosen art, Arthur Machen surely deserves our special respect and honor for being the truly classic Odd Man Out, raised to the nth degree. This kind and courageous man, retaining as much good cheer and quiet self-humor as possible, found and developed the strength of heart and mind and character to transcend both personal tragedy and artistic failure, as well as both popular and critical neglect, in a truly remarkable way. Although he killed himself (so to speak) as a practising writer before this final phase, he ended his life as the archetypal Great Old Man of Letters, often visited by sympathetic admirers who sometimes came from afar and who appreciated Machen's genius as unique to their times. He was, incidentally, a wonderful host and raconteur. If nothing else, Machen had developed into a great human being; moreover, one who had rendered the humanities an awesome service by pre-serving, in a singularly pure and intrinsic way, something of the an-cient British-Keltic spirit into an alien age (the twentieth century). In his own peculiar and proper way he had lived much of his best creative life as an artist-martyr or as a hermetic alchemist of letters, becoming his own best book (or work of art) himself in the end. A wondrous transformation, indeed!

In addition, he had achieved through his fiction, at the only truly popular moment of his entire writing career, what only another and earlier Welshman had been able to accomplish. (We must emphasize here that a true Welsh person is descended from the really British or British-Keltic race existing in England, as well as in the Scottish Lowlands, before the Saxons and other ancestors of the present-day English had invaded the island.) This other and earlier Welshman had been the bishop Geoffrey of Monmouth, and thus of Machen's own homeland of Gwent. Geoffrey (at least to himself) certainly was no conscious forger, but he had his *Historia Regum Britanniæ* (or *History of the Kings of Britain*, written originally in Latin prose about 1135) a deliberately mythopoetico-historical account (a personal poetic myth, if you will) "published" and accepted immediately among a majority of his contemporaries as actual history. His fantastic history begins with the well-chosen fiction that Britain was first settled by Brutus, the great-grandson of the Trojan hero Aeneas, and then finishes with an astonishing account of King Arthur, whom Geoffrey portrays as the conqueror of Pict, Scot, Saxon, and Roman. The book proved a brilliant success for that time.

Geoffrey's magnificent main chronicle of an imperial King Arthur conferred (or so it seemed to his contemporaries) an authentic historical dignity on the Arthurian myths and legends. Although he does not go so far as to state the analogy in such obvious terms, he implies that Arthur (as an archimperial figure and as a military leader fighting for decades against savage invading outlanders) was indeed comparable to Charlemagne, High King of the Germans and the Franks, Restorer of the Roman Empire of the West, and (hence) Holy Roman Emperor (as crowned at the hand—and therefore certainly with the pronounced official approval—of Pope Leo III on Christmas Day, 800 A.D., in Rome).

In some strange and subtle way the distinct feeling haunts Geoffrey's pages (although he is nowhere so bold as to state this explicitly) that Arthur had in a sense functioned, at least symbolically, as the

Last of the Roman Emperors of the West. The chronicle depicts Arthur as head of a brilliant, imperial, cosmopolitan court centered in ancient Caerleon-on-Usk (Arthur's coronation capital) and as master of Western Europe including certain portions of the Scandinavian world (e.g., Denmark and Norway) in addition to large islands in the West (e.g., Ireland and Iceland).

Up to a certain point Geoffrey seems plausible enough (apart, of course, from the obvious accounts of hypernatural marvels). Recent "Arthurian" archaeology and recent reconsideration of the Arthurian Mythos would seem to bear out, at least in broad terms, some of Geoffrey's allegations. But he loses credibility with the modern reader when he depicts Arthur as master of a vast empire stretching from Iceland to Norway (in the north) and from Ireland to Britain and Gaul (lying further south). What might actually lie behind such a grandiose allegation? Arthur evidently reunited the Britons everywhere (whether in Britain or in Brittany across the Channel) under a strong central government centered in Western Britain. He had restored in effect the former province of Britannia. Considering the time in which he lived and the peculiar difficulties under which he had to operate, that was a tremendous thing to do! By reuniting the Britons everywhere and then acting as their suzerain, Arthur would have ruled over a fair piece of turf, at least the areas Cambria (what we today call Wales), Cornwall, Devon, Somerset, Dorset, Cumberland, Westmoreland, Lancashire, Cheshire, the Scottish Lowlands, the two isles of Mona in the Irish Sea (today called Man and Anglesey), Brittany, Armorica (later called Normandy), the Channel Islands, as well as those fragments presumably left over from the lost land of Lyonnesse, the Cassiterides of Roman times, the 500 islands and islets of the Scilly archipelago lying immediately due west or southwest of Land's-End at the tip of Cornwall.

Now all this would have constituted an "empire" of some kind. Arthur may also have fostered strong ties, both political and cultural, with the Irish or Goidelic Kelts (the Gaels), to whom he and his fellow Britons were related as "cousin" Kelts. Geoffrey may have worked from written or oral traditions that, taking all these "facts" and factors into account, could not have avoided construing Arthur in other than "imperial" terms. Geoffrey would then have been merely continuing and developing further this "imperial" tradition in a perfectly logical way. Granting the basic premise of Arthur's Brythonic empire, what would have struck the imagination of someone like Geoffrey, living as he did so much closer to Arthur's time than ourselves? Arthur had in effect restored more than the former province of Britannia: he had thus restored a substantial and strategic fragment—to wit, the actual north-western corner—of the former Roman Empire of the West. Again, that was a tremendous thing to do! Given these premises, it is easy to see how Geoffrey and his contemporaries, whether they were actually conscious of the process or not, would have instinctively conceived of Arthur in terms of the departed splendor and pomp of the imperial Caesars. Given these terms, we cannot only generously pardon, but we can actually applaud Geoffrey for extrapolating Arthur's "real" empire into a vast North Atlantic and Western European domain.

This then was the deliberately mythopoetic "fact" that Geoffrey perpetrated, an imperial myth still potent in the reigns of the Welsh-descended Tudors (particularly Henry VII, Henry VIII, and Elizabeth I). This last period significantly marks the span of the English Renaissance: from 1485, when Henry VII took power, to 1603, when Elizabeth I died (although some scholars extend the span to 1625, thus including the reign of James I, the first of the Stuart kings). Geoffrey's account formed the inner core (the so-called Matter of Britain) around which so much myth and legend had already cycled and from which the romancers of the High Middle Ages were to borrow many hints. His "history" was accepted, quoted, and followed by most later historians; and credibility in it was maintained into the Late Middle Ages and the early Continental Renaissance. This imperial myth had proven equally potent in the reigns of the earlier Anglo-Norman kings beginning with William the Conqueror, and it is obvious that Geoffrey formulated the myth the way he did purposefully for his fellow "Britons" (*exoterically* for the inhabitants of England living in his own time, but *esoterically* for his *true* fellow Britons: the Welsh, the Cornish, and the Bretons).

Now Machen during World War I had written and published one short fantasy—a poetic parable more mystic than patriotic in any narrowly chauvinistic or jingoistic sense—which his English contemporaries had immediately picked up as a historical report of an actual miracle; to wit, "The Bowmen." This was in 1914. In this brief and, in its way, brilliant story, he hymns some ghostly bowmen from Crécy and Agincourt necromantically evoked out of England's earlier days but now fighting in the British ranks during the retreat from Mons in France in 1914. His imaginary tale was accepted as factual by much of the British public; and when garnished with sword-brandishing saviors on horseback, this became the celebrated legend of those "Angels of Mons" fighting on the British side. So, in effect, Machen too had created, willy-nilly, a myth for his fellow Britons. Next to Geoffrey of Monmouth's *History,* and possibly on an equal footing with it in this regard, Machen's tale can be described as one of the most successful works of fiction ever composed.

However, Machen never received just recognition for this exploit. It did not really help his writing career, which would be over and done with by the later 1920s/1930s, when he achieved a considerable vogue in the U.S., thanks to such discriminating American enthusiasts as Vincent Starrett and Carl Van Vechten. To the end of his life he would be described as the man who claimed to have invented the tale of the Angels of Mons!

Machen had been born on March 3rd, 1863, in Caerleon-on-Usk, in southeastern Wales, not far from the "Severn Sea" to the south or southeast (the inner estuary of the Severn River), and the very heartland of ancient Britain. Machen, the inheritor of a vast and immemorially old spiritual legacy from the Welsh, the true Britons, described his birthplace in various novels and stories, but possibly he has done so the most compactly in the "Novel of the Black Seal," one of the major narrative units in the picaresque "gallimaufry" *The Three Impostors* (1895). Here he shadows his own Caerleon under the name of "Caermaen"—and here are the relevant passages, in some of his at once most simple and most lyrical prose:

> It was one evening after dinner that the word came.
> "I hope you can make your preparations without much trouble," he said suddenly to me. "We shall be leaving here in a week's time."
> "Really!" I said in astonishment. "Where are we going?"
> "I have taken a country house in the west of England, not far from Caermaen, a quiet little town, once a city, and the headquarters of a Roman legion. It is very dull there, but the country is pretty, and the air is wholesome."

I detected a glint in his eyes, and guessed that this sudden move had some relation to our conversation of a few days before.

* * * * *

The days passed quickly; I could see that the professor was all quivering with suppressed excitement, and I could scarce credit the eager appetence of his glance as we left the old manorhouse behind us and began our journey. We set out at midday, and it was in the dusk of the evening that we arrived at a little county station. I was tired and excited, and the drive through the lanes seems all a dream. First the deserted streets of a forgotten village, while I heard Professor Gregg's voice talking of the Augustan Legion and the clash of arms, and all the tremendous pomp that followed the eagles; then the broad river swimming to full tide with the last afterglow glimmering dustily in the yellow water, the wide meadow, the cornfields whitening, and the deep lane winding on the slope between the hills and the water. At last we began to ascend, and the air grew rarer. I looked down and saw the pure white mist tracking the outline of the river like a shroud, and a vague and shadowy country; imaginations and fantasy of swelling hills and hanging woods, and half-shaped outlines of hills beyond, and in the distance the glare of the furnace fire [of the setting sun] on the mountain, growing by turns a pillar of shining flame and fading to a dull point of red. We were slowly mounting a carriage drive, and then there came to me the cool breath and the secret of the great wood that was above us; I seemed to wander in its deepest depths, and there was the sound of trickling water, the scent of the green leaves, and the breath of the summer night. The carriage stopped at last, and I could scarcely distinguish the form of the house as I waited a moment at the pillared porch. The rest of the evening seemed a dream of strange things bounded by the great silence of the wood and the valley and the river.

The next morning, when I awoke and looked out of the bow window of the big, old-fashioned bedroom, I saw under a grey sky a country that was still all mystery. The long, lovely valley, with the river winding in and out below, crossed in mid-vision by a mediaeval bridge of vaulted and buttressed stone, the clear presence of the rising ground beyond, and the woods that I had only seen in shadow the night before, seemed tinged with enchantment, and the soft breath of air that sighed in at the opened pane was like no other wind. I looked across the valley, and beyond, hill followed upon hill as wave on wave, and here a faint blue pillar of smoke rose still in the morning air from the chimney of an ancient grey farmhouse, there was a rugged height crowned with dark firs, and in the distance I saw the white streak of a road that climbed and vanished into some unimagined country. But the boundary of all was a great wall of mountain, vast in the west, and ending like a fortress with a steep ascent and a domed tumulus clear against the sky. (*CF* 1.372–73)

This then was the country of Gwent, or Monmouthshire, the ancient Siluria. This then was the town of Caerleon, the "Castra Legionis" or fabled "City of the Legions" where Machen was born; and according to Geoffrey of Monmouth, one of the imperial camelots or capitals of Arthur, King of the Britons.

II. In the Forest of Nodens

Siluria, or southeastern Cambria, was thus the country of the Silurians, the ancient British-Keltic folk of the woods and forests. Most of the Brythonic Kelts lived originally as forest folk, and many of the Silurians still dwelt in the forests and mountains of southeastern Cambria all through the Roman occupation. The Silurians were hunters, fishermen, and skilled iron-miners, and they hunted, among other prey, both the red deer and the wild boar. Their skill as hunting men made them dangerous and unpredictable foes. Yet the Silurians were also skilled fishermen and were definitely at home in the water, paddling about in their peculiar braided and caulked coracles. To this day one of the greatest forests in this region that have survived is the old Forest of Dean, formerly the Forest of Nodens (the hunter-god Nuada of the Silver Hand) whose shadowy depths preserved his chosen people, the Silurians, from the worst effects of the successive invasions of Britain by outlanders, beginning with the Romans.

The Forest thus protected them from complete colonization and pacification by the Romans, such as obtained over most of lowland Britain. Make no mistake about it: the Romans did materially change the face of the British land with the network they founded and developed of cities, towns, and forts all the way to the Antonine's Wall lying north of Hadrian's by a good piece of ground. Antonine's Wall stretched from the Firth of Clyde on the west to the Firth of Forth on the east. The Forest of Nodens similarly protected the Silurians from the worst immediate effects of the continuing invasions by the Saxons. These Germanic barbarians were primarily cattle-herding people and country-dwellers who preferred the open grasslands to the Roman towns and villas, and who also preferred to live in their own tribal communities in the lowlands beside the rivers with their heavy but fertile soils favored for Saxon agriculture. For these basic reasons they settled early in the extensive open country of Kent south of London, or in the central-to-southeastern stretch of Britain's southern coast (the "Saxon Shore" separated from the continent of Europe by the "Narrow Seas").

In 1018 Canute, the Danish king of England, granted the Forest a royal charter, upholding the ancient Verderer's Court which persists to this day. The Forest of Nodens again preserved this ancient Cambrian people from the worst conditions resulting from the Norman Conquest of England under William the Conqueror in 1066. The now Forest of Dean became one of William's favorite hunting grounds. Since it was a royal forest, the inhabitants of Dean were spared much of the degradation of petty feudalism.

The Silurians then witnessed a long succession of English kings in their more pleasant moods. Now there ensued the pageantry of the royal hunt as the king would pursue the red deer and other wild creatures of the woods. Eventually the Silurians witnessed a Welsh-descended prince, one of their own ancient British-Keltic race, ascend to the throne of Britain (in fulfillment of an elder prophecy) and found an imperial dynasty, the House of Tudor. The last Tudor monarch in direct line of descent ruled as Elizabeth I, one of England's finest sovereigns, and the mystical Astraea returned to turn "dull time" for a substantial respite into a golden and goddess-inspired age.

"Happy the eye / 'Twixt the Severn and Wye." The bare outline of the Forest of Dean's history is endorsed in this old rime, reminding us of how the old woods have indeed palpably preserved and protected the Silurians from the worst effects of Time's changes. In the ancient forest depths, in the shadow of the olden oaks and beeches, something of the original British-Keltic spirit still remained as if by some predestined magic, and passed uniquely to Arthur Machen, born in Caerleon-on-Usk, and one of antique Wales' most illustrious offspring.

This Caerleon, the little town in which Machen was born, had once stood in Roman times as Isca Silurum, or "Isca of the Silurians," and as possibly the single most distinguished city in southern Wales. Although Caerwent, or Venta Silurum (8 to 10 miles to the east, just inland along the northern shore of "Severn Sea")—the "Market of the Silurians"—was the "cantonal" or local administrative capital for southern Cambria; Caerleon was one of the three legionary fortresses for the whole of Britannia: the other two were located at Eburacum, or York, in the Midlands, and at Chester, or Caerleon-upon-Dee, called Ceva by the Romans, and located in northeastern Cambria. Isca was, moreover, a cosmopolitan community thanks to the presence of the Imperial Augustan Legion, or "Legio II Augusta," a cosmopolitan gathering of professional soldiers who had brought with them their altars and cults of such gods and goddesses as Mithras, Isis, Horus, Osiris, Diana (the Artemis of the Ephesians on the west coast of Asia Minor), and Jupiter Dolichenus, a Syrian divinity.

Although the Romans had been in the country in one way or another since 55 B.C., it was not until about a hundred years or so afterwards that they began to settle and civilize Britain in earnest. The central Roman government maintained some official representation or control in this province until about 410 A.D. Britannia protected the northwestern sector of the Imperium Romanum.

III. "Caer Nodentis"

North and east of Isca Silurum there stretched the mysterious Forest of Nodens. East of Venta Silurum, further up the Severn, again along the river's northern shore, and just within the southeastern corner of the Forest (which virtually came to the water's edge), there stood the imposing Temple of Nodens upon its own hill.[1] This was an elaborate and quite sizable temple compound comprising various buildings and

---

1. The main axis of the Hill of Nodens is more northeast and southwest than north and south. However, we have presented the discussion of the Hill and Temple (area) of Nodens in simple terms of north and south for ease of presentation as well as for ease of understanding. The ground-plan accompanying this monograph (for which sketch we are indebted to Jack Hesketh of New Ash Green, near Dartford, Kent, England) indicates the specifically correct compass directions.

set within an older, pre-Roman, Iron-Age fortress, a spot sacred to Nodens from time immemorial.

South of the temple compound, across the Severn, all along her eastern and then southeastern shore (stretching from Glevum or Gloucester on the north to the great southeastern "bend" in the Severn Estuary, more or less marked by the mouth of the River Brue or Uxella), there lay the great estates of the landed Britanno-Roman gentry (actually large farms) with their elegant and stately villas, which were also well-heated, well-watered, well-ventilated, and quite livable, comfortable, and eminently "modern." The Britanno-Romans had carefully modeled their country houses upon the Roman villa, which they skillfully modified to suit the new non-Mediterranean surroundings. The placement of "Caer Nodentis" (as we shall call it after the Welsh fashion) virtually on the river facilitated all approaches by water. The temple served as a focus for the immediate countryside on both banks of the river, and it was common for people to ferry back and forth.

Caer Nodentis was the greatest of all Romano-British temples, a center of healing and pilgrimage, with an elaborately appointed hostelry, or "villa," with baths, healing cubicles, priests' quarters, and so forth—and all built in the fourth century A.D. within the prehistoric earthenwork fortress and above the remains of an early Roman iron mine.

To the ruins of this temple located on its own hill within Lydney Park, the present writer (then in Britain during a long sojourn of half pleasure and half business) came early in the first week of April 1972, together with two English friends Jack and Audrey Hesketh, during our pilgrimage to the Arthur Machen country and to the West Country at large. First on our itinerary was the Temple of Nodens, not far from the new Severn Bridge that goes over the river just west of Bristol, one of the largest modern cities in the West Country. We had first been apprised of this Britanno-Roman relic through its mention by Machen in a number of his tales as well as in various autobiographical materials. But we were eager to see the temple not only because of this association with and mention by Machen but just as much for its own intrinsic and unique historico-cultural interest.

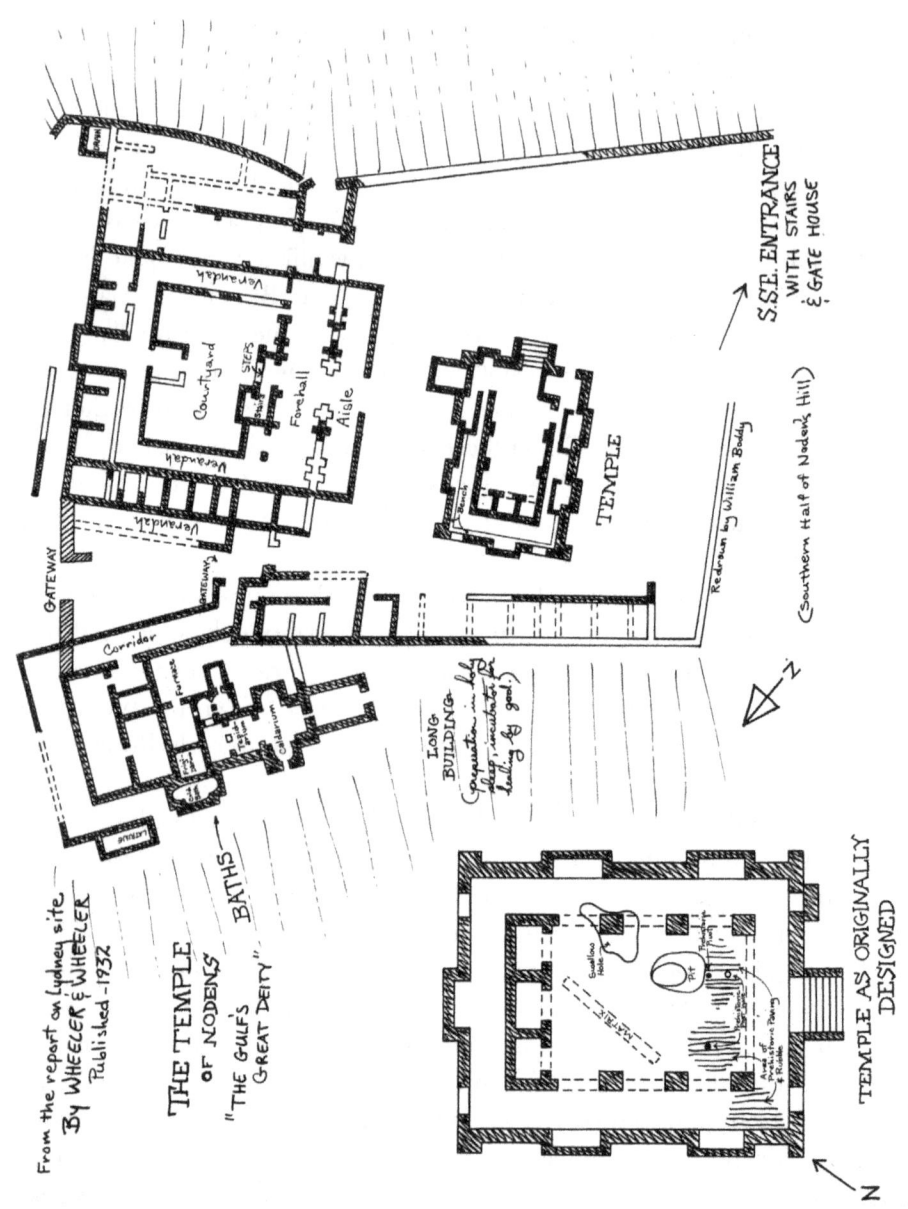

THE TEMPLE
of NODENS
"THE GULF'S
GREAT DEITY"

BATHS

From the report on Lydney site
By WHEELER & WHEELER
Published 1932

Redrawn by William Boddy

(Southern Half of Nodens Hill)

S.S.E. ENTRANCE
WITH STAIRS
& GATE HOUSE

TEMPLE

LONG
BUILDING

GATEWAY

Corridor

Veranda

Courtyard

Forehall

Aisle

STEPS

TEMPLE AS ORIGINALLY
DESIGNED

Here was centered the cult of the Severn river god Nodens, "Lord of the Abyss" and "the gulf's great deity" and also (in another of this divinity's attributes) Nuada of the Silver Hand, god of the forest and the forest-depths. The Severn is presumably named after Sabrina, the daughter of Locrine, who, when pursued by her angered stepmother Gwendolen, drowned herself in the river to which she bequeathed her name. Nodens was the greatest god of the Silures, or Silurians. But Nodens was also a marine divinity and the particular genius loci of the Bristol Channel, or Gulf of Nodens, with the inner gulf, or Severn Sea, extending west about as far as Cardiff, and with the outer gulf extending as far west as St. George's Channel on the north and the Atlantic Ocean on the south.

In addition to the Hill of Nodens (and now Camp Hill), there stands another smaller hill, once crowned by a Roman watchtower and separated from Camp Hill by a ravine some 28 yards in width. Although the location functioned primarily as a shrine, the civil authorities in Caerwent, or Venta Silurum, maintained a military station here, as well as in the watch-tower on the smaller adjacent hill (for the practical, everyday purpose of protecting the shrine from any immediate man-made perils and alarms), through most of the Roman occupation of Britain. The ravine forks below the temple park. Since the river once came to the foot of Nodens Hill, the tide would have gushed into the creek that flows down from the hills farther to the north. Today, between the base of the main hill and the edge of the Severn River (lying thus on the southeast), there lies an alluvial plain given over to farming. Among the present native trees marking the temple site are some huge, well-matured oaks and beeches, 300 or 400 years old, and well garlanded with mistletoe, that mystic plant cherished by the ancient Gallic and British Druids. The only alien among the native trees here is the Spanish chestnut brought over by the Romans from the Continent, along with the "fallow deer."

As noted, Nodens had at least three main but related attributes: he was a sea god, a river god, and a forest god, and was thus three times a god of the abyss or of the depths. But in one further significant and quite literal aspect he functioned as lord of the void, or voids. Most gods have their benign and overt attributes, their outer selves, imaged as divine men or women or both; this represents their exoteric side. However, they also have their unknown and mysterious attributes, and sometimes possibly malign; this represents their esoteric side. The former administers to the worshippers and is often and usually the object of popular cults. The latter administers as it were to the secret and unknown concerns of the initiates, priests, and mysteriarchs. This esoteric aspect is your true "unknown and unknowable god," and Nodens too had his hidden and unknown self who presided over and within the manifold caves and caverns that abound in the hills and mountains of Wales (including those of southern Cambria), either opening to the outer air or located in hidden places far underground. Over these upper caverns and these subterranean places, Nodens presided as the unseen, unheard, and unknown deity, truly the Lord of the Abyss (a divinity whose presence is *known of* and *felt* but who yet remains *unknown*). Appropriately enough, there is at least one (and partially man-made) hollow space beneath the Temple of Nodens, to wit, an early Roman iron mine, abandoned during the later Latin occupation and presently walled off with cement.

The Severn River's tidal bore presented a palpable manifestation of the god's divinity. His priests, once they learned how to foretell the arrival of the mystic wave peculiarly associated with Nodens, gained the confidence of simple men, and thus the cult grew. The Temple of Nodens was at once the largest and yet most intimate relic of its type in the whole of Roman Britain, and his shrine is more than an ordinary ruin. Barring its firing by the Saxons (an event that may or may not have happened), the buildings would have continued in use in some way throughout the Middle Ages and into the Renaissance, like a great deal of Roman architecture both in Britain and in Europe. Already commanding a large popular cult during the earlier Roman times in Britain, the Lord Nodens became even more popular (especially as a healer) during the "Keltic Revival" of the latter 300s and early 400s.

This revival came about as a direct result of the first major Saxon and related Germanic attacks on Britain's eastern and southeastern shores during the years 367, 368, and 369. These attacks (which the Britanno-Romans vigorously repulsed, and which had no real effect on the continuing prosperity of the province) also had another and singularly practical result: the Britanno-Romans now proceeded to erect walls around most of their cities, towns, and villas. Walls already existed around the great legionary fortresses and the smaller camps that were situated all over Roman Britain, as well as around those towns located near such dangerous milieux as Hadrian's Wall or the mountains in the west or northwest where the Roman influence had at best proven superficial. But most of the towns and cities were not protected by walls because hitherto they had proven unnecessary: the civil communities had had the security afforded by the highly mobile presence of the three great legions stationed in the island. One by one, the legions were to be called away for duty on the Continent, where the Western Roman Empire was crumbling beneath the attacks of barbarian invaders. But now the Britanno-Romans with commendable and sensible dispatch erected walls and bastions around most of their settlements. A major series of maritime defenses and forts—established earlier in the 300s against Saxon pirates—continued in use along Britain's eastern and southeastern shores, all the way from the Wash (about 100 miles almost directly north of London) to the Thames, and then from the Thames to the white cliffs of Dover, and then finally from Dover to Portsmouth and the Isle of Wight; to the same earlier period there also belonged a new fort at Cardiff southwest of Caerleon and a fleet station at Holyhead on the Isle of Anglesey just off the northwestern coast of Wales. Thus, with good reason, the Hill of Nodens and the adjacent hill with watch-tower possessed their own garrisons and substantial fortifications.

It must be remembered that, although the upper classes in Britain had become largely Christian (at least superficially), following the imperial example of Constantine the Great (sole emperor 323–337), himself proclaimed emperor in Britain, yet the British cult of the young Nazarene carpenter-god Jesus Christ was at best only minimal at that time, and only one of many religions. The Christian cult was, in addition, only the latest in a long series of "exotic" religions imported from the Orient and including the cults of Isis, Horus, Osiris, Mithras, the Asiatic Diana, and Jupiter Dolichenus. It should not surprise the reader therefore that in times of such genuine peril, whenas not only a people's way of life was threatened but also its very life stood in danger of annihilation, the people should have turned to their own native divinities with renewed trust and inspiration. The religious life of the province was especially rich and variegated, and formed three main groups of cults: the official or imperial cults (these involved at least the dead emperors deified while alive, the living emperor or emperors, and the imperial household); the imported cults (these involved at least the main divinities from the Oriental, Greek, and Roman pantheons); and the native cults (these involved all the local British deities throughout the island, an amazing and typically Keltic multiplicity of gods and goddesses). These various kinds of religious life survived all over the country up to the latest period of Roman Britain, especially in the southwest.

Although the cult of Nodens became even more elaborate during Late Roman times, here was the site of an oracle and a shrine long before the arrival of the Romans. But it was particularly during the Keltic Revival of the later 300s and early 400s that Caer Nodentis received its greatest following and appanage. Replacing the much older Keltic shrine but still honoring the same god or principle, the Romano-Britons now constructed in 384 A.D. a splendid congeries of buildings in Roman style primarily on the southern half of the hill. The entire hill itself was protected on the north (where it joins a wooded plateau) by a double fortification, each with its own outer fosse. The outer wall was pre-Roman and built of earth, the inner wall was Roman and built at least partially of stone. Heavy gates led through both walls.

The northern half (for the most part unexcavated) of the hilltop was evidently used as a courtyard but possessed few structures and was probably naturally landscaped. The southern half of the hill was dominated by the temple building itself and by the large-scale two-story luxurious hotel-villa where both ordinary pilgrims and important dignitaries could find lodging. The temple itself, built to be used in winter, was originally enclosed and was not of the colonnaded Mediterranean type. It measured 93 feet in length and 76 feet in width, and was unique for the period in having six side chapels.

Nodens was depicted in typical Roman mosaic design on the floor of his temple, surrounded by salmon and sea serpents (or conger eels, much esteemed as a comestible by the Romans). He was portrayed as coronetted and rising up from his own river, standing in his chariot drawn by four horses and accompanied by Tritons bearing coracle paddles. In appearance Nodens resembled the Roman god of the sea, Neptunus, but without the beard. As a marine god, he held or inspired the gift of prophecy, and as such he was definitely a power or divinity to be propitiated.

Popularly Nodens was a god of health and healing in the manner of the Greek deity Aesculapius. Like Mercury, he was also a god of good luck. According to the *interpretatio romana,* the Romans likened him, in his "sylvan" aspect, to Sylvanus, one of the Latin divinities of the woods. Originally in the temple floor there was located the so-called Oracle of Nodens, a circular opening 9 inches across and environed by a broad red band in turn enclosed by two other bands of blue. The coins recovered from within the temple floor (and close to this oracular orifice) range from the reign of Augustus to that of Arcadius (about 377–408), the Roman Emperor of the East, from 383 into 408 A.D.

In addition to the gates opening onto the forest at the north, there was also an entrance to the hill-top located with stairs and gate-house at the southeast (for the devotees coming by river). Here, after climbing the stairs, one would find himself in an open area bounded on the west by the temple. The main entrance into the temple building (which runs more or less on an east–west axis) is on the east. There was also an open area to the north of the temple, and between the temple and the hotel-villa. West of the temple there lay a long low building, the healing house or *abaton,* with individual rooms or cubicles where the devotees of Lord Nodens (many of them cripples and other kinds of invalids) would await the healing presence of the god. Indeed, the evidence suggests that Caer Nodentis was a kind of British-Keltic Lourdes, and many miraculous cures resulted there over time. North of the *abaton* and west of the hotel-villa there arose the obligatory bath building which, like the *abaton,* overlooked the ravine (separating the Hill of Nodens from the watch-tower hill) and which included the caldarium, tepidarium, and frigidarium. The pilgrims who came to Caer Nodentis would first negotiate with the resident priesthood, would probably find lodging for the night if they had come for "the cure," and before retiring to their individual chambers in the *abaton* to await the god, would go through a complete cleansing ritual in the baths.

There were also other and smaller edifices, such as the quarters where the priests and acolytes lived, studied, and maintained their own private cults and mysteries. The buildings were roofed with heavy, Mediterranean-type red tile, bits of which one can still easily see scattered here and there on the southern half of the hill-top. Altogether, the Shrine of Nodens presented an imposing and rather mysterious appearance, half hidden by the primordial Forest of Nodens, which stretched away from the temple to the north and west. Wales, like most of Britain at that time, was heavily covered with all manner of huge, beautiful, and olden trees, most of them deciduous: the spring and autumn glory of leaves much have been breathtaking. Not even the truly splendiferous temple and great baths dedicated to Lady Sulis, sovereign queen above all waters, and the presiding divinity of Aquae Sulis (or Bath), formed a more magnificent architectural entourage than "Caer Nodentis." The Romans likened this goddess of the hot springs and medicinal waters to Minerva, or Pallas Athena. It is indeed an odd coincidence that in Roman Britain—as in the Britain of later times—the great metropolis was London, and the fashionable spa in the West Country was Bath (or Aquae Sulis), which stood south-southeast of Caer Nodentis and the northwestern bank of the Severn.

Long after the last official Roman legion had departed from Britain and the Latin speech itself had become a dead language, the name of Nodens was remembered, until his own river gradually wandered away from the shrine now left standing alone amid the low forested hills that marked the southeastern corner of the Forest of Nodens.

The Forest, once a vasty and primordial woods, became in time only a fragment of its former self, but it had more than served its purpose by preserving Nodens' chosen people into an age completely different from that which had known his charismatic worship. The unknown and potentially malign aspect of the god would not have been directed against his own people, the Silurians and other forest folk, but (on behalf of their preservation) against the successive tides of outland invaders.

There is the possibility that the Saxons fired the temple compound in their final push westward and after the golden age of peace and order brought about by King Arthur's victories. But there is no conclusive evidence for such a burning, and in all likelihood the buildings would have continued in use into the Renaissance. We think the Saxons would have respected Caer Nodentis (as they did the shrine at Glastonbury or Avalon) and would have allowed it to function in its own immediate locality as previously. However, the fact remains that both Caer Nodentis and Caerleon continued under the direct political control of the Welsh until the Norman Conquest, that is, for half a millennium.

Both Cambria, or Wales, and Cornwall maintained a quasi-independent status for centuries before their eventual absorption into what was to become the mainstream of English culture and life. Both the Welsh and the Cornish managed to maintain much of their own peculiar way of life into modern times: their language, their customs, their arts, their poetry, and their music.

In 1670, the Hill of Nodens, now Camp Hill, was enclosed in Lydney Park, just south of the little town of Lydney. As recently as the eighteenth century, many of the walls in the old temple compound were still at least 8 feet high. Today they are only about 3 feet high, but still demonstrate the solid building skill of the Britanno-Romans. One can still clearly see how they constructed the walls with forest stone well cemented together. Today Caer Nodentis is still part of Lydney Park, Lydney, Gloucestershire, on private property owned presently by Lord and Lady Bledisloe, who live in the (comparatively) modern manor house on the hill just to the east of the old Hill of Nodens.

Before we proceed on our pilgrimage from the Temple of Nodens on into ancient Caerleon-on-Usk, we mention in passing—for the benefit of interested readers—two basic books to apprehend properly the archaeological site and its cultural significance. First, the *Report on the Excavation of the Prehistoric, Roman, and Post-Roman Site in Lydney Park, Gloucestershire,* by Messieurs Wheeler and Wheeler, and published by Oxford University Press, 1932. Second, the *Roman Antiquities at Lydney Park, Gloucestershire,* by Reverend William Hiley Bathurst, and published by Longmans, Green & Co., London, 1879. The former is an excellent report on the exemplary excavations conducted by Sir Mortimer Wheeler in modern times. Unfortunately it completely or virtually ignores the considerable folklore relative to Nodens in the immediate neighborhood of Camp Hill and handed down orally from generation to generation. The latter title makes up for the cultural/anthropological omissions of the modern report and forms a fascinating compendium of the vicinage's oral traditions as extant in Bathurst's lifetime. This is a book that would have been known to the young Arthur Machen, since his references to Nodens in both his fiction and his autobiographical materials draw upon virtually the same folklore.

IV. Caerleon-on-Usk

And now at last we come to "Caer Leon" or "Castra Legionis" on the river Usk, whereby there hangs full many a tale; indeed the full ROMANtic heritage of which, like wings summoned out of time, descended upon the exquisite sense, sensibility, and sensitivity of Arthur Machen.[2]

Although Julius Caesar came into Britain in 55 B.C., the Romans did not begin their conquest in earnest until sometime just a little less than one hundred years later under the emperor Claudius in 43 A.D. In a scant thirty years the Romans succeeded in superimposing their civilization over most of what is now England. The reduction of Cymru, or Cambria, the western mountain heartland of ancient Britain,

---

2. As in the case of the Hill and Temple (area) of Nodens, the main axis of the Roman fortress as well as the city of Isca Silurum (that is, the two thus lying side by side) is really northeast and southwest and not north and south. We present the discussion of Britanno-Roman Caerleon in simple terms of north and south for ease of presentation and of understanding. The illustration accompanying this monograph and showing "Early Isca Silurum" clearly demonstrates the half-circle of the river Usk sweeping on the south around the city.

It has only been since after World War II and after Machen's death that modern archaeologists have known for a certainty (thanks to recent discoveries) that the city (as distinct from the fortress) did exist, and did indeed constitute a fair-sized community. However, when Machen grew up in Caerleon and then later when he wrote *The Hill of Dreams*, he had to work from local traditions about the Roman antiquities and from his own artistic intuition. It is clear from his descriptions of Isca Silurum that he knew perfectly well that the town itself existed in the form that modern archaeology has discovered and confirmed. This last revelation represents one of the great archaeological finds of the twentieth century.

remained until the last. Then in 75 A.D. the commander Julius Frontinus began the conquest of the Silurians. About the same year the Romans built the foundation of the fortress at Isca Silurum, the Isca or Usk of the Silurians, taking the name thus from the river.

The Silurians had already marked the general position of the fortress as one of strategic value by the presence of the 17-acre prehistoric Iron-Age earthenwork fort (today called Lodge Camp or Belinstock) on the hill just to the northwest (and possibly the original for Machen's "hill of dreams"). The Romans moreover chose the site for its approachability by river and for its command over the coastal area as well as of the routes into the hinterland, that is, the wilder and more remote mountainous areas of northern and central Wales. A network of smaller (auxiliary) forts in southern and central Wales depended upon the fortress at Caerleon.

A large rectangle with rounded corners, the fortress measured 1630 feet (running east and west) and 1375 feet (running north and south), and covered about 50 acres. It occupied a terrace in a broad bend of the Usk, and together with various other stone buildings, it accommodated some 6,000 men in 64 substantial barrack blocks.

The wall or walls (mainly a rampart of clay with thick stone facing and superstructure) environing the fortress rose about 20 feet to a crenellated parapet, with a ditch moat 30 feet wide and 8 feet deep in turn surrounding them, providing thus for both defense and the removal of effluents. Attached interval and corner turrets rose every 150 feet. A gateway stood symmetrically situated in each side of the rectangle, and each gate had twin arched portals between towers.

In addition to the 64 barracks the fortress possessed numerous administrative offices, stores, and other buildings. The subsidiary streets had side drains and the major streets had deep central sewers. Seven-inch lead pipes provided the running water. All the buildings (including the towers and turrets) possessed heavy, Mediterranean-type tile roofs, and were grouped in three main sections or divisions.

The headquarters or *principia* lay in the middle of the central section. It had a chapel of the standards or *aedes,* and its great basilica measured 210 feet by 90 feet. Its great courtyard lies principally beneath the parish church and churchyard of St. Cadoc's, which in turn lies virtually at the heart of modern Caerleon.

To the rear of the headquarters (that is, toward the west) there stood the residence of the commander, or *legatus*. The real King Arthur would certainly have inhabited this building among other imposing residences within the overall area of camp and city combined. In the central section the workshops or *fabrica* lay to one side of the commander's residence, and a drill hall (flanked by "magazines") lay on the other.

Twenty-four barracks lay in the western section and a like number lay in the eastern one. Each barracks block typically measured 250 feet long, with one third of its area appropriated for the centurion; the remaining area provided for the men's quarters, with a veranda in front.

The front or eastern section included a large hospital of typical legionary pattern measuring about 230 feet square, together with a commodious bath-house (containing a long exercise hall, lavish cold-water and hot-water baths, and a *palaestra* with a sizable swimming pool 135 feet long, 19 feet wide, and 4 feet deep).

Both south and north of the headquarters there lay a group of eight barracks each, the southern group lying just adjacent to the principia, and the northern group lying adjacent to the fortress's northern gate. Between the northern group and the principia there lay the stabling for the 120 mounted scouts who made up the full legionary complement. This would later have provided the stables for at least some of Arthur's "knights" or *equites cataphractarii.*

We have described the fortress in some detail since this part of Caerleon would have played an especially important role in the life of Arthurian Britain.

South of the fortress (between it and the river now flowing west), the Romans began building the town of Isca about 100 A.D. The settlement covered more than 100 acres and accommodated some 12,000 people. It soon possessed a wide range of impressive buildings.

The town, incidentally, did not develop (like so many communities of the Western American frontier) willy-nilly as a random agglomeration of buildings but as a planned settlement. It boasted handsome temples to Diana, Mithras, Jupiter Dolichenus, and other divinities both native and imported, an indication of its cosmopolitan character.

Southwest of the fortress there lay a walled parade ground 700 by 500 feet for the use of the resident legion, and one of the few areas within the city proper which would have been available for new construction during the regimes of Aurelius Ambrosius and Rex Artorius.

Across from the parade ground, and southeast of the fortress, there stood Isca's military amphitheatre used for both military and civic events. It measured 222 feet long 192 feet wide, and some 30 feet high, thus overtopping the fortress walls. Immediately southwest of the amphitheatre there lay a large public bath-house. South of the walled parade ground and the city's forum there lay the principal area of the civilian settlement. East and south of the city, along the banks of the Usk, there lay the military and civilian warehouses with their wharves.

Unlike Venta Silurum, the cantonal capital to the east or northeast by some 8 miles, Isca Silurum flourished as something more than a marketplace or administrative center. Its preeminence and entire characteristic development was due completely to the fact of its being one of the three permanent legionary bases and specifically the home of the Second Augustan Legion. Curiously, the official emblem of the Second Legion duplicates one of the standard symbols of modern astrology: the Capricorn, that elegantly mythical creature compounded of half-goat above and half-fish below.

Isca Silurum, almost from the very beginning of the Roman occupation of Britain, was thus an important and strategic provincial city of the Roman frontier. But, as noted, it also very much possessed a charisma and mystique all its own. However similar it may have appeared in a general way to other Roman cities, it retained (according to a variety of reports then and later) a character very much its own, and that curious atmosphere of "otherwhere" typical of the West Country.

The civilian settlement at Isca, like that of so many classical Roman cities, had two main streets (one running east and west, the other north and south) that bisected each other at right angles. This bisection resulted in four uneven quarters. The great walled parade ground dominated the quarter on the northwest, and in the northeastern quarter, near the fortress's southern gate, the legionary amphitheatre (flanked just south or southwest by the good-sized public baths) stood at the entrance to Isca's forum, which lay beyond surrounded with basilicas, theatres, temples, and other civic buildings. Most of the civilian population lived in the two larger quarters on the south: east of the southeastern quarter as well as south of this same quarter, and then of the quarter on the southwest, Isca's considerable waterfront area with wharves and warehouses (mixed in with civilian residences and probably military stations, particularly at the water's edge) lay generously displayed.

After or around the time of the first severe barbarian assaults of 367-69 A.D., the Britons living in Caerleon refurbished the substantial walls (with attached interval and corner turrets placed probably every 150 feet) around the city proper similar to the defenses enclosing the fortress lying just to the north. The waterfront areas too would have received some kind of fortification system consisting of divers bits of walls and towers and turrets alternating with portcullis-type gates and smaller pastern-type doors. The Britanno-Romans, we can be confident, made sure of Isca's defenses.

When Caesar Honorius (then in Ravenna north of Rome) declared Britain a free province in 410—when much of the former Western Empire had already collapsed—Isca Silurum as a Roman city was thus more than three centuries old.

The Welsh derived the very name of the town in later times from "Castra Legionis" (the Camp or Camps of the Legion): Caerleon, or "Caer Leon" (the Castle or Fort of the Legion). Hence, by Late Roman and certainly by Arthurian times, the civilian and military communities had fused together to be transformed into that golden and glittering "capital" deep in the west of Britain, the legendary "City of the Legions" where something of the ancient imperial splendor still abode.

Mention has already been made of Caerleon's military amphitheatre, whose arena measured 184 feet by 137. It could accommodate around 6,000 persons, or an entire legion (for the purposes of military education). And legend has associated it with King Arthur's Round Table (whatever may have lain originally behind *that*). Certainly, had there been a real "emperor and leader in battles" named Artorius, and had he made Caerleon one of his camelots or capitals, this ancient monument (today maintained for the public by the Department of the Environment) would have played its part in large public gathering during the time of Arthur's Britain.

The later Welsh historian Geoffrey of Monmouth, writing in his *History of the Kings of Britain* in the twelfth century, depicts Caerleon as the setting for King Arthur's imperial coronation. Although some scholars and critics have considered Geoffrey "a reckless forger" and his magnum opus a fable pretending to be history, recent research suggests that, allowing for some pardonable *cultural* or patriotic exaggeration on the good bishop's part, he may very well have worked from some genuine historical sources no longer extant (and not only just that certain ancient book in British that he cites, which could have really existed, when all is said and done).

Now, when Geoffrey knew Caerleon the city would still have had a fair show of ancient architecture. Even the less imaginative Gerald of Barry (who saw Caerleon in 1188) writes of temples and theatres, immense palaces, remarkable hot baths, and other buildings, all enclosed in fine walls; in short, a town of prodigious size and substantial architecture that would have impressed a sensitive and knowledgeable person of that time as a considerable "relic" left over from the former Roman Empire.

It is worth noting some peculiar coincidences here. Geoffrey of Monmouth's father had Arthur for his name. His son derived his greatest fame in writing about *King* Arthur. According to Geoffrey as well as various local traditions, Caerleon was one of the British war-chief's headquarters. And *Arthur* Machen, who was to extend and extrapolate certain elements and aspects of the Arthurian Mythos in his poetic fantasies (possibly most notably in "The Great Return"), was born in Caerleon and, it will be noted, largely from ancient British-Keltic stock.

V. Roman Britain and the Western Roman Empire

But now Caerleon must be seen against the larger background of Roman Britain and the Western Roman Empire. By 410 A.D., when much of the Western Roman Empire had already collapsed, and when Caesar Honorius (the puppet emperor of the Romanized barbarian general Stilicho until the latter's death in 408) declared to the

Britons that the defense of their province now depended upon their own initiative (and that in effect Britannia was now a free realm), the impossible happened.

The general Alaric with a large barbarian host entered and sacked the great imperial city of Rome, an event that, while perhaps unavoidable, caused a profound shock throughout the Roman and Romanized populations in what was left of the Western Empire. The emperor Honorius and his court had taken refuge in Ravenna in the north of Italy, and it was plain that if Mother Rome could herself no longer look to her own defenses, then the Romans themselves could have no thought for the safety or protection of Rome's far-away northwestern frontier.

Ironically enough, the latest surviving Roman coin found in Caerleon does not honor Caesar Honorius but dates to the reign of Arcadius (but before 395). During the time of the first major sacking of Rome, whilst Honorius had removed to Ravenna, Arcadius was ruling from Constantinople, the ancient Byzantium, as the Eastern Emperor. Two further major sackings of Rome were to occur in the mid-400s and mid-500s. In 476 the barbarian Odoacer deposed the last official Western Roman Emperor, Romulus Augustulus. By 547 it is written that for a while the city of Rome remained actually deserted!

Meanwhile the Romano-Britons were having their own problems. Britain, or Britannia, during the fourth century A.D. had remained a wealthy and integral part of the Roman Empire. Left to its own devices in 410, the government of Roman Britain during the 420s evidently enlisted Saxon warriors from Germany to strengthen the British defenses.

But sometime during the 420s to 440s the Saxon and other Germanic barbarians rebelled—that is, *mutinied*—against the nominal Britanno-Roman dominion. A contemporary Gallic chronicle could even say that in 441–42 Britain (actually East Britain) had been reduced to the dominion of the Saxons. This report would have of course been greatly exaggerated, but it undoubtedly captures something of the dread felt by British refugees making the report. The Romano-Britons (from Eastern Britain) fled into Western Britain and into Armorica, the ancient double peninsula of Brittany and Normandy, on the northwest of Gaul.

The Britons then made the signal mistake of hiring further Saxons to fight and contain the rebelling Saxons already in Britain. These mercenaries in their turn rebelled or mutinied, and in collaboration with further Germanic barbarians took the occasion evidently to mount a full-scale invasion and settlement of at least Eastern Britain.

Three main routes of penetration by the Anglo-Saxons (along estuaries and other waterways) are prominent: along the Thames, the Wash, and the Humber. The invasion up the Thames in particularly linked with the Jutish heroes Hengest and Horsa, and with their dealings with the chief British ruler Vortigern in the mid-fifth century. The later English scholar Bede places the time of Hengest and Horsa's invasion somewhere between 450 and 455. Hengest and his son (or grandson) Aesc established the Jutish kingdom of Kent, or Cantwara, a name borrowed from the British tribe of the Cantii. The wars of Hengest and Aesc seem principally to concern their conquest and settlement of Kent.

From the writings of the sixth-century monk Gildas (associated with the early Christian monastery at Glastonbury), as well as from other contemporary or near-contemporary accounts, we may vaguely perceive a great federated attack by the Saxons and other Germanic tribes (and not just into Eastern Britain) in the later fifth century. This attack ruined what remained of the Roman towns at least in much of Eastern Britain and spread devastation over vast stretches of the country. The Britons now drew back into their mountain strongholds in the west, the southwest, the northwest, and the north of Britain, while probably still holding both York and London. Between them and the Saxons in the east, a desolate no-man's-land ran down the middle of the country.

The fifty or sixty years between the mid-fifth to the early sixth century, many of them grim for the Britons, were years of intermittent warfare that destroyed much of the Roman economy and technology. Whilst something of Roman civilization still survived in the west, most of Eastern Britain now lay beyond the effective recovery and repair of the Britanno-Romans. The net result of the ravages (beyond the destruction of Eastern Britain and the settlement of Brittany by the Britons or Bretons) was to thin out virtually to extinction the educated Romanized classes: their last efforts, decisive and considerable, produced the careers of Ambrosius Aurelianus and Arthur, the fabled "King of the Britons." The post-Arthurian Welsh kings and tribes surviving in the west were Britons with but an inconsiderable trace of Roman civilization or language. The ravages that occurred circa 450–500/510 had one further important result. Because of the devastation spread over large areas of the country, there was now plenty of room for the settlement of the Saxons and other invaders.

In that long struggle with the barbarians the Britons found two outstanding and ingenious leaders from the Romanized remnant. Of Ambrosius Aurelianus it may be said he made a successful resistance; and on the foundation of this defense the Britons chose Arthur again and again to lead them against the invaders. This series of twelve great battles culminated in a signal victory at Mons Badonicus around 500 or 510, and won for the Western Britons some thirty or forty years of peace or semi-peace.

Thus the British won the war under Arthur's leadership, and Arthur restored the forms of Roman imperial government. They contained the Saxons within substantial and clearly defined reservations. Arthur's "empire" of united Brythons on both sides of the "Narrow Seas" lasted some thirty to fifty years (estimates vary). At his death his realm fragmented into a large number of small independent successor states.

Also, sometime following his death, starting in 547 and gaining new impetus in 552, the Anglo-Saxons continued the expansion of their territory westward, and always at the expense of the Brythons. The Saxon and other Germanic federates rebelled once again (say, from the mid-fifth century on into the early seventh). In one generation they subdued most of the former province of Britannia and began its transformation into England. (Some authorities give the approximate dates 552–615 for this further period of conquest by the Saxons.)

From that time onward, the independent native British were confined to the west (mainly Cambria and Dumnonia or Cornwall, Devon, and Somerset) and to the north (areas such as the Scottish Lowlands and the Lake District).

According to a recent monograph devoted to the subject, *The Age of Arthur* (1973), John Morris sums up the achievement of the real historical Arthur or Artorius in the following words:

His triumph was the last victory of western Rome; his short-lived empire created the future nations of the English and the Welsh; and it was
during his reign and under his authority that the Scots first came to Scotland [from northern Erin or Ireland]. His victory and his defeat turned
Roman Britain into Great Britain. (xiii)

What then were the basic British holdings during the regimes of Aurelianus and Artorius?

There were some five or more principal Welsh "kingdoms" or
geographical areas that spread from southwestern Britain all the way
up through the Scottish Lowlands to the Grampian Mountains north
of Antonine's Wall (this latter is in the same latitude as Edinburgh).

There was Cambria or Wales with three main kingdoms: Gwynedd or Venedotia in the north, Dyfed in the south, and between them
(lying more in the east of central Wales) Powys. There was also the
area in southeastern Cambria, Siluria or Gwent, which included Caerleon and Caerwent and the Forest of Dean. To the east and north of
Gwent, there lay the great protected inner valley of the Severn (mainly
north of Glevum or Gloucester).

The Britons held Cheshire and Lancashire and then further
north Cumberland and Westmoreland. These last two areas southwest of Hadrian's Wall comprised the kingdom of Rheged.

North of the Wall (that is, in the eastern Scottish Lowlands) there
was the large kingdom of Gododin (also called Manau Guotodin) or
Lothian; in the western Scottish Lowlands there were other smaller
kingdoms. Drawing a line from the Tyne or the Tees to Silchester
(west of London)—virtually down the middle of Britain—we may regard everything east as belonging to the Anglo-Saxons and other invaders.

The Britons would probably still have held the land just around
Eburacum or York, say, somewhere between the Humber River on
the south and the Tees River on the north.

They would still have held Winchester, Vindocladia, the Isle of
Wight, Calleva or Silchester, London, and the naval control of the
Thames to Vagniacae and Rutupiae and in the series of Roman forts
built along the lower Thames out to the "German Sea" (lying on the
east or northeast of Britain).

They would still have held the heavily forested Chiltern Hills, which lay north and northwest of London, and which served as a natural defense against the settlements of the Northern Angles in the land just north of the Wash as well as those of the East Angles and the East Saxons inhabiting the lands northeast of London, that is, lying between the Wash and the general London area.

The heavily fortified Britanno-Roman city of Londinium served of course as its own defense against the South Saxon settlements in southeastern Britain, particularly the chieftain Aelle's own isolated but populous kingdom in Sussex between the "Narrow Seas" and the uninhabited forest of Anderida, or the Weald. Aelle founded his own kingdom sometime between 477 and 491, when he stormed and sacked the fortified town of Anderida or Pevensey.

VI. Arthurian Britain

It has only been recently that more and more scholars have come to realize that a real historical figure does indeed stand behind the King Arthur of myth and legend, and that for excellent reasons he should be legended. In restoring for the nonce a substantial portion of the Western Roman Empire, Arthur as a Britanno-Roman hero deserved—indeed could not have avoided—the mythicizing that for centuries and centuries kept his name and something of his real ancient renown alive in people's imaginations in lieu of any actual historical evidence available to the modern world until recently. A pretty piece of magic for someone who has been described as "a semi-barbaric chief"!

The following collation of dates and events in regard to Arthurian Britain is the present writer's own personal interpretation, and represents a conflation of varying sources (history, legend, archaeology, traditions, folklore, and summaries of divers schools of thought). While many of the dates are frankly tentative, we have tried nonetheless to create some kind of consistency between the historical Artorius and the legendary "King Arthur" by aligning them with certain main outlines and facts of that almost obliterated and certainly chaotic period of history.

According to Geoffrey of Monmouth, Arthur was born in 505 and died in 542. However, the consensus of modern scholarship suggests around 470 for Arthur's birth. This date would allow a more extended period of time than 505, in order to accommodate the press of events in Arthur's lifetime, but we shall use this latter date elsewhere. Arthur was crowned king in Silchester (the Calleva of Roman times) at age fifteen. This would give us 485 or around 485, a year in which we may also posit the death of Arthur's father Uther Pendragon (if there is indeed any historical reality to such a kingly father-figure for Arthur's own immediate progeniture), as well as the first of Arthur's "twelve great battles" against the Saxons. These last three events might all be connected.

At least one modern novelist, Mary Stewart in her best-selling novel *The Hollow Hills* (1973), has adroitly and astutely connected them. In her telling Uther Pendragon, virtually on his deathbed, commands the British forces against the Saxons in a great battle near Hadrian's Wall at Caer Luguvallium. Arthur literally saves the day for his own British by the heroism and fiery enthusiasm of his fighting. Uther dies during the subsequent victory feast within the old Roman fort. Arthur is recognized as king by virtue of a magic sword in a mysterious forest chapel. All these events transpire during the same day and night. The year is around 485.

The neighborhood of Caerleon-on-Usk witnessed Arthur's ninth great battle against the Saxons: we shall posit 505 for this event. If the myths and legends relative to this battle at Isca Silurum reflect any truth, the defense of this proud and ancient city (the one-time military capital) would have called forth an especially valiant display of desperate and heroical fighting on the part of Arthur and the Britons.

The prolonged and intermittent fighting betwixt Saxons and Britons lasted from 450 into 500 or 510, and culminated at last at Mount Badonicus where the British won overwhelmingly against the Saxons, returned them to their clearly defined reservations, and presently enjoyed a long period of peace or semi-peace before the inevitable reduction of most of Britain to the dominion of the Saxons.

Various dates have been suggested for the battle at Mount Badonicus (also called Mount Badon, Mons Badonicus, and Badon Hill): 490, 500, 510, 512, 514, 516. We have chosen the year 510, as this would allow more than thirty years for the "imperial reign" of Arthur, a respite of peace that, in retrospect, would appear a magical and "golden" age. The precise location of Mount Badonicus is not known, but it may have been at Bath, or possibly somewhere southeast of Bath, or possibly it might have been Salsbury Hill at Batheaston.

Twenty-five years of Arthur fighting victoriously against the Saxons (circa 485 to 510) does not seem a necessarily unrealistic length of time for what must have proven a bitterly desperate struggle for the beleaguered British. Charlemagne spent thirty years in subduing the Saxons in the later 700s on the basis of intermittent warfare.

We would posit 510 or 512 as the year in which Arthur would have been crowned as Caesar Augustus Artorius—the Roman Emperor of the West—at "Caer Leon" on Usk. As a proper military, administrative, commercial, and courtly ambiance it would naturally have suggested itself to the British of that time. It was a former military capital, a wealthy community with a long-established cosmopolitan character, a well-protected municipality (that is, a Roman town still extant and intact as compared to many Roman towns in Eastern Britain that lay desolate and ruinous), and a seat of the ancient Brythonic stock situated in the still unconquered West Country of Britannia (and moreover in the very mountain heartland of Cymru or Cambria). Arthur came along just in time to take advantage of all the previous Britanno-Roman efforts against the Anglo-Saxons, and his twenty-five years of vigilance against the barbarian invaders represents approximately the latter half of the fifty or sixty years between 450 and 510.

At the time of his imperial coronation Arthur would have numbered among his contemporaries the following key historical figures: Symmachus, the Pope at the Lateran Palace in Rome; Theodoric, King of the Ostrogoths, and the Byzantine Emperor's Viceroy in Italy; Anastasius I, Emperor of the East, ruling from Constantinopolis and surrounded by imperial splendor; and Kavadh I, the Shah of Iran and the Sasanian Empire, ruling from the double city of Ctesiphon (on both sides of the lower Tigris River) in ancient Mesopotamia (20 miles southeast of the later Bagdad) and surrounded by no less imperial magnificence.

Whether or not any of these would have recognized (or even

been aware of) the Welsh *ameráudur* or emperor is today a moot question, since early in the fifth century the Teutonic conquest of Gaul had virtually cut Britain off from Rome and the Mediterranean.

There in the "sunset realms" of Britain the Britanno-Romans would have been conscious of preserving a cultural continuity directly from Late Roman times. By the time of Arthur's Britain they were already far enough away from those irremeable days that they would certainly have perceived with acute nostalgia the vanished peace and order of the Imperium Romanum and the whole way of life that had gone with it.

Whilst Arthur's reign (imperial or merely royal) would have marked a revival of Keltic art and architecture, and the earliest transformation of Late Roman society into "proto-medieval," the Romano-Britons would especially have reverenced the forms of Roman imperial ritual as a charismatic survival from the Western Roman Empire. This would have represented in effect some of the earliest ROMANticism—properly speaking—even though most modern phases of Romanticism stem from the High Middle Ages and the whole way of life symbolized through the metrical romances of the trouvères, and the songs of the troubadours and minnesingers.

As one of the three former legionary bases in Britain, Caerleon would have retained a strong civic pride as a custodian and protector of the Late Roman culture as well as of the revised Kelticism symbolized by such a *native* ruler as Arthur, a revised Kelticism also seen in the contemporary hero-cult in verse concerning Arthur fostered and maintained by the native Welsh bards according to immemorial custom.

The mixed Roman and (revived) Keltic style that would have prevailed in the Romano-British world in the age of Arthur might be symbolized best for us by the following simple and purely verbal examples. Segontium became Caer Segontium, then later Caer Seint, then still later Caernarvon (after the Welsh "Caernarfon," i.e., Caer yn Arton, the fort in the land over against the island of Mona or Angelesy). Venta Silurum became Caer Venta or Caerwent. Isca Silurum, Caer Legionis or "Caer Leon." Maridunum, Caer Maridunum, then Caer Myrrdyn, then finally Carmarthen (this area is strongly associated with the poet–prince–magician "Myrrdyn" or Merlin, the name so closely linked with Arthur's in later legend).

This curious mingling of the classical (Roman) with the native (Keltic) continued on in various forms during most of the Middle Ages. Geoffrey of Monmouth brought a strong "classicizing" influence upon the Arthurian lore bequeathed to the Britons of his time, and from this peculiar mixture the later Arthurian Mythos derives much of its characteristic aesthetic (together with a considerable admixture from the Age of Chivalry, it must be emphasized).

In the saga of the historical Artorius there remains now to record only the final Battle of Camlann, or Camlaun (identified by some scholars as "Camogdelanna")—"in which Arthur and Medraut fell"—dated by some to 537, and by others (including Geoffrey of Monmouth) to 542. Compare this with the Arthur of legend, reported as "sore wounded" whilst fighting against Medraut (or Mordred) in a last battle on the River Camel in Cornwall. And this is the last we hear of the Welsh *ameráudur*—in any kind of historical way—until the High Middle Ages and Geoffrey of Monmouth.

At the time of Arthur's death Justinian the Great was reigning from Byzantium as Emperor of the East (he had succeeded Justin I, who in turn had succeeded Anastasius I), and Chosroes or Khosrau I (at least as great a ruler as Justinian) had succeeded his father Kavadh I as the Shah of Iran and the Sasanian Empire. Then sometime between 547 (signalized by the death of King Maelgwyn of Gwynedd) or 552 and 615, the Saxons conquered further but always (it should be stressed) against the fierce opposition of the British, or as the newcomers called them, the Welsh who lived in the west and the north. By 570 the Welsh still held a little less than half of Britain, although they evidently had lost London by this time.

VII. The Arthurian Country at Large

We have now pursued the career of certain elements and locales in the work and life of Arthur Machen as related to Caerleon and what we may call the specifically *local* Arthur Machen country. Next we shall continue to follow some of these (mainly certain aspects of the Arthurian Mythos) into what we might call the Arthur Machen (and surely the "Arthurian") country *at large*. To wit, the world (cultural and geographical, and surviving through radically diverse political sys-

tems over a period of millennia) of the Brythonic or British-Keltic
empire, and then, beyond that, the Keltic world of Gael and Brython
combined, including most particularly ancient Erin, or Ireland, the
Hibernia or Ivernia of Roman usage.

First, we open an atlas to the British Isles and quickly focus in on
the country around the Bristol Estuary and the western end of the
English Channel. Glance at Scotland, Ireland, and the Isle of Man
(called Mona in Roman times) in the upper Irish Sea; here have lived
from ancient times the Goidelic or Gaelic Kelts, cousins to the Brythonic Kelts. Now look over Wales (including also the Isle of Anglesey, just northwest of Wales, and also called Mona in Roman times)
bounded by the Dee and the Severn (and at one time by Offa's Dyke,
the Anglo-Saxon wall connecting the two rivers, and keeping the
Welsh within the traditional boundaries of their native mountain
heartland), Monmouth or Monmouthshire, Gloucester, Somerset,
Devon, Cornwall, and the Scilly Isles. And then glance over to Brittany and Normandy (the ancient Armorica), and just west of Armorica,
the Channel Islands. These are some of the ancient lands where the
Brythons have dwelt since both before and after the decline of Roman Britain; and according to myth and legend, these lands form but
a fragment of Arthur's Empire, which in its own turn had been but a
fragment of the Western Roman Empire, which in yet its own turn
had only been the other half of the Imperium Romanum, stretching
from the British Isles on the far west to venerable Mesopotamia on
the far east. Both the Gaels and the Britons had myths and legends
that told of their Avalons and Avilions, remarkably Hesperides-like or
Atlantis-like islands arising from those depths of the North Atlantic
Ocean that lay to the west or southwest of Britain and Gaul.

(Between 500 and 550, the Brythonic Kelts primarily inhabited
the western peninsulas and highlands from Cornwall and Wales on
through the scenically spectacular Lake District (an old Keltic mountain heartland from which the much later English Romantic poets
were to derive both inspiration and a name) and then on through the
Scottish Lowlands about as far north as Antonine's Wall and "Caer
Eidyn," or Edinburgh.)

Secondly, we draw a line from Caer Nodentis in Lydney Park,
Gloucestershire (this would be a point roughly midway betwixt the

Wye and the city of Gloucester on the Severn) south-southeast to the city of Bath (the Aquae Sulis of Roman times); then, another line from Aquae Sulis but going southwest to Glastonbury (the ancient island-valley of Avalon); and then, another line from Avalon (or "Glastonia"—one of its names in medieval Latin) but going northeast or north-northeast back to "Caer Nodentis." Thus you will have a triangle that lies at the very heart of the cultural Brythonic empire, and which keynotes an immediate area where extraordinary spiritual and mystical activity has taken place from pre-Roman to post-Christian times and into the twentith century. This area is moreover intensely connected with certain main aspects and elements in the Arthurian Mythos. Keep this triangle in mind, since it will serve as the geographical touchstone or triangular homebase (as it were) from which we shall now explore some of those same principal aspects, elements, and locales important in Arthurian Britain.

By an odd coincidence, the distance between the Wye and the city of Gloucester on the Severn—upon a line running from southwest to northeast—measures roughly the same as the distance between Caer Nodentis and Aquae Sulis, and then between Aquae Sulis and Glastonbury; that is, the original distance is approximately the same in length as the "eastern" or "southern" sides of our triangular homebase.

VIII. Cadbury Castle

Straight in a line as the bird flies, about 12 miles southeast of Glastonbury, we come into the neighborhood of the River Cam and the village of Queen's Camel (formerly known as just Camel) and thus to Cadbury Castle. This earthenwork fort (pre-Roman Iron-Age, like that to the northwest of Caerleon, or like that at Caer Nodentis) stands on a solitary hill some 500 feet high and overlooks the Vale of Avalon with Glastonbury Tor in the distance to the northwest. During the reign of Henry VIII, the antiquarian John Leland recorded the fact that the local people referred to Cadbury Castle as "Camalat" and as once the home of King Arthur. Out of all the sites that might have been the original for the legendary Camelot, this particular place has one of the best claims to a real enduring tradition.[3]

The question of Camelot seems to be curiously intertwined (linguistically at least) with that of Camlann or Camlaun, as well as with other places and place-names where *cam* or *camel* occur. If *cam* or *camel* has any meaning in Welsh or Cornish beyond "twisted" or "crooked," it may have been a generic word for stream or river in that the course of most rivers is twisted, or twisting, or making loops or "esses." Curiously enough, in many poems and stories that depict or mention Camelot, there is usually a river that goes near or fairly near its walls, and that features rather prominently in the given narrative.

According to legend, Camelot was the capital where King Arthur ruled over the Britons, during the time of the terrible Saxon invasions but before the overall Saxon conquest of England. The oldest existing records or stories of Arthur do not mention Camelot. He is first mentioned as ruling there in *Lancelot,* the metrical romance by Chrétien de Troyes, written sometime between 1160 and 1180, and hence after the first appearance in Latin prose (c. 1135) of Geoffrey's *History of the Kings of Britain.* "Camelot" happens to make a good rime with "Lancelot" in Norman French (where the final "t" is pronounced) as well as in modern English. Chrétien de Troyes may simply have picked up the name of Camel, or Camlann/Camlaun (or as Camalann/Camalaun), and Frenchified it easily enough into "Camelot."

In *Le Morte d'Arthur* (published in 1485), his classic redaction of the Arthurian Mythos in English prose, Sir Thomas Malory depicts Camelot as the chief metropolis of the realm (rather like London), sometimes equated with Winchester but in one context located north of Carlisle (Caer Luguvallium). Some scholars have proposed the modern city of Colchester as the site of Camelot; in Roman times it bore the name of Camulodunum; but since that area of East Anglia was occupied by the barbarian invaders almost from the start of the Germanic invasions, the Britons would have needed to spend a great deal of energy to make Camulodumun an important capital for Arthur so far from the West Country still occupied and controlled by

3. The principal source for this chapter is the article "Camelot and Arthurian Britain" by Geoffrey Ashe in *Man, Myth and Magic.*

the Kelts. Thus, beyond the purely linguistic coincidence of the name, Camulodunum has little to recommend it as Camelot.

Just north of Antonine's Wall and then due west of the inner Firth of Forth (not far from Caer Eidyn; i.e., Edinburgh) there once rose a Roman fortress called Camelon or, in the Keltic style, "Caer Camelon." This general area saw some considerable Arthurian activity; immediately outside Caer Eidyn is the mountain called Arthur's Seat (from whose summit he is supposed to have surveyed the surrounding countryside) not far from which Arthur and his Britons fought one of his "twelve great battles" against the Saxons. The name of Camelon is (coincidentally) close to that of Cam(a)laun, and whilst this Roman frontier fortress was probably no more Camelot than Colchester, it seems safe to assume that the Arthurian Britons may have used it to defend their own realm's northern frontier inherited from the Romans. It may even have figured in some signal way in Arthur's own saga.

Yet another theory places Camelot near Tintagel where in a pre-Norman castle Arthur is supposed to have been born. Again, without placing absolute credence in the legend of his birth, or in the theory that here in this particular spot there once a rose the legendary Camelot, so much tradition has associated Tintagel with Arthur that it does seem safe to assume it did possess some real and important connection with him.

If Camelot does have any meaning beyond a generic usage as capital or headquarters (and any particular town and/or fortress under Arthur's rule could have functioned in that capacity even if only temporarily), then the two best geographical candidates must share the specific honor between them, as they often do in some of the legends. We stress the double honor, since the overall concept of Camelot has at least two main aspects as Arthur's capital.

In some accounts Camelot is primarily a great castellated palace with a village or town attached in order to serve the needs of Arthur's court. In other accounts Camelot is a genuine and heavily fortified city similar to London (although nowhere near as large) with Arthur's "gorgeous palace" featured as one of the main architectural attractions. The best candidate for Camelot as a genuine city is probably Arthur Machen's own birthplace Caerleon-on-Usk. The city is located on, and derives its Roman name from, the Usk; and while no site as yet discovered at Caerleon has preserved any vestiges of Arthur's royal palace, we cannot presently rule out the possibility that such may not have existed there.

The best candidate for Camelot as a "great castellated palace" is undoubtedly Cadbury Castle. The River Cam and the village of Queen's Camel lie close enough to the Castle so that they figure geographically in the traditional local references to, and accounts of, King Arthur. Thus it remains Cadbury Castle "in the neighborhood of" or "not far from" the River Cam and the village of Camel or Queen's Camel.

The Castle's ramparts enclose an area of 18 acres atop the 500-foot-high hill, and the summit plateau (which local folklore of vast antiquity calls King Arthur's Palace) did actually support at least one elaborate timber structure once upon a time. During the first quarter of the sixth century (a part of Arthur's presumed period) a wealthy and powerful British lord or leader did use the hill-top as a stronghold, and erected at least one substantial timber building on the summit plateau. This edifice (as visualized in basic restoration on paper) has an immediate affinity with the great hall of later medieval usage. Recent archaeology has revealed a large rectangular ground-plan (wider east and west than north and south) and with about the eastern third of its area originally walled off by some kind of screen. (This last feature also has its mediaeval affinity.)

Moreover, the same British ruler and/or war-chief secured his woodland fortress with strong fortifications indeed. He completely refurbished the original, pre-Roman, Iron Age defenses of earthenwork by superimposing an enormous "drystone" type of rampart (featuring a type of tower both similar to and yet different from that of the Roman fortress-camps) and all done in a peculiarly Keltic style of architecture. These walls remain without "known contemporary parallels anywhere else in Britain" (Cavendish 331). The war-chief lived quite securely and comfortably within what must have been (from the available evidence) an elaborate series of mounds upon the summit plateau, enclosed as they were inside the far-reaching round of outer battlements. It is known that either the lord or his household acting for him imported luxuries from the eastern Mediterranean and also probably from the Middle East.

This "Camalat" was then easily the largest, strongest, and most elaborate of all the known British fortresses in Arthurian times (apart, of course, from the walled cities and forts in the West Country left over from Late Roman days). The remaining usable acreage on top of the hill could easily have accommodated (within tents and pavilions) a large entourage, military and otherwise, whenas circumstances relative to the omnipresent Anglo-Saxon threat served to gather them there (this last must have been fairly often). Details of the specific buildings and fortifications still possess distinct analogies with Britanno-Roman architecture (but not the placement of the entrance to the great hall at the southwest and northeast). But the overall conception of the stronghold would have definitely appeared to us as non-Roman, however obvious its ultimate immediate evolution from Roman models in certain selected aspects. The typically native Brythonic, purely timber architecture of the main group of buildings, as well as the general plan of the fortress (a kind of donjon or inner castle surrounded by a series of vast outer courtyards, in turn environed by "many-towered" ramparts of mixed stone and timber construction), rather curiously foreshadows the typical castle of the later Middle Ages.

It is not hard to imagine the Welsh *ameráudur* living in this typically British woodland fortress of the early Dark Ages—this Brythonic Versailles, as it were—attended by an entourage of British warriors and knights, bards and minstrels, astrologers and priests (whether Christian or Druid, or both).

Recent archaeology suggests a genuine historic link between this Brythonic stronghold and Glastonbury Tor some 12 miles to the northwest. Significantly, both places lie within sight of each other. In the graveyard of early Glastonbury Abbey—according to an ancient local tradition—his followers buried "Rex Arthurius" after his famous last Battle of Camlaun in 542 A.D. Although it may seem at first as though we are straying far afield from Arthur Machen and from matters strictly Machenesque, we must spend some little time and space next at Glastonbury.

In its own right it is a mystical milieu of supreme importance—it has been termed quite properly a prime spiritual "acupuncture point" on the planet Earth—and during the High Middle Ages, Glastonbury's greatest period, it contributed tremendously both to the local renown and the international cult centered around King Arthur.

IX. Glastonbury and Avalon

The Tor, or Avalon Tor, rises high above the small town of Glastonbury in Somerset, internationally famous for its ruined Abbey, one of the greatest Christian foundations in all Western Europe.[4] The town lies upon (or actually just off) the River Brue. Like "Camelot" or Cadbury Castle some 12 miles to the southeast, this hill attains a height of some 500 feet above sea level and looks out over a broad stretch of low-lying country on all sides, the ancient island-vale of Avalon. Built more specifically on the site of the island proper of Avalon, Glastonbury Abbey is allegedly the first Christian foundation in Britain and the last resting place of King Arthur. In addition, the Abbey is the focus of a large tapestry of myth and legend, and in some special sense a repository of pre-Christian mysteries.

The main legend relative to the Abbey tells how in the first century A.D. Joseph of Arimathea (the rich man who buried Christ) transports the Holy Grail (used at the Last Supper of Christ and his apostles) to the Island of Avalon. In obedience to a vision Joseph and his companions build a wattle chapel, the so-called Old Church dedicated to the Virgin Mary, and still standing in the High Middle Ages as an object of the profoundest veneration. How did this Arimathean story come about? Was it a symbolic literary fiction, a deliberate monastic fraud, or a genuine rediscovery of an elder tradition?

The main legend relative to the Tor is that of the ancient Isle of Avalon. The original "island" of Avalon and its immediate neighborhood have served as a holy place, a burial ground, and a residence. To the original Brythons it was a place of the greatest religious awe, the literally *enchanted* Isle of Avalon, consecrated to the shades of the dead: the "ynys apfalon" or "ynysapfalon annwn." The Abbey site itself is rich in both Christian and pre-Christian burials; this evidently was the original burial site for which Avalon was first used and from

---

4. This chapter is heavily indebted to the article "Glastonbury" by Geoffrey Ashe in *Man, Myth and Magic*.

which there evolved much of the "otherworldly" character of the Avalon legends. The earthwork of Ponter's Ball (to the east) may be a vestige of the Keltic sanctuary's boundary that defined the original limits of the island.

As for "Avalon," this is usually interpreted as the "place of apples" like the Garden of the Hesperides in classical mythology; the Irish Kelts (the Gaels) also told of an Avalon as Isle of the Blest, and a "place of apples" likewise, lying somewhere in the Atlantic Ocean west or southwest of the British Isles. A later name was no longer "ynys apfalon" but "ynys vitrin" or the Isle of Glass ("Glastonbury" is an Anglo-Saxon version of this): that is, an "Isle" reflected in the "Glass" or mirror of the surrounding waters.

Geology would seem to indicate quite definitely that before drainage, and especially during Late Roman times and the subsequent Dark Ages, the Tor with its environing lesser hills must often have been virtually isolated. Indeed, most of this region used to be subject to flooding, with permanent lagoons, marshes, and forested islets. Thus at the beginning of the Christian era Glastonbury was almost a true island, surrounded as it was by lagoons and rivers: with its original flora and fauna the area must have presented an appearance of wild "primordial" beauty.

The island of Avalon, the otherworldly apple orchard, was thus a pre-Christian religious center and for the Brythons an "Isle of the Dead" and a Gate into Annwn, the realm of shades and faery folk. In some of the Brythonic folklore Avalon is indeed equated with Annwn, and to distinguish it from other Avalonian concepts the real Avalon should therefore be more properly termed Avalon Annwn. Apple trees have grown on the Tor at various times, and in the pre-Christian era wild apple orchards may have originally flourished here. Any apples from such sacred trees would have possessed a mystical signifiance for the Kelts. At least one surviving legend (relative to the Welsh saint Collen) preserves presently undatable folklore about the Tor as an entrance to Annwn the Underworld, and as a home for Gwyn-ap-Nudd, lord of the faery folk, leader of the Wild Hunt, and sometimes the "son" of Nodens (hence, a later aspect or incarnation of the same principle or divinity).

Gwyn-ap-Nudd and his "home" on Avalon may preserve a

memory of a shrine to Nodens or some closely related god here in Roman times. There may have been tales or legends of the Tor as a hollow hill. Hence, Nodens or Nudd, Lord of the Abyss or of the "void" (the "hollow place" lying below the earth's surface), provides an easy and logical transition to—and transformation into—Annwn the Underworld (and part of the Keltic concept of the *Other*world). We can safely postulate therefore a pre-Christian shrine on the Tor. Significantly, the Christian monks during the later Middle Ages built a chapel with a tower on top of the Tor and dedicated it to St. Michael, vanquisher of the "evil powers." Only the tower still stands.

Traces of inhabitants on the Abbey site in Roman times have been recently found but no indication of their religion. This might have been some kind of simple residence for pre-Christian holy men, say, a hermitage or abbey of Druids. Recent excavations on the Tor have revealed human settlement there also, notably around 500 A.D., part of the Arthurian period. Indeed, in the time of Arthur a typical timber-built citadel stood atop the Tor. We shall call this stronghold "Caer Avalon Annwn" after the Welsh fashion. Such a citadel would have safeguarded this holy spot from overt physical damage during the early Dark Ages, above all a period of turmoil, danger, and chaos. Since Christianity was still only one religion among many and had not as yet become paramount in the Western world, we could have seen (during the age of Arthur) both on the Tor or close to it—that is, existing at one and the same time—the Keltic pre-Christian shrine, the Brythonic citadel, and the early Christian monastery with the Old Church.

A Keltic pre-Christian monastery would have more than likely stood on the future site of Glastonbury Abbey (just as the well-organized colleges of Druids among the Irish Kelts were easily converted to Christian monasteries). By the sixth century Christian hermits were living on the spot and worshipping in the Old Church. The simultaneous presence of a Christian Keltic monastery near the Tor, and of a timbered Brythonic citadel atop the Tor, is closely paralleled by that of the Christian Keltic monastery on Tintagel Headland, as well as of the presumed Brythonic citadel upon whose site the later Norman castle was built.

As for Glastonbury Abbey it was certainly founded by British

Christians on the present site before the Saxon conquest. Archaeologically a date early in the sixth century appears likely. Although St. Patrick reorganized the little community and gave it a monastic rule, no saint of the Dark Ages is credited with Glastonbury's foundation. The monastery is simply there in some form, its origins unexplained and further back still. Hence it is arguable that the Old Church and a small group of hermits may have been there *before* the 500s. Or it is equally arguable that the Church and Abbey were founded within a pre-existing Druid abbey; or, if the latter had been destroyed, then upon the site of the same pre-Christian hermitage.

The West Saxons conquered central Somerset in 658. Their Christian king Cenwalh maintained Glastonbury without a break. It thus became the first major institution in which Teuton and Kelt co-existed and cooperated. It is the one place in Britain with Christian continuity stretching back without a break to King Arthur, to the Romans, and to the apostolic age itself. It is a kind of national shrine, with a spiritual character uniquely its own. The British monks were unable to tell the Saxons any clear story of the Abbey's foundation; this had already been lost in antiquity.

Whenever its foundation, and whatever the site's pre-Christian antecedents, one fact from the Abbey's earlier history seems to remain a fact. According to a very old local tradition, King Arthur was buried in the Abbey's graveyard after his famous last battle, wherever that took place. His alleged exhumation in 1190 served to affix the name of Avalon on the map after it had evidently been lost to the general recognizance.

In 1184 most of the then Abbey (including the Old Church) burnt down, and in the course of the rebuilding the monks who were digging at the site discovered a coffin together with a stone slab and a lead cross, inscribed HIC IACET SEPULTUS INCLITUS REX ARTURIUS IN INSULA AVALONIA: "Here lies ensepulchred the famous King Arthur in the Island of Avalon." The coffin, made from a hollowed-out oak log, contained the bones of a large man with a damaged skull, as well as some smaller bones (and some tresses of blond hair) understood to be those of Queen Guinivere, Arthur's second wife. Perhaps the most valuable contemporary account of this exhumation is that of Geraldus Cambrensis; he was a skeptic about

King Arthur at a time whenas most people were indiscriminately credulous.

The monks appropriately enshrined the relics in a casket that Edward I re-interred before the new high altar. However, the contents of the casket were tragically dispersed and lost at the Abbey's dissolution in 1539 during the reign of Henry VIII. The Abbey's dissolution in itself constitutes a tragic loss of the first magnitude: the main church alone, whether as an ecclesiastical locus or simply as a piece of superb Gothic architecture, was in every way at least as great as the cathedral of Westminster Abbey.

In 1962 and 1963, C. A. Ralegh Radford re-excavated the area of the original disinterment, and among other evidence he discovered "the stone lining of an important grave at a great depth." Ralegh Radford was thus able to prove (though not conclusively—which, given the particular evidence, should not be surprising) that this may very well indeed have been the original grave of the real Arthur.

If it is indeed true that Cadbury Castle near Queen's Camel forms the original locus for the legendary Camelot, its closeness to Glastonbury may be more than a mere coincidence.

Before we leave Glastonbury, we must note certain aspects of the Arthurian Avalon legends inspired ultimately by the pre-Christian Isle of Avalon. There are two main concepts of Avalon: there is the island-vale of Avalon Annwn where the real King Arthur was buried, and there is the Avalon depicted by Geoffrey of Monmouth as an Island of the Blest in the Atlantic Ocean rather like a Garden of the Hesperides. This last idealized Avalon is very similar to—if not the same as—the Avalon legended by the Irish Kelts to lie in the western ocean (i.e., somewhere in the Atlantic). Just as the historical Arthur was taken to the real geographical Avalon, Geoffrey's idealized Avalon in the Atlantic is again Arthur's last earthly destination, where he is taken for his wounds to be healed. This occurs in a later work of Geoffrey's, his *Vita Merlini*. Geoffrey possessed (it should be emphasized) an especially poetic quality of imagination, and in its pronounced *poeticalness,* distinctly Welsh or Keltic.

In some versions the idealized (ocean-situated) Avalon is ruled over by Morganne Le Fay. Could she be a memory of a "lady of Avalon" who once lived in Caer Avalon Annwn, or a goddess peculiar to Avalon?

Here we see a fictional/mythical extrapolation in the classic "scientific-tional" manner. The real island of Avalon is removed to an unspecified location in the Atlantic, and the Brythonic goddess (possibly Morrigu) is extrapolated into a medieval enchantress. Whatever else the real Avalon may have been, it remained for the Keltic imaginative tradition a place of great magic-making, as well as a perfectly logical "smithy" for the production of Caliburn or Excalibur, Arthur's magic sword.

As a traditional burial ground sacred to the British Kelts (not even Christianity could prevent that particular pre-Christian cultural continuity) it was close enough to Arthur's last great battle (whether near "Camelot" at Cadbury Castle, or near "Camelot" at Caerleon-on-Usk in Gwent, or near Tintagel and Camelford in Cornwall) to be the officially logical choice for the inhumation of Caesar Augustus Artorius with due mystical and imperial splendors. The traditional barge in most of the legends, which bears the dead or dying Arthur to Avalon, is very likely the reminiscence of a real vessel that did bear Arthur to Avalon for burial there.

Looking back through the mists of time, can we not somehow see that military flotilla with Arthur's funeral barge in its midst proceeding just off the northern coast of Devon and then into the mouth of the River Brue that flows by Glastonbury? This was the gloriously sad and ultimate public moment in Arthur's career: the little navy paddling up the river into the haunted island-vale of Avalon Annwn, past the forested islets and the brooding marshes, over the great misty lagoons, directly to the Isle of the Dead, and the Gate into Annwn the Underworld or *Other*world.

X. Cornwall and Tintagel

Now going due southwest, we leave Glastonbury, pass through Devon, and come into the ancient land of Cornwall (or "Cornua"), proceeding immediately to Tintagel Headland, a place of unique and spectacular senic beauty high above the western sea.[5] In the later 400s

---

5. Sometime after the presumed Brythonic hill-top stronghold but before the later Norman castle, another castle was built (this is archaeologically attested), thus indicating a virtually continuous residence by politically eminent persons upon Tintagel Headland.

A.D., and before the final ascendancy of the Brythonic Kelts under the aegis of King Arthur, great numbers of the Romano-Britons had fled before the invading Saxons from eastern and southeastern Britain into the West Country and beyond, settling in Wales, Cornwall, Devon, Westmoreland, Cumberland, lower Scotland, and Brittany. Indeed, Cornwall together with Wales and Brittany remained a sanctuary for the Britons long after most of England had yielded to the dominance (political and cultural) of the Anglo-Saxons. The Cornish preserved their own language virtually into modern times, and even much of their culture into the twentieth century.

If Arthur were indeed born at Tintagel, as many traditions and legends aver, then the area would naturally have loomed large during his early manhood and later maturity, especially during his career as *imperator atque dux bellorum.* The strategic position of Tintagel far in the west of England (the Brythonic territories par excellence) alone would have assured its importance during the Arthurian period. Although no trace has yet emerged of the pre-Norman "castle" where Arthur was reputedly born, it has now become a fact (thanks to recent archaeology) that the Headland certainly did have inhabitants at this period. A community of British monks (Christians, not Druids) lived here then, and the imported pottery used by their monastery has provided paramount clues to the dating and interpretation of other places, including Arthur's "Camelot" at Cadbury Castle.

The later medieval castle at Tintagel stands close by the remains of the Keltic monastery, and it may very well have been constructed upon the remains of a typical Brythonic hill-top citadel dating from Arthur's time or somewhat before. This Headland is in many respects a very special area, and while it may not have been a place of sacred awe to the Brythons in the manner of Avalon Annwn to the northeast, it does possess its own unique aura. The spot is a natural one for habitation of some kind, and especially desirable as a location for some Arthurian chieftain's hill-fort. Such a fortress (and let us call it "Caer Tintagel" after the Welsh fashion), like Caer Avalon Annwn, would have afforded protection not only to the monastery also on the Headland but to the overall area as well. The simultaneous presence of Christian monastery and Brythonic citadel in the same immediate area is closely paralleled (as we have noted earlier) by that of the monastery and stronghold on the ancient Isle of Avalon.

At a further hill-top dwelling in Cornwall—to wit, Castle Dore—recent archaeology indicates that a Brythonic stronghold (similar to, but not as large as, Cadbury Castle) stood there during the sixth century, i.e., during Arthur's period. Some West Country chieftain built a timber hall within a preexisting Iron Age earthenwork hill-fort, like that at "Caer Nodentis," or like the 17-acre hill northwest of Caerleon's Roman fortress, or like the 18-acre hill of Cadbury Castle. Some scholars have suggested that this chieftain may have furnished the original (historical) model for the King Mark figuring in the romance of Tristram and Yseult. Further hill-top dwellings and strongholds of Arthur's period are known to have existed in both Cornwall and Wales.

Tintagel Headland lies only some 5 miles northwest of the small town of Camelford and the River Camel area. This overall neighborhood is literally permeated with the atmosphere of the sea lying immediately to the west. Again, like Caer Nodentis and the island-vale of Avalon Annwn, this vicinage possesses its own haunted and haunting aura. According to various legends as well as local traditions, the River Camel region is the general area where Arthur fought his famous and fatal "last battle." Certainly, like most of Cornwall, it would have provided a striking background for such an event. The bards at least were following a sound story-telling instinct when they located the last battle here.

The rugged and rocky Cornish coast, the farms on upland plains and in river valleys, the desolate marshes and moors near the sea, the brooding moors lying inland, the outbreaks of stone on old hills and mountains, the variegated clumps of wood, thickets, and other shrubbery—the "poetic" coloring with gemlike hues of blue and/or green pervading the sea, the sky, and the land on a clear day—all possess a wonderfully picturesque quality well suited to the "spirit" of the legend, even if not necessarily to the "letter" of any available historical evidence.

Apart from his final voyage to Avalon, this is the last we see of the real historical Arthur (by now in his later sixties or early seventies) while he is yet alive: the great Welsh *ameráudur* riding forth from Caer Tintagel to the "Last Great Battle of the West"—an event that will loom in later legend like a Brythonic Ragnarok, poignantly symbolizing the final moments of the British-Keltic revival as well as its twilight, which transpired at one and the same time during the period circa 500–550 A.D.

XI. Lyonnesse and Brittany

Now we leave the land of that final fatal encounter of Brython against Brython, and heading again due southwest we pass the towns of Camborne ("Cam-Bourne"), St. Ives, and Penzance, and then come directly to the southwestern extremity of Britain, that curious rocky promontory sculptured by wind and wave into fantastical shapes, to wit, Land's End, with the western sea immediately beyond.

Just some 25 miles due west southwest of Land's End (at the westernmost tip of Cornwall) there lies the small archipelago called the Isles of Scilly; and according to ancient Cornish tradition, they represent the fragments of a larger land called Lyonnesse long lost beneath the waves, but which once stretched from Land's End up to the Scillies, and which also included St. Michael's Mount not far from Penzance.

These islands possess at times a semi-tropical climate, and to the ancient mainland Brythons they must have seemed a veritable paradise. They once contained valuable deposits of tin which both the Phoenicians and the Romans mined; and from this fact there came their Latin name of the Cassiterides, or Isles of Tin. There inheres something peculiarly "Atlantean" in the name of Lyonnesse (as in that of Yss, the island-city that appears and submerges in Breton legendry), vaguely suggesting a survival of some kind from the far-off Empire of Atlantis (such as Plato hath devised), as though Lyonnesse or the Isles of Scilly were somehow the actual remnants of a former Atlantean colony. Lyonnesse (easily semi-independent by virtue of her environing waters and treacherous reefs and rocks) would nonetheless have borne fealty to Arthur, since the inhabitants of the Scilly Isles were at least kindred to the mainland Brythons.

Now we depart from Lyonnesse and head southeast, crossing over the western reaches of the English Channel (or the "Narrow Seas" as they were known in Roman and post-Roman times), and then coming to the peninsulas of Brittany and Normandy, the Armorica of Roman times. An earlier (pre-Keltic) race had lived in Brittany and had built such curious and mysterious megalithic monuments as menhirs, dolmens, and cromlechs; these are most numerous at Carnac and Morbihan. Thus, even before the arrival of the Britons, the peninsula already possessed its own unique aura of otherworldly myth and magic.

The ancient Keltic people in the region of Brittany came under Roman control in 51 B.C. Brittany, or Little Britain, received its name from the Britanno-Roman tribes who settled in Armorica during the second half of the 400s, fleeing before the Anglo-Saxon invaders of eastern and southeastern Britain. By Armorica (from *ar-mor* or *on sea*) we mean Brittany and Western Normandy. It was the lower peninsula that became known as Brittany, with an Upper Brittany and a Lower Brittany, and the home of the "Bretons" (i.e., Britons), or Armorican Brythons. According to various traditions and legends, these definitely counted as among the lands over which King Arthur ruled as Brythonic suzerain. The Channel Islands, just west of Normandy or Upper Armorica, also purportedly formed part of Arthur's Empire.

Before, during, and after Arthur's time, Western Britain and Brittany carried on considerable cultural exchange. Ireland, Britain, and Gaul all possessed varying types of Druids and Druidry, as they later did of Christians and Christianity. On the southern coast of Cornwall and not far from that country's western tip at Land's End, there stands St. Michael's Mount just offshore from the little town of Marazion. (Again, according to ancient Cornish tradition, this Mount represents a remnant of the lost land of Lyonnesse.) The Gulf of St. Malo lies between Brittany and Normandy, and in its (inner) southeastern corner there stands the majestic mass of Mont-Saint-Michel, again just offshore. During the High Middle Ages, these two Benedictine abbeys were closely connected: in name, religion, and general monastic culture.

Rennes, the immemorial capital of Brittany, was named after the Gallic tribe of the Redones or Redonians once resident there. In Roman times the city was known as Condate, or Condate Redonum (the "Condate of the Redonians"). The Forest of Paimpont lies southwest of Rennes; this is the modern remnant of the ancient Forest of Brocéliande, so closely associated in the Arthurian Mythos with Merlin and Arthur (as is much of Brittany). According to one legend the Lady Vivienne ensnared none other than Prince Merlin (the "uncle" and advisor of King Arthur) and imprisoned him in one of the hoary oaks of Brocéliande.

It was here in Brittany (as well as in Western Normandy) that the earliest cycles of poetic narratives about "li re Artus" (first in Breton and then in Norman French) developed subsequently to Arthurian Britain. Thus, "The Bretons have a strong Druidic and Arthurian tradition from classical and mediaeval times . . ." In addition to the enchantments of the Forest of Brocéliande, they had their famous prophecying "Druidesses" on the Ile de Seine.

> It was only at the beginning of the present century, however, that Druidry became an organized force in Brittany. For several years now the annual August Eisteddfod [that peculiarly Keltic gathering of bards, musicians, and entertainers] has been held beside the beautiful lake at Paimpont, in the midst of the old forest area of Brocéliande. (Cavendish 6.723)

The Breton mythology in general has characteristics uniquely its own, just as modern Breton literature written in French is unique in modern French literature for its keenly mystical and cosmic feeling and quality. Thus, Brittany can justly and proudly claim the distinction of acting as the first medium for the transmission of the Arthurian Mythos into the culture of the High Middle Ages, and for thus influencing (in a signal manner) the subsequent development of romance in general throughout Europe. Moreover, the Bretons' bardic and musical culture has remained alive and vigorous into the twentieth century, and has produced outstanding and highly original harpist–singer–poets, some of them popular at least throughout Europe.

XII. Bards, Druids, and Arthur's Later Fame

This then was the Arthurian country at large: the world (cultural and geographical, and surviving through radically diverse political systems over a period of millennia) of the Brythonic (or British-Keltic) empire, and then, beyond that, the Keltic world of Gael and Brython combined, including Ivernia or Ireland.[6]

---

6. This chapter is heavily indebted to the two articles (under the uniform heading) "Druids," the first by Stuart Piggott and the second by Ross Nichols, respec-

This cultural Brythonic empire, stretching from the Grampian Mountains in Scotland on the north all the way to Brittany across the "Narrow Seas" on the south, may then actually reflect a Britanno-Roman dominion once ruled by a Rex Imperator Artorius. Even if not politically, at least *culturally* he would have claimed kinship with all these Brythonic lands and peoples to whom he certainly would have been known contemporaneously. The real King Arthur, however great he may actually have been during his life, became infinitely greater after his death, thanks to the peculiar cycles of myth and legend that the various Brythonic peoples wove around his name and exploits.

However, this particularly Keltic tradition would have commenced in Arthur's case whilst he was very much alive, and in fact early in his public or military career. Arthur's court would naturally have attracted the greatest bards, musicians, and sages of his time. Hence the Arthurian Mythos would have begun in the age of Arthur itself.

Throughout the post-Roman Keltic world of Western Europe (whether Gaelic or Brythonic) the bards and seers, unlike the more famous but also more mysterious Druids, continued in positions of power and authority. Certainly in Arthurian society, with its curious and unique mixture of transformed Romanism and revived Kelticism, the bards occupied a singularly important place. The traditions relating to the Druids are curiously intertwined with those relating to the bards. Even though the Druids are supposed to have been abolished or driven underground (that is, either exterminated or banished to divers hinterlands devoid of political or economic importance to the Romans), various of their traditions continued on in specific ways: thus, for example, the bards evidently captured something of the particularly "Druidic magic" in their poetry.

Geoffrey Ashe has well summarized the importance of the bards in Arthurian times:

A great chieftain's title depended partly on the appropriate bard's knowledge of his ancestry. The loyalty of his vassals depended on the bard's success in keeping them convinced of his prowess, wisdom, and

---

tively, in *Man, Myth and Magic.*

generosity. Poet-sages of legend like Merlin and Taliesin have real if shadowy originals. It is because of these highly respected figures . . . that the tradition of Arthur himself, and of a British heroic age associated with him, was handed down to supply the material of mediaeval romance. (Cavendish 1.393)

The condition of the Druids during this post-Roman period of revived Kelticism is (due to lack of direct evidence) more problematical, since they are frequently confused with the bards and seers. The Druids often incorporated within themselves the functions of bards and poets, and like the bards they spent anywhere from twelve to twenty years in the oral tradition of memorizing verses (as recorded by Julius Caesar in *De Bello Gallico*).

The Druids—the priestly caste in Gaul, Britain, and Ireland—were originally (before the arrival of the Romans) the authoritative class in Keltic society, and in Ireland at least they took precedence over king and warriors.

The Keltic or Druidic beliefs in regard to the immortality of the soul evidently seemed rather outré to the classical world (and pointedly unfamiliar): an otherworld that was a magic recreation of life just as on Earth but in another place. Hence an Avalon "here" has as its counterpart an Avalon "there" or "otherwhere." To accommodate this concept within classical thought, the Graeco-Roman philosophers used the Pythagorean doctrine of the transmigration of souls, although Druidic belief nowhere implies this.

Druidry has consistently claimed a considerable antiquity, going back at least to the New Stone Age. In Stonehenge, Avebury, and other stone circles throughout the West Country, modern Druids recognize the elder temples in which their forebears regarded the sun, moon, and stars with wonder and awe. Specific connections with India's early Aryan culture seem clear: reverence for the sun, moon, and other heavenly bodies; circle dancing in a clockwise direction; the existence of a sacred caste composed of sages; the burning of the dead; wisdom-teaching and the imparting of sacred lore through the medium of long memorized poems; and the cult revolving around certain animals.

According to Julius Caesar, "The young are taught to repeat a great number of verses by heart and often spend twenty years upon this institution. . . . The Druids teach likewise many things related to the stars and their motions, the magnitude of the world [that is, the cosmos] and of our Earth, the nature of things, and the power and prerogatives of the immortal Gods" (*De Bello Gallico* 6.15). Both Britain and Ireland rather than Gaul, evidently, were the traditional training places of this caste who knew, and presided over, the contemporary arts and sciences and imparted them, who acted as political advisers to rulers, who were exempt from war and who often acted as heralds of peace, as well as being priests of a religion.

The term *druid* or *dru-wid* presupposes a Gallic *druvis* (from *druvids*) and probably relates to the Greek *drus*—an oak tree—with the ending the same as the Inda-European root *wid* or "to know" (and surviving in modern English in such a phrase as "to wit"). In his depiction of the Druidic mistletoe ceremony, Pliny makes an immediate link between oak trees and the Druids; in this ritual the Druid would cut mistletoe from an oak tree with a knife or sickle of gold upon the sixth day of the new moon. The oak tree in some mystic way evidently symbolized (for the Druids) wisdom or at least knowledge. Hence, *dru-wid* can mean either deep knowledge or knowledge of the oak *or* both. Of course, *deep* knowledge can be the same as, or can lead to, true wisdom.

Woodland sanctuaries are characteristically Keltic, such as those at Caer Nodentis and Avalon Annwn. According to Julius Caesar, there was an Archdruid for the whole of Gaul who convened annual meetings in a sacred woodland sanctuary within the territory of the Carnutes tribe. Archaeology does indeed bear witness to such sites, generally just simple cleared areas in the forest (identified in Gaul by such names as nemeton), sometimes enclosed with a palisade and/or bank and ditch. A reasonable possibility exists that there was an Archdruid for the entirety of Britain as well as a similar ecclesiastic for Ireland, both of these probably elected by constituent groups of sages and elders.

The noble classes largely supplied the personnel for the Druid caste. Their instruction in the oral tradition of memorizing verses could last anywhere from twelve to twenty years. Such traditional instruction for bards and poets was archetypally Keltic. It continued in Ireland up to the late 1600s and in Scotland up to the 1700s.

The Druids thus functioned as the acknowledged repositories of traditional lore and wisdom, particularly of customary law. They also incorporated within themselves something of the prophetic powers of the seers due to their practical knowledge of the calendar. They were directly responsible for animal and human sacrifice when they required that for their magic-making. To judge from the surviving fragments of a monumental calendar-inscription from Coligny in Gaul and other evidence, the Druids possessed considerable calendrical expertise, and they had long recognized the practical problems of reconciling the solar and lunar cycles. Like most shamans, they also possessed considerable knowledge of herbs and their medicinal properties.

Modern archaeology would seem to vindicate the traditional Druidic beliefs at Stonehenge and other stone circles; and we can add the obvious deductions from their structure: circular dancing, fivefold teachings, processions, and a death-and-rebirth cult of the sun, together with male and female emblems. These phenomena would seem to indicate a cult remarkably like that of traditional Druidic ideas.

The Druids urged their peoples to fight the Romans when Julius Caesar invaded Gaul and Britain. In Gaul the Druids rapidly lost influence as the Roman military advanced. The Latins either exterminated them or forced them to flee, knowing them immediately for a dangerous and seditious influence. It was their seditious influence, just as much as their practice of human sacrifice (and sometimes on a large scale, it might be added), which caused the Romans to proscribe their religion, and to banish and/or exterminate them with no mercy shown.

However, numerous Gallo-Roman altars and shrines, together with various inscriptions, demonstrate that cult functionaries of lesser standing (who could also be considered Druids) continued to preside at the various native temples and holy spots throughout the non-Christian period of the Roman Empire. In Britain the Roman general Julius Agricola destroyed the Brythonic Druids in 78 A.D., but the Gaelic Druids continued in Ireland until their conversion to Christianity during the 400s.

Again, in Britain as in Gaul, lesser cult functionaries (again, virtually the same as Druids but posing no threat to the civil authorities of the Roman administration) continued at native shrines (such as at "Caer Nodentis," Aquae Sulis, or the island-vale of Avalon Annwn) before as well as during the first and largely superficial Christianization of the Britons (the Late Roman and Arthurian periods).

It is fascinating and important to note that there were great Druidesses as well as great Druids. In Gaul and in Ireland at least they often enjoyed considerable prestige and power, sometimes comparable to what the male Druids enjoyed. The essential function of the ancient Druids then was clearly to sustain—by magical or "shamanistic" means—the prosperity of tribe and land. As the tribal repositories of traditional Keltic learning and sentiment, the Druids embodied the specific "barbarian" element that classical civilization could not assimilate and naturalize.

How far was Druidry driven out by the Romans? It survived in the remote parts of Wales, in Scotland beyond the Lowlands, and in Ireland. It developed the deeply poetic traditions of the fifth, sixth, and subsequent centuries, the same poetic traditions that later were to nurture the Arthurian legendry.

Later references depict the remnants of the original Druids as no more than magicians and medicine-men on the fringes of Roman-Keltic culture, and even Druidesses appear as no more than common fortune-tellers. The original Druidry may also have survived by simply going underground: that is, in the Romanized areas much of the former priesthood may simply have continued on under the guise of being lesser cult functionaries at the native shrines, or they may have transformed themselves into bards, seers, and so forth.

And now we come to the question of the Druids *vis-à-vis* the Christian monks during Late Roman, Arthurian, and post-Arthurian times. Apart from the one great difference in their respective central conceptualization of deity—the one Christian god versus the Keltic multiplicity of gods and goddesses—there are a number of reasonably close parallels between them. For example, the Holy Trinity of Christian doctrine versus the curious use of, and emphasis upon, the "triad" within the Welsh storytelling tradition of Arthur's time and after (possibly stemming originally from Druidic poetic practice). For a more strategic example, the Christian concept of an immortal soul and an afterlife is not that dissimilar (in broad outline) from the Druidic beliefs of an immortal soul and a Keltic otherworld. Many articles of faith among the Kelts before the advent of Christianity seem to have prepared the way for the later Jesus cult. There is the distinct implication of some kind of cooperative coexistence then between the native Druidry and the early Keltic Church of the British Isles.

The Keltic Church in Britain and Ireland (almost out of touch with the Church in Europe) developed along its own lines and possessed its own (and rather different) character. Monasteries rather than dioceses provided its foundation; abbots rather than bishops furnished the main authority; the monks rather than the secular clergy set the tone. The three chief Christian centers of Arthurian Britain were evidently Llantwit Major (in southern Wales), Amesbury, and Glastonbury; these were all monasteries, and no bishop claimed any of them as his seat.

The Keltic monks of the British Isles had far greater freedom than their Continental brethren. More democratic in outlook, they wandered widely, and because their importance made the Keltic nuns important as well, Keltic society held women in greater esteem than among European Christians. In scholarship and literature the Keltic monks of Britain and Ireland excelled and produced outstanding manuscripts.

In Ireland as well as in the less Romanized western parts of Britain, the Church did not need to contend—as formerly on the Continent—with a powerful and firmly established non-Christian priesthood. The Keltic monks did not view their old religion as "Satanic," and preserved much mythology and speculation of a type that passed into virtually permanent eclipse elsewhere.

The greater freedom, greater individuality, and more democratic outlook of the Keltic Church in the British Isles than of Christianity in Europe—as well as the superior esteem accorded women and women ecclesiastics—probably reflect a natural evolution from the times and conditions of the Druids and of Druidry.

In early Irish literature (surviving through Christian sources) the Druids or "Magi" who are depicted as malignant magicians bitterly opposed to the introduction of the new faith probably represent the die-hard remnant of those Druids not easily converted or convertible to the new cult. The *filid* or "seers"—who also practiced divination and are often confused with the true Druids in the early Irish hero-sagas—assumed an honored place in early Irish Christian society as literary men and historians. Significantly many contests between Druids and Christians take place over the possession of land. This (besides its literal meaning) could easily signify the struggle between the two creeds for the domination over the territory of souls.

Just as the well-organized colleges of Druids among the Irish Kelts were easily converted into Christian monasteries, Druidic abbeys may more than likely have stood on the future sites of Glastonbury Abbey and the monastery inhabited by British monks on Tintagel Headland. It is also a distinct and logical possibility that Druidic abbeys may have preceded the Christian monasteries (at least) at St. Michael's Mount near Marazion in Cornwall, at Mont-Saint-Michel just northeast of Brittany, at Iona Island just west of Scotland, and so forth.

In the event that he does not symbolize a real historical personage, what then precisely would the poet-sage and poet-magician Merlin have represented at Arthur's court *if not the Druidic element itself par excellence?* Significantly, Merlin is never shown in the later legendry as in conflict with Christianity. The strongest and most fascinating *magical* elements in the Arthurian Mythos are but rarely Christian; they are primarily *non*-Christian.

It could only have been with the full cooperation of all classes indigenous to the Brythonic society of his time that the historical Arthur would have been enabled to achieve what he did. Needless to say, he would most particularly have needed the active support of the Druids, bards, and seers, in addition to the support and approbation of the wealthy and noble classes on the one hand and of the Keltic Church on the other. In both Britain and Brittany (or Little Britain) it was the bards who kept Arthur's immediate *later fame* alive.

The Eisteddfod—the Welsh musical convention and contest—goes back to an unknown date, at least before the reign of King Hoel the Good (circa 950 A.D.), whose Pencerrd or Chief Poet already had a special chair in the court. Some kind of Eisteddfod, patronized by Lord Rhys, took place at Cardigan Castle in 1176, but nothing is later recorded until 1450 at Carmarthen (indubitably under the excorporate aegis of Prince Merlinus, whose presence at least consistently in legend has always been closely linked with Caer Maridunum). The next recorded meeting took place at Caerwys in the north in 1523, and then another in 1568 when a committee (appointed by Queen Elizabeth) examined bards and granted licenses to wander and earn money by performances. Assuredly is it significant that this happened in the reign of Elizabeth I; the Tudors, it will be remembered, claimed Welsh nobility among their immediate ancestry. Thus, apart from these few recorded Eisteddfods, the earlier tradition against written records has prevented our knowing much more until the eighteenth-century almanacs begin to advertise meetings.

Organized with the assistance of Wales, the modern Bards of Cornwall form a considerable group that revives the extinct Cornish language (among other activities). The Bards are of two classes, language and non-language members. Uniquely bardic, their impressive robes are of deep blue. They implement some of their usual ceremonies at the stone circles of Cornwall or in the great halls of Arthur built at Tintagel in the twentieth century for the Arthurian Order.

In view of the Keltic imaginative concept (quintessentially Druidic) of the immortality of the soul that will continue living in an otherworld, it is easy to understand how an Avalon "here" or in Britain can also be an Avalon "there" or somewhere indefinite west of Britain in the North Atlantic (the Avalon in Geoffrey of Monmouth's *Vita Merlini* as well as that island sacred to the mystical consciousness of the Irish Kelts). But . . . this Avalon located in the western ocean as conceived by Gaelic or Brythonic Kelts . . . could this not be some kind of racial memory of an Atlantis long since submerged beneath the ocean's waves?

XIII. A King Arthur Summary

Conjectures about Arthur's mail-clad cavalry are based on the facts of fifth-century warfare and revolve around the conception of Arthur as the creator of a band of knights. Now "knight" is a word that for us in the twentieth century, as in the nineteenth (the Romantic period par excellence), has a preeminently medieval coloring. However, the knight of the Middle Ages was in fact only a survival or revival of the

Late Roman *eques cataphractarius,* clad in a shirt of mail, with arm-pieces and leg-pieces attached. This armor (embryonically "medieval," it will be noted) made the Roman horseman "invulnerable" (according to the Roman historians Ammianus and Vegetius).

Thus, one of the best popular theories explains the knights of the Round Table by contending that the historical Arthur turned the tide against the Germanic invaders with an innovative cavalry force, a personal corps of armored riders. It is a fact that the Romans developed heavy mailed cavalry during the last period of the Western Roman Empire. It is also a fact that the Anglo-Saxons were not horsemen (at least at first), and thus a highly trained group of armored British horsemen, possessing therefore a militarily technological advantage, could well have put them to flight.

From clues in early Welsh poetry, and from the results of recent excavation, an explicit picture is formed of Arthur's knights. They went into combat wearing coats of mail over thick leather tunics with thick leather breeches attached. They carried lances, long-bladed swords, and circular shields. They rode horses that were sometimes also armored. The actual style of armor would have developed from the Late Roman mode of heavy mail, to which would have been added typically Keltic and therefore largely abstract patterns of decoration. Many of the knights would have been Christian (at least nominally). These would have attended Christian service before battle. Their non-military clothing would have consisted of breeches, tunics, and robes of simple but colorful design. They wore golden ornaments and jewelry.

While the civil authorities would probably still have tolerated and even protected the native cults and cult sites, the new Christian faith would have provided a unifying and inspirational impetus of which the older native beliefs were incapable. The Grail stories, while superficially Christian, actually reflect the Druidic preoccupation with the inherent Keltic sense of otherwhere. Thus, while Christianity was probably already well on its way to becoming the principal religion of the land, the older and increasingly dispossessed native religion began to show up as an unmistakable element in the continuing Brythonic mythology of Arthur's period. Some of this early Christian activity was unusual enough to harmonize with the strange "otherworldly" atmosphere of the later Grail romances, if not with their imagery in detail.

The upper Britanno-Roman classes, for the most part Christian somewhat before the end of Roman rule, produced such outstanding figures as St. Patrick. The containment of the Anglo-Saxons during Arthur's reign permitted a much wider flowering of Christianity and Christian culture both in Britain and in Ireland than what would otherwise have obtained. Ireland above all became the most cultured and most thoroughly Christianized country of Western Europe during the Dark Ages and owed much to the British-Keltic saints.

In his monograph *King Arthur's Avalon,* Geoffrey Ashe has adroitly summarized the case for a "great" historical Arthur with unusual clarity and insight, and he deserves to be quoted in full:

> The salient point about the mass of Arthurian oddments is the grandiose geography. Nobody else except the Devil is renowned through so much of Britain. From Land's End [in Cornwall] to the Grampian foothills [in Scotland], Arthur's name "cleaves to cairn and cromlech." We hear of the Cornish fortress at Kelliwic; of a Cornish hill called Bann Arthur and a stream called the River of Arthur's Kitchen; of Cadbury and its noble shades; of the lake Llyn Bertog in Merioneth, where Arthur slew a monster, and his horse left a hoof-print on the rock; of a cave by Marchlyn Mawr in Carnarvon, where his treasure lies hidden (woe to any intruder who touches it); of a cave at Caerleon, and another near [Mount] Snowdon, where his warriors lie asleep till he need them; of still another cave in the Eildon hills, close to Melrose Abbey, where some say he is sleeping himself; of the mount outside Edinburgh called Arthur's Seat; of Arthur's Stone, and Arthur's Fold, as far north as Perth; and many more such places. Arthur seems to be everywhere.
>
> The first natural deduction is that Arthur really was everywhere: that he flashed from end to end of his crumbling country on that terrible armoured charger, rallying the faint hearts, reconciling the factions [no mean task, *that!*], and pouncing on the bewildered heathen; with Kay and Bedivere riding beside him. And the second deduction . . . is that the man who bequeathed such a towering legend was no ordinary human being. Even if most of the Arthur stories were borrowed or fabricated, it is still necessary to explain why they should ever have been attached to Arthur. Even if the bards vested him with the attributes of a god, the question still remains: Why him in particular? To which there is no adequate answer but the readiest one—because he deserved it. (91)

Thu s, it can be readily seen how Arthur's historical period and court could easily have prompted at least something of the immediate imagery and narrative "staples" (to say nothing of the "strange" atmosphere which is peculiarly Keltic) featured in the later medieval romances. Also, it can be readily seen how in a genuinely historical way the British culture or manner of living in Arthur's period foreshadows the later Middle Ages and contains in a fashion more than embryonic much that will become common in medieval times. Nor can there be much doubt that the peculiar coloring of the Arthurian Mythos, especially in its grand and Ragnarok-like finale, reflects something of the real poignancy and nostalgia that would gather—retrospectively in myth and legend—to the period of British history circa 500–550, a period which was after all, in a strict historical sense, the Keltic Twilight.

Nor is it at all bizarre that Geoffrey of Monmouth should have stressed the "imperial" characteristics of King Arthur and his dominions. While this "imperialism" may reflect something of a historical reality peculiar to Arthur and his times, it surely reflects the real British-Roman imperial tradition before Arthur, and which he would have inherited as a natural consequence of historical evolution: beginning at least with Constantine the Great (proclaimed Caesar Augustus at Eburacum or York) and continuing later through Magnus Maximus (Spanish-born but an "adopted" Briton) and then later through Aurelius Ambrosius (or as the later myths fashion his name, Ambrosius Aurelianius), one of Arthur's immediate Britanno-Romanized predecessors.

Arthur's career may be divided into three main parts; and again we must emphasize that these dates are purely provisional. From 470 into 485 he would have been prince; from 485 into 510/512, king, from 510/512 into 537/542, emperor. In many tales about Arthur (including various modern novels), the first fifteen or sixteen years of his life are deliberately "mysterious." To avoid being murdered or harmed in any way, and so that he can have a "normal" childhood and adolescence, he is taken out of Britain and raised by foster parents, with his identity remaining a secret. Later still, he returns (still young) and spends time away from the political centers and factionalism of the Britons. Then he appears miraculously and as a great fighter at around the age of fifteen or sixteen. This could be fiction, but it could also reflect some folklore or genuine historical tradition known to earlier periods but lost before our modern era.

Spenser in his great epic-romance-allegory *The Faerie Queene* (published 1590-1609) presents, among other main narrative threads, a myth of "Arthure, before he was king" and as "the image of a brave knight." He therefore depicts *Prince* Arthur during his lengthy sojourn in "Faerie lond." Now it is a fact that in the characterization of *his* fictional Faeryland Spenser would have portrayed not only something of his native Britain but also, and particularly, something of his "adopted" country of Ireland, or Ivernia (which he personifies in Book V as "Irena"), where he lived for long periods of his adult life (approximately 1580-89, 1591-95, and 1597-98), if not the majority of his adult life. Thus, in ways both subtle and overt, Spenser's Faeryland is an uniquely Irish one; and it must be admitted that the Irish countryside to this day can be "heartbreakingly" beautiful. Now, depicting Prince Arthur as adventuring in Faeryland, which is Ireland in particular, may have been based by Spenser on some Arthurian tradition current in his contemporary Britain (the Age of Elizabeth I) but lost since that time. Not that the tradition would have necessarily emphasized Ireland to the neglect of other Keltic lands. The tradition may have preserved a memory of Arthur passing most of his first fifteen or sixteen years in the various Brythonic or Gaelic realms: Cornwall, Brittany, the Channel Islands, Lyonnesse, modern England's northwest (i.e., Westmoreland and Cumberland), the Scottish Lowlands, the Isles of Man and Anglesey, the Hebrides, the Orkneys, and of course Ireland.

There are still some remaining aspects relative to the Arthurian Mythos that we need to discuss before we return to Caerleon-on-Usk and Arthur Machen.

As a concept of the creative collective imagination of Western man, the Arthurian Mythos has passed through two principal stages. The early Welsh tradition celebrated an idealized Britain or Britannia where Arthur and his knights had flourished. England was then "Logria," and the Cymry or Welsh had the dominion over it. Then the Cymry lost Logria, and the West Country (notably Wales and Cornwall) almost alone preserved the lingering vestiges of Arthurian splendor. Some day, however—or so it was prophesied—Arthur would come back as a Keltic Messiah and would then subdue the English or Anglo-Saxons. This then was the tradition promulgated by Geoffrey of Monmouth when, in the 1130s, he indited and published his *History of the Kings of Britain*; this compilation did everything to implant an exaggerated and highly glamorized Arthurian realm in the minds of readers outside Wales.

The second principal stage began with the popularization of the Mythos by non-Keltic romancers. However, with this popularization Arthur became something far more than a purely regional hero. The Plantagenet kings of England claimed to possess his birthplace, his chief cities, and his grave, and they posed as his legitimate successors in their dominion of the whole of Britain. Edward I displayed Arthur's alleged remains at Glastonbury to demonstrate once and for all that he would never come back as the Keltic or Welsh Messiah. Significantly, no Welshman ever disputed Glastonbury's claim to possessing Arthur's grave.

Geoffrey Ashe has again well summarized the final purely political formulation of the Mythos as follows:

> Both aspects of Arthur were adroitly united by Henry Tudor. He stressed his own Welsh ancestry, and marched to overthrow Richard III under the standard of the Red Dragon. When he became king as Henry VII, he allowed his propagandists to construe the event as fulfilling the prophecy of Arthur's return—meaning, now, not that the Welsh had conquered the English, but that a true "British" prince had saved the whole land from civil war and restored its ancient Arthurian glory. (Cavendish 1.396)

The great poetic exponent of this Tudor myth is Edmund Spenser who, in *The Faerie Queene,* portrays the England of Elizabeth I as the magnificent kingdom of the Britons restored.

Spenser would have of course been familiar with the classic redaction of the Arthurian Mythos in English prose *Le Morte d'Arthur* by Sir Thomas Malory, published more than a century before in 1485 in London. William Caxton, the first English printer, had printed and published that particular masterpiece, the first great surviving piece of English literary prose. Malory had evidently written *Le Morte d'Arthur* during the last twenty years of his life, which he spent in prison. From Book XXI we quote Chapter VII in full:

OF THE OPINION OF SOME MEN
OF THE DEATH OF KING ARTHUR

Yet some men say in many parts of England that King Arthur is not dead, but had by the will of our Lord Jesu into another place; and men say that he shall come again, and he shall win the holy cross. I will not say it shall be so, but rather I will say: here in this world he changed his life. But many men say that there is written upon his tomb this verse:

Hic jacet Arthurus, Rex quondam, Rexque futurus.
[*Here lies Arthur, the once and future King.*]

The original inscription on the lead cross found during the exhumation of King Arthur in 1190 at Glastonbury Abbey had read: *Hic iacet sepultus inclitus rex Arturius in insula Avalonia.* It is fascinating to see how Malory has refashioned the original inscription to read: *Hic iacet Arthurus, rex quondam, rexque futurus.* (The Welsh and English forms of Arthur's name have changed the original Latin form of Artorius or Arturius into Arthurus.) Thus, his regal title contains the ancient Welsh prophecy within a singularly compact form: "King formerly, and King to be."

In fact—and in a sense not quite foreseen by Geoffrey of Monmouth and his contemporaries of the twelfth century—the later generations of the Middle Ages vindicated the ancient Brythonic prophecy. King Arthur had indeed returned and was to enjoy a greater and longer reign than any he had enjoyed in his own proper and historical period—in the minds and imaginations of not only his fellow later "British" peoples but also, and more extensively, in minds and imaginations throughout Western Europe.

From the twelfth to the fifteenth centuries, the "magick" of Arthur and his Britain grew greater with every retelling in verse and prose from generation to generation—no matter the transformation in externals—and in a truly marvelous fashion not even those early Welsh prophets, bards, and seers could have conceived.

Thus, when people began to doubt his historical reality in modern times (say, from the first Elizabethan age to the first half of the twentieth century, and then on into the Second Elizabethan Age)—at least on the scale (more symbolic than actual) indicated by Geoffrey of Monmouth and the medieval romancers—the myths and legends were to keep Arthur's name and the "glamor" of his Britannic realm necromantically alive. And that is indeed as fair a piece of magic as ever prophesied by any Brythonic poet-sage!

Thanks to recent archaeological investigation, no longer is it possible to maintain (after at least a disbelieving first half of the twentieth century) that "the original Arthur, if he lived at all, must have been a semi-barbaric Celtic chief" (Grebanier 1.207).

XIV. Back to Caerleon

Two years after Machen published for the first time his short fantasy "The Bowmen" in the London *Evening News* for September 29, 1914—thereby creating the twentieth-century legend of "the Angels of Mons"—a book appeared that contains an interesting citation apropos of Caerleon. This was *A Tennyson Dictionary,* compiled by Arthur E. Baker.

> An ancient town in Monmouthshire on the river Usk. [. . .] This "city of Legions" with its golden domes and magnificent churches, and its gorgeous palace, with its giant tower
>
> > from whose high crest, they say,
> > Men saw the goodly hills of Somerset,
> > And white sails flying on the yellow sea. [i.e., Severn Sea]
>
> is supposed to have equalled Rome in splendor. It was one of the principal residences of king Arthur, where he lived in splendid state, surrounded by his knights, and where he held his court.
>
> > For Arthur on the Whitsuntide before
> > Held court at old Caerleon upon Usk.
>
> King Arthur's ninth great battle against the Saxons was fought here. (87; the quotations are taken from Tennyson's *Idylls of the King*)

Now, on the face of it, the statement—"This 'City of Legions' . . . is supposed to have equalled Rome in splendor"—seems patently absurd, since it is a matter of plain historical fact that Rome was incomparably the largest and greatest city of classical antiquity. How could such a provincial *town* as Caerleon (no matter its own charisma and mystique) even be mentioned in the same breath as the archimperial *city* of "Mother Rome" upon the River Tiber? Nevertheless, this statement (which really stresses magnificence rather than size) reflects an older British tradition and is by no means without its basis in historical fact.

This tradition clearly dates back to the time of Arthur (as well as before and after), when Caerleon would have served quite logically as capital of Western Britain. By the time of Arthur's imperial coronation (c. 510 or 512) as High King of Britain and Armorica, Rome had endured two major sackings (one by the Goths under Alaric in 410 and the other by the Vandals under Gaiseric or Genseric in 455). In 476 another barbarian chieftain, Odoacer, deposed the "last" Roman Emperor of the West, Romulus Augustulus (an event often deemed "the Fall of Rome"). By 547 the great imperial city was actually deserted for a while. After Arthur's death in 537 or 542, Rome underwent a third and last major "sacking" of a most peculiar kind. Totila, king of the Ostrogoths, captured Rome in the middle of December 546 *and evacuated everyone out of it,* but perpetrated no material plundering. Thus, by late 546 and early 547 the city lay deserted and solitary: if one single event could be said to symbolize the death of the classical Rome of antiquity, this would be it. The city was still subjected to occasional plundering by barbarians later in the same period. By the time of Geoffrey of Monmouth, the ancient city of Rome was a vasty ruin, inhabited by herders and their flocks, and by a few great feudal families—a wreck that had foundered on the reefs and shoals of inimical Time.

Thus, allowing for some pardonable patriotic exaggeration on the part of British commentators, but keeping in mind the actual *physical* deterioration of Rome's great municipal architecture, it is possible to see how Caerleon by a curious fluke of historical accident could have been conceived as equalling Rome in splendor during Arthur's period. This tradition would have had even greater weight in the twelfth century (the time of Geoffrey of Monmouth and Gerald of Barry) when Caerleon still possessed an impressive array of ancient architecture, and whilst Rome had become an enormous and catastrophic wreck overgrown with weeds and thickets, and infested with desperadoes and bandits.

As we have previously established, the best candidate for Camelot as a genuine city remains Machen's own Caerleon. Within the old "Castra Legionis" proper, the former residence of the Roman legionary commander would have served quite well as one of King Arthur's own palaces. However, we cannot rule out the possibility of a special residence being built for the "Briton King"—in addition to Arthur's using the *domus legati* as well as any other especially fine residences already existing in the city proper.

During Arthur's period Caerleon would have presented a splendiferous appearance as a city. Both the *civitas* and the old "Castra Legionis" would have been girdled by walls at least 20 feet high with crenellated parapets and with attached turrets or towers at least every 150 feet. It is a distinct possibility that these walls were refurbished and then heightened further during Arthur's reign by means of a second smaller wall (also with turrets and crenellated parapets) superimposed upon the original Britanno-Roman defenses. Further stories may have been added to many of the original edifices in both city and camp at this time. This further building up (both walls and added stories) may have been of a mixed stone-and-timber construction or of a purely timbered style (more typically Brythonic). As capital of Western Britain and as a gathering place for the British refugees from eastern and southeastern England, Caerleon would have seen its population increase dramatically during the period 440/450–500/510 and then to a lesser extent during the period 510/512–550.

Southwest of the Roman fortress there yet lay the old walled parade ground (700 by 500 feet), one rare open area within the city proper that would have been available for new construction during the reigns of Ambrosius Aurelianus and Caesar Augustus Artorius. Here there may have arisen that special residence, the legendary "gorgeous palace" proper to King Arthur. If we postulate a typically Brythonic and purely timber-built edifice, it is not hard to see why no vestiges of it have survived the passage of time into the twentieth century.

What possible shape might such a royal palace as Arthur's have taken? This would probably reflected the architectural tradition (but magnified considerably, as would seem appropriate) of such wooden woodland citadels as Castle Dore in Cornwall, Caer Tintagel upon Tintagel Headland, Cadbury Castle near Queen's Camel in Somerset, and Caer Avalon Annwn within the island-vale of Avalon. This "Caer Imperatoris" (let us call it after the Welsh fashion) would probably have reflected as well certain details and elements from the Britanno-Roman architectural tradition. Thus we can postulate a great central towered hall rising donjon-like from the midst of subsidiary halls and towers, in turn environed by a series of inner courtyards and various outbuildings, and all set within an outer line of towered and/or turreted fortifications, superimposed upon the original boundaries of the old walled parade ground. We can also safely assume a highly sophisticated wooden architecture; it is much easier to be fanciful and elaborate in wood than in stone and cement. One of the likeliest places to look for some kind of example—which would give us at least some idea, some archetype, to image by—would probably be among the so-called stave churches found throughout Scandinavia; and such a specific example as the stave church at Heddal in Norway would serve as well as any. (The form of the stave churches is thought to preserve that of the pre-Christian Norse temples.) The postulation of such a typically Brythonic and purely timber-built edifice is a perfectly logical choice in view of the mixed Keltic and Roman culture characteristic of Arthurian times.

Close to the southern gateway symmetrically situated in the southern wall of the Roman fortress there still arose Caerleon's military amphitheatre, which would certainly have played an important part in large public gatherings during Arthur's period. It may have been domed or somehow roofed over at this time in a typically Brythonic and purely timbered fashion with some kind of carapace, even if only temporarily for Arthur's coronation. However, with or without roof or carapace, the amphitheatre would surely have been the logical choice for Arthur's imperial coronation since it could easily accommodate around 6,000 persons.

Sometime after his death Arthur's realm fragmented into a large number of small independent successor states. Quite apart from its traditional status as one of his former seats, and apart from its rank as the metropolitan see of Wales before the establishment of St. David's, it is a fact that Caerleon continued as a Welsh princely capital up to the time of the Norman Conquest of 1066 A.D. Subsequently it became a Marcher lordship but principally in Welsh hands until 1235; a sizable motte and a tower of its castle survive. During the Middle Ages and later, Caerleon became a borough, and enjoyed a considerable coastal trade, eventually destroyed by the development of the railways (characteristic of Victorian times) as well as that of the city of Newport, which lies 3 miles southwest of Caerleon.

Considerable expansion occurred in the Caerleon area following World War II, and on December 15, 1947, Arthur Machen himself died, at the age of eighty-four, as one of Caerleon's most illustrious natives.

The Welsh had long agone lost their dominion of Britain, and whilst the West Country (notably Wales and Cornwall) almost alone had preserved the remnants of Arthurian splendor, had not King Arthur himself become a dubitable myth, a mere legend concocted from some mystic Welshman's fertile imagination, and an insubstantial fable compounded in equal parts of empty air and restless wind? Why, who could place credence in those old stories, the artless testimony to the dreams of rude and barbaric ages?!

When Arthur Machen was born on March 3, 1863, Queen Victoria had already reigned on the throne of England since 1838, that is, for some twenty-six years. By this time Caerleon—"once a city, and the headquarters of a Roman legion"—had shrunken into "a forgotten village." Moreover, "the Augustan Legion and the clash of arms, and all the tremendous pomp that followed the eagles"—did not all these form part of a dim and fading past? The "quiet little town" lay in "the long, lovely valley" of the lower Usk "crossed in mid-vision by a mediaeval bridge of vaulted and buttressed stone." Here, of an evening, in the twilight following sunset, one could see "the broad river swimming to full tide" and "the pure white mist tracking the outline of the river like a shroud." Then "across the valley, and beyond, hill followed on hill as wave on wave": altogether then, "a vague and shadowy country" with "imaginations and fantasy of swelling hills and hanging woods, and half- shaped outlines of hills beyond." Now "here a faint blue pillar of smoke rose . . . from the chimney of an ancient grey farmhouse, there was a rugged height crowned with dark firs, and in the distance . . . the white streak of a road that climbed and vanished into some unimagined country. But the boundary of all was a great wall of mountain, vast in the west, and ending like a fortress, with a steep ascent and a domed tumulus clear against the sky."

This then was the Caerleon into which Machen was born, and

this then was the countryside surrounding it at the time of his birth and later childhood. The great courtyard of the headquarters or *principia* of Caerleon's old Roman fortress lay then, as it still lies, beneath the parish church and churchyard of St. Cadoc's, which is thus located above the very center of the "Castra Legionis" and which stands also virtually at the heart of modern Caerleon. Machen was born here in a house owned by his grandmother (and not at the small parish of Llanddewi Fach—some five miles north of Caerleon—where his father presided as the resident clergyman). Most of the then "quiet little town" or "forgotten village" was thus contained within the area once bounded by the walls of the Roman fortress-camp.

Not far to the west of St. Cadoc's there had long agone stood the *domus legati* and in all likelihood one of the headquarters of King Arthur within the ancient "City of the Legions." Caerleon's present-day Legionary Museum is located not far away to the north or northeast of St. Cadoc's; this is one of the best institutions of its type in all modern Britain.

So to the town of Caerleon the present writer came early in the first week of April 1972 (on a Tuesday, to be exact, following the Monday spent at the ruins of Caer Nodentis in Lydney Park), together with two English friends Jack and Audrey Hesketh, during our pilgrimage to the specifically local Arthur Machen country as well as to the West Country at large. We had driven into the area from near Chepstow-on-Wye (immediately adjacent to Caerwent, the ancient "cantonal" capital and market-town of Venta Silurum) and had gone via the city of Newport, whose modern suburbs rise upon the hills environing Caerleon to the south; these suburbs encroach increasingly upon the elder community.

We visited a local pub, made a few inquiries under the guise of refreshing ourselves with the local ale and cider, and then continued on into Caerleon. First, we visited St. Cadoc's without disturbing the present occupants of the rectory and lingered for a brief while in the church, proffering our silent devoirs on behalf of Machen's spirit. From there we motored to the Legionary Museum where again we lingered for more than a little, imbibing as much historicity as we could in the short period at our disposal.

But the highlight of the visit came next, as we reconnoitered to the ancient military amphitheatre and part of the old fortress's southern (or actually southwestern) wall nearby. The amphitheatre survives amazingly intact, being (we would say) about one half its former size or height. To the three of us, upon that early afternoon, while a brisk wind was blowing out of the west and under cool gray skies, it seemed a haunted and haunting place, endowed still with strange occulted splendors left over from Arthurian and Late Roman times as well as from Machen's own immediate period, the Victorian Age.

Then Tennyson, the poet laureate of the British Empire, had located various portions in his series of epic-narratives *Idylls of the King* within this ancient "City of the Legions" where local traditions yet maintained a connection betwixt the amphitheatre and Arthur's regime. Once again, the elder mythopoetic Keltic magic welled up from dark depths, to inform and guide intuitively the vision of an imperial poet laureate on the one hand and on the other the vision of a young prose-poet who was himself Keltic, descended most particularly from the ancient Brythons, and actually born in this former seat of King Arthur's.

XV. An Arthur Machen Summary

Looking back from California to that visit in Wales, the present writer finds himself arrested again and again by certain facts of Machen's own mundane life (especially relative to certain facts or factors in his creative or *dream* life) and also, and above all, by the overall significance of the *aesthetic pattern* peculiar to Machen's life-period.[7]

We have already considered certain prime elements and factors from Machen's immediate (as well as extended) native environment: elements and factors that contributed tremendously to his personal

---

7. This chapter is heavily indebted for many basic biographical and bibliographical data to David Ieuan's biography "Arthur Machen: 1863–1901" and "Arthur Machen 1901–1947," which appeared in the British periodical *Balthus,* Numbers 3 and 4, respectively (edited and published by Jon M. Harvey, Cardiff, Wales). The quotation from the speech of Chief Seattle in 1855 is taken from its redaction in the issue for July 15, 1975, of *East West Journal.* Chief Seattle, who was born in 1786, died on June 7 1866.

and artistic development. But now let us look directly at certain salient facts of his biography.

He was born as the only child of a clergyman; he developed into a
dreamy, introspective boy, a solitary, and a mystic; and he grew up very
much attached to his native land of Gwent as well as to the Arthurian
legendry indigenous to Caerleon. His father was descended from a
long line of Welsh clergymen that can be traced back at least to the
last quarter of the eighteenth century.

Machen had a sound classical education (Greek and Latin) both
in school and then out on his own. His own later writing (essays or
fiction or miscellanies) is rife with classical reminiscence. But he also
had a knowledge (in both writing and speaking) of Welsh, and evidently something of the immemorial poetic usages native to the Brythonic bards.

His first period of exile from his beloved Wales occurred when
he went away to school to pursue that training that would enable him
to continue the unbroken ecclesiastical tradition of his father's family.
He attended Hereford Cathedral School from January 1874 until
April 1880 (with the exception of six months in 1876 when he remained in the Caerleon area). While still at school Machen had sub-
mitted a poem in blank verse based upon the Arthurian legends to
the *Gentleman's Magazine,* but the periodical rejected it.

It is significant that Machen's first serious effort as a writer should
concern the Arthurian legendry so dear to his childhood and adolescence, thus reflecting his reaction to the vestiges of Arthurian splendor still remaining in his native Caerleon.

The Reverend Jones-Machen had planned to send his only child
to Oxford, but increasing poverty prevented this. Without such higher education both the clergy and the teaching profession were closed
to his son Arthur Llewelyn.

At the instigation of his family Machen then made his first journey to London in June 1880, when he appeared before the examiners
for entrance into the Royal College of Surgeons. Quite sensibly they
did not accept him as a candidate.

After his return from London he wrote another long poem titled
Eleusinia in a mixture of rhymed and blank verse; this concerned the
pagan rites at Eleusis in ancient Greece. It was printed and published

locally in a limited edition largely financed by his family. Later Machen suppressed this pamphlet.

His second period of exile (far more difficult than the first) occurred when he went to live in London (again at the instigation of his family) to pursue a career in journalism, or so they thought and hoped. This called for a profound readjustment on Machen 's part, as he instinctively preferred the superior physical quality of country living. London was then, as it still is to this day, "the City" par excellence.

Even stated generously, his early career there proved almost repulsively wretched, but it found exquisite artistic reflection in his later creative writing (especially the often highly autobiographical novel *The Hill of Dreams*). During this early London period (from the summer of 1881 into the late autumn of 1885), although he suffered often from acute loneliness and intense melancholia, he somehow got by: for a while as a clerk in a publishing house, then as a teacher (that is, as a private tutor), later as an assistant to a genealogist, and finally as some kind of freelance writer. His life appears to have been at times only slightly less dreadful than the London career of his alter ego Lucian Taylor in *The Hill of Dreams*.

Two excellent books emerged from this period, however. *The Anatomy of Tobacco* reflects Machen's dual passion for tobacco and the occasional pint of ale or beer; this book is an early masterpiece in what we may term the peculiarly Machenesque genre of the miscellany. He published it (significantly enough) under the pseudonym of "Leolinus Siluriensis." He was now twenty-one, and he had come of age in the same year (1884) as his first real book's publication. Machen then devoted most of 1885 and 1886 to the creation of his first bona fide and full-length piece of fiction, *The Chronicle of Clemendy,* a highly original imitation of certain fictional procedures and formulations as found in the *Gargantua and Pantagruel* of François Rabelais. The singularly varied and adroitly picaresque narrative in *The Chronicle of Clemendy* demonstrates the enchantment created for Machen by his native land of Gwent (in which, apart from one scene, the action of the book takes place).

In 1884 he had undertaken his first major translation for the publisher of *The Anatomy of Tobacco,* and he devoted much of that year to the project. This was a translation of *The Heptameron* from the

French of Queen Marguerite de Navarre. In the late autumn of 1885 Machen returned from London to Caerleon and Llanddewi Fach; his mother was dying. His father, declared a bankrupt, became apathetic after his wife's death and progressively deteriorated. Machen stayed in Gwent until January 1887.

Then in that same month he returned to London, making the great city now his home. In August 1887 he married his first wife, Amelia Hogg. (She was to die in the summer of 1899.) Those twelve years were as happy for Machen as his first London period had been painful and lonely. A few weeks before his marriage his father had passed on. Arthur and Amelia then spent a little while in Caerleon and Llanddewi Fach, clearing up various family affairs. The couple then returned to their home in London. In 1887 and 1892 Machen received a number of legacies from some long-lived Scottish relatives on his mother's side of the family. This added income enabled the couple to live much more comfortably than what otherwise might have obtained. During the later 1880s Machen was working as a cataloguer of second-hand books, and for his then present employers he undertook his next major translating project.

He devoted his days during the greater part of 1888 and 1889 to translating the interminable *Memoirs* of Casanova (they fill twelve volumes in all); Machen's has become the classic English translation of this work. During the same period of time he devoted his evenings to yet another translation from the French, *The Way to Attain* (*Le Moyen de Parvenir*, literally *The Way to Succeed* or "get ahead") by Beroalde de Verville (an imitator of François Rabelais). All these translations were professional work (even if Machen's rate of pay might seem rather low to us today), but the last was printed privately. He put a great deal of time and effort into these translations.

In 1890 he wrote, or began the writing of, *The Three Impostors;* this did not see publication until 1895, In 1894, the year previous, he had published two of his most famous tales "The Great God Pan" and "The Inmost Light" in one book (with illustrations by the great English Decadent artist Aubrey Beardsley). Despite the fact that Machen was a serious creative writer of genuine integrity and even of real genius, none of these books already mentioned received any critical hurrahs from the contemporary English press.

Although he was officially a member of the Anglican Church, there is an undeniable Roman Catholic quality to much of Machen's writing; perhaps from this there may have stemmed much of the antipathy to his work demonstrated by the London-area and largely Protestant-dominated English press. Machen was both Welsh and (aesthetically) Catholic, and these factors could have contributed to an unsympathetic reaction on the part of his critics in the 1890s and early 1900s.

Following the publication of *The Three Impostors* in 1895, Machen gave definitive artistic expression in his magisterial novel *The Hill of Dreams* to the agony and pain he had undergone as a dedicated creative artist during his first London period. Now during the middle to later "Yellow 'Nineties" he recreated the aching loneliness and alienation of that earlier life; and at the same time he passed through the agony of recreating his own proper prose style, in order to do justice to this unique compendium of dream-life and reality combined. The book, surely Machen's masterpiece of full-length fiction, had to wait ten years for publication in book form, that is, until 1907. *The Hill of Dreams,* in a somewhat abbreviated version, had appeared serially in *Horlick's Magazine* during the last six months of 1904 under the title *The Garden of Avallaunius.*

Machen was later to write, and justly, in his autobiographical volume *Far Off Things* (1922) the following pivotal words: "I shall always esteem it as the greatest piece of fortune that has fallen to me, that I was born in that noble, fallen Caerleon-on-Usk, in the heart of Gwent. My greatest fortune, I mean, from that point of view which I now more especially have in mind, the career of letters. The older I grow the more firmly am I convinced that anything which I may have accomplished in literature is due to the fact that when my eyes were first opened in earliest childhood they had before them the vision of an enchanted land" (*FOT* 8).

In *The Hill of Dreams* Machen succeeded in retrieving not only something of his own immediate past but just as much (especially in the "Roman Chapter") a glorious period from the early history of Wales. Moreover, he succeeded in capturing, in significant token form, something of the tremendous yearning of the Welsh for their own magnificent past, as well as their almost religious attitude toward their own past and language and culture and musico-poetic arts.

This almost religious attitude of the Welsh toward the mythical and historical totality of their own way of life is not that dissimilar—in a general way—to the attitude displayed by Chief Seattle, the head of the Suquamish and Duwamish tribes, in his speech on the occasion of the founding in 1855 of the city that bears his name in the state of Washington. Here he speaks of their religion (and then elsewhere he prophesies with tremendous pathos of the inevitable passing of the Amerindian way of life): "Our religion is the traditions of our ancestors—the dreams of our old men, given them in the solemn hours of night by the Great Spirit, and the vision of our sachems, and is written in the heart of our people."

Following the completion of Machen's fictional magnum opus (whose creation took from late 1895 to the middle of 1897), he created his single outstanding piece of nonfiction (apart from his later volumes of autobiography), *Hieroglyphics: A Note upon Ecstasy in Literature.* In this treatise he developed and illustrated his theory of great literature as "ecstasy." Completed in the summer of 1899, this appeared in book form in 1902.

The Hill of Dreams and *Hieroglyphics* probably represent the *crème de la crème* of Machen's literary output, together with his autobiographical volumes. But they also represent something more than that. In the late 1800s and early 1900s, a momentous event was happening in Anglo-American letters. This was nothing less than the final flowering of Late Romantic, and peculiarly British, Kelticism. This particular final flowering—represented by such poets and authors as William Butler Yeats, Lord Dunsany, Padraic Colum, etc.—is symbolized perfectly in both *Hieroglyphics* and *The Hill of Dreams.*

The new generation of eager or clever young writers at this time was either hostile or indifferent to, or ignorant of, this event; or else they were totally blind to anything beyond their own new and narrow and uniquely modern anthropocentrism. The English Decadents (a group that definitely does not include Machen)—to judge, for example, by the remarks of Oscar Wilde on some of Swinburne's later poetry—were not hostile to this Keltic spirit but merely indifferent to certain larger aspects and considerations of this same spirit, particularly its vast epic-imaginative qualities. They were too busy being clever and "up-to-date" as well as involved in trivial aspects of "art for art's sake."

The death from cancer of his first wife Amelia in the summer of 1899 plunged Machen into a period of intense depression. The turn of the century found him seemingly unsuccessful as a professional writer as well as depressed and short of money. For a brief while he became an occultist. Together with such respectable figures as W. B. Yeats and George Moore, he joined the Hermetic Order of the Golden Dawn, more or less presided over by his great and good friend, the expatriate American A. E. Waite. Machen considered investigating Satanism, but fortunately he became infatuated instead with a young actress Pierpont Vivienne, whom he called his "Shepherdess." Although they were good friends, she did not return his love but married someone else instead (a musician).

However, by now Machen had already started a leave of absence (as it were) from his creative writing when in January 1901 he first went on the stage. He possessed as a mature man a deep sonorous voice à la Dylan Thomas (another and later Welshman), and this served him well as a Shakespearian actor when he joined Frank Benson's Shakespeare Company, mouthing the "tremendous" lines of Elizabethan rant, rhetoric, and poetry. Thus, he became an actor at thirty-nine and began a whole new life for himself, which lasted from 1901 to 1905, a remarkable achievement for a middle-aged man.

Moreover, he married—again in middle age—one of the actresses in the Benson Company, Dorothy Purefoy Huddleston, on June 25, 1903. From this union, his second marriage, there emerged two children, a boy and a girl. The year 1906 saw Machen return for a while to his creative writing when he published *The House of Souls.* Finally in 1907 he published *The Hill of Dreams.* That year also saw him on the stage for the last time as a regular trouper. Late 1907 marked his final and lasting return to writing of all kinds, and thus there began his last major period as a creative artist, renewed and replenished by his experience on the stage as well as by his second marriage.

For the next few years Machen wrote for various periodicals: the *Academy* (owned and edited by Lord Alfred Douglas), the *Neolith,* and *T.P.'s Weekly.* In 1906 and 1907 he had put together *The Secret Glory,* a patchwork of material accumulating over the last dozen years; it did not see publication until 1922. Then almost at the age of fifty he became a journalist, a profession he detested, writing for the (London) *Evening News,* beginning around 1911. The newspaper encouraged him to do his own creative writing, which they also published in addition to his purely journalistic pieces.

The year 1914 saw the "Great War"—or World War I—commence its destructive and stupid course. During these war years (ending 1918), a time of great physical and spiritual danger for many Europeans and Englishmen, Machen accomplished some of his finest fiction, in addition to perpetrating willy-nilly a myth for his fellow Britons with his tale "The Bowmen," first published in 1914. *The Angels of Mons: The Bowmen and Other Legends of the War* appeared in 1915 and proved to be Machen's greatest commercial success. *The Great Return* (1915), although a masterpiece of artistic reserve and balance, as well as his most important story of supernatural joy, proved to be one of his least successful publications from a purely popular viewpoint; cast in the form of a newspaper report, this tale narrates the manifestation of the Holy Grail in a lonely Welsh town by the sea. *The Terror,* first appeared in 1917, is one of his most potent stories of supernatural horror.

After nearly a decade as a regular contributor—he was almost sixty—Machen resigned in 1921 from the *Evening News.* The next five years were a time of great happiness for the veteran writer. He and his family had moved to a new house in London (at 12 Melina Place). Here he and his wife Purefoy developed a kind of salon on Saturday evenings, for punch, games, and good conversation. This became a kind of tradition with them for quite a while.

Meanwhile in America that publisher of unusually good taste, Alfred A. Knopf of New York City, had in the early 1920s begun publishing Machen's works in those handsome yellow editions that one can still see today in used bookstores as well as in private and public libraries. Machen had by now issued the three volumes of his unique autobiography (one of the finest things in his overall oeuvre): *Far Off Things* in 1922, *Things Near and Far* in 1923, and *The London Adventure* in 1924. The first two volumes in particular surely rank with the best he ever wrote.

For the first time in his life Machen was enjoying a considerable vogue, principally in the U.S., thanks to the Knopf editions and thanks to certain preeminent proselytizers. Among his more outstanding American enthusiasts active at this time (as well as later) were Vincent Starrett, Carl Van Vechten, Robert Hillyer, James Branch Cabell, H. P. Lovecraft, and Clark Ashton Smith, but not (alas!) H. L. Mencken or Edmund Wilson, those two arbiters of literary "elegance."

Machen was at last rewarded somewhat for the long hours he had put into his translation of *The Memoirs of Casanova* when an agreement was negotiated for a Casanova Society edition of the memoirs in 1922. Martin Secker of London issued in nine volumes the "Caerleon Edition" of Machen's novels, tales, and memoirs in 1923.

Machen took advantage of this unexpected but certainly welcome vogue for his work by issuing in book form four miscellanies, a genre in which he was a natural and intuitive master: *Strange Roads* in 1923, *Dog and Duck* in 1924, and lastly *Notes and Queries* together with *Dreads and Drolls* in 1926. Other books of this same general time were *The Glorious Mystery, The Canning Wonder,* and *Precious Balms* (this last being a collection of all the adverse book reviews Machen had received since the 1890s).

His remaining books of creative fiction appeared over a period of twelve years: *The Shining Pyramid* in 1924, *The Green Round* in 1933, and then *The Cosy Room* and *The Children of the Pool* in 1936. *The Green Round,* his last novel, received its first American publication in 1968 by Arkham House; August Derleth, its owner-editor, had championed Machen's cause on many occasions.

In 1929 Arthur and Purefoy Machen retired from London to Old Amersham, Buckinghamshire, in the Chiltern Hills, northwest of London. Here, where Arthur and his first wife had lived for a few years in the early 1890s, the olden beechwood forests linger to this day from Britanno-Roman and pre-Roman times. By 570 A.D. London had been lost to the Romano-Britons but some real British-Keltic influence remained longer here in the Chilterns than in any other area of Eastern Britain. Indeed, the Chilterns by virtue of their forested heights and uplands (forests and hills were always favored areas for the original Brythons) had served in their aggregate as a kind of citadel or bulwark against the Saxons and other Germanic barbarians, thus to preserve the ancient "Augusta" or "Londinium" for a much longer period of time than what would have otherwise obtained. London had belonged to the Britons during the regime of King Arthur and immediately subsequent to his death.

So to this ancient stand of beechwood trees that had also functioned as an ancient stand of the Romano-Britons, Machen and his wife Purefoy retired to live in Old Amersham. His books had never earned him any real livelihood, and substantial recognition (even if only of a highly specialist kind) had not come to him until he was a comparatively older man. Writing had always been a torture to him: his own creative writing had proven a virtual torment to him for the most part; and journalism (usually writing trivial items for hire) proved an aesthetic horror for him, however manfully he did it and however much his income benefited from it at the time.

In the later decades of his life, as pleasant and enjoyable as his early London career had proven bitter and painful, Machen could have reflected that during his lifespan he had indeed become a variety of things just as a Jack-of-all-trades literary. Perhaps foremost as a writer of weird fiction (especially tales of supernatural horror and supernatural joy, and always of the secret ecstasy inherent in mortal existence). But he had started out as a none-too-successful poet in verse with the subsequently suppressed *Eleusinia.* Later he developed into a fascinating and often superb essayist, as well as a sovereign translator, particularly from the French (of two different centuries, the 1500s and the 1700s). Since he had a mystical outlook on life, he functioned in his writing as a literary mystic, a sort of Druidic poet in prose. He had been a serious critic of literature, but he became a professional journalist late in his life: his parents had originally sent him off to London to become just that at the very beginning of his long career. He developed into an autobiographer of especial excellence. Although he had never had a great commercial success (apart from *The Bowmen and Other Legends of the War* in 1915), he remained a great master of English prose, even though the ecstasy that burns at the heart of it is distinctly Welsh, that is to say, distinctly Brythonic. At his best he was an eminently successful poet in prose. Then, after all the difficulty and great lonely pain of his first major creative period (ending around the turn of the century), in the last decades of his life Machen became his own self-legend, with himself as his own best book, or work of art; or in the hermetic language of the Middle Ages that he loved so discerningly, his own alchemy and alchemist into a happier and more enlightened state. And it is distinctly significant that he deliberately killed himself (so to speak) as a writer in his early sixties. He still did some work, interesting and valuable as all his writings are, but not major in the sense of "The Great Return" or *The Hill of Dreams.*

In the very last decade of his life Machen received a number of signal honors, and we must say that they were certainly well deserved by this time. On March 3, 1937, that is, upon his seventy-fourth birthday, he sat at a luncheon in his honor put on in the city of Newport by his home county of Monmouthshire with many local dignitaries on hand. They presented Machen with a check for 20 guineas. In the autumn of 1937 the National Liberal Club in London held a dinner in his honor.

In 1939 World War II broke out. The war effort in Britain immediately commenced, and Machen made his own contribution by editing the book *A Handy Dickens.* He passed eighteen months in the selection of his favorite chapters from the works of Charles Dickens, and wrote an introduction for each chapter thus chosen. This personal anthology appeared just before Christmas 1941. In the spring of 1942 his great and good friend A. E. Waite died at the age of eighty-five; he and Machen had been close friends for fifty-five years.

As the war years dragged on, the financial condition of Arthur and Purefoy became increasingly straitened. Certain stalwart friends (a number of them quite influential) determined to rectify this once and for all. Inspired by Desmond MacCarthy and administered by Colin Summerfield, an appeal was made six months before Machen's eightieth birthday. This appeal appeared in the national press as a letter signed by twelve well-known literary figures: Max Beerbohm, Algernon Blackwood, Walter de la Mare, T. S. Eliot, John Masefield, Bernard Shaw, Arthur Quiller-Couch, Compton Mackenzie, Edward Marsh, A. E. W. Mason, Michael Sadlier, and Desmond MacCarthy. This appeal proved a remarkable success (particularly considering that it was wartime), and Machen's home county of Gwent or Monmouthshire organized a separate appeal that also proved successful.

Meanwhile, Alfred A. Knopf in New York City organized yet another appeal that also yielded a considerable sum of money. The overall fund finally closed at well over £2,000.

On Machen's eightieth birthday on March 3, 1943, in a Hungarian restaurant in London, Desmond MacCarthy presented Arthur with a check for 1,200 guineas, the first installment of the fund. The archetypal Great Old Man of Letters held the seat of honor surrounded by a distinguished company indeed. This was probably the single greatest public moment of Machen's life. Neither Arthur nor Purefoy would want for money for the rest of their lives.

On March 30, the Palm Sunday of 1947, Purefoy died quite suddenly. After his wife's death Machen's health deteriorated, and his children established him at St. Joseph's, a nursing home operated by nuns in Beaconsfield, just south of Old Amersham. Not far from Beaconsfield the great Puritan poet John Milton had written *Paradise Regain'd,* the sequel to *Paradise Lost.* Machen firmly stated his desire to his daughter (Mrs. Janet Machen Davis), who had come to see him, to go live with her and her family at her home in Bristol, back in his beloved West Country, once his health improved enough to allow this. But this was not to be. In the early morning of December 15, 1947, Arthur Llewelyn Jones-Machen died in the presence of his daughter and Colin Summerfield.

In 1948 Alfred A Knopf published Machen's *Tales of Horror and the Supernatural,* selected and edited by Philip Van Doren Stern, who had written in the "Introduction" apropos of Machen's work as follows:

> A taste for his work has to be acquired; the writing is polished and elaborate, the thinking is subtle, and the imagery is rich with the glowing color that is to be found in medieval church glass. His style does not belong to our period of stripped diction and fast-moving prose; it stems instead from the latter part of the nineteenth century, and preserves some of the formality of that age when authors were learned people who had to undergo long apprenticeships to master their profession. (v–vi)

Also, as pointed out perceptively by Stern, Machen's art "is firmly based on the belief that the mystical interpretation of life is the only one worth holding. Machen is the artist of wonder, the seeker for something beyond life and outside time, the late-born disciple of

Christianity who sees the physical world as the outer covering of a glowing inner core that may someday be revealed" (xi). During the last decades of Machen's life, H. P. Lovecraft, writing in his now classic study "Supernatural Horror in Literature," penned what must surely rank as some of the most judicious, perceptive, and eloquent praise in honor of his literary achievement.

> Of living creators of cosmic fear raised to its most artistic pitch, few if any can hope to equal the versatile Arthur Machen, author of some dozen tales long and short, in which the elements of hidden horror and brooding fright attain an almost incomparable substance and realistic acuteness. Mr. Machen, a general man of letters and master of an exquisitely lyrical and expressive prose style, has perhaps put more conscious effort into his picaresque *Chronicle of Clemendy,* his refreshing essays, his vivid autobiographical volumes, his fresh and spirited translations, and above all his memorable epic of the sensitive aesthetic mind, *The Hill of Dreams* [. . .] his powerful horror-material of the 'nineties and earlier nineteen-hundreds stands alone in its class, and marks a distinct epoch in the history of this literary form. (81)

But it should be pointed out that Lovecraft, writing most attractively about Caerleon-on-Usk and Machen's masterpiece, actually misrepresents *The Hill of Dreams.* Lovecraft cites the novel as one "in which the youthful hero responds to the magic of that ancient Welsh environment *which is the author's own,* and lives a dream-life in the Roman city of Isca Silurum, shrunk to the relic-strown village of Caerleon-on-Usk" (81; emphasis added). Lucian Taylor's dream-life in Isca Silurum is most vividly and amply described in Chapter IV—the so-called "Roman Chapter"—but it is true that its immediate artistic effect is adroitly adumbrated in the first three chapters, and then haunts the remainder of the book. Incidentally, the "Roman Chapter" can stand on its own in any anthology as a classic of English prose and must take rank with some of the noblest passages in English literature, including not only those of Thomas De Quincey (of whom Machen was a great admirer) but the last and most celebrated chapter (the fifth) of Sir Thomas Browne's *Hydriotaphia,* or *Urn-Buriall* (1658). Lovecraft gives the impression from his description (completely authentic otherwise) that the overall book is largely concerned with the hero's dream-life in the Late Roman town and fortress combined (which it is not): the "Roman Chapter" is only one chapter among a skillfully juxtaposed mosaic of seven chapters, even though its effect does haunt at least half the book (especially the beginning and the end), if not indeed most of the book.

Lovecraft had an instinctive understanding *in depth* of such a signally cosmic master artist as Machen, as (for example) when he writes: "Of utmost delicacy, the passing from mere horror into true mysticism, is *The Great Return,* a story of the Graal, also a product of the war period" (87). Then immediately he continues: "Too well known to need description here is the tale of 'The Bowmen'; which, taken for authentic narration, gave rise to the widespread legend of the 'Angels of Mons'—ghosts of the old English archers of Crécy and Agincourt who fought in 1914 beside the hard-pressed ranks of England's glorious 'Old Contemptibles'" (87).

But perhaps Lovecraft is at his most eloquent when he sums up some of the apparatus of Machen's interior fantasy life as a writer.

> Mr. Machen, with an impressionable Celtic heritage linked to keen youthful memories of the wild domed hills, archaic forests, and cryptical Roman ruins of the Gwent countryside, has developed an imaginative life of rare beauty, intensity, and historic background. He has absorbed the mediaeval mystery of dark woods and ancient customs, and is a champion of the Middle Ages in all things—including the Catholic faith. He has yielded, likewise, to the spell of the Britanno-Roman life which once surged over his native region; and finds strange magic in the fortified camps, tesselated pavements, fragments of statues, and kindred things which tell of the day when classicism reigned and Latin was the language of the country. (82)

And thus has Mr. Lovecraft opined, and justly, apropos of Mr. Machen.

There is something peculiar about the Keltic element in modern English that should be mentioned here. Although relatively few Keltic words remain directly in modern English, many writers have opined that, in place of an immediate transference of words into English, the Keltic spirit exercised a much more profound and subtle influence on later English literature. Matthew Arnold, for one, has maintained that this Keltic spirit represents a species of "natural magic"—a magic which has accounted for some of the abilities possessed by Spenser, Marlowe, Shakespeare, Keats, Coleridge, and other poets. And it is

peculiar that although the work of Arthur Machen is the very essence—the *quint*essence (to use the alchemical diction of the Middle
Ages)—of Late Romantic (British) Kelticism, it was almost completely
misunderstood at the time by the contemporary press, especially in
England. Its real and genuine significance has remained, for the most
part, unknown or presumably too vague and "cloudy" to define aright.
But this fact—that Machen's work embodies the quintessence of Late
Romantic Kelticism—explains in large measure why so many historic
layers, so many mystic auras, and so many spiritual or aesthetic
splendors, are subsumed into Machen's viewpoint and his art.

As a writer in the highest sense Machen may be seen in various
roles; and these would form some of them. As a Welsh "bard" in
highly musical English prose (rather than verse), his own usage of poetic prose parallels that of the French Decadents and Symbolists, and
anticipates the poetic prose once again so popular in written fantasy.
As a "mythographer" or myth-maker, he continues both the Welsh
and the classical (Greek and Latin) traditions of myth in an unique
and autochthonous synthesis of his own. As a Druid or high priest of
literature (conversant with strange medieval rigors and mortifications
of the flesh, many in description and a selective number in practice),
he skillfully mosaicks into the English of his narratives incantatory
passages of truly "hermetic" meaning in Latin, Welsh, and Greek.
Above all and always—and this is the collective art which permits all the
other functions—as a paramount master of English prose, he stands beside Thomas De Quincey, Sir Thomas Browne, the Robert Burton
who penned *The Anatomy of Melancholy,* the super-aesthete and
pedagogue Walter Pater, and selective others.

Arthur called Machen was well named indeed: Arthur the Maker—yes, Arthur the Myth-Maker—as "fabulous" a figure in various recondite aspects as Merlin and Taliesen themselves, or as Geoffrey of
Monmouth, from Machen's own native country of Gwent.

By being born in Caerleon-on-Usk, Machen inherited the various
historic layers or traditions associated with that ancient town (as well
as with southern Wales), and which he subsumed into his own unique
genus of Kelticism: first, the lore relative to the pre-Keltic "Little People" (later transformed into "féerie" or Faerie); then the British-Keltic
or Brythonic culture; the Britanno-Roman culture; the Dark Ages;

the Middle Ages; the Renaissance; the early Romantic period, middle Romantic or Victorian, and Late Romantic or Late Victorian; and then on into the 1920s, which were to witness the first major triumphs of the then new "modernism."

Like a last of the Romano-British bards displaced in both time (Victorian England, *not* Arthurian Britain or Late Roman Britain) and space (London, *not* Wales), Arthur Machen—by preserving, and by necromantically evoking, various ancient and then later historical "splendors"—became, in a deep, subtle, and innermost sense, truly "The Last of the Arthurians" himself. Alienated in his own time and space for much of his life (and we are speaking here in a mystical or spiritual sense), he was moreover descended from people, the Welsh, who had once maintained their dominion over the whole of Britain, who had become dispossessed of most of their ancient national patrimony, and who had thus been transformed themselves into "aliens" in most of their former realms. Nor could they forget this. However, they had endured, as Machen himself was to endure.

Toward the last of his first major creative period, "Leolinus Siluriensis" had achieved his own self-myth as a dedicated and painstaking "artist-martyr" when he had to become the Lucian Taylor of his own romance, *The Hill of Dreams*. But whereas Lucian dies of an accidental overdose of laudanum (perhaps symbolic of Machen writing "finish" to his early London career and all that it represented in terms of his earlier, less experienced, but certainly more purely idealistic self), Machen merely went on living in that determined and persevering way of his, and continued writing his books, articles, and reviews.

If the splendor that his work reflects in a symbolic or actual (historic) way could be summed up in one word or phrase, it might be either "Arthurian" or "Late Roman." And if we finally decided that it might be Arthurian, then it would be with the understanding that it subsumed within itself at least the various historic layers or traditions just previously adumbrated. His early training at Hereford Cathedral School, with which he was originally to continue that unbroken ecclesiastical tradition peculiar to his father's family, prepared him instead uniquely well indeed for his real career or destiny: that of creative literature of a completely individual class. By receiving his earliest and greatest influence from Caerleon and from the presumably "mythical" age of King Arthur—Arthur, "the Bright Light of the Dark Ages"— Machen thus became supremely well equipped to create his own expression of the Keltic spirit, a spirit at once mystic and magical.

Machen, it must be emphasized, evolved into his own kind of *modern* romancer. His powerful supernatural stories of the 1890s and early 1900s have elements akin to the "scientific romances" of the same period. For just one salient example, Machen's novella "The Great Return" is a *modern* story of the Holy Grail (a story that takes place completely in Wales, a fact that is noteworthy in that Machen's native country remained the single greatest sanctuary for the Arthurian traditions and magnificence) *with no mention of Glastonbury.* In his handling of such a well-known property of medieval romance, Machen is notable for the purity of his approach: the Grail is simply used as a kind of supernal catalyst for inducing a sense of deep and inner spiritual splendor in those who come into contact with it, a type of paradisaical serenity or sublimity, the "peaceable kingdom" restored.

Throughout Machen's oeuvre and balancing the great fears "captured" in his most powerful tales of horror and the supernatural, there is the curious and ironic emphasis on splendor and enlightenment (often purchased at great loss or expense within the given stories), as indicated by some of his titles and main images: "The Inmost Light," *The Secret Glory,* "The Shining Pyramid," *The Glorious Mystery.*

The Holy Grail in "The Great Return" is refulgent with strange transdimensional glories. Whilst originally in the medieval romances it was a symbol of "grace," in our own time it has developed into simply a symbol for that lost or Arthurian splendor so persistently associated with the San Graal in myth and legend. In Machen's work overall it is the cup of wonder and marvel overbrimming with great joy and great awe, with otherworldly magnificence, and with a lost and Atlantean exaltation.

Despite his birth in eminently "Arthurian" Caerleon, this is one of the few instances (virtually unique) within the canon of his oeuvre where Machen permits himself, as a mature artist, to use such a preeminently Arthurian property: significantly it is the San Graal, the symbol par excellence of Keltic mysticism.

Machen's own artistic preoccupation with the ultimate sunset of the Arthurian splendor (which in its own turn seems but a reflection or continuation of the still potent Late Roman Imperial magnificence) is indicated in the highly autobiographical pages of *The Hill of Dreams,* where he again shadows his own Caerleon under the name of "Caermaen," and is particularly highlighted at the beginning and the end of the novel by the tremendous image of the setting sun likened to the fire in a great brazen furnace. But the final statement of this image is projected within the open eyes of the writer Lucian Taylor who is dead at his writing table and thus literally "amort" with splendor. In some incredibly elusive way the artist's spirit has passed into the splendiferous world of his vision . . . the dreamer has passed into his dream. . . .

Just as he had given over the best part of his adolescent imagination to relating the various local Arthurian traditions and legends immediately to his native environment of Caerleon, so did Machen devote the best part of his first major creative period as a mature artist (from the early 1800s up to 1899) to the imaginative reconstruction of Late Roman life in Isca Silurum.

In his later novella "The Great Return" he was to use the Arthurian splendor to retrieve a paradisaical presence or immanence, a notably "Christian" endeavor on the part of the author, and very much in keeping with the overall tradition of the legend in question. But in his fictional magnum opus, *The Hill of Dreams,* Machen is above all notable for his use of the Arthurian splendor to recapture (paradoxically enough) a pagan glamor. Machen's heritage of Arthurian dream and wonder from old Caerleon becomes the specific window or focus through which he perceives the rich and variegated world of Roman British life in Isca of the Silurians.

In his introduction to the 1923 Alfred A. Knopf edition of *The Hill of Dreams,* the author gives us a fascinating description of the overall origin of his novel, as well as of the specific creation of the "Roman Chapter."

The required notion came at last, not from within, . . ., but from without. I am not quite sure, but almost sure, that the needed hint was discovered in an introduction to "Tristram Shandy" written by that most accomplished man of letters, Mr. Charles Whibley. Mr. Whibley, in classifying Sterne's masterpiece, noted that it might be called a picaresque of the mind, contrasting it with "Gil Blas" which is a picaresque of the body. This distinction had struck me very much when I read it; and now as I was puzzling my head to find a spring for the book that was to be written, Mr. Whibley's dictum occurred to me, and applying it to another eighteenth century masterpiece, I asked myself why I should not write a "Robinson Crusoe" of the soul. I resolved forthwith that I would do so; I would take the theme of solitude, loneliness, separation from mankind, but, in place of a desert island and a bodily separation, my hero should be isolated in London and find his chief loneliness in the midst of myriads of myriads of men. His should be a solitude of the spirit, and the ocean surrounding him and disassociating him from his kind should be a spiritual deep. And here I found myself, as I thought, on sure ground; for I had had some experience of such things. For two years I had endured terrors of loneliness in my little room in Carendon road, Notting Hill Gate, and so I was soundly instructed as to the matter of the work. (*CF* 2.522-23)

Machen had received the overall conception of his novel toward the end of October 1895, but it was not until early February 1896 that he began the actual writing. He encountered arduous difficulties and problems but persevered and resolved them, very much to his credit as a painstaking craftsman. He details further in his introduction something of the specific creation of the celebrated Chapter IV.

Then I found somewhere or other, the recipe for the "Roman Chapter," an attempted recreation of the Roman British world of Isca Silurum, Caerleon-on-Usk, the town where I was born, and soaked myself so thoroughly in the vision of the old golden city—now a little desolate village—and listened so long in the deep green of Wentwood for the clangour of the marching Legion and for the noise of their trumpets that I grew quite "dithery" as they say in some parts of England. I would go out on my dim Bloomsbury strolls, deep in my dream, and would "come to myself" with a sudden shock in Lamb's Conduit Street or Mecklenburgh Square or in the solitudes of Great Coram Street, realizing certainly, that I was not, in actuality, in the Garden of Avallaunius or delaying in the Via Nympharum or on the Pons Saturni—it is called Pont Sadwrn to this day—but utterly at a loss to know exactly where I was or what I was doing, without the faintest notion of the various positions of north and south, east and west, and not at all clear as to how I was to get home to Gray's Inn and my lunch. And it was in this queer way that the fourth chapter was accomplished. I was somewhat proud of it, and went on gaily … (*CF* 2.525-26)

The composition of *The Hill of Dreams* required from first to last a period of eighteen months, from February 1896 to July 1897. It first appeared in book form in 1907, ten years after its completion.

The sentence that opens this magisterial romance of alienation is remarkable for its utter simplicity: "There was a glow in the sky as if great furnace doors were opened" (*CF* 2.9). Further on in Chapter I, Machen describes Lucian Taylor's progress away at school; this evidently reflects something of the author's own experience at Hereford Cathedral School.

> Lucian went slowly, but not discreditably, up the school, gaining prizes now and again, and falling in love more and more with useless reading and unlikely knowledge. He did his elegiacs and iambics well enough, but he preferred exercising himself in the rhymed Latin of the middle ages. He liked history, but he loved to meditate on a land laid waste, Britain deserted by the legions, the rare pavements riven by frost, *Celtic magic still brooding on the wild hills and in the black depths of the forest,* the rosy marbles stained with rain, and the walls growing grey. The masters did not encourage these researches; a pure enthusiasm, they felt, should be for cricket and football, the dilettanti might even play fives and read Shakespeare without blame, but healthy English boys should have nothing to do with decadent periods. (*CF* 2.12-13; emphasis added)

However, Machen reserves some of his most skillful writing, his finest descriptive powers, for the "Roman Chapter" wherein he adroitly juxtaposes and contrasts the modern and rather asinine Victorian life in Caerleon with the wonderfully sensuous and certainly sensual world of Isca. The author shadows Caerleon under the name of "Caermaen" and adumbrates his own self as Lucian or, in his Late Roman incarnation, as Avallaunius. The chapter's opening is memorable for its poetic and evocative description whose imaginative qualities would not have been lost on either H. P. Lovecraft or Clark Ashton Smith.

> In the course of the week Lucian again visited Caermaen. He wished to view the amphitheatre more precisely, to note the exact position of the ancient walls, to gaze up the valley from certain points within the town, to

imprint minutely and clearly on his mind the surge of the hills about the city, and the dark tapestry of the hanging woods. And he lingered in the museum where the relics of the Roman occupation had been stored; he was interested in the fragments of tessalated floors, in the glowing gold of drinking cups, the curious beads of fused and coloured glass, the carved amber-work, the scent-flagons that still retained the memory of unctuous odours, the necklaces, brooches, hairpins of gold and silver, and other intimate objects which had once belonged to Roman ladies. One of the glass flagons, buried in damp earth for many hundred years, had gathered in its dark grave all the splendours of the light, and now shone like an opal with a moonlight glamour and gleams of gold and pale sunset green, and imperial purple. Then there were the wine jars of red earthenware, the memorial stones from graves, and the heads of broken gods, with fragments of occult things used in the secret rites of Mithras. Lucian read on the labels where all these objects were found: in the churchyard, beneath the turf of the meadow, and in the old cemetery near the forest; and whenever it was possible he would make his way to the spot of discovery, and imagine the long darkness that had hidden gold and stone and amber. All these investigations were necessary for the scheme he had in view, so he became for some time quite a familiar figure in the dusty deserted streets and in the meadows by the river. (*CF* 2.71)

Then, further on, Machen elucidates the purpose behind his hero's numerous visits and investigations.

All these journeys of his to Caermaen and its neighbourhood had a peculiar object; he was gradually levelling to the dust the squalid kraals of modern times, and rebuilding the splendid and golden city of Siluria. All this mystic town was for the delight of his sweetheart and himself; for her the wonderful villas, the shady courts, the magic of tesselated pavements, and the hangings of rich stuffs with their intricate and glowing patterns. Lucian wandered all day through the shining streets, taking shelter sometimes in the gardens beneath the dense and gloomy ilex trees, and listening In the course of the week and trickle of the fountains. Sometimes he would look out of a window and watch the crowd and color of the market-place and now and again a ship came up the river bringing exquisite silks and the merchandise of unknown lands in the Far East. He had made a curious and accurate map of the town he proposed to inhabit, in which every villa was set down and named. He drew his lines to scale with the gravity of a surveyor, and studied the plan till he was able to find his way from house to house on the darkest summer night. On the southern slopes about the town [i.e., across the river] there were vineyards, always under a glowing sun, and sometimes he ventured to the furthest ridge of the forest, where the wild people still lingered, that he might catch the golden gleam of the city far away, as the light quivered and scintillated on the glittering tiles. And there were gardens outside the city gates where strange and brilliant flowers grew, filling the hot air with their odour, and scenting the breeze that blew along the streets. (*CF* 2.75)

Still further on, Machen gives us—from a vantage point high on the steep slope south of the town across the river—a wonderful "impressionistic" panorama of Isca Silurum as seen through the eyes of his hero Lucian still in his Late Roman incarnation as Avallaunius.

At other times it was his chief pleasure to spend a whole day in a vineyard planted on the steep slope beyond the bridge. A grey stone seat had been placed beneath a shady laurel, and here he often sat without motion or gesture for many hours. Below him the tawny river swept round the town in a half circle; he could see the swirl of the yellow water, its eddies and miniature whirlpools, as the tide poured up from the south. And beyond the river the strong circuit of the walls, and within, the city glittered like a charming piece of mosaic. He freed himself from the obtuse modern view of towns as places where human beings live and make money and rejoice or suffer, for from the standpoint of the moment such facts were wholly impertinent. He knew perfectly well that for his present purpose the tawny sheen and shimmer of the tide was the only fact of importance about the river, and so he regarded the city as a curious work in jewellery. Its radiant marble porticoes, the white walls of the villas, a dome of burning copper, the flash and scintillation of tiled roofs, the quiet red of brickwork, dark groves of ilex, and cypress, and laurel, glowing rose-gardens, and here and there the silver of a fountain, seemed arranged and contrasted with a wonderful art, and the town appeared a delicious ornament, every cube of colour owing its place to the thought and inspiration of the artificer. Lucian, as he gazed from his arbour amongst the trellised vines, lost none of the subtle pleasures of the sight; noting every *nuance* of colour, he let his eyes dwell for a moment on the scarlet flash of poppies, and then on a glazed roof which in the glance of the sun seemed to spout fire. A square of vines was like some rare green stone; the grapes were massed so richly amongst the vivid leaves, that even from far off there was a sense of irregular flecks and stains of purple running through the green. The laurel garths were like cool jade; the gardens, where red, yellow, blue and white gleamed together in a mist of heat, had the radiance of opal; the river was a band of dull gold. On every side, as if to enhance the preciousness of the city, the woods hung dark on the hills; above, the sky was violet, specked with minute feathery clouds, white as snowflakes. It reminded him of a beautiful bowl in his villa; the ground was of that same brilliant blue, and the artist had fused into the work when it was hot, particles of pure white glass.

For Lucian this was a spectacle that enchanted many hours; leaning on one hand, he would gaze at the city glowing in the sunlight till the purple shadows drew down the slopes and the long melodious trumpet sounded for the evening watch. Then, as he strolled beneath the trellises, he would see all the radiant facets glimmer out, and the city faded into haze, a white wall shining here and there, and the gardens veiled in a dim, rich glow. On such an evening he would go home with the sense that he had truly lived a day, having received for many hours the most acute impressions of beautiful colour. (*CF* 2.79–80)

Through his focus onto the pagan world of Isca Silurum, the true purpose of life—to wit, the simple acceptance and enjoyment of its wonder, mystery, and beauty—has become apparent to Lucian Taylor; and the "Roman Chapter" concludes with his full and expanded understanding of this revelation.

To Lucian, entranced in the garden of Avallaunius, it seemed very strange that he had once been so ignorant of all the exquisite meanings of life. Now, beneath the violet sky, looking through the brilliant trellis of the vines, he saw the picture; before, he had gazed in sad astonishment at the squalid rag [i.e., "the dull modern life"] which was wrapped about it. (*CF* 2.89)

The "Roman Chapter" records thus the best and brightest period in Lucian Taylor's life, his imaginative sojourn within the marbled confines of ancient and beautiful Isca (with all its transcendent emotions and sensations) when he had lived the life of a Late Roman aesthete. The seventh and ultimate chapter of *The Hill of Dreams* describes, on the other hand, his delirium and descent into death through an overdose of laudanum. Machen's narrative of his hero's final "trip" contains some of his most powerful and poignant passages of prose, culminating of course in Lucian's death, the final revelation.

Without, the storm swelled to the roaring of an awful sea, the wind grew to a shrill long scream, the elm-tree was riven and split with the crash of a thunderclap. To Lucian the tumult and shock came as a gentle murmur, as if brake stirred before a sudden breeze in summer. And then a vast silence overwhelmed him.

A few minutes later there was a shuffling of feet in the passage, and the door was softly opened. A woman came in, holding a light, and she peered curiously at the figure sitting quite still in the chair before the desk. [. . .] She put her hand to his heart, and looked up, and beckoned to some one who was waiting by the door.

"Come in, Joe," she said. "It's just as I thought it would be: 'Death by misadventure';" and she held up a little empty bottle of dark blue glass that was standing on the desk. "He would take it, and I always knew he would take a drop too much one of these days." [. . .]

The man took up the blazing paraffin lamp, and set it on the desk, beside the scattered heap of that terrible manuscript. The flaring light shone through the dead eyes into the dying brain, and there was a glow within, as if great furnace doors were opened. (*CF* 2.155, 156)

The Hill of Dreams closes with the same directness and simplicity with which it begins; indeed, with virtually the same words. The novel's final pages possess a rare pathos and grandeur, a genuine epic dignity as the narrative moves to its inexorable finish. Moreover, the tremendous image with which the story opens and then ends is not actually the setting sun but is instead the sunset's immediate aftermath, that is, the afterglow that just precedes the twilight and then the ultimate night.

Behind the definitive artistic expression contained within his *Robinson Crusoe* of the soul, there lay the bitter actuality of the agony and pain that Machen had undergone as a dedicated creative artist—as well as the aching loneliness, the intense melancholia, and the profound alienation which he had experienced simply as a person—during his first London period (from the summer of 1881 to the late autumn of 1885).

The reality of those two full years in particular, during which (as he later wrote) he "endured terrors of loneliness" at his then home (his little room) in Clarendon Road, Notting Hill Gate, London, formed the crucible in which Machen's character as well as his personality as a mature creative artist were fired and tested. But like the Welsh in general, he was to endure, and emerged from his ordeal as a better and a stronger person. He had survived the worst part of his self-imposed apprenticeship both as a person and a writer. All this then was part of the actuality of real experience which lay behind his fictional magnum opus, and which gives the novel its especial flavor of authenticity.

Machen then in his most characteristic creative writings is a peculiar mixture of hard-edged realist and poetic fantaisiste. Just as the critical respect and admiration for him as a man of letters has always been more pronounced in America than in England, his influence as a writer on other writers has apparently always proved greater in the U.S. than in the United Kingdom, and has always been limited to writers of a similar temperament as well as of similar tastes. The true connoisseur of Machen's works is your genuine lover of *mystery*—that is, mystery that remains fundamentally inviolate despite all hints and adumbrations—and is not necessarily by any means the same as the lover of conventional mystery tales, or detective stories, wherein the unknown is reduced at the end to something perfectly well known and even commonplace.

Machen exercised a profound and undeniable influence on both H. P. Lovecraft and Clark Ashton Smith, an influence not only deep-reaching but subtle and selective as well. Lovecraft, it will be remembered, was a lover of Latin and classicism in general, and Smith was no less a lover of the classical than Lovecraft but also, by process of strict historical evolution, a Late Romantic poet of the most pronounced kind. For such sensitive and unique artists as these, Arthur Machen would have provided a source of pure and undiluted ROMANticism.

Both Lovecraft and Smith learned from the elder writer, but whereas Lovecraft, as a "photographic realist" in his own most characteristic stories, would have studied more closely the realistic aspects of Machen's fiction, Smith would have studied more attentively the poetic or lyrical aspects of Machen's art. However, we can be sure that both Lovecraft and Smith would have equally appreciated these two major aspects of Machen's most idiosyncratic fiction.

In a number of profound and significant respects there is perhaps a greater kinship between Machen and Smith than between Machen and Lovecraft. Machen and Smith in regard to a given story of their own respective creation possessed an instinctively more lyrical or poetic approach than Lovecraft, although Machen is probably more obviously human and humane than Smith. However much Smith came to the writing of his own most characteristic prose fictions as a result of his own interior artistic evolution, it is curious and striking how the conclusion of *The Hill of Dreams*—which features the death of Lucian Taylor—anticipates many of Smith's own short stories, the majority of which always end with the death of their protagonists.

However, apart from such a selective albeit profound influence as that on Lovecraft and Smith, both Arthur Machen and *The Hill of Dreams* will probably remain *sui generis* and basically inimitable.

Postlude

No matter that most of the Late Romantics were to end their days—even as most of them had passed their lives—in obscurity or near-obscurity. They had accomplished a brave and courageous work in the very teeth of a cuttingly hostile counterreaction on the part of the modern anti-Romantic establishment (artists and critics alike). Especially had some of them developed further, and indeed achieved the preservation of, literary fantasy in the grand manner on into the twentieth century. And certainly few other Late Romantics had achieved as much as Arthur Llewelyn Jones-Machen, prose-poet par excellence.

Machen would surely have been beloved of *Elen,* the Welsh goddess of the sunset. And did he not indeed receive at least some token guerdon—toward the sunset of his own life—for labor lovingly designed and accomplished often in the face of singular bitterness and (on occasion) breadless days?

Machen is that particular poet of wonder and romance who sings the tremendous and kaleidoscopic glories invoked by the ultimate sunset of the Arthurian splendor. All through the best part of his first major creative period (specifically the "Yellow 'Nineties") he was transfixed and enraptured by that especial moment "like some eternal sunset brave with gold," to quote from "Fetlain's *Elegy for Vixeela*" by Clark Ashton Smith.

Off the west of Europe, and from the west of Britain, specifically from ancient Wales, "Leolinus Siluriensis"—virtually alone, unknown, and unhonored (at least in a comparatively larger sense)—was to preserve something of the ancient British-Keltic spirit, the elder Brythonic magic in a singularly pure and intrinsic form, into an alien age until such time as wonder and romance would find again a later cyclical and mystical rebirth.

In the far west of the United States of America, the Californians (native or adopted) were also to preserve something of this ancient epic-imaginative spirit, this Arthurian or Atlantean splendor of romanticism.

When the new romanticism surged up exuberantly in the late 1960s and early 1970s, the collective work of the Late Romantics had somehow survived to remain as a valuable heritage of beauty and inspiration for the practitioners of the new romanticism (as well as for the general public, of course), and from this new romanticism's immediate, hitherto largely unknown but recently discovered or rediscovered past. In that collective *living* museum which is the mind of the Western world, this heritage remains an unique and radiantly magical treasure somehow miraculously left over from an otherwise irrevocably lost Atlantis.

Works Cited

Ashe, Geoffrey. *King Arthur's Avalon.* New York: E. P. Dutton, 1958.

Baker, Arthur E. *A Tennyson Dictionary.* London: Routledge, 1916.

Cavendish, Richard, ed. *Man, Myth and Magic: An Illustrated Encyclopedia of the Supernatural.* New York: Marshall Cavendish, 1970. 24 vols.

Grebanier, Bernard D., et al. *English Literature and Its Backgrounds.* 1939. Rev. ed. New York: Holt, Rinehart & Winston, 1949. 2 vols.

Lovecraft, H. P. *The Annotated Supernatural Horror in Literature.* Ed. S. T. Joshi. New York: Hippocampus Press, 2nd ed. 2012.

Morris, John. *The Age of Arthur.* New York: Charles Scribner's Sons, 1973.

Stern, Philip Van Doren. "Introduction." In *Tales of Horror and the Supernatural* by Arthur Machen. New York: Alfred A. Knopf, 1948. v–xvi.

A FINAL LAUREL WREATH OF LYRICS

For Lin Carter

(In memoriam)

To you who viewed so much with pristine vision,
Who also called attention and acclaim,
And saved them from neglect and from derision,
To many names out from forgotten fame,
And rescued all of them from any blame,
To you we give our heartfelt thanks in turn,
And seek to save your name in turn from shame,
To bring it back like ashes from an urn,
To make it with a deeper flame a little while to burn.

Your constant and more brilliant light has long since lit our route,
And thanks to your clairvoyance how much more can we discern
As we go down our path as if with trumpet, drum, and flute.

You leave a gate, a beacon, and an open sesame,
A key for unknown land, for unknown sky, for unknown sea.

Inspiration

O minnesinger, troubadour, trouvère,
With eagle's quill you pluck the gut-strung lute,
And state the tune, a strong straightforward air:
You seek and choose the notes that seem to suit
The weft or web of sound, in close pursuit
From one note to the next, a phrase in point:
The tune goes on its way, its forthright route,
A moment's treasure, but not out of joint,
This melos or this melody that does not disappoint:

You make one big note at a time—big, bold, and bare—
Now low, now high, and thus in strictest counterpoint,
Searched out, selected out, with forethought and with care:

This older mode of making sound serves as a case in point,
However much it might appear disjunctive or disjoint.

Ayery-Fayery

Where might survive somehow the faeries,
Concealed in what woods or what wilderness,
Or perched somewhere on palaced aeries?
Like some unsung Olympus more or less,
A point whose locus no one could confess,
If known, the longitude and latitude?
But past the prophet or the prophetess,
For which we feel such humble gratitude,
The place appears but only to poetic aptitude.

My sensum of direction has become un-compassing:
Am I not faithful to myself, my own desires, my mood?
Always outrageous, overwhelming, all-encompassing.

Airy-fairy, a palace perched upon an eyrie,
Fairy-airy, what other place could be more eerie?

Pomgarnet Wine

Apples of garnet and of garnet-wine,

The pomegranate wine brewed in the cask,

Could not assuage or quench this thirst of mine:

So that in ripe contentment I might bask,

Beyond the need to answer or to ask,

A state of gnostic equilibrium:

Perhaps a mode of grace poured from a flask,

Or yet a mood, a realm, a kingdom come

As of its own accord, beyond the need to think, to sum:

Is this too much to ask the power of pomegranate wine,

Of any wine, of anything, in booze or liquor-dom,

A state almost divine, somewhat divine, beyond divine?

The flavor or the savor of these apples of the garnet

Is as powerful in their mode as anything carved in granite.

Nor Cleopatra Nor Helen of Troy

"Is this the face that launched a thousand ships?"
—Christopher Marlowe, *Doctor Faustus*

Nor Cleopatra nor Helen of Troy
Could have had launched for them an ampler fleet
Than what they had at Actium or at Troy!
A thousand ships is not something effete,
Something with which to argue or compete,
Colossal effort in the ancient world!
And even if they both led to defeat,
A countenance with features gnarled and knurled
Could not have stirred such fate as one with loveliness empearled.

Grandeur can stir up so much more than just the commonplace,
As when the storm tide hits the river's mouth with waves a-swirled,
Like some sea god imperious with his mighty scepter-mace.

Unless but mere celebrities who do not rank or rate,
Do not disparage or depreciate the truly great.

No Safe Refuge

They sailed from Rome bound for Byzantium,
With manuscripts inside a treasure-chest;
The past without them would stay mute or dumb.
They asked astrologers what time were best
To write their fate upon time's palimpsest—
They left per sign or pointer horoscopal.
To seek a better refuge formed their quest—
Each script more dear than any pearl, or opal,
Or other gemstone safe inside high-walled Constantinople.

Alas, their future brethren would have need to move once more:
If they could but have peered ahead with vision telescopal,
To find somewhere secure but westwards of wherevermore?

But well before the fatal year of Fourteen Fifty-Three,
They knew to flee Constantinople over land and sea.

The Emperor Steps Down:
Uncommon "Comme il faut"

(Akihito surrenders his office to Naruhito)

At eighty-two he wanted to retire;
To abdicate he needed to resign.
How could he then hand on that sacred fire,
How could he still maintain his holy line,
How could his duty with his wish combine?
His nation's diet fixed it so he could,
Since different laws pertain to things divine,
And all things came out well, as well they should,
For emperor as father or the son, and for the common good.

In majesty and honor in contrast to minuscule,
With sacred rite, per sacred custom, still as understood,
In dignity and modesty beyond yet majuscule:

The father did return the treasures that were three—
The mirror, the sword, and the jewel, intensified by three.

Confessional

O brave new cosmic-astronomic world—
Are we the only species to explore
The stars and suns and planets all unfurled?
Rare privilege indeed, and what is more,
With script or rescript handed out the door,
To navigate this awesome cosmic-scape!
The evermore, wherevermore, and more,
And is it thus that we dream to escape
On into other worlds, or gulf, or isle, or bay, or cape?

With big wide mouth agape, as at the agapé,
One *Homo sapiens* as *the* all-purpose ape,
Wonder-struck I remain, today, tomorrow, yesterday.

Let us now seek those further shores, beyond the known unknown,
Where cosmic blooms, luxuriant, wax blown or overblown.

A Blessing or a Curse

Elixir of elixirs, alcohol!—
Quintessence of an essence in a vat,
The chief component being ethanol:
Yes, booze has always been where it is at,
Along with salt, with sugar, and with fat—
Did they have cocktails in antiquity,
Or only potent wines, and that was that?
How came the label of iniquity,
Through injudicious use, or more, through its ubiquity?

Could it have been a simple substitute of this for that,
Or yet a tertium quid, a tertiary quiddity,
Or still once more a case of tat for tit, or tit for tat?

Wine, beer, and spirits are much more a blessing than a curse,
Except that each can eat away the exchequer and the purse!

Nyctalops

Dedicated to Prince, and in memoriam.

Twin words that hold my fancy: nyctalops,
And nyctaloptic, nyctaloptical—
Somewhat aligned with opulence and ops,
And secretly encyclopaedical:
Night-vision, or night-visioned, overall
Confers some benefits not quite the same
As phony Vicodin with fentanyl:
Thus Prince deceased, but haply without blame,
An accidental overdose, heroic, with no shame:

Prince could see deep, and well, within both dark and light—
But not his own decease, a vision not the same—
He need not fret, he has gone back sans oversight:

Prince has escaped both censure and the patient graveyard worms,
Transcending to the Other Side, and thus on his own terms.

(P.S. A free spirit, both until and beyond the end.)

A Random Enquiry and Something More

Does everything perchance take place by chance,

Despite the best-laid plans of mice or men,

That is, by no more than sheer happenstance?

Not flattering to men, but then again

Would this please more from megaphone, from pen,

Or yet again by other overt means,

To blaze in public place for public ken?

Is this a thing inherent in our genes,

And as a something engineered in us more like machines?

In such a case it serves like destiny or fate

That none or nothing contradicts, or contravenes,

A *force majeure* that naught or cipher could abate.

Could everything take place by nothing more than happenstance?

Or thus it would appear, and thus perchance by only chance?

Impermanence and Permanence

With cupola and widow's-walk around it,
It stands, a typical New Bedford house,
With towering and leaf-topped elms that bound it:
Attended at the base by gull or grouse,
And not exempt from rodents—rat or mouse—
This lordly habitation sits extant:
No harm from household pest—cockroach or louse—
The house is made of wood, not adamant;
Its essence cannot long survive the termite with the ant.

But still the structure stands, withstands the battling elements,
Those elements and their incessant change or rage or rant:
Yet how remote all that seems from a place of temperance!

Just the same as of when in the eye of a tropical storm,
The winds and rains around it whirl and swirl and endlessly swarm.

Sunset Sail

(For Gail Fryer Scannell.)

With jib, with mast, with mainsail, and with boom,
The two sailboats offshore glide under sail,
For other boats they leave a lot of room.
The open seas inhere beyond the pale,
Beyond the earth-bound wall, and without fail
The open seas have freedom without end.
And far beyond the reach of whip or flail,
To no king's will might they be made to bend,
An outcome that forced King Canute to comprehend.

So let this handsome view, these sunset boats, exemplify
The limitless kaleidoscope that never has an end,
The boundless liberty, untrammeled, of the sea and sky.

And with this utmost liberty we choose to make us one—
The soul need not have barriers below the moon or sun.

Adrift

We drifted as a consciousness
Above the star-filled seas of space
Without an ego more or less;
But still with mind and heart in place,
How free we felt with no disgrace,
No second thoughts to spoil the fun!
Thus nothing did we need efface,
While we stared boldly at the sun,
No spectre at the feast, nor where there could be none!

Immersed inside this dazzlement of sight and sound,
How could this overwhelming overview not stun?—
While we stay thunderstruck past barrier or bound!

The best reaction is a quiet wonderment
For one who has lived in the City too long pent.

Averonne

(An imitation *Amithaine*.)

Who views the towers of Averonne,
Sharp-etched and limned against the dawn,
Shall have a glimpse of paradise,
The highest point of thrice by thrice:
Who views the towers of Averonne
Shall have a trove to draft upon.

With sunrise-gonfalons outspread,
With raptures to wake up the dead,
Her towers and turrets lift and loom
Beyond the dark of doom and gloom:
Shall sunset morph into sunrise?—
To stir our hearts with rare surmise?

Amid her gardens Averonne
Hath verdure that greens on and on,
An alchemy beyond our sun,
Beyond our moon's oblivion:
So thus we gaze at Averonne,
Her towered and spired phenomenon.

And who might be the châtelaine
Of that high castle's choice domain?—
Where only people pure of heart

Might reach by masterpiece of art,
By care and vigilance at least,
By endless quest to west from east.

The fanfares blaze in Averonne
Against the coming of the dawn
In high-pitched, clear fortissimo,
Proclaiming weal, but never woe,
To god and goddess, nymph and faun,
To come abide in Averonne.

Who views the towers of Averonne,
Sharp-etched and limned against the dawn,
Shall have a glimpse of paradise,
The highest point of thrice by thrice:
Who views the towers of Averonne
Shall have a trove to draft upon.

In Appreciation of Publius Vergilius Maro

Upon reading Gilbert Highet's *Poets in a Landscape* (1957).

From these our elder years to those your nights and days,

We bow or nod, or at least give a little dip

From this our brow, resolved in mind to praise your praise

Of herdsmanship, of husbandry, of warriorship,

With such voice as we have, to serve with tongue and lip,

Your *Bucolics,* your *Georgics,* and your *Aeneid:*

You held onto your genius with an earnest grip

As for your ego, your libido, and your id,

With calm restraint you kept them all beneath an iron lid.

In spite of later blame your works remain superior,

And in your epic poem your genius you outdid,

All negative critique can only seem inferior.

You made a nobler fable than

     the one of Ariadne and of Theseus—

You made a grand romantic myth,

     the tale of Dido left behind by Aeneas.

Enigmatic

The Vernal, or Vertumnal, Aequinox,
The true New Year, reminds or minds us all,
"How life is change, how different from the rocks"
How must we heed our Mother Nature's call,
To spring to life, or elsewise back to fall,
Before we leave that Other Side once more:
The choice is ours to make, or not at all,
Before we pass again on through that door,
To take up life, to live that life, its essence, yes, its core.

We leave behind that exitus, the gate of no return,
Before we might accost that unknown shore, that farther shore,
Back to that certain inmost heart, the source for which we yearn:

Enigma of enigmas, or
    elixir of elixirs, and
        the source from which we drink—
By this we have existence, yes,
    our sense of life and beauty, and
        by this we feel and think.

Mittel Europa in One Single Pile

(For Lou and Sue Irmo, con amore.)

Behold Chicago's castled Water Tower,
The single shaft of which lifts up on high,
And at the top a domed and cozy bower!
The four round corner towers hit the eye
Down on the ground like castles in the sky,
Perhaps too castellated to be real:
At first reluctant, or a little shy,
The eye soon travels over all with zeal,
So much to note, so much detail with which to deal:

So many little towers or turrets everywhere,
Foursquare kaleidoscope by which to dream or feel,
This pile should be approached with piety and prayer.

Is this a temple to some god, some hydro-deity,
For whose life-giving source of strength we should bear fealty?

Note for "The Emperor Steps Down"

Then eighty-two, Akihito as the Emperor of Japan, after two surgeries, told his nation in 2016 that he wanted to retire, to step down, from the Chrysanthemum Throne. By special dispensation (or indulgence) the National Diet (or parliament) released him from the law that kept him as emperor, kept him in office, until he died of the natural causes of old age. In May 2019, the nation granted him his wish in an elaborate ritual, or ceremony, at sunrise, steeped in tradition and gracious protocol, whereby the emperorship, or empery, passed from father to son.

The gist of this material derives from *The Week* (the periodical), 21 June 2019 (Friday), p. 11, a succinct article on the condition or status of "Modern monarchy"—good or great, and certainly strong. We quote:

> "Presidents come and go," said Kenneth W. Gunn-Walberg, head of
> the International Monarchist League's chapter for the Eastern U.S.
> "There's continuity, a sense of history with a monarchy."

APPENDIX:
CLARK ASHTON SMITH, AS PERCEIVED BY
TWO CONTRASTING POETS

Foreword

As assembled and quite capably edited by Scott Connors, the publication (by Hippocampus Press) of *The Freedom of Fantastic Things* (2006), the first collection of critical pieces on Clark Ashton Smith as poet and fictioneer, marks not only a major step in the evolution of fantasy and science fiction criticism, but in fact in the annals of modern imaginative literature overall.

As outstanding contributors to *Weird Tales* (1923-54) and other pulp magazines of the 1920s and 1930s, Ashton Smith's two principal confrères, H. P. Lovecraft and Robert E. Howard, have both had many critical articles written about them and their fiction and poetry, not to mention several books (compilations) apiece, consisting exclusively of critical pieces on their specific writings.

In a sense such a collection as *The Freedom of Fantastic Things,* devoted exclusively to Smith, certainly seems like something long overdue. Scott Connors has thus fulfilled a strategic function in gathering and editing such a compilation. Oddly and inexplicably, the more than able editor did not include in the contents of his volume two of the longest and most outstanding of such critical essays.

First, as written by the then eighteen-year-old Donald A. Wandrei (of the Twin Cities, Minnesota), and appearing in the mid-1920s, his essay surveying Smith's three major early poetry collections (1912, 1922, 1925) achieved publication in the *Overland Monthly* for December 1926. This came about thanks to the editorial influence of George Sterling as a prominent contributor to the same prominent magazine, the equivalent on the West Coast of the *Atlantic Monthly* on the East Coast. The publication of this major essay marked the last major effort on behalf of Smith as his poet-protégé. The elder poet had only deceased in the month, November, immediately preceding.

Also thanks to Sterling those three major early collections—*The Star-Treader, Ebony and Crystal,* and *Sandalwood*—had garnered their fair share of positive reviews and other critical pieces at their respective time of publication. Although Sterling considered Wandrei' s essay, "The Emperor of Dreams," far too encomiastic—beautifully written, its enthusiasm is highly contagious!—recent poetic history seems to have completely justified Wandrei's apparently outrageous praise.

Thanks exclusively to Derrick Hussey and his Hippocampus Press, Ashton Smith seems to have founded an entire new school of poets, mostly traditionalist, as influenced by Smith and his poetry! Witness the biannual *Spectral Realms* (same press), the poetry magazine. Witness also the three big volumes of Smith's *Complete Poetry and Translations* (as gathered and edited by S. T. Joshi and David E. Schultz, a colossal task), same publisher, 2007–08. Even the British have apparently now claimed Ashton Smith as one of their own, given the Anglo-Britannic origin of his father Timeus.

A traditionalist, and in his own turn strongly influenced by Smith, Wandrei as poet and critic was then living through the poetically tumultuous 1920s thanks to the emerging prominence of T. S. Eliot, Ezra Pound, and Harriet Monroe, who had already founded her innovative and quite influential *Poetry* magazine, and which she edited during the second, third, and fourth decades of the twentieth century.

Wandrei meanwhile would become a leading contributor to *Weird Tales* and the other pulp magazines of the 1930s and 1940s. His early appreciation of Smith's (early poetry) collections, thus written at the very start of Wandrei's own literary career, and first published in late 1926, still certainly stands out as much today as it did back then.

Introduced to Smith's poetry and prose by D. Sidney-Fryer, Marvin R. Hiemstra—as a modern, innovative, and highly original poet in his own right, and very much in the tradition of T. S. Eliot, Ezra Pound, not to leave out Walt Whitman, but above all e. e. cummings—managed to read and assimilate the entirety of Smith's then literary output in book form during just a few months before Hiemstra wrote his outstanding appreciation of Smith (as poet and fictioneer) under the title of "Cosmic Master Artist."

This happened in San Francisco during the later 1960s, created purposely for inclusion as the final piece in Sidney-Fryer's C.A.S. bibliography, accepted for publication by Donald M. Grant (then living in Rhode Island, and now deceased). The acceptance took place in the same later 1960s, but not so published until 1978, which resulted as the more propitious occasion to bring the monograph out.

Thoroughly acquainted in depth with literature ancient and modern, Marvin Hiemstra[1] achieves in his critical piece in his own turn, at once exceptional and profound, an almost iconoclastic revelation. If it remains the single best essay on Ashton Smith thanks to Hiemstra's wide-ranging literary and intellectual genius, then Wandrei's own "Emperor of Dreams" assuredly follows close behind, if not in fact running a close parallel.

D. SIDNEY-FRYER

West of Wherevermore,
East Sandwich, Massachusetts,
Tuesday evening, 9 July 2019.

N.B. We must mention (as definitely included by Scott Connors in *The Freedom of Fantastic Things*) the extended essay on Ashton Smith by Brian Stableford as equally outstanding as are the appreciations or interpretations by Donald Wandrei and Marvin Hiemstra.

---

1. Originally from Pella, Iowa, but resident in San Francisco for many years.

The Emperor of Dreams

Donald A. Wandrei

In 1912 there came from the press of A. M. Robertson, in San Francisco, a slender book of poems. Had that volume come from a well-known writer, it would have ranked him with the immortals. Had it come from a rising author, it would have spread his fame far and wide. It came from neither. It was little advertised, for it had no financial backing and the author had neither influential friends nor acquaintances among those who determine what the public may read. No attempt was made to popularize it. The book shortly passed from sight, almost unknown save to a few fortunate people who possessed copies. The book was, "The Star-Treader and Other Poems;" its author, Clark Ashton Smith, a young poet, not yet twenty, who had already dreamed and dared to dream as few men have in a lifetime. That book of poems is one of the great contributions to American literature. It contains some of our finest pure poetry, some of our best imaginative lyrics. A few of them would now be famous, had they been written by a Keats or Shelley, and a cause of laurels. The critics have ignored the volume. The literary pontiffs have passed it over. Today, not many persons know it, even by title. Yet the same critics decry the anaemic state of American letters, its lack of enduring works. A genius—in the true, not abused, sense—appears, his eyes on the other side of eternity, his poems of eternity, his work the kind that endures. He is unnoticed. He is given no encouragement. American poetry is still anaemic.

A thousand years hence, when the people of that distant time survey the accumulated mass of all literature, they will place high up on the role of honor the name, Clark Ashton Smith; and looking backward, they will ask why the world of that age long ago did not appreciate him when it had him. Perhaps this is as it ought to be. The man of letters should be the possession of those who do appreciate him. It is not given to ordinary man to walk with the gods; nor, when it is so given, does he usually avail himself of the opportunity unless he is one of that group which is the justification of himself, the cornerstone

379

of the arts, and the prophet of. immortality.

A poet cannot live on visions, on dreams, on a prospect of future fame. He must live on something more material. And one cannot write when it is necessary to earn a sustenance. Perhaps this was the reason that ten years elapsed before another book appeared under the poet's name. Or perhaps it was the neglect, popular, which is of little importance, and critical, which may be of the greatest importance, given his first book. Or perhaps the dreamer lived in his own realm, indifferent to ephemeral external life, writing seldom and then mainly for his own pleasure. Or perhaps . . . One trembles at the thought. "Ebony and Crystal" was published in 1922. Its fate is akin to that of "The Star-Treader." Not many persons know it. Those who do regard it as worshippers a sanctum sanctorum, as connoisseurs a rare tapestry, as jewellers a priceless pearl.[1]

There is no place in contemporary prose and poetry for genius.

Was "Ebony and Crystal" worth the labor of ten years? It is a larger volume than the first and contains twice as many poems, one hundred and fourteen against fifty-five. Did eleven poems a year, and those not of unusual length, with one exception, justify the author a place among the front-rank poets? If fame is the criterion, no. If excellence, yes. "Ebony and Crystal" is the finest volume of pure poetry that has appeared in America since the opening of the twentieth century, perhaps the finest since the time of Edgar Allan Poe. Not until its publication did any of our poets approach him in imaginative power. "Ebony and Crystal" belongs on that shelf with Poe, Coleridge, Blake, Shelley, Baudelaire. In that group where each is coequally supreme, he may justly take his place.

Imagination is his god, beauty his ideal; his poems are an offering to both. He is the poet of the infinite, the envoy of eternity, the amanuensis of beauty. For even as beauty was deity to Keats and Shelley, so it is to him, and in its praise has he written. But he has not celebrated it as an abstract term or an aesthetic quality, but as a more

---

1. I have since been informed that the silence was due to the destruction of imperfect poems, and to ill-health. It is hard to believe this statement in a day when the least is treasured by those whose best is mediocre. But it explains the uniform excellence of his work, the lack of a single weak poem.

tangible substance. He has constructed entire worlds of his own and filled them with creations of his own fancy. And his beauty has thus crossed the boundary between that which is mortal and that which is immortal, and has become the beauty of strange stars and distant lands, of jewels and cypresses and moons, of flaming suns and comets, of marble palaces, of fabled realms and wonders, of gods, and daemons, and sorcery. Time and Space have been his servants, the universe his domain; with the stars his steeds and the heavens his tramping ground, he has wandered in realms afar; and he has found there a wondrous beauty and a strange fear, the goal of his early dreams and the enchanted road to greater, all manner of things illusory and fantastical.

Some of his poems are like shadowed gold; some are like flame-encircled ebony; some are crystal-clear and pure; others are as unearthly starshine. One is coldly wrought in marble; another is curiously carved in jade; there are a few glittering diamonds; and there are many rubies and emeralds aflame, glowing with a secret fire. Here and there may be found a poppy-flower, an orchid from the hot-bed of Hell, the whisper of an eldritch wind, a breath from the burning sands of regions infernal. The wizard calls, and at his imperious summons come genie, witch, and daemon to open the portal to the haunted realms of faery; and their wonder is transmuted so that those who can open the door may listen to the murmuring waters of Acheron, or watch the passing of a phantom throng; and the fen-fires gleam; and the slow mists arise; and heavy perfumes, and poisons, and dank odors fill the air. A marble palace rises in the dusk, a treasure-house of gold, and ebony, and ivory; soft lutes play within; fair women, passionless and passionate, wander in the corridors; silks and tapestries adorn the walls, and fuming censers burn a rare incense. And fabulous demogorgon and hippogriff guard the golden gateway to the hoarded wealth. The sky is black. But now and again white comets blaze, or suns of green, or crimson, of purple, flame across the firmament with silver moons. The sky is burning. Stars hurtle to destruction or waste away. All mysteries are uncurtained. One may watch a landscape of the moon, the seas of Saturn, the sunken fanes of old Atlantis, wars and wonders on some distant star.

There is no place in the poetry of Clark Ashton Smith for the conventional, the trite, the outworn. It is useless to search his work for offerings to popular desire. Some authors pander to the public taste; their books may have a huge sale, but die with the author. Some writers have skill and ability but desire wealth or immediate fame; their work has not so great a popularity but endures longer. A very few have what is called "genius." They write primarily for themselves, or with a certain small group of people who know literature in mind. They are artists, word artists; and they fashion their prose or poetry with care and labor. They are seldom appreciated in their lifetime, and never have widespread popularity, but the highest minds of every age enjoy their work. These are ones who speak to us across the ages, who will speak across the ages to come. It is to this class that Clark Ashton Smith belongs. One will examine his poems in vain for the commonplaces that have so largely crept into our literature; and by so much as he has avoided ephemeral and written of immortal things, by so much the longer will his work endure.

II

"The Star-Treader" was his earliest volume, and it shows the effects of imagination in its first exuberance. Stars and suns and comets parade in all their majesty; Chaos. Infinity, and "the eldritch dark" are ever present; and the wonder, the inexplicable mystery of the Universe form the background of the book. It was then that the young poet wrote "The Song of a Comet;" it was then that he fashioned "The Song of the Stars;" and from his pen came "The Wind and the Moon." Of the fixed forms, the sonnet was his favorite, and nearly a third of the poems have its form. In most of them he strove to obtain single, dominant effects, to limn one unforgettable scene, as in "The Last Night," "The Medusa of the Skies," and "Averted Malefice." Occasionally, he was content with a single quatrain, or a pair, as "The Maze of Sleep" and "The Morning Pool." But he had a greater chance to display his power in the longer, more sustained poems, such as "Saturn," "The Star-Treader," and "The Masque of Forsaken Gods." They would have been accomplishments for a man of maturity, for one who had long written poetry, as the work of a youth they are remarkable achievements. The entire book has this note of maturity; it was a world-weary youth wise beyond his years who wrote these poems beautiful, fantastic, sometimes bitter and more than once inexpressibly terrible in their suggestion. "The Star-Treader" was published in 1912. Not for ten years did another book come from the poet.[2] What had he been doing those ten long years? Had the neglect of his first book compelled him to turn his mind into other channels? It is hard to say, but "Ebony and Crystal" is not a large volume for the work of ten years.

There is a great difference between the two, in imagery, in tone and subject, and in metrical skill. The first was, to some extent, experimental; the second, a fulfillment of the promise in the foreshadowing work. The craftsmanship of these later poems is well-nigh flawless; the volume is rich in perfectly planned, perfectly fashioned jewels. It is jewel-cutting that he was engaged in those ten years. Here may be found "such stuff as dreams are made of," and the dreams themselves; here the utterance of god and witch, the harmony of the spheres, the strains of immortal music, the unveiling of an imagery unparalleled. The beauty of these poems is intoxicating, for the poet who wrote them was haunted and intoxicated by loveliness immaculate and incarnate, by all beauty. And the poems are couched, not in ordinary language, but in an English filled with curious and archaic forms, rare or obsolete words, unusual diction; and they have been given flowing rhythms and unforgettable melodies; and they move in measured intonation, and in cadence, and in musical sweep that are seldom found in poetry. They are whispers of the unearthly, rather than mortal work. They are enduring forms of unenduring dreams and ideals and desires. They are the unattainable, set in deathless words of gold. They are time-outlasting marble; they are lotus and poppy; they are fadeless amaranth and asphodel, pure, perfect shadows of the pure and perfect, eternal, aeonian. They are star-dust and starshine, caught by a dreamer of the ages, fashioned in ebony and crystal. They are nectar and ambrosia, nepenthe, Lethean draughts to drown the world

---

2. "Odes and Sonnets" was privately issued by the Book Club of California in 1918. The odes are from "The Star-Treader"; the sonnets were included in "Ebony and Crystal."

in forgetfulness and oblivion. They are the waters of paradise.

The poems are laden with a pagan, exotic beauty and imagery. Sometimes this takes the form of light and shadow, as in "Arabesque." Sometimes it deals with the lands of romance, as in "Beyond the Great Wall:"

> Beyond the far Cathayan wall,
> A thousand leagues athwart the sky,
> The scarlet stars and mornings die,
> The gilded moons and sunsets fall.
>
> Across the sulfur-colored sands
> With bales of silk the camels fare,
> Harnessed with vermeil and with vair,
> Into the blue and burning lands.
>
> And, ah, the song the drivers sing,
> To while the desert leagues away—
> A song they sang in old Cathay,
> Ere youth had left the eldest king.
>
> Ere love and beauty both grew old,
> And wonder and romance were flown.
> On fiery wings to worlds unknown,
> To stars of undiscovered gold.
>
> And I their alien words would know,
> And follow past the lonely wall,
> Where gilded moons and sunsets fall,
> As in a song of long ago.

Occasionally it reverts upon itself as in "The Melancholy Pool" and "Solution:"

> The ghostly fire that walks the fen,
> Tonight thine only light shall be;
> On lethal ways thy soul shall pass.
> And prove the stealthy, coiled morass.
> With mocking mists for company.

On roads thou goest not again.
To shores where thou hast never gone,—
Fare onward, though the shuddering queach
And serpent-rippled waters reach
Like seepage pools of Acheron,

Beside thee; and the twisten reeds,
Close raddled as a witch's net,
Enwind thy knees, and cling and clutch
Like wreathing adders; though the touch
Of the blind air be dank and wet,

As from a wounded Thing that bleeds
In cloud and darkness overhead—
Fare onward, where thy dreams of yore
In splendour drape the fetid shore
And pestilential waters dead.

And though the toad's irrision rise,
As grinding of Satanic racks,
And spectral willows, gaunt and grey,
Gibber along thy shrouded way,
Where vipers lie with livid backs,

And watch thee with their sulphurous eyes,—
Fare onward, till thy feet shall slip
Deep in the sudden pool ordained,
And all the noisome draught be drained,
That turns to Lethe on the lip.

But usually it takes the form of a rich imagery, oriental in its profusion and splendour, unlimited in its concept and scope, imperishable by reason of its supreme, its unearthly, its alien perfection. "In Saturn"—

Upon the seas of Saturn I have sailed
To isles of high, primeval aramant,
Where the flame-tongued sonorous flow'rs enchant

The hanging surf to silence: All engrailed
With ruby-colored pearls, the golden shore
Allured me; but as one whom spells restrain,
For blind horizons of the somber main,
And harbors never known, my singing prore

I set forthrightly: Formed of fire and brass,
Immenser skies divided, deep on deep
Before me,—till, above the darkling foam,

With dome on cloudless adamantine dome,
Black peaks no peering seraph deems to pass,
Rose up from realms ineffable as Sleep!

"The Kingdom of Shadows," "The Land of Evil Stars," "A Precept," "Chant of Autumn," Requiescat in Pace,"—but it is useless to try to select fine poems from a volume which has room for none other.

There is one long poem, however, that deserves special attention. It is "The Hashish-Eater," containing many hundred lines of blank verse. But it is far different from what is usually called blank verse, from what, one knows as ordinary iambic pentameter. This has always been a stately metre, capable of impressive effects; and in his hands, with the aid of his boundless imagination and descriptive powers, besides his technical skill, it has become the implement of a poem-colossus, gigantic in theme and treatment, told in a heavy, sonorous English that sweeps onward in measured roll with an ever-swelling rhythm from the imperial summons of the opening lines:

Bow down: I am the emperor of dreams:
I crown me with the million-colored sun
Of secret worlds incredible, and take
Their trailing skies for vestment, when I soar,
Throned on the mounting zenith, and illume
The spaceward-flown horizons infinite.

And at the very end of a volume, which will one day be a prized literary heritage, is the sombre and morbidly magnificent prose-poem, "The Shadows," a poem told with such care that no word is lost or wasted, and so well that it lingers in the memory as a sable fantasy enshrined, a rare perfume, darkly odorous and darkly poisonous, clinging to a bit of strangely shapen ebony.

III

In October, 1925, came the third of his published books, "Sandalwood," a volume which, though slender, contains more poems than his first. After "Ebony and Crystal," not much could be added to his laurels, but had that volume not existed, "Sandalwood" might have taken its place to a large extent. It is different from "Ebony and Crystal" in that the poems are less ambitious with regard to the depicting of strange, vast splendour, but more songlike, lyrical, and spontaneous, though the mastery of technique and the metrical skill displayed admit of neither spontaneity nor its attendant roughnesses. The poems may be divided into several classes, including nineteen translations from Baudelaire, and four songs from the uncompleted romantic drama, "The Fugitives," And there is a poem of six stanzas, "We Shall Meet," told in an original or very rare but very beautiful verse form. But to one who has read the early work of Clark Ashton Smith, his later poems remain beyond praise. One may go into ecstasies at a vision of glory; but the greater glory surpasses description. And he who has sate on the ramparts of Heaven and Hell is mute before magnificence and pageantry that shame the speech.

No critic and no criticism can do justice to the work of this poet. There are some things which are beyond the reach of both, and in this rare group belongs the work of Clark Ashton Smith. For there are books so distinctive, so excellent, that they cannot be compared with others of their class, by reason of their perfection. For them, there is no standard of judgment, and one can only admire what one is helpless to censure or to sanctify. To use homely language in estimating such work is to do it an injustice; and yet, superlatives are equally useless, for they have been so carelessly employed that nowadays they deprecate the work they are meant to extol.

Earlier in this essay, certain other poets of the romantic-imaginative group were mentioned. But Clark Ashton Smith cannot be associated with any particular one. Each within that class was original, and by virtue of a similar originality, this modern poet deserves his rank. The great poets neither follow nor imitate; they create. And he has created, on a cosmic scale. The greatest indictment of contemporary verse is its lack of form, its deliberate exclusion of the most vital quality of a work of art, a quality which every book that aspires to greatness must have, above all else, if it is to endure. Substance-form; form-substance; of the two, form is by far the most important. And this element—including, as it does, diction, style, presentation, euphony, craftsmanship—is present in the poems of Clark Ashton Smith to such an extraordinary degree that, had there been no substance, had he produced only rainbows and iridescent bubbles, he would still have deserved lasting attention. Indeed, the sole flaw in his poems is occasionally form in too great a degree. His gifts are so much beyond those of average poets, and his vocabulary is of such enormous content that the desired word is often an uncommon one. Yet even this lends a curious charm, a singularly effective atmosphere to the poem, at worst, it may only be considered what would be a god-send to the lamentably word-base verse of the Philistines. It is an example of his innate power of concentration, his ability to say best and to say beautifully the things that deserve to be clothed in costly raiment.

Just where the place of this emperor of dreams will ultimately be fixed in poetry cannot, of course, be fixed in poetry, cannot, of course, be foretold, save that it should be very high. Nor can one prophesy the day he shall receive the recognition he has earned. It took the world forty years to appreciate Thomas Lovell Beddoes; it took longer for it to appreciate William Blake; Arthur O'Shaughnessy is still almost unknown; and few even of those occasional persons who have read "The Book of Jade" could tell the name of its author, Park Barnitz. And now, Clark Ashton Smith.

Five Approaches to the Achievements of Clark Ashton Smith, Cosmic Master Artist

Marvin R. Hiemstra

To the Sun

Thy light is as an eminence unto thee,
And thou art upheld by the pillars of thy strength.
Thy power is a foundation for the worlds;
They are builded thereon as upon a lofty rock
Where no enemy hath access.
Thou puttest forth thy rays, and they hold the sky
As in the hollow of an immense hand.
Thou erectest thy light as four walls,
And a roof with many beams and pillars.
Thy flame is a stronghold based as a mountain;
Its bastions are tall, and firm like stone.

The worlds are bound with the ropes of thy will;
Like steeds are they stayed and constrained
By the reins of invisible lightnings.
With bands that are stouter than iron manifold,
And stronger than the cords of the gulfs,
Thou withholdest them from the brink
Of outward and perilous deeps
Lest they perish in the desolations of the night,
Or be stricken of strange suns;
Lest they be caught in the pitfalls of the abyss,
Or fall into the furnace of Arcturus.
Thy law is as a shore unto them,
And they are restrained thereby as the sea.

Thou art food and drink to the worlds;
Yea, by thy toil are they sustained,
That they fail not upon the road of space,
Whose goal is Hercules.

When thy pillars of force are withdrawn,
And the walls of thy light fall inward,
Borne down by the sundering night,
And thy head is covered with the Shadow,
The worlds shall wander as men bewildered
In the sterile and lifeless waste.
Athirst and unfed shall they be,
When the springs of thy strength are dust,
And thy fields of light are black with dearth.
They shall perish from the ways
That thou showest no longer,
And emptiness shall close above them. (*ST* 76)[1]

Clark Ashton Smith's viewpoint as a creator of cosmic adventures is the viewpoint of an all knowing and beneficent cosmic pedagogue. Very simply, he radiates understanding. It is as if Smith has at his command at all times the remarkable power of "The Plutonian Drug" as Dr. Manners so aptly explains that multi-perceptual power to the sculptor Rupert Balcoth.

Under the influence of plutonium, you were able to extend the moment of present cognition in both directions, and to behold simultaneously a certain portion of that which is normally beyond perception. Thus appeared the vision of yourself as a continuous, immobile body, extending through the time-vista. (*LW* 294)

Clark Ashton Smith would instruct his reader to plumb the mystery of the multidimensional experience that is each tale.

Imagination's eyes
Outreach and distance far
The vision of the greatest star
That measures instantaneously—

---

1. The following abbreviations are used herein:

AY	*The Abominations of Yondo* (1960)	*OST*	*Out of Space and Time* (1942)
DC	*The Dark Chateau* (1951)	*PP*	*Poems in Prose* (1965)
EC	*Ebony and Crystal* (1922)	*S*	*Sandalwood* (1925)
GL	*Genius Loci* (1948)	*S&P*	*Spells and Philtres* (1958)
LW	*Lost Worlds* (1944)	*ST*	*The Star-Treader* (1912)
OS	*Odes and Sonnets* (1918)	*TSS*	*Tales of Science & Sorcery* (1964)

Enisled therein as in sea—
Its cincture of the system-laden skies. (*ST* 32)

As this intrepid vision from "Ode on Imagination" outlines the astounding force of imagination, so is the willing reader carefully led to the full power of his imagination and beyond. Christopher Chandon, the Smithian adventurer-hero in "The Eternal World," finds a position of complete absorption in the miraculous, far beyond "the safe, monotonous certitudes of earthly life" (*GL* 38). "He was beyond awe or surprise or bewilderment. As if in some cataclysmic dream, he resigned himself to the unfolding of the swift miracle" (*GL* 51). Quick thereon follows the resplendent and fantastic action that is the manifest gift to the reader who explores the various creations of Clark Ashton Smith.

Complete functional beauty of style and complete accuracy of emotional flux in each tale proclaim the urgent wish of Clark Ashton Smith to affectionately offer the receptive reader an ample Smithian slice of cosmic wisdom. Despite some of the most ingeniously bizarre situations and characters in all of literature, Clark Ashton Smith writes in the light of an adroit clarity to evoke a full, meaningful vision. It is never his aim to confuse or tease the reader as is the wont of many writers (take for example J. D. Salinger in his transcendental, if opaquely offered, *Nine Short Stories*) who delight in presenting an attractive aesthetic shard of obscurity to politely evade the readers while they, the token creators, luxuriate privately in their deepest secrets or their lack of the same.

Smith offers meaningful views of cosmic wisdom to his eager neophytes in a suprahistorical chain of logic that constantly astounds. "The Dark Age" is one of the finest extended metaphors applicable to the power technology versus human emotion joust which is practiced with ever increasing frequency in our society. "The laboratory was like a citadel" (*AY* 161). "Apparatuses of a hundred forms, whose use the young barbarians could not imagine, littered the paved floor and were piled along the walls" (*AY* 174). Ironically the last custodian of the laboratory poisons himself rather than accept the friendship of Torquane and the barbarian youths who had in fact saved the laboratory from the onslaught of senseless aliens.

For a vital caricature of political and social attitudes to rival Swift's

poignant chalk sketches in *Gulliver's Travels* or the exotic societal in-
version painted by Li Ju-Chen in the Chinese encyclopedic classic
Flowers in the Mirror, Smith's "The Letter from Mohaun Los" records one of the most audacious and delightfully informative journeys
to a fantastic civilization ever recorded. The wisdom that blossoms
from the few pages of that letter has seldom been equalled either in
exquisite clarity or in relevance to the very uneasy state of man.

Clark Ashton Smith is careful to warn his neophyte reader, the
would-be connoisseur of the full life in the cosmos, of the superhuman perils to which the ardent seeker of Absolute Experience is
subject. "The City of the Singing Flame" appears as a complete exploration of man's quest to stand in the superdimensional vista of
cosmic being. "It was as if we no longer existed, except as one divine,
indivisible entity, soaring beyond the trammels of matter, beyond the
limits of time and space, to attain undreamable shores. Unspeakable
was the joy, and infinite the freedom of that ascent, in which we
seemed to overpass the zenith of the highest star" (*OST* 86). Unfortunately, the "ability to recognize unknown colours and non-
Euclidean forms" (*OST* 86–87) is only a rather temporary accomplishment since the Flame that engenders the ability is destroyed and
the men must return through "greyish-green columns" (*OST* 99) to
the mundane existence which is the fate of the human animal. In
"The Light from Beyond" Dorian Wiermoth experiences a similar
trip to the infinite world of sensual awareness and returning to terra
firma pays the price. Dorian suffers minor corporal damages. "But in
all other senses, I was, and still am, a mere remnant of my former
self. . . . Among other things, I soon found that my artistic abilities
had deserted me" (*LW* 388). "I have become as it were, a clod" (*LW*
388). Lemuel Sarkis in "A Star-Change" has his body physically altered so that he may become more receptive to the sensory splendors
of the planet Mlok. When he must return to earth, Lemuel is de-
voured by "terrific hallucinations" (*GL* 102) which lead him to a
quick death.

The extent of Clark Ashton Smith's superterrestrial wisdom is un-
fathomed. The thoroughly effective manner in which he conveys this
wisdom and the necessity, for the mundane neophyte, of a temperate
approach to this wisdom is no less a marvel. The title, *Man is the only*

One who found Everything, of Hartmut Lincke's etching that offers a view of man's limitless psychic vision might be an apt label for the man Clark Ashton Smith as visionary creator of unearthly tales. The joy to be found is in Smith who can so skillfully present his discoveries, his Everything to the receptive reader.

To an extraordinary extent the tales gain their interest and impetus through Smith's intense concern with the precise psychological state of the protagonist throughout the taunt happenings of each tale. Although Smith creates a selection of the most aesthetically concrete otherworld fantasy absolutely out of space and time in a completely convincing manner, the strength of this achievement is more than doubled by the completely accurate presentation of the protagonist's mental eruptions as he is abruptly confronted by alien vistas. This truly uncanny awareness and this uncanny stylistic sketch of the hero or anti-hero's turmoil often elevates the tales to become on one level flawless symbolic landscapes of the human psychic dilemma assuming an artistic, philosophical, and psychological proto-value far beyond the elaborate and intriguing stimulus, in Smith's case the fantastic situation, that precipitates the psychic dilemma. Let the following examples speak more eloquently for Smith than my excess of jargon has succeeded in doing.

A typical Smithian landscape often stands as a fiery sketch of the abnormal emotional extremes to which the protagonist (or protagonists) has fallen. The frightening journey into unreasoned lust is undertaken by Adèle and Oliver as they yield willingly to the forbidden part of the forest in one of Clark Ashton Smith's most psychologically accurate excursions, "The Satyr."

> There was a strange perfume on the windless air, coming in slow wafts from an undiscernible source—a perfume that seemed to speak insidiously of love and languor and amorous yielding. Neither knew the flower from which it issued, for all at once there were many unfamiliar blossoms around their feet, with heavy bells of carnal white or pink, or curled and twining petals, or hearts like a rosy wound. Looking, they saw each other as in a sudden dazzle of flame; and each felt a violent quickening of the blood, as if they had drunk a sovereign philter.
> They dared not look at each other; and neither of them had eyes for the changing character of the wood through which they wandered; and

neither saw the foul, obscene deformity of the grey boles that gathered on each hand, or the shameful and monstrous fungi that reared their spotted pallor in the shade, or the red, venereous flowers that flaunted themselves in the sun. The spell of their desire was upon the lovers; they were drugged with the mandragora of passion; and everything beyond their own bodies, their own hearts, the throbbing of their own delirious blood, was vaguer than a dream. (*GL* 159)

The deus ex machina, the satyr triumphant, is a just dessert for both Adèle and Oliver and the incensed husband, Raoul.

The shrieks and laughter died away at some distant remove in the green silence of the forest, and were not followed by any other sound. Raoul and Oliver could only stare at each other in complete stupefaction. (*GL* 161)

Desire rampant is also the subject of "The Third Episode of Vathek," a painfully honest chronicle of the path of incest—from the childhood affection to the final consummation.

Now, lord, we wait, even as you, the moment when our hearts shall be kindled with the unconsuming fire, and shall burn brightly as the tail of the baboon—but, alas! shall derive unutterable anguish, like the hearts of all other mortals, from that flame in which is the ecstasy of demons. (*AY* 222)

And it is the subject of "The Maker of Gargoyles," a taciturn misanthropic artisan in stone whose grotesque creations spring to life with their maker's hate and satyr-lust, ravage Vyônes, and finally destroy their maker and animus.

Blood lust colors another of Clark Ashton Smith's painterly masterpieces, "Murder in the Fourth Dimension," an adroit view of a man's psyche as he enters the unique world of the murderer.

Some obscure need of confessing my crime and telling my predicament to others led me to an act of which I should never have believed myself capable, for I am the most uncommunicative of men by nature. Apart from the satisfying of this need, the composition of my narrative is something to do, it is a temporary reprieve from the desperate madness that will surge upon me soon, and the grey eternal horror of the limbo to which I have doomed myself beside the undecaying body of my victim.' (*TSS* 119)

"The Return of the Sorcerer" serves the murderer with a more vital revenge, the return of a most thoroughly disembodied victim to demand literally an eye for an eye with knife and saw. But the torture before the final retribution displays most keenly the murderer's mental schist.

> "It is more than a week—it is ten days since I did the deed. But Helman—or some part of him—has returned every night. . . . God! His accursed hands crawling on the floor! His feet, his arms, the segments of his legs, climbing the stairs in some unmentionable way to haunt me! . . . Christ! His awful, bloody torso lying in wait! I tell you, his hands have come even by day to tap and fumble at my door . . . and I have stumbled over his arms in the dark." (*OST* 249)

The paralyzing effect of complete emotional surrender to terror is drawn so well by Smith in his various views of Medusa. In "The Gorgon" the hero's positive will power allows him to escape. "I had closed my eyes instinctively, but even through my lids I felt the searing radiance. I knew, I believed implicitly the fate which would be mine if I beheld Medusa face to face" (*LW* 323). But the old man, who had given "an instant fascination, an immediate terror" (*LW* 314) to so many eternally, falls victim to the same eternal stone despair. This involvement with terror is a threat to the individual in "The Medusa of Despair" ("I may not mask forever with the grace / Of woven flow'rs thine eyes of staring stone"; *OS* 27), to a civilization in Medusa—

> As 'round an altar-base
> Her victims lie, distorted, blackened forms
> Of postured horror smitten into stone,—
> Time caught in meshes of Eternity—
> Drawn back from dust and ruin of the years
> And given to all the future of the world. (*ST* 16)

and in the aspect of the moon to the entire world in "The Medusa of the Skies"—

> O'er rigid hills and valleys locked and mute,
>   A pallor steals as of a world made still
> When Death, that erst had crept, stands absolute—
>   An earth now frozen fast by power of eyes
> That malefice and purposed silence fill
>   The gaze of that Medusa of the skies. (*ST* 80)

Panoramic vistas of hope and possibility, often dissolving to a monochromatic blur as the vista expires, offer the eager protagonist problematic situations in another type of Smithian landscape. "The Abominations of Yondo" is perhaps the most direct catalogue of man's innate rack of mental anguish and dread in all of Clark Ashton Smith. Caught in the very vicious circle of attraction/repulsion the hero driven to penetrate farther and farther into the domain of the sundry atrocities . . . "Terror lent me new strength" (*AY* 59) . . . with the dim hope of escaping. Inevitably the positive impetus is not rewarded and the hero's goal is violently reversed.

> Back, back through aeons of madness and dread, in a prone, precipitate flight, I ran from those fumbling fingers that hung always on the dusk behind me; back, back forever, unthinking, unhesitating, to all the abominations I had left; back in the thickening twilight toward the nameless and sharded ruins, the haunted lake, the forest of evil cacti, and the cruel and cynical inquisitors of Ong who waited my return. (*AY* 61)

"The Last Incantation" displays a protagonist, Malygris the magician, with a desperation even more chronic than the anguish of the wayfarer in Yondo. Malygris's anxiety is fed by ennui. It is the futile wish of the aged occult sophisticate for a return to the fresh, naive ardour of guileless youth. Malygris would recapture the spring verdure of the innocent's spirit. His attempt only dashes him farther into the mental state which is the natural result of his prolonged experience with dreadful enchantments, preoccupation with the chaotic void.

> The soul of Malygris grew sick with age and despair and the death of his evanescent hope. He could believe no longer in love or youth or beauty, and even the memory of these things was a dubitable mirage, a thing that might or might not have been. There was nothing left but shadow and grayness and dust, nothing but the empty dark and the cold, and a clutching weight of insufferable weariness, or immedicable anguish. (*LW* 89–90)

Exquisite rendering of fortune's agility as it denies all hopes appears in the patterns of Smith's magnificently beautiful "Chinoiserie." The merciless cross affections that Nemesis so matter-of-factly dictates to those who pray that their interest and affection in another be returned is given flawless expression in this magnificent double portrait (*AY* 223).

Two of Smith's finest psychic landscapes are painted in the love poems, "The Hidden Paradise" and "Love Is Not Yours, Love Is Not Mine." "The Hidden Paradise," "deep in the vales where vernal leaves are young, / and the first poppies loiter" (*EC* 41), offers one of the most precariously hopeful conclusions that the mind might be able to conceive.

> . . . Though the breath
> Of all the gods a bolted storm prepare,
> And blood-red gloom of thunders blind the sun,
>
> Shall we not turn, with clinging kisses there,
> And, laughing, quaff some dreamless wine of death—
> Triumphant still, in mere oblivion? (*EC* 41)

And yet the poem is love, built with images that transcend the abstraction l o v e and the individual experience of love to become love. Another equally valid perspective rendering, "Love Is Not Yours, Love Is Not Mine" sketches the illusion of love in a mode beautiful beyond words. Perhaps only in the painting of William Turner does such a vital presentation of the circumstantial dilemmas that waft across and blur the path of the human spirit also find expression.

> Love is not yours, love is not mine:
> It is the tranquil twilight heaven
> Through which our pauseless feet are driven
> Into the vast and desert noon.
>
> Love is not mine, love is not yours:
> It is a flying fire that passes,
> Perishing on the blind morasses,
> After the frail and perished moon. (*EC* 67)

The final dilemma of each man's psyche, the comprehension of extinction, is sketched by in two intriguing alternatives. "The Last Hieroglyph" records a simple, graphic, absolute estimation of the final human experience. Each man is at last only a cipher on the book of Vergama, Fate. In sharp contrast we view Xeethra, a testament of the reoccurring chain of incarnations, open to the individual. It is the archetypal wish of man who believes he would do well if placed by fortune in another setting.

> In a high-domed city, gates of burnished metal would open for him, and fiery-colored banners would stream on the perfumed air; and silver trumpets and the voices of blond odalisques and black chamberlains would greet him as king in a thousand-columned hall. (*LW* 220)

Xeethra, the curious goat boy, becomes the glorious ruler of his dreams only to wish again for the "passing of wind over lonely hilltops" (*LW* 233). "There the world's turmoil and troubling were lost upon measureless leagues of silence, and the burdens of empire were blown away like thistle-down" (*LW* 233). He returns to become again the goat boy. But his desolation has only been doubled to match the knowledge of his two attempts at life.

As Smith excels in the artful pictorial graphing of man's psychic balance, he finds an uncanny province in his ability to draw the supernal outlines of the scales of cosmic justice. Many of the core situations in the tales concern an outrageous defiance of natural order. The intent neophyte learns precisely what will happen to a man in the cosmos, if the man decides to turn sharply to the right or left of the man's natural ordained path regardless of the quest or the apparent success of the action. To quote from Smith's *Black Book,* his journal of intriguing illuminations, "It is better to go to hell in one's own proper and personal way than to go to heaven in someone else's proper and personal way."[2] The major portion of the Clark Ashton Smith canon explores the outcome of a hero's ill-conceived quest. As man moves beyond his natural jurisdiction, he is consequently subject to forces beyond his control. The following list of cosmic errors coupled with the cosmic consequences is only an abbreviated sample of the immeasurable cosmic wisdom within Smith. "The Ice-Demon": Quanga and the avarice prone jewelers defy the inevitable, the great glacier, and instead of gaining King Haalor's glorious rubies they are captured by the ice flow. "The Voyage of King Euvoran": Euvoran, the cruel unworthy king, seeks the symbol of his office, the symbol that he has forfeit, the rare gazolba-bird. When at last he discovers the habitat of the fowl, he is compelled to end his days on that island with the gazolba-bird as his monotonous diet. "Master of the Asteroid": Three anti-social spacemen leave their company for the unknown where the irrational forces unbridled cause Gershom to commit suicide, Colt to kill himself as a sacrifice to atone for Gershom's act, and Beverly to

---

2. *The Black Book of Clark Ashton Smith,* ed. R. A. Hoffman and Donald S. Fryer (Sauk City, WI: Arkham House, 1961), Item 216.

be worshipped as unwilling God on a distant planetoid until he is destroyed by the real deity. "The Chain of Aforgomon": Calaspa, for an insane memory of desire, disturbs the order of Aforgomon, God of Minutes and Cycles, and therefore is doomed to many cycles of suffering only to end as he, in a later incarnation, is burned by "iron chains, heated to incandescence, . . . wrapped about him" (*OST* 146). "The Weird of Avoosl Wuthoqquan": The antihero's uncontrollable greed allows him to be literally swallowed by a Greed even more insatiable. "The Empire of the Necromancers": Mmatmuor and Sodosma bring an entire empire back from the dead for their own pleasure and for this acute violation of the natural order the two necromancers "quartered bodies crawl to and fro to this day in Yethlyreom, finding no peace or respite from their doom of life-in-death" (*LW* 170).

In the fullest sense cosmic justice, for Smith, is merely and significantly a natural balance of desperate forces, a constant shuffling of polar opposites, the dark versus the light, life and death, the birth and the final anxious moment of planets and of suns. "The Eternal World" perhaps charts best the cosmic overview that permeates the visionary's tales and images. In this adventure we see the various levels of hierarchy that dwell in the cosmos with the inevitable struggle for power and the even more inevitable outcome of each momentary cosmic imbalances.

———————

There is no room in any town . . . / To house the towering hugeness of my dream. / It straitens me to sleep in any bed / Whose foot is nearer than the night's extreme. (*DC* 43)

Of my dreams I have made a road, / And my soul goeth out thereon / to that unto which no eye hath opened, / nor ear become keen to hearken— / to the glories that are shut past all access / Of the keys of sense. (*ST* 86–87)

My dreams are like a caravan that departed long ago, with tumult of intrepid banners and spears, and the clamour of bugles and brave adventurous songs, to seek the horizons of perilous untried barbaric lands, and kingdoms immense and vaguely rumoured, with cities beautiful and opulent as the cities of paradise, and deep Edenic vales of palm and cinnamon and myrrh, lying beneath skies of primeval azure silence. (*PP* 12)

Each tale that blooms from the pen of Clark Ashton Smith embodies the intricate depth, raw beauty, and immeasurable wisdom of the most meaningful dream crystalized into art, or rather into the creation of absolute expression. Each story is the essence of a satisfactory working dream. The lack of opportunity to resolve conflicts within the dream estate, as scientific experiments have shown,[3] quickly produces an extreme disorientation in the mental balance of the individual thus deprived. Often the artistic, psychological, and philosophical success of a particular tale lies in the fact that Smith has explored fully and honestly the experience of the human psyche and in the fact that Smith has employed the natural human device for such exploration, the dream state.

Within a spectrum from the most jubilant wish projected daydream to the most dire throes of the subconscious's chasm, Smith utilizes the human dream in the full cosmic scope of variation as a functional and sublime metaphor for the condition of man. For the writer whose own dream state served him ravishing material,[4] the dream opens man to all of life. The dream vision within "The Mirror in the Hall of Ebony" suggests the depth of the complete revelation within the body of Smith's work.

> And in the mirror I beheld the haggard face that was mine, and the red mark on the cheek where one I loved had struck me in her anger, and the mark on the throat where her lips had kissed me in amorous devotion. And, seeing this, I remembered all that had been; and the other dreams of sleep, and the dream of birth and everything thereafter, alike returned to me. And thus I recalled the name I had assumed beneath the terrene sun, and the names I had borne beneath the suns of sleep and of reverie. And I marvelled much, and was enormously troubled, and all things were most strange to me, and all things were as of yore. (*PP* 32)

George D. Painter suggests that for Gide the *Pastoral Symphony* "is a realization that the Devil, if one has the intelligence to understand him without being his dupe, can be a valuable instructor in ethics and psychology."[5] *The Hashish-Eater; or, The Apocalypse of Evil* most graphically portrays the goal of Clark Ashton Smith's emperor of dreams—it is the complete discovery and the absolute recognition

---

3. W. Dement, "Effect of Dream Deprivation," *Science* (June 10, 1960), 1705–07.

4. Evidence for Smith's utilization of his own dreams appears in several of his letters and in memoirs or articles about him by Ethel Heiple, Donald Sidney-Fryer, and George F. Haas.

5. George D. Painter, *Andre Gide: A Critical Biography* (London: Weidenfeld & Nicolson, 1968), 83.

of evil in all its infinite variety. It is the evil of the cosmos. It is the evil of the human psyche. "The Crystals" reflect the close relationship between these two prime evils.[6]

> Raptly as one who would divine the perilous eyes of Sleep, and the dreams and mysteries which lurk therein, I sought to fathom the gulf-enclosing orb of the crystal. . . . But soon the light was centered to a star, and the crystal itself, as if pregnant with the Infinite, became a tenebrous and profound abysm, thro which a teeming myriad of shadows, vague as incipient dreams, or luminous with a glimpse of vision not prefigurable, fled in an ever-changing phantasmagoric succession about the star: from out those vortical and swirling glooms, where only the central star was constant, I saw the pallor of innominable faces emerge—faces that broke like bubbles; and forms that were strange as conceptions of an alien sun, with the eidolons of things which were imageless before, swam for a little in that phantasmic wave. But all the multifold mysteries which were manifest therein, I knew for the hidden thoughts and occluse, reluctant dreams of mine under-soul—thoughts and dreams now shadow-shown in the gulf-revealing orb of the hollow crystal. (*PP* 30)

It is the terror of the cosmos. It is the terror of the human psyche.

The vision of "The Nameless Wraith," as the vision within "The Crystals," suggests that the content of dreams is based on a subconscious transformation of a difficult past.

> Ruins, and wrecks of many a foundered year,
> Doubtfully known, bestrewed the unvisioned verge,
> Where, from unsounding reaches of blind surge,
> Some nameless wraith of beauty fluttered near. (*S&P* 14)

Smith in "The Return of Hyperion" offers us an extended metaphor using the dream state and the successful release therefrom to suggest Dark conquered by Light. This metaphor, to my mind, represents the brilliant release experienced by one who reads and concludes a Smithian fantasy.

> The night is as some terrific dream,
> That closes the soul in a crypt of dread
> Apart from touch or sense of earth,
> As in the space of Eternity.

---

6. For other examples see "Said the Dreamer" (*S&P* 12–13) and "In Slumber" (*DC* 55).

[. . .]

The night is loosened from the land,
As a dream from the mind of the dreamer.
A great wind blows across the dawn,
Like the wind of the motion of the world. (*ST* 54)

A comprehensive study of evil as it is presented on the stage of dreams in the fantasy of Clark Ashton Smith might fill several volumes. The following examples only hint at the variety and the more than remarkable achievement of Smith in the artistic expression of the subconscious's strenuous endeavors. "The Outer Land" pictures a man strayed from the exquisite valleys of pure love into the chaotic dreamlike state of uncontrollable lust. The landscape is a triumph as a rendering of the psyche's delirium (*DC* 58–60). In "Morthylla" Valzain's lust for an all absorbing passion is satisfied. "It was like a dreamer's acceptance of things fantastic elsewhere than in sleep" (*TSS* 251). The reality of Beldith causes Valzain to kill himself with a knife to replace the mock lamia's teeth. Significantly Valzain makes his own dream of the lamia's embrace come true in his experience after death. Perhaps the finest portrait of ill-channeled affection in Smith's work appears with awesome mastery in "The Garden of Adompha." From the archetypal clearing of Eden to the medieval *Romance of the Rose* to the contemporary cocktail party psycho-questionnaire (If you could choose, what would the gates of your garden be like? The path to the center? The wicker table in the center? The vase on the wicker table? What would the shape of the key to the gates of your garden be like?) the garden has symbolized the most profound exchange of affections, the rightful bower for love's fulfillment. Adompha, with the aid of Dwerulas's dire wizardry, explores perhaps farther than any man the terrifying schism between the relentless curiosity of the human intellect (the Apollonian individual stance) and the natural and necessary affection of humans for each other (the Dionysian flow to unity). The garden grows as a terrifying trophy of Adompha's amorous adventures and it is more than inevitable that the garden, grafted with terror, should annihilate its master. "A Rendezvous in Averoigne" is a nightmare experience of mutual affection thwarted, complete with magnificent levels of confusion. The Evil is laid to rest and Fleurette at last finds the arms of her lover Gérard. "She was dazed with wonderment like one who emerges from the night-long labyrinth of an evil dream, and finds that all is well" (*OST* 42).

The ultimate significance of the dream vision in Clark Ashton Smith as in human experience is the key that the dream vision offers to man's understanding of his juxtaposition to life and to death. At least indirectly the misdirected amorous action in "A Rendezvous in Averoigne" and other tales is involved with these two ultimate concerns. Smith speaks more explicitly in "Maya" where life is discovered as a dream, "illusion of illusion," that will end when death lulls us to the "last delirium" (*S* 24). "Laus Mortis" presents the case for "the last and ultimate desire" (*EC* 93). "O, solace of all weary hearts and wise!— / The dream which Satan hath for anodyne, / Which is to God a sweet and secret wine" (*EC* 93). Herbert in "The Ninth Skeleton" has a vision at one of the happiest moments of his life, as he is about to enjoy a tryst with his beloved. "A horror that was more than horror, a fear that was beyond fear, petrified all my faculties, and I felt as if I were weighted down by some ineluctable and insupportable burden of nightmare" (*EC* 93). The parade of skeletons carrying skeleton children plagues him until one skeleton touches his arm. He swoons, but, of course, it is Guinevere, his beloved, who brings him back to touch. Smith has achieved a brilliant method of definition within the structure of the tale. The pageant of death enacted just when life means so much to Herbert explains more accurately than any words could precisely what life is—the glory and the limitation. "The Gorgon" appears in the mirror as the "final mystery. I was terrified, appalled—and fascinated to the core of my being; for that which I saw was the ultimate death, the ultimate beauty. I desired, yet I did not dare, to turn and lift my eyes to the reality whose mere reflection was a fatal splendor" (*LW* 322). This indirect confrontation with superhuman suffering grants the hero wisdom just as the dream state instructs man before he must return to the mundane reality. "Anticipation" offers a vision of death less disquieting, the thought of sleep undisturbed by the dream that is life.

> The thought of death to me
> Is like a well of waters, deep and dim—
> Cool-gleaming, hushed, and hidden gratefully
> Among the palms asleep

At silver evening on the desert's rim.

Or as a couch of stone,
Whereon by moonlight, in a marble room,
Some fevered king reposes all alone—
So is the hope of sleep,
The inalienable surety of the tomb. (*EC* 120)

In the preface to the collection *Ebony and Crystal,* in which the poem "Anticipation" appears, George Sterling paid Clark Ashton Smith a very knowledgeable tribute.

Because he has lent himself the more innocently to the whispers of his subconscious daemon, and because he has set those murmurs to purer and harder crystal than we others, by so much longer will the poems of Clark Ashton Smith endure. (*EC* i)

It is this remarkable ability of Smith to heed and to transform his daydreams and nightmares into meaningful artistic expression in the poems and in the tales that will never cease to astound his very fortunate reader.

What Dante accomplished in the field of the understanding of the human psyche employing the ethical traditions of religion as a touchstone, Clark Ashton Smith has accomplished by employing a vast spectrum of scientific knowledge as a touchstone. Both concerned individuals used the Prime Hell of their age to clarify the crucial subtleties of human experience, to instruct their neophyte readers in the significant dogma: for Dante knowledge of a God centered universe, for Smith the wisdom of an individual's imaginative perception of Essentiality in the Cosmos (*ST* 34). As Virgil leads Dante through the graduated levels of human disorientation in *The Inferno,* Dante makes this plea—

O poet, my true guide,
Consider if my courage will suffice
Ere you commit me to such high endeavor.[7]

As Smith leads the reader through the graduated levels of human disorientation in the maelstrom of his poetry and prose, he asks the

---

7. Dante, *The Inferno,* trans. Lawrence Grant White (New York: Pantheon, 1948), 2.10–12.

reader to assume the highest courage, the courage of complete honesty in the face of inevitable existential consequences. The "Interrogation" of the beloved might also serve as a suitable address to the eager neophyte who would approach the immeasurable wisdom, wisdom of the celestial cosmos and wisdom of the complete cosmos within each human spirit, in the work and the thought of Clark Ashton Smith.

> Love, will you look with me
> Upon the phosphor-litten labour of the Worm—
> Time's minister, who toils for his appointed term,
> And has for fee
> All superannuate loves, and all the loves to be?
>
> Love, can you see, as I,
> The corpses, ghosts and demons mingled with the crowd?
> The djinns that men have freed, grown turbulent and proud;
> Alastor, Asmodai?
> And all-unheeded envoys from the stars on high?
>
> Know you the gulfs below,
> Where darkling Erebus on Erebus is driven
> Between the molecules—atom from atom riven,
> And tossing to and fro,
> Incessant, like the souls on Dante's wind of woe?
>
> Know you the deeps above?
> The terror and the vertigo of those who gaze too long
> Upon the crystal skies unclouded? Are you strong
> With me to prove
> Even in thought or dream the dreadful pits above?
>
> Know you the gulfs within?
> The worms and dragons of the charnel caves undared?
> The sombre foam of seas by cryptic sirens shared?
> The pestilence and sin
> Borne by the flapping shroud of liches met within? (*S* 24–25)

It is the superhuman understanding of the human psyche and of the terror inherent in the imbalance of the human psyche appearing often in the brutality of a nightmare thralldom that Clark Ashton Smith transforms into an art of absolute meaning and absolute beauty.

Works Cited

The Abominations of Yondo. Sauk City, WI: Arkham House, 1960.

The Dark Chateau. Sauk City, WI: Arkham House, 1951.

Ebony and Crystal: Poems in Verse and Prose. Auburn, CA: Auburn Journal Press, 1922.

Genius Loci. Sauk City, WI: Arkham House, 1948.

Lost Worlds. Sauk City, WI: Arkham House, 1944.

Odes and Sonnets. San Francisco: The Book Club of California, 1918.

Out of Space and Time. Sauk City, WI: Arkham House, 1942.

Poems in Prose. Sauk City, WI: Arkham House, 1965.

Sandalwood. Auburn, CA: Auburn Press, 1925.

Spells and Philtres. Sauk City, WI: Arkham House, 1958.

The Star-Treader and Other Poems. San Francisco: A. M. Robertson, 1912.

Tales of Science and Sorcery. Sauk City, WI: Arkham House, 1964.

Acknowledgments

"Afterword" to *As It Is Written* [as by Clark Ashton Smith] (Donald M. Grant, 1982).

"Arthur Machen and King Arthur, Sovereigns of Dream,"*Nyctalops* Nos. 11/12 (April 1976).

"Averoigne: An Afterword," in *The Averoigne Chronicles* by Clark Ashton Smith (Centipede Press, 2016).

"Captain Volmar and Crew: An Afterword," in *Red World of Polaris: The Adventures of Captain Volmar* by Clark Ashton Smith (Night Shade Books, 2003).

"Dark Oracles Indeed," *Spectral Realms* No. 12 (Winter 2020).

"Eblis in Bakelite" (by James Blish) and "James Blish vs. Clark Ashton Smith; to Wit, the Young Turk Syndrome: A Riposte," in *The Freedom of Fantastic Things,* ed. Scott Connors (Hippocampus Press, 2006).

"Emeraude Indeed," in *As Green as Emeraude: The Collected Poems of Margo Skinner* (Dawn Heron Press, 1990).

"The Emperor of Dreams," by Donald Wandrei, *Overland Monthly* (December 1926).

"Five Approaches to the Achievements of Clark Ashton Smith, Cosmic Master Artist," by Marvin R. Hiemstra, in *Emperor of Dreams: A Clark Ashton Smith Bibliography* by Donald Sidney-Fryer (Donald M. Grant, 1978).

"Grim News from the Far Future," in *The Last Continent: New Tales of Zothique,* ed. John Pelan (ShadowLands Press/Bereshith Publishing 1999).

"H. P. Lovecraft—Beacon and Gateway," *Lovecraft Annual* No. 12 (2018).

408   ACKNOWLEDGMENTS

"In Defense of 'Little Boys,'" *The Cimmerian* (December 2005),

"Introduction: Crimson Pages from the Future Perfect Past," in *The Crimson Tome* by K. A. Opperman (Hippocampus Press, 2015).

"Introduction" to *Diary of a Sorceress* by Ashley Dioses (Hippocampus Press, 2017).

"Introduction" to *Etchings in Ivory: Poems in Prose* by Robert E. Howard (Glenn Lord, 1968; courtesy Dennis McHaney).

"Klarkash-Ton, High Priest of Atlantis," in *Poseidonis Cycle: The Age of Malygris* by Clark Ashton Smith (Pegana Press, 2014).

Letters to "The Lion's Den," *The Cimmerian* (February, December 2005; March, July, August 2006; August 2007; June 2008).

"Not Quite Atlantis: Foreword," in *Not Quite Atlantis* (PS Publishing, 2010).

"A Poetic Original," *Spectral Realms* No. 10 (Winter 2019). "Dark Oracles Indeed," *Spectral Realms* No. 12 (Winter 2020).

"The Phosphor Lamps of Clark Ashton Smith" (with Ron Hilger), *Chronicles of the Cthulhu Codex* No. 17 (Winter 2000).

"Shadows and Light," *The Cimmerian* (December 2008).

"Thibaut di Castries, Revenant," in *The Pale Brown Thing* by Fritz Leiber (Swan River Press, 2016).

All other items appear here for the first time.